The High Kâhl's Oath

More Warhammer 40,000 from Black Library

• DAWN OF FIRE •

Book 1: AVENGING SON
Guy Haley

Book 2: THE GATE OF BONES
Andy Clark

Book 3: THE WOLFTIME
Gav Thorpe

Book 4: THRONE OF LIGHT
Guy Haley

Book 5: THE IRON KINGDOM
Nick Kyme

Book 6: THE MARTYR'S TOMB
Marc Collins

Book 7: SEA OF SOULS
Chris Wraight

Book 8: HAND OF ABADDON
Nick Kyme

Book 9: THE SILENT KING
Guy Haley

• DARK IMPERIUM •
Guy Haley

Book 1: DARK IMPERIUM
Book 2: PLAGUE WAR
Book 3: GODBLIGHT

LEVIATHAN
Darius Hinks

DAY OF ASCENSION
Adrian Tchaikovsky

BRUTAL KUNNIN
Mike Brooks

VOID KING
Marc Collins

OUTGUNNED
Denny Flowers

THE FALL OF CADIA
Robert Rath

The High Kâhl's Oath

Gav Thorpe

A BLACK LIBRARY PUBLICATION

First published in 2024.
This edition published in Great Britain in 2025 by
Black Library, Games Workshop Ltd., Willow Road,
Nottingham, NG7 2WS, UK.

Represented by: Games Workshop Limited – Irish branch,
Unit 3, Lower Liffey Street, Dublin 1,
D01 K199, Ireland.

10 9 8 7 6 5 4 3 2 1

Produced by Games Workshop in Nottingham.
Cover illustration by Grant Griffin.

The High Kâhl's Oath © Copyright Games Workshop Limited 2025. The High Kâhl's Oath, GW, Games Workshop, Black Library, The Horus Heresy, The Horus Heresy Eye logo, Space Marine, 40K, Warhammer, Warhammer 40,000, the 'Aquila' Double-headed Eagle logo, and all associated logos, illustrations, images, names, creatures, races, vehicles, locations, weapons, characters, and the distinctive likenesses thereof, are either ® or TM, and/or © Games Workshop Limited, variably registered around the world.
All Rights Reserved.

A CIP record for this book is available from the British Library.

ISBN 13: 978-1-83609-164-6

No part of this publication may be reproduced, stored in a retrieval system, or transmitted in any form or by any means, electronic, mechanical, photocopying, recording or otherwise, without the prior permission of the publishers.

This is a work of fiction. All the characters and events portrayed in this book are fictional, and any resemblance to real people or incidents is purely coincidental.

See Black Library on the internet at

blacklibrary.com

Find out more about Games Workshop
and the worlds of Warhammer at

warhammer.com

Printed and bound in the UK.

This book is dedicated to everyone that asked,
'When Are Squats Coming Back?'.
Thanks for keeping the dream alive.

For more than a hundred centuries the Emperor has sat immobile on the Golden Throne of Earth. He is the Master of Mankind. By the might of his inexhaustible armies a million worlds stand against the dark.

Yet, he is a rotting carcass, the Carrion Lord of the Imperium held in life by marvels from the Dark Age of Technology and the thousand souls sacrificed each day so his may continue to burn.

To be a man in such times is to be one amongst untold billions. It is to live in the cruelest and most bloody regime imaginable. It is to suffer an eternity of carnage and slaughter. It is to have cries of anguish and sorrow drowned by the thirsting laughter of dark gods.

This is a dark and terrible era where you will find little comfort or hope. Forget the power of technology and science. Forget the promise of progress and advancement. Forget any notion of common humanity or compassion.

There is no peace amongst the stars, for in the grim darkness of the far future, there is only war.

PROLOGUE

'Go!'

Orthônar's bellowed command caused the High Kâhl to break into a body-wracking fit of coughs. His grey beard was matted with drying crimson, his left eye almost swollen shut. Rivulets of fresh blood trickled from scabbed lacerations that criss-crossed his face, a ruddy scowl framed within a gorget-seal of orange void armour. The suit, its interlocking plates forge-crafted from the best bastium alloy, had sustained even more battle damage than its owner. It creaked and shuddered as the High Kâhl adjusted his grip on his ornate plasma axe; his combi-bolter had been lost in the fighting some time ago.

'I can't.'

Dori Hûltvan, champion of the Eternal Starforge Kindred, was frozen to the spot. His immobility was not due to fear for his life but to a dread far deeper and more piercing than self-preservation: the terror of failure.

He looked past his lord, along the broad, pillared hall, into the fire-rimmed shadows where the orks were attacking again. Their war bellows and bestial grunts reverberated from the high vaults and distant walls as they hurled themselves through the gunfire-lit darkness of the massive vault. Larger war engines clanked behind the mobs of snarling green-skinned aliens, weapons aglow with strange energies, sparks erupting from crude electrics to illuminate the oily smog from dozens of smokestacks. Their fungal stench blotted out the stink of blood and death.

Orthônar held up his axe in a gloved hand. A great ruby glimmered on a ring around the High Kâhl's index finger. With his other hand he pulled the ring free and thrust it into his champion's grip.

'Fulfil my oath. It is my will.'

Uttering the words made Orthônar wince with pain, but his champion flinched even harder at their intent. A shout of defiance welled up from the Einhyr of the Kindred, Dori's company of warriors. The crash of alien cleavers and stout Kin-wrought hammers added to the clamour of desperate war. The champion saw a towering beast of a figure leading the latest charge: the ork warlord. Orthônar's bodyguards packed closer, trying to stem its advance. Dragging his eyes back to the High Kâhl, Dori swallowed, his spit like acid in his throat.

'I am your champion, first of the bodyguard. My place is at your side.'

'Your place is where I bloody well say it is,' snapped the High Kâhl. With effort he grabbed the front of Dori's armour and pulled him closer. His blue eyes were bright, bloodshot, their stare like two aumorite borers drilling into the champion's soul. 'Take my oath back to the Kindred.'

'Send another,' the champion pleaded, laying a hand on his master's forearm. 'You named me Ironhelm. I swore an oath to serve you until death. I cannot live while you fall. Please, send someone else.'

Orthônar's gaze did not relent. He turned his head for a moment to spit blood, but returned his eyes to his champion without a hint of softening.

'You also swore to obey my righteous command. Do so now. I trust only you to do this for me.'

A voice crackled over the communicator channel, warning that the orks were breaking through.

'You are my oathkeeper now, Ironhelm,' Orthônar continued. 'It is your burden until you die or you pass it to another. If the orks overrun us, there's no way back to the ship. Go *now*. That is my last command to you.'

Tears welled in Ironhelm's eyes as his lord stomped away, rejoining the much-diminished lines arrayed before the great gate of the main hall. From the rest of the second line of Einhyr – the bodyguard Ironhelm had led for half his life – magna-coils thrummed the air and lit the dark with their gleam.

The weight of duty sagged Ironhelm's shoulders. If he failed, these warriors would die forever here, their experiences wasted, their memories lost to the great wisdom of the Votann. He carried more than the High Kâhl's oath back to the Kindred. He carried the accumulated existence of his companions.

The champion stiffened as a cannon boomed from the far end of the hall. The alien gunner's aim was wayward, a shell striking high upon one of the hundred pillars supporting the vastness of the ancient settlement. Kin and foe were locked in battle wherever he looked.

Tearing his gaze from the scene, Ironhelm turned and broke into a lumbering run, headed for the landing field.

CHAPTER ONE

Friends in Bad Places

Immense detonations wracked the carapace-like hull of the bioship as another fusillade from the *Grand Endeavour*'s gun batteries thundered into its crater-pocked flank. Almost twice as large as the Kin Pioneer ship, the gigantic living vessel spilled globules of freezing ichor into the void amid a shower of carapace fragments left trailing in the wounded void-beast's wake. Among the organic debris ejected by explosive decompression were the corpses of smaller creatures, spinning and turning on their haphazard courses through the vacuum.

Observing the destruction from the piloting compartment of a gunship was Myrtun Dammergot of the Kindred of the Eternal Starforge. She had earned many titles in her long life: Scion of the Trans-Hyperian Alliance, Gatemistress of the Ebon Channel, Voidmaiden of the Nêrn Straits. The one she prized the most was Commander of the *Grand Endeavour*. Myrtun knew that the damage was mostly superficial. Given time the bioship would heal, the majority of its deadly cargo kept secure within armoured gut-vaults deep within layers of flesh and chitin. Which was sort of the point – as soon as the ship died, the most useful parts of it would start to wither and lose value.

For millennia, the deepest hatred of the Kin had been reserved for the ork savages that had bedevilled their worlds and expeditions since the time of the first Votann. Yet these ancestral enemies paled in comparison to the genekillers that had swept into Kin territories of late. Voracious, single-minded world hunters, the genekillers didn't just slay Kin; they stole their skein-data to create more hyper-evolved monstrosities. To be slain by the genekillers was to have everything taken away – memories, Votann-ordained genes – denied the chance to become one with the vastness of the Votann after death. This was why there was another name for them.

The Bane.

Rarely did profit and pleasure come together so neatly as when dismantling a bioship. Myrtun had manoeuvred the *Grand Endeavour* into position without the shields being overloaded by the huge biocannons studding the recessed lateral weapons integumentary tracts that ran two-thirds of the alien ship's length. Now a complex dance of bioship and prospector continued, with the latter burning thrusters to remain in the blind spot for as long as possible while the gunships carrying the boarding teams covered the void between.

Like the rest of the boarding party, the expedition leader wore a heavy void suit of black and orange, capped by a dome helmet. Inside the transparent hemisphere Myrtun looked as though she might have been formed of cooled lava, dark of skin and heavily etched with age. Her white hair was much thinned and worn in a long scalp lock. Her eyes were dark brown, bloodshot but piercing, a short stare from which was more than enough to unsettle all but the most strong-willed. Her left ear was missing, replaced with a bionic device wired down to her jawline that acted as a hearing device and transmitter-receiver.

A notification blinked on her wristpanel, indicating a transmission on her private frequency. She already knew who it would be as she pressed the assent button.

'The messenger, the one from the Hold ship, is almost here,' said Lutar, her Wayfinder and, more importantly, her lifelong aide and companion. Myrtun imagined the Ironkin back on the bridge of the *Grand Endeavour* checking and rechecking the bioscans, the lights of the panels reflected on the glassy dome of his armoured form. *'Are you sure you want to proceed?'*

'Sure enough,' she replied, keeping a sigh from her voice. 'Also sure Fyrtor's message means we're just a watch or less from being ordered back to the Hold ship.'

There was no reply, but Myrtun could read as much from Lutar's silences as she could from the spoken word.

'You want to know what's wrong? Why I'm dodging Fyrtor?'

'So there is something wrong?'

'No, not wrong.' Myrtun looked up at the dark bulk of the bioship blotting the stars. 'Distracting. You know the Hold ship has been nagging on at me for a while.'

'Jôrdiki told me that you are ignoring them. Not even reading their messages.'

'Jôrdiki should know better than to gossip,' growled Myrtun. 'It's my business alone.'

'She did not confide the contents of the missives, which she does not know. Only their existence. And her concern.'

'Concerned that she can't get me to do their bidding?'

A slight pause, the vocal equivalent of a frown.

'Concern for you. The bidding of whom? The High Kâhl? The Votann?'

'Of course not! I always listen to the Votann.' Myrtun's shoulders hunched at the thought, and she flexed the metal fingers of her artificial left arm within her void suit. 'I don't... I'm not a tamed hound, to come running back at a call.'

'Or to be collared and leashed. I understand, my jewel-star.' Lutar's use of his personal term for Myrtun softened her demeanour.

'Yes, you do understand me, my star-guide.' She smiled as she uttered the last words. 'Like nobody else does.'

'More than a hundred orbits have passed since you last returned to the Kindred. Longer than ever before. And we have been further from the Hold ship than any Prospect has ever been. Perhaps it is time that you allowed some of the Hernkyn to return, and brought in fresh recruits. There are some here that should be leading their own Prospects, or pursuing their lives in other ways.'

'I can't go back, not until I'm all settled with Orthônar. He sponsored this ship and I'm still owing. And now he's reeling me back in to the Hold ship.'

'You've earned more than any other Hernkyn Prospect ever.'

'And spent more getting out there. We were supposed to do more than break even this time. A good haul from the bioship puts us in good stead on the balance sheet.'

'So why would the High Kâhl want to recall you?'

'I don't know… I just have this feeling.'

'Paranoia?'

His subtle tone conveyed a smile that his synthetic body could not replicate, and Myrtun found herself feeling a little foolish.

'Might be. But I can't shake the idea that this is my last journey. I'm old, but these are my best days yet.' As she spoke, Myrtun became more animated. It was as if the last hundred orbits had fallen from her. 'I want to go beyond. Further than the charts. Maybe–'

She cut herself off, eyes glistening, breaths coming quickly.

'I'm scared, my star-guide,' she confessed. Her animation receded, time weighing down on her again. 'Scared that if I go back to the Hold ship they will see this tired old ragbag of bones and skin, and they'll not let me go again. They'll give the *Grand Endeavour* to someone younger, better suited to this life. Maybe even Fyrtor will get it for his fleet. Perhaps that's why he's been dogging my heels these past three systems. Then what for me? Piddling about the Hold ship, boring the grit out of everyone with stories of my glory days.'

'Or perhaps an esteemed retirement, advisor to the High Kâhl?' suggested Lutar.

'Esteemed retirement?' Myrtun's expression hardened. 'Sitting around jabbering all day about nothing and everything? Like I said, I'd be pining for the old times and giving the High Kâhl an earful about how it was all better back then, like all the other greyheads. No! That's not for me! Not for us.'

'Us?'

She wanted to take the word back; it had slipped out of its own accord. But it was too late now.

'Yes, *us*, of course. You're a Wayfinder, meant to be out on a ship cruising the starways, guiding a Prospect or a Kinthrong across the warp sea. That's what the Votann made you for.'

'*Made me?*' The hint of offence in his voice felt damning to Myrtun, who knew Lutar was rarely nonplussed by anything. *'The Votann make us all, Myrtun. Your cloneskein and mine are different only in material. Synthetic circuitry for me, flesh and nerves for you. They had intentions for both of us, but the Votann are not gods or fate. You have fulfilled their intent a score of times and more. I could choose to stay with you. Would that be so bad?'*

Myrtun thought about his question for a few moments, not saying anything. She disliked how most folks spoke first and let their brains catch up. She liked to weigh her responses.

'Neither of us would be happy,' she said at last.

Everything was ready for the final approach, and Myrtun knew the time had come to make her move. Before that, she needed to address the Prospect. Each of them would get their share from this adventure, and she liked to remind them of their duty.

'Lutar, have me patched through to main comms.'

* * *

'The galactic core has been beset by warp storms the like of which even the Votann have not seen for ten thousand years.' As she spoke, Myrtun could feel the attention of hundreds of Kin across the transmission waves, in their void suits or listening at communal speakers back on the Prospector. Her voice was being carried from the engine rooms to the command bridge and everywhere in between. 'Aliens, the Imperium, and slaves of the warp powers encroach everywhere on the territories of the Votann. War reigns supreme. Let us remember for a moment those no longer with us, who have been returned to the Votann.'

Silence fell upon the broadcast, lasting just a few heartbeats before Myrtun spoke again, her voice rising to a triumphant volume.

'And let us all embrace this time of great opportunity!'

'*Opportunity!*' hundreds of voices roared back, dulled by the auto-senses of her bionic.

Taking her final words as a command, the crew on the *Grand Endeavour* fired the main cutting laser. A beam of flickering yellow and red, more commonly employed to dissect asteroids and drill into moons, now speared from the prow to slice open the exposed flank of the gene-killers' vessel. Strata of muscle tissue and fat parted like a finely cooked *bovi* steak. Flanked by two smaller landers, the gunship sped towards the open wound.

'Closing for final approach,' the pilot announced to the void-armoured Kin aboard, her words simultaneously transmitted to Lutar on the *Grand Endeavour*.

'Ready?' Myrtun asked as she stepped back into the main compartment.

Twenty of her best warriors waited in two squads, two neutron charges floating just above the deck between them, glowing suspensor units built into their black cases. Brôkhyr Thôrdi stepped forward, a staff-like giant autowrench in one hand, his bristling grey whiskers pale in the helm lights of his suit. The Iron-master gave a thumbs up and motioned for the warriors to take up their burdens. Four came forward from each squad, lifting the charges like pall bearers at a funeral. At another command Thôrdi's two E-COG units, far less complex cousins to Lutar and other Ironkin, floated up beside the Iron-master. The E-COGs were a little shorter than Thôrdi, resembling animated busts of Kin warriors held aloft by their suspensors, weapons ready as he turned towards the disembarkation hatch.

The communicator buzzed into life, Jôrdiki Ortdott's voice sounding distorted within the dome of Myrtun's helm.

'Urgent communication from Fyrtor,' said the Prospect's Grimnyr. *'The* Canny Wanderer *has exited warp and is heading to our position. He is requesting an immediate audience.'*

'I'm busy here, Grimnyr.'

'That was what I told him, but he says he's been bound to speak to you as soon as possible.'

Myrtun looked back through the door of the control chamber and out to the greatness of the bioship that almost filled the view. She could see ice-encrusted lumps drifting past like a ruddy micro-asteroid field, and beyond that, the flaps of the wound in the creature's side, already hazy with small organisms swarming over the tattered flesh, the glistening of secretions catching distant starlight as they started to weave a healing membrane across the cauterised layers. It would not be long before they started webbing across the gap into the interior.

'Well then, tell him I'll see him in the guts of this beast, and to bring his best warriors.'

'I'll be sure to pass on your regards.' Jôrdiki sounded resigned more than anything else. *'I'll let you know his decision. Fight proud. The Ancestors are watching.'*

The last comment brought a wry smile to Myrtun's lips as the link severed with a click. Save for the Grimnyr, there were few Kin alive today who were closer to the Ancestors than Myrtun; some of the most recent Ancestors had been created and died within the span of her existence.

'Scanners picking up larger life forms in the entry cavity,' warned the co-pilot, Hengfr. Like everyone else, the flight crew wore void suits of the Kindred's customary orange lined with black, but his visor was golden, shielded against starglow and plasma blindness. A screen on the console showed red blips amid a backwash of duller orange from the bioship. 'Two dozen, increasing in number.'

Myrtun nodded, though inside the spacious dome of her helm the movement was hidden to all but the co-pilot, who could see through the faceplate. She tapped a control on the wristband of her suit to activate the comm.

'Hostile landing. Fire-team to the front. Preparatory strafing and simultaneous alighting. No dallying about, we need to get deep enough for the charges to do their job before the enemy gather their numbers. Take too long and we'll be neck-deep in the grit.'

The co-pilot activated the weapons controls and the gunship's familiar harmony of vibrations changed to incorporate the motors of the dual HYLas beam cannons mounted in its nose. Glancing out to the left and right, Myrtun saw the lighters carrying the rest of the force coming alongside, their stubby wings heavy with rocket pods.

'Beginning attack run in five... four...' said Hengfr.

Myrtun turned her attention back to the bioship while the countdown continued.

'...two... one... Open fire.'

Rockets streamed in pairs from the lighters, a score flaring out towards the enormous gash that was the landing site. A strange feeling of detachment came over Myrtun as she watched soundless explosions filling the wound. The whine of primed energy cells forewarned of the HYLas barrage, a moment before streaks of crimson pierced the fresh cloud of ichor and ruined alien flesh. Breaking her gaze away from the behemoth ahead, Myrtun checked the scan display, waiting for the data to refresh. When the screen flickered with the next sweep, more than half the returns had disappeared.

'Landing run initiated,' the pilot reported, easing the gunship into a slow roll with a short burst from the lateral thrusters and guiding them past the expanding cloud of organic debris. 'Matching course and speed. Hatch locks disengaged.'

Myrtun moved to join her warriors in the transportation compartment, carried by a long, gravity-less stride. Ahead of her, Theyn Lordun activated the hatch controls. The door swung upwards to reveal a brief glimpse of starfield before the view filled with tattered fleshy nodules and cracked alien carapace thicker than the hull of a battleship. Burn marks scorched the edges of a severed transport artery, within which floated the las-mauled bodies of smaller creatures frosting in the void.

'Assault group, on me,' barked Lordun. Myrtun felt the judder of attitude thrusters bringing the gunship closer, and at the edges of her view through the hatch she caught a reflected gleam from the accompanying lighters.

Disengaging his mag-locks Lordun jumped through the hatchway, a small flare from his void armour's propulsors carrying him forward. Nine other Hearthkyn followed, becoming a cluster of sparks in the distance, their positions marked out in Myrtun's visor by ident-tags and artificial auras.

'Charge bearers, it's time.' Myrtun pushed forwards against the drag of her boots, cutting off the mag-locks just as she felt she would fall forwards. Her momentum carried her clear of the opening, and she followed in the wake of the Hearthkyn. More dome-display data hinted at the flanking positions of her Pioneers – more lightly void-suited than the Hearthkyn. She was similarly aware of the remaining Hearthkyn following behind, the two neutron charges borne between them. Ahead, the flash of weapons fire announced contact with the surviving Bane.

With her comm-piece switched off, it almost felt as though she was watching a holo with no sound, the splashes of brightness that threw flares across her vision resembling interference static. If she concentrated on one thing for too long, Myrtun felt like she had come to a standstill and the whole universe was moving towards her, such was the lack of sensation. She wondered if this was anything close to the experience of the Votann – whether their timeless, formless intellect watched the turning of aeons with the same graceful serenity that she approached the firefight.

The feeling ended the moment she switched on the communicator. A flood of warnings, battle cries, and orders overlapped in her artificial ear. The thrum of ion weapons and the ejection coughs of bolters sounded in the background, muted behind the gruff, stark voices of her companions. Iyrdin Cabb's sharp tones cut through the chatter with the arrival of the Pioneers. While the Hearthkyn set up a perimeter into which Myrtun drifted with the charge bearers, the Hernkyn Pioneers floated ahead, moving into the leftward stretches of artery, heading deeper into the bioship's innards.

There was no decking for mag-locks here, and so a short burst of void-armour jets brought Myrtun to a relative standstill, just inside the severed end of the artery tunnel. The tunnel was six times her height, curving downwards and to the right, its walls ridged with cartilaginous growths. Her suit picked up atmospheric agitation as more air leaked from deeper within the genekillers' vessel.

Sensor readings relayed back from the Pioneers appeared as a rough schematic in the corner of Myrtun's vision – a swathe of interconnected pipeways running broadly prow to stern, branching into more complex structures towards the interior. The image shimmered and she saw a ripple pass along the tunnel, fresh drops of ichor expelled from the severed tissue around her.

She recognised what it was from previous encounters. It was a reminder that she was just a bug crawling into a cut – one organism of an invasive species intent upon laying explosive eggs.

A monstrous pulse.

'Securing junction designate fourteen lateral. Second squad moving to dorsal promontory designate fifteen dorsal.'

Listening to the reports from Iyrdin Cabb gave Lutar little idea of the scene inside the bioship. He knew from past conversations with Myrtun and others what the innards would be like: aspiration chambers full of cloying fog, slick lubrication tubes and throbbing ichor pumps, hot hall-like exhaust ventricles expelling the accumulated heat of a creature that, by any Kin understanding of biology, should not be able to exist. Despite this, and holo-recordings of previous expeditions, he found it impossible to create a proxy simulation of an environment even more alien than a gas giant's storms or the depths of a helium sea.

Fortunately, the scan data from the boarding party provided a better geo-topographical interpretation for him to work with. A holo of the triangulated readings hovered just above the sensor station, overlaid against a translucent rendering of previously encountered bioships stored in the *Grand Endeavour*'s Fane – at least those that Jôrdiki had been able to coax from its records. The similarities were clear. Even though this exact configuration – species? – of the Bane had not been encountered before, its internal layout formed equivalent, reasonably predictable patterns.

With this information Lutar was able to place a virtual marker in the displays of the assault teams, highlighting an area previously identified as the statocystic chambers. The best minds of the Leagues had studied captured bioships and determined much of their anatomy, but the exact functioning of many organs and systems was still conjecture rather than fact. Lutar knew that the statocystic chambers, typically four of them in symmetric organisation, affected the movement and sensory abilities of a bioship in a similar way to those of waterborne invertebrates found all over the galactic core. However, in the depths of space with minimal gravity to impart directionality, it was not known to what force the primary statocysts responded. Some thought they were potentially attuned to the warp plane in some way.

While the theory was very much up for debate, the practical application of this knowledge had been tested many times since the Bane had invaded the Leagues. Disruption – preferably destruction – of the statocystic chambers rendered a bioship unmanoeuvrable. Returning to its inter-system biostatic state, the ship was then an easy target as it drifted lifelessly across the void.

Destroying the organs was, however, a far from easy task. And even then, other creatures within the bioship had to be dealt with.

'There should be a coil-route heading vertically up and down from fifteen dorsal,' Lutar told Iyrdin. 'You need to climb up through the aortic channel and then cut open a membrane across an opening on your left.'

'Understood. Beginning ascent.'

Small pulsing runes moved on the display, clustered around the brighter rune of Myrtun. Lutar tried not to fixate on that particular symbol. He knew that every Kin fulfilled a life worthy of the animus given them by the Votann, from kâhl to reactor technician, Grimnyr to hydroponics farmer. He also knew that he was functionally incapable of the kind of emotion that other Kin might feel for a special individual. And yet…

His thoughts were interrupted by Duri at comms.

'Receiving signal from the *Canny Wanderer*. It's Fyrtor.'

Lutar gave a nod and the comm-speakers crackled as the intership link was established.

'I'm on? Right. This is Fyrtor, commanding the Canny Wanderer *for the Hernkendersson Prospect. I seek audience with Myrtun, Gatemistress of the Ebon Channel, Voidmaiden of the–'*

'She isn't here,' Lutar cut in as he checked the scan of the bioship. The expedition were almost completely past fifteen dorsal and making their way through the cut membrane into the superior amphibowel. The quickest way to their objective was unfortunately through part of the immense creature's digestive tract. 'She's busy, I'm afraid.'

'Myrtun's actually on that Bane monstrosity? Now? Did she not get the message?'

'She received your missive, but judged this matter of higher priority. I am sure you would agree that securing such a valuable prize and preserving Kin life are our foremost concerns?'

'Er, yes, of course. I saw that she had sent over a boarding action, but figured that perhaps she wouldn't have gone herself.'

The juxtaposition of this assumption with everything Lutar had stored on Myrtun in his databanks set off a short cascade of processor reactions, culminating in a brief but loud laugh.

'You haven't met Myrtun?'

'Once, when I was much younger.'

Lutar had been left strict instructions for this eventuality.

'I assure you that Myrtun will attend to your message the moment she has returned to the *Grand Endeavour*,' he said.

'She really would rather hide herself in the guts of a Bane monster than hear what I have to say? This is ridiculous!'

'Your comms appear to be working well, I do not understand the problem.'

'I have to guarantee that she has received the message. There can't be any room for doubt.'

'Then I am afraid you'll have to wait.'

'You don't understand,' answered Fyrtor, his frustration growing. *'I have to deliver this message in person, as soon as possible. I was tasked with this by the Hearthspake.'*

'And if they hear that you did not do your utmost to fulfil their wishes, you think they might withhold payment?'

Silence was the only answer Lutar needed. He rapidly assessed the situation and surmised that Fyrtor was intent on joining the boarding action. It was in everybody's interest that the two forces were coordinated in their efforts.

'I can share our tactical data with the *Canny Wanderer* if you wish?'

'No need, I've been tracking the attack since we came within range. Going for the shut-down-and-loot approach?'

'That's the plan, yes.' Lutar ran a quick evaluation through the scanners. He was not programmed for combat leadership, but tactical thinking was mostly a matter of informed pathfinding anyway. And he had quite a wealth of data to use.

'A dorsal entry would divert a considerable proportion of the mounting opposition,' he suggested.

There was no reply for a short while. Haeven at the scanner reported that the *Canny Wanderer* was manoeuvring into position above the bioship, their trajectory taking them close to a cluster of spiracles just under the rim of the forward edge of the main shell.

'Let Myrtun know we're on our way. Fyrtor out.'

Kin had only a residual natural sense of the warp and its tenuous connection to mortals, but Grimnyr Jôrdiki Ortdott had been clonewrought to have a fraction more psychic sensitivity. This was aided by the empyric runes carved into her staff and studding the charms and amulets that adorned her. Like the lenses of a microscope bending light waves, the runes magnified her rudimentary connection, and through their arcane technology she could feel the immense yet blunt consciousness of the bioship itself.

More and more of the Bane were waking.

Against the backdrop of its dull presence were pinpricks of other awareness. Each was an individual, each signature possessing no more psychic potency than the mighty ship, but a part of a more nebulous and powerful whole. Where scanners were blocked by cartilage, muscle and bone, Jôrdiki's mindsense gave a less accurate but further-reaching warning of the emerging threat. With every waking organism the shadow-cloud of awareness grew darker and sharper, guiding more creatures towards the intruders.

So far they had encountered the least potent organisms – worker things and minor battle constructs that had either fled or attacked on instinct, neither proving much of a threat. Even in the swarms that gathered about organs and nerve clusters like nesting beasts they were uncoordinated and ineffective, either dying to the bolters of the Kin in disjointed wave attacks or cut down where they cowered in the folds of flesh and bone-vaulted chambers.

But that was changing.

Jôrdiki pushed forward to catch up with the Prospect's leader. She did not wear bulky void armour like her companions, its mass too much of an interference to the subtle empyric waves that her runes needed to operate. Instead, she wore her robes as normal, safe within a complex weave of wards projected by her runic gear. It was enough even to shield her against the potentially corrosive atmosphere of the bioship's innards as they moved through digestion slurry with long zero-gravity leaps, bounding from fleshy wall to fleshy wall.

She was flanked by two CORVs – basic thinking machines that looked like elaborate E-COGs, each with an extravagant crest that arced up from the back and over the blank dome of the head, containing empyric resonators. They were equipped with bolters to guard the Grimnyr. The guns were a precaution against physical threat, but the CORVs' primary means of protecting her were the complex empyric circuits housed inside their rounded shells. Synced with her runic talismans, the constructs acted like psychic fuses, placing a breaker mechanism between Jôrdiki and the warp, from which she drew her powers.

'Myrtun, trouble's coming,' the Grimnyr warned.

'When isn't it?' Myrtun replied. Her armour was marked by ichor and gore, the livery partly hidden beneath smeared viscera, but otherwise not a dint nor scratch marked it.

'The Bane groupmind is strengthening. Nexus beasts are waking. You know what that means.'

Myrtun's grunt confirmed that she did indeed know what that signalled – more coordinated attacks and the imminent arrival of more dangerous warriors.

'We're almost at the valveway to the target. Our guns and blades will handle whatever's in front, I need your wards to shield our backsides.'

'It's as good as done,' Jôrdiki assured her.

'Kinna, you're on rearguard with Jôrdiki.'

'Aye, as you say,' replied the veteran squad leader.

Ten Kin peeled away from the others and joined the Grimnyr, bringing up the rear of the advancing expedition. One of them carried a portable scanner and checked its glowing screen while they pulled themselves up the incline of the slickly floored tunnel and floated through drifting post-digestion particles. Though her mindsense was not as precise as the scanner, Jôrdiki knew they were in no immediate danger. The closest of the Bane nexus beasts was still some way behind, at the centre of a coalescing mass of other organisms.

Several others were more distant still, one of them far sharper and stronger than the rest. As though she was looking through a heavy veil, the Grimnyr could broadly sense the psychic channels between the nodes of awareness – hardlines in a biological comm-network, connecting transmitters that rebroadcast a pulsing signal over their local areas. It was always unnerving to feel the consciousness of aliens in this way. The Bane filled her with an empty dread – an emotionless groupmind not even hating its foes, driven on by a single uniting predatory need. A hunger that entire galaxies could not sate.

Pulling herself back to her surrounds, Jôrdiki watched as the lead squad used cutting lasers to slash an exit out of the tract into a fatty, foamy layer of cells. The first of them pushed their way in as liquid and oval globules slumped out of the wound.

'This is the tissue around the statocystic chambers – cushions them against impact,' reported Iyrdin Cabb, passing on the information being fed to her from the *Grand Endeavour* by Lutar. 'Nearly there.'

Moving through the protective layer was more like swimming than anything else, visibility reduced to the wake left by the warrior in front. Jôrdiki became aware of a sense of alertness close at hand just a moment before the scanner in Kinna's hand started to ping violently.

'Something in here with us!' the squad leader warned.

Sinuous shapes moved effortlessly through the globules, eyeless and sheathed with chitinous plates. They brushed past the Kin, unaware of them until they touched something solid. At this, they spasmed, coiling instinctively around whatever they had discovered. The calls of entrapped Kin bounced back and forth over the comm-net, while sporadic barks of bolters vibrated dully through the oily morass. For a few heartbeats confusion reigned, and Jôrdiki found herself alone but for the domed shapes of the CORVs cutting through the cells to either side of her.

A suited figure emerged from the slick, their horrified face illuminated by her suit lamps – an old-timer called Vargn. One of the creatures was wrapped around her right arm, its tail whipping back and forth as it tried to find something else to ensnare.

'Get it off me!' Her expression was becoming more and more panicked. 'It's cracking open my armour!'

Jôrdiki saw that where the creature's plated armour rasped against Vargn's void suit, splinters were breaking away. The snake-thing coiled tighter and tighter, sending stress fractures creeping along the warrior's arm. Jôrdiki's CORVs pivoted left and right, responding to thrashing movements elsewhere in the mass of cells.

+Target detected. Firing solution unavailable.+

Jôrdiki dragged herself forward, reaching out her hand to grab the tail of the creature. She missed and the barbed tip whipped towards her, sending a flare of ward power sparking outwards just a finger's breadth from her face. Trying again, she flailed and twisted, finding no purchase in the oozing semi-liquid.

The endosymbiote renewed its attention on Vargn, slamming its tail repeatedly against her chest and faceplate. Vargn gasped with every impact, the pitch of her exhalations increasing with each blow. In desperation, she grabbed the worm with her other hand and immediately its remaining length coiled around her wrist, binding her like shackles. The creature flexed and Vargn screamed, her forearm protruding from the creature's coils perpendicular to its natural angle.

Vargn's predicament was also her salvation. Jôrdiki was able to grasp the undulating attacker, her wards like a layer of electricity between her and the organism. Through this she summoned empyric power, channelling energy via the circuitry of the CORVs. Sparks danced in her eyes and rivulets of flame flowed along her arm, the energy coursing into the defence organism. White fire rippled along its length, bursting free from within, consuming the creature in a series of detonations that sent shock waves bulging out through the bioship's fatty tissue.

'Is your suit intact?' the Grimnyr demanded. Vargn's eyes were looking everywhere but at Jôrdiki, fixed in disbelief at her freed arms, and then fixated on her broken wrist.

It took several more attempts to get Vargn to focus, but at last some clarity entered her dull gaze. She nodded and allowed Jôrdiki to grab the front of her armour and drag her forwards. After a couple of moments, Jôrdiki felt Vargn kicking alongside her and let go, her companion almost returned to her full faculties. She still held her bolter in her good hand, the left cradled protectively against her midriff.

They came across others in the fleshy morass. Most living, but spooked. A few dead. Cracked faceplates seemed to be the common cause, though a couple had missing arms or legs where the snake-things had constricted tightly enough that they had ripped off limbs. Their corpses were tied together in a grisly caravan and towed through the fatty sludge. In time they would be returned to the Votann, not abandoned to the genekillers. Dozens of the immune-system creatures floated in the gunk, hacked apart by blades or torn asunder by bolts.

Guided by flashing beacon signals, the expedition gathered again around an opening cut into the wall of the nearest statocystic chamber. Myrtun was waiting there, assessing each follower as they pulled themselves out of the protective tissue.

'That was new,' Jôrdiki said as she came up on her leader. 'Nothing in the records about snake beasts there.'

Myrtun hid her concern well, but Jôrdiki saw the telltale flexing of the crow's feet beside her eyes and the slight deepening of the lines around her mouth. Not only that, in such close quarters the Grimnyr's empyric sense was just about sharp enough to detect an aura of uncharacteristic uncertainty emanating from Myrtun.

'I think they've been learning,' the old Kin replied after a moment's consideration. 'You tell me there's a great big mind links them all up, yes?'

'That's right.'

'Seems to me that we, the Kin, have pulled this trick enough times the Bane have caught on. Started growing defence measures against us.'

'I'm not sure how I feel about that,' admitted Jôrdiki. She floated to one side as Kinna and the remaining warriors of her squads dragged themselves into the chamber. They had another body between them, its domed helm cracked like an egg, the lifeless face of the Kin within almost unrecognisable, a mass of blood and crushed bone. The Grimnyr returned her attention to Myrtun. 'It's horrifying that they can evolve like that. But… that's quite a reaction we've forced.'

'Makes it feel like we've hurt them?' Myrtun had already reverted to her normal attentive, confident demeanour. There was a ghost of a smile on her lips that was infectious.

'Aye, something like that,' said Jôrdiki.

'Right, let's get this sorted out and get about our business,' said Myrtun, her words now carried to everyone on the comm-feed. 'Iyrdin, form up the squads and reorganise. These filth are getting wise to our intent, and you can be sure as stars sparkle that worms aren't the worst of their tricks. Keep a watch like the Ancestors themselves.'

War has casualties because no profit comes without first incurring cost, Myrtun thought as she watched the deceased being strapped together into an uneremonious but practical spherical mass that would be taken back to the *Grand Endeavour*. It was a truth that she had learned early in her life in the hardest way possible. A Kin that was created, lived, and then returned to the Votann had partaken in a productive – some would dare say profitable – existence. Their matter would live again and their experiences had become immortalised. The Votann in their wisdom had never eradicated fear from the Kin. As a biological drive it was exceptionally motivating, and as long as it was honed with training and discipline, it was absolutely essential. Self-preservation, when under control, brought all decisions into sharp focus.

Yet the Votann had gifted the Kin a lack of existential dread. Not for them questions of the afterlife, whether souls existed, how to live a good life. Every Kin knew where they came from – the gene databanks and Crucibles in the Holds of the League – and that they would, if returned home, end up in the bio-recyclers with their consciousness uploaded to the Ancestor Cores. There was no mystery to confuse, no questions that might bring doubt.

Which was why Myrtun had never allowed herself to become wholly comfortable with death. It was to be accepted, but Kin lives were not simply existence tokens to be expended for gain. Each was a potentiality for further experience, with the ability to exploit new opportunities for the Leagues, and live new experiences for the Votann. So disparate were all the Kin, even within just her Prospect, that every death altered the future trajectory of her people – most in minor ways, but some Kin might have gone on to greatness that would never be realised. Each of the bodies bundled up with mag-belts might have been a future Prospect commander, a future kâhl, or even High Kâhl. The cloneskein in each of them may have pushed them in a direction, be it Hernkyn or Brôkhyr, Cthonian miner or Grimnyr, but it was not a preordained fate.

Death was transformative, though. She had led her people here to turn the threat of a bioship attack into a profitable source of materials. It was not lost on her that some who had started that journey were no longer going to benefit from their share. But they knew that the life of the Hernkyn was one of greater risks than most. And usually, until a couple of disastrous near-misses, Myrtun capitalised on that. But now that she felt the grip of the Hold ship dragging her back, she had to push those risks a little more. She did not need her crew's permission to make such decisions. None of them had signed up to return empty-handed.

She looked past the floating corpse mound to where Jôrdiki and the rearguard waited at the edge of the chamber, bolters ready for any monstrosity that emerged from the sea of goop, the crackle of ward runes occasionally flaring around the Grimnyr. Myrtun wondered what Jôrdiki thought of life and death, how she saw the servants of the Votann.

The Prospect commander had always shared her thoughts with Lutar but guarded them from others. Now it seemed natural to her that she would unburden herself to an Ironkin that might understand her but did not risk becoming weighed down by her baggage, yet as she knew the evening of her life was firmly moving into the night-time, a closer connection to the Votann and the heart of her people would not be amiss. Was there some worth in spending more time with her Grimnyr? Learning more about her than was spoken at the council?

'Found it!' Iyrdin's triumphant call shattered Myrtun's chain of thought, bringing her smartly back to the present. 'Bring the charges up.'

With no need for Myrtun's supervision, the Hernkyn and Hearthkyn fell into position, the small attitude jets in their suits manoeuvring them into place as they moved the charge coffins forward. Theyn Lordun and the bodyguard warriors kept close to Myrtun, but from long experience knew better than to crowd her. It was time to press on.

'Jôrdiki, come with me. Rearguard, keep close.'

Myrtun did not wait to see if her command was obeyed; she simply turned and pushed herself away from the slicked cartilage of the floor and floated after the others. Glowing slightly as her wards filled in for armour thrusters, Jôrdiki came alongside. Myrtun looked across to the Grimnyr.

'What's your mindsense telling you?'

'Nothing unusual. Waking sentience. Growing alertness. One of the greater node beasts is moving towards us, gathering forces.'

Myrtun cocked a glance towards the Grimnyr. 'You should lead with that sort of information!'

'It's already on Iyrdin's scanners.'

'Of course,' said Myrtun, though she wondered how she could have missed the Hernkyn theyn's report. Getting distracted by the nearness of Fyrtor, the recall looming like a shadow over her. She connected her comm to the *Grand Endeavour*.

'Lutar, how long before the genekillers reach us?'

There was a delay before the reply came through, and the signal seemed muffled, as though the mass of the creature between her and the Ironkin physically blocked the noise.

'It would seem that the main transport artery does not run directly towards the statocystic cluster. I suspect the Bane will need to cut their way through to you, as you are doing to reach the statocysts. I can't say how long, it would just be a guess.'

'If you guessed, would it be longer or shorter than the time needed to place and prime the charges?'

There was another pause. Myrtun wasn't sure if it was a communications delay or simply the Wayfinder making the necessary calculations.

'I would project that the Bane will take longer, but not by much of a margin. Avoid any delays.'

'Thank you. And how is Fyrtor doing?'

This time the reply was almost instant.

'Very well. His Prospect is attacking perpendicular to your line of advance and will shortly be within tactical communications range. The Bane have responded in part, but it seems they are treating you as a priority threat. I can use a relay to put you in touch with him, if you'd like?'

'No, but if you could ask that he push a bit closer, that'd be nice. Maybe try and get that big node beast to pay him some attention.'

'I'll pass on your suggestion. I will also remind you that as the genekillers approach and merge with your heat and movement signatures, and given the general scanning diffraction caused by the mass of the bioship on our life signals trackers, your localised scanners will be more useful than what I can see here.'

'You're saying to keep an eye out? You think we're just wandering about, sightseeing?'

Another pause.

'Just… be careful.'

Myrtun suppressed the urge to throw back something glib. Lutar was entitled to his concern, and she respected that.

'Myrtun out.'

They carried on across the space of the outer statocystic chamber, its darkness only broken by the beams of suit lamps shining from particles and myriad tiny organisms suspended in the air, dancing into whorls at the passage of the Kin like plankton in a deep sea. It was not so vast as even the council hall of the *Grand Endeavour*, but its space seemed to swallow the light, the limits of its volume only sporadically revealed as a beam passed over the wall of the roughly ovoid space.

'Everyone, hold position.' Iyrdin's sharp command brought a flurry of thruster flares gleaming across the chamber. Suit lamps turned in all directions as each squad moved to cover its quarter, weapons at the ready. A pencil-thin stab of light picked out one of the Hearthkyn advancing close to the wall. The warrior rotated amid a puff of motive gas, the irregular ovals of lamplight distorting across the chamber surface. 'Who's that over there, just in front of Gârnr Hammerbrow? Durskor? Pan your lamps along the wall, just to your right.'

The warrior stopped, lamp beams gleaming on a growth in the wall, like a scar but too regular to be the result of an injury. 'There!'

Calls from some of the others, all around the chamber, reported that similar lesions were dotted at regular intervals across the whole surface. Myrtun felt a twinge of revulsion, reminded that she was inside another living creature.

'Don't remember seeing these before,' said Iyrdin. 'Anyone know what they are? Lutar?'

Negative responses filled the comm until Lutar's transmission broke across the local links.

'There's nothing like them in the datacores. As best we can tell from here, they seem to be attachment points for some kind of denser ligament tissue in the surrounding flesh. They run off directly away from the chamber. Purpose unclear.'

'Stay alert, but keep going,' Myrtun announced, unsure what to make of this development. She was usually excited by novelty, but the worms that had already killed seven of her Kin and injured a few others warned that anything new here couldn't be trusted. 'Pick up the pace if you can – I want those charges placed and prepped as soon as we can manage it.'

With light beams tracing back and forth more frequently, the Kin ascended, following the narrowing sides of the chamber towards an opening above. With a stutter of vector thrust Myrtun spun whilst still travelling in the same direction. Behind her the rearguard were also ascending backwards, bolters pointing down into the gloom, their lamplight swallowed by the depth. Myrtun expected to see fanged maws and dead eyes lunging into the spread of lights, swarming up from below, but all seemed clear.

Turning to face forward again, she wondered what was making her so jittery.

CHAPTER TWO

Loss and Profit

It was more than the oppressive darkness that weighed heavily on Jôrdiki's thoughts. Her mindsense was not so much alive with signals as overwhelmed by a single crushing presence. It had grown so slowly and steadily that she had not noticed it until seeing the doubt and concern in Myrtun's face. Then she'd become aware of the pressure of the omnipresent psychic assault, like a slow, grinding drill head boring away the resolve of the Kin. She felt no direction or target for the attack; it was simply everywhere, a stifling effect of the Bane groupmind's warp-based shadow.

She tried her best to push back against the darkness, but her influence did not stretch far, encompassing herself, Myrtun and the closest of the Hearthkyn and Hernkyn. Such was her concentration on this task as they neared the opening at the top of the chamber that she almost missed the sudden sensation of awareness that suffused the giant entity around them.

'The walls! Check the walls!' she called, her wards blazing into luminescence at her command, a cone of blue light flaring towards the skin of the chamber not far away. The wardlight settled on one of the odd muscle structures, which, now she was closer, she saw was about four times the height of a Kin, a circle of compressed nodules. It trembled, the flesh around it shuddering as though about to convulse.

Cries from the other side drew everyone's attention. Jôrdiki swivelled in time to see flashes of six-limbed monsters skimming through criss-crossing lamp beams. Some held gun-like bioweapons, puffs of exhaling gas freezing in the air as they vomited forth a hail of flesh-boring organisms that spattered bloodily off the void suits of the closest Hernkyn. Others had scythe-like claws tipping their upper four limbs, each as long as a sword, the razor-sharp fangs in their slender jaws gleaming in the yellow light, their bulbous heads catching the glow on five overlapping chitin plates. Behind them, the wavering beams swung across dark pits surrounded by fibrous tissue – openings where the sinew growths had been. Larger warrior-forms pulled their way into view, dragging themselves from quivering orifices like obscene births.

The harsher light of bolter fire and ruddy detonations bleached out the scene, explosive rounds tearing apart the first wave of the Bane. As the Hearthkyn turned in response to the attack on their lightly armed and armoured cousins, there came the flare of other weapons: the red strobe of HYLas auto rifles, the blue glint of charging magna-coil accelerators, the combustion trails of foe-seeking missiles. The quickly coordinated response slashed through the closest aliens, blowing them apart, incinerating them with beams of plasma and shredding them with white-hot shrapnel.

Undeterred, the larger warriors launched themselves into the battle, obscene fleshy guns spitting deadly beetle-like ammunition, serrated bonesw0rds shimmering with bioelectric energy. The comm burst into life, Myrtun snapping out orders, Iyrdin adding her own directives to the charge bearers. Jôrdiki felt her gaze drawn everywhere: to the ongoing firefight, to the other nodule openings that were spasming into life all around the expedition, to the charge teams hauling their loads out of the chamber into the throbbing tunnel beyond.

And then her attention was drawn to a new presence, just below her.

'Myrtun!' she yelled, but the Prospect leader didn't respond, snapping off shots at a group of smaller genekillers emerging from an orifice behind the charge teams. 'Myrtun, something's coming! Something powerful!'

Jôrdiki directed her wardlights towards the growth as Myrtun turned. The opening dilated, shuddering apart to reveal a broad-crested head, almost as large as any Kin, nearly too big to fit through the gap in the flesh. It forced its way forward, tearing at the sphincter to thrust out a heavily carapaced body, arms sheathed in chitin. Growths like chimney stacks jutted from the thick covering across its shoulders and back, streaming a swarm of particulate matter that swirled with a life of its own.

Kinna's Pioneers opened fire, engulfing the emerging monstrosity with bolt shotgun rounds. Oblivious to the whirling metal fragments scratching across its face and armour, the node lord dragged free a tubular bioweapon that bulged with hideous sacs where the creature's long fingers meshed with its flesh. The symbiote convulsed, coughing forth a spray of mucus with a seed-like projectile at its heart. Jôrdiki watched with growing horror as the pellet expanded like a grotesque plant, uncoiling whiplike tendrils in the moments it arced across the space before impacting the chest armour of Kinna. The Hernkyn squad leader spun from the blow, barbed sinews burrowing into the soft sheathing between plates of bastium alloy.

Her scream blotted out the other comm-links, becoming a panicked sob.

'It's inside…! Votann's mercy, it's in–'

Kinna exploded.

From her bloody remains tendrils lashed at the nearby Kin, a frenzy of flailing hooks and spines that latched on to Nûrburyk, ripping away his arm with a sudden death spasm. A heartbeat later and the thing was already dead, shrivelling away to wiry fronds.

'Pull back!' Myrtun shouted, her combi-bolter unleashing a storm of fire against the node lord. 'Protect the charges!'

The beast had to contort its body to free its other arms from the fleshy wreckage of the connective passage, bringing forth a bonesword twice as tall as Jôrdiki, while a writhing whiplike organism uncoiled from its fourth hand. The Grimnyr brought up her staff and called the two CORVs forward, interlacing their empyric fields. The runework in her gear flared into blue light, projecting a barrier between the oncoming monstrosity and the retreating Kin. The whip lashed out, striking golden sparks of warp power from the shield. Jôrdiki flinched, glad for the protection of her wards.

Through the effort of keeping the shield intact, the Grimnyr felt the pulsing energy of the psychic shadow-cloud coalescing around the node creature. Winged horrors burst from other tunnels around it like bats from a brood tower, greeted by a fusillade of bolt-rounds and laser. Psychic power crackled across the chitinous plates of the command creature, leaping from spore chimney to spore chimney like chain lightning in a Brôkhyr's laboratory.

'I ain't having that,' grunted Jôrdiki, reaching into the ethereal web linking her to the empyrean through her runes and CORVs. She mentally took hold of the gathering alien psychic energy and wrenched it away, as if she were ripping the cables from a conduit. The bio-lightning faded, pitching the node creature into sudden blackness.

Around and behind Jôrdiki, there was barely room for the Hearthkyn and Hernkyn in the narrowed opening. Forced together, the Kin had to lessen their fire, allowing squads to pass by into the tunnel to their objective. Clawed beasts and filth-trailing projectiles followed them without relent, a second wave of larger warriors not far behind.

Jôrdiki turned, breath tight in her chest as she swept wardlight to the left and right, seeking the huge creature. She found it a few desperate heartbeats later, its emotionless eyes given a predatory glint by the reflected gleam. The node lord closed in while winged terrors slashed at Jôrdiki's wards, claws flaring trails of white fire from every impact. Pressure was building inside the Grimnyr's head, the effort of maintaining the shield making her feel faint.

The node lord was looking directly at her, its attention drawn by her interference. She wished she caught a buzz of hatred, a brief glimmer of anger, but she sensed nothing beyond emotionless, unwavering focus. The Bane mind shadow assumed a regular pattern, becoming a singular purpose. A predator locked on to prey.

More psychic power pulsed around her, summoned by the node lord. The creature raised a bonesword, the tip pulsing with multicoloured energy. Too late, Jôrdiki tried to intervene, but her CORVs were still dissipating the fallout of the last psychic shunt. A blast of raw power slammed into withdrawing Kin. The detonation engulfed two Hernkyn, burning through their void suits, turning flesh black with withering power. Missiles streaked back in response, fired by the Hearthkyn standing at the lip of the exit. Blossoms of fire swallowed the monster, their muffled booms reaching Jôrdiki through the thin air moments later. The node lord emerged from the blasts with pieces of chitin hanging off its form, one side of its face charred and ripped, revealing enormous fangs in a spine-chilling half-grin.

It turned its head towards its attackers, bonesword coruscating with power once more. A detonation in such packed confines would kill a dozen Kin.

'Look at me, you skein-stealing filth!' Jôrdiki cried, and sent a beam of fire leaping from her staff, splashing against the sword arm of the beast. 'Come at *me*.'

The node lord was obliging, turning its terrible cannon and the glimmering bonesword in Jôrdiki's direction. Gripped by the incontrovertible sight of her impending death, she panicked and snatched at all the etheric power she could reach.

Her shields burned white-hot from the stranglebeast's impact and a blast of psychic power. Beside her, one of the CORVs shuddered, sparks erupting from its empyric circuitry. Its suspensors malfunctioned, sending it into a spiralling loop away from the Grimnyr, trailing blue energy until it disintegrated into glowing shards.

'One down, still one left,' Jôrdiki growled, her free hand forming a fist, flames licking from her fingers.

'Lutar, get me a signal to Fyrtor.'

It was the first clear message that had come through the commpanel for some time, and it brought a sense of relief to Lutar, which quickly returned to one of apprehension as he realised that Myrtun's continued survival was far from guaranteed.

He looked over to the comm-station and received a nod from Duri, who was already tapping at the control screen.

'We're setting it up. Waiting on reply from the *Canny Wanderer*.' Lutar looked at the melange of data on the three-dimensional scanner projection. Transponders, life signals, and route markers all merged into an incoherent mess around the objective point. 'What's happening over there?'

'Placing charges. Don't think we can get out. Where's that link?'

The feed was oddly quiet, the periods of connection happening against a muted background of near-continuous weapons fire.

'Where's the link?' Lutar repeated to Duri, though she had clearly heard Myrtun. The comms attendant gave him a look he interpreted as 'cool your forges' and turned back to her station.

'Hello?' Fyrtor's voice was no clearer than Myrtun's. *'Myrtun?'*

'We're nearly ready to prime the charges. There're going to be damage spasms across the bioship, so you need to get back out before they blow.'

Lutar's temporal dampeners kicked in hard, stretching out every moment of the conversation. His processors went into overdrive, calculating and recalculating routes back out of the bioship. With the Bane already inside the statocystic system, none of the solutions looked good. And he knew he was working on flawed data. This ship had superior transit and immuno-defences around the vulnerable point. It had been bred to resist such attacks.

'I can't do that,' replied Fyrtor.

'Why not?'

'I've a message for you, from the Hold ship. Swore an oath to the Votannic Council to deliver it in person.'

'Well, bloody tell me it while you pull out,' Myrtun snapped.

'In person means just that,' Fyrtor insisted. *'I'm coming to you.'*

'That's just ridiculous,' said Lutar. 'Just give us the message.'

'You'll die here too.' Myrtun's assessment almost froze Lutar's artificial synapses altogether. *Too.* She was already resigned to her end.

'It wasn't me that bloody picked the guts of a genekillers' ship to meet in.' It was hard to tell over the poor-quality feed whether Fyrtor was genuinely furious or making light of it. His voice cut in and out, the comm-link dampened to suppress nearby spikes of noise: explosions and bolter barks. *'Where's the node beast? Is it still with you, Myrtun?'*

Lutar's rapid processing kept looping back to a possible solution.

'Fyrtor, just below you are the dorsolateral entrances to the tubular vessels that the genekillers are using to reach the statocystic chamber.'

'We can follow them to Myrtun?'

'Don't you bloody dare! I know it was stupid of me to make you come here, don't make it worse.'

'No, you can both make it out,' insisted Lutar. 'Where is the node lord?'

'We hit it hard with plasma beams and drove it back. Jôrdiki thinks it might be regenerating, though. It's distracted, and we've destroyed the main warrior-forms, so the lesser creatures are all over the place. But we have only a short time before that node lord recovers, or another gets here.'

'Fyrtor, follow the node lord up through the transit pipes. Withdraw your drillers and come in again from the dorsolateral side nearest to the *Grand Endeavour*. Have them keep going until they reach the chamber.'

'They'll be stuck in here with us,' Fyrtor replied.

Lutar eyed the display again, running the numbers a few more times to be sure. He looked over to Hôrfyk at the gunnery console.

'I can give you a quicker route out. The mining laser can cut away a portion of the bioship.'

At the controls Hôrfyk's eyes widened at the suggestion, but he voiced no protest.

'You get that wrong, lad, and you'll slice through all of us.' Fyrtor's assessment was accurate but unhelpful. Hôrfyk swallowed hard and nodded.

'Trust me,' said Lutar.

'I do.' Myrtun's calm assurance made everything suddenly seem crystal clear. Two words stopped the vague sense of vertigo that had beset Lutar since the Bane had launched their attack. *'Fyrtor,*

if you want to deliver that message and live to take the reply back to the Hold ship, do what Lutar says.'

The next few heartbeats dragged past.

'Right. Lutar, give us those attack coordinates and vector. Myrtun, hold on. Don't prime those charges yet. We're coming to you.'

'Don't take long.'

The comm-feed fell quiet and Hôrfyk turned in his seat. 'You have a firing solution for me?'

'Not yet. I need the energy signature of the drillers as a locking point to fix on Myrtun's location. When they're ready to board, I'll send you the target details. Duri, pull our landing craft away from the target zone. Fyrtor's craft should be enough to get everyone out of there. Watch for the biocannon kill-zones, that ship can still wreck us with a few good salvoes.'

Lutar knew the plan could work, though the margins were slim and there would be more casualties. There was no way to know who might be among them. He also knew Myrtun would not risk failing to cripple the bioship, even if it meant being caught in the blast of the charges, or crushed by reaction paroxysms within the vessel itself.

It didn't help that she had survived similar – possibly worse – situations before. Hundreds of times he had been on the bridge while she was off putting herself in danger, and it never became routine for him. The strange connection he had felt when he had first rescued her, an indefinable attachment that seemed counter to his mechanical creation, had never gone away. The laws of probability could often look like laws of inevitability the older she became and the more dangerous the situations she placed herself in. To Myrtun that was a rewarding life. To Lutar it was an unavoidable stress, but one he also actually relished.

That confounding dissonance was how he knew he was Kin.

* * *

'Running low on bolts and energy cells.'

Iyrdin's report came as no surprise to anyone holding the line on the lip of the statocystic chamber, and Myrtun accepted it without comment. The tunnels behind were filled with drifting, fist-sized rocks that acted much like the inner ear of a Kin, helping the bioship keep stable and orientate itself, though Jôrdiki detected a faint resonance from the shifting stones that suggested they interacted with warp space as well as gravity. The charge teams had pushed their way into the cloud and had positioned their burdens close to the central ganglia relay that connected all four of the outer statocysts.

They were primed and the countdown was already ticking. Myrtun would leave nothing to chance – the charges would go off whether anyone was left to give the command or not.

It was hard to tell dead foes from living, the area in front of the chamber opening filled with the corpses and body parts of the Bane. In places the organic debris was thick enough to act as cover for the incoming wave attacks. Though wounded, the node lord had not spared its minions any relent, massing together various beasts into assault waves that scrabbled along the chamber wall and leapt through the dead-cloud with only a single intent. Each attack was met with a wall of bolts and plasma. On the last two, survivors had made it as far as the line of Kin, slashing with hardened chitin blade-digits, firing corrosive arthropods from flare-muzzled bio-rifles.

And there were more and more coming. Jôrdiki had said she could feel the whole bioship waking to the threat of intrusion. Soon another node lord would arrive and the chance to escape would pass.

A sudden flurry of signals on the scanners heralded the timely arrival of Fyrtor's warriors. Bursting out of the pipelines to Myrtun's left, about a third of the way down the chamber, the Hearthkyn of the Hernkendersson Prospect arrived with a fresh blaze of HYLas beams and rocket strikes. Fyrtor and a knot of heavily armoured Einhyr led the charge, boosting away from the side wall directly towards the enemy. Myrtun caught a glimpse past them of something larger moving behind the scattered viscera and broken chitin: the wounded node lord.

The fresh assault that had been swelling now moved as one, scything towards the new threat.

'Push after them, meet up with the Kenderssons.' Myrtun was already plunging off the flesh ledge as she gave the order, combi-bolter raining rounds into the backs of the foe.

'For the Ancestors!' cried Iyrdin, jetting past with thrusters on high burn, her Hearthkyn around her.

'Show the strength of the Eternal Starforge's battle-wrought!' exhorted Jôrdiki as she joined the attack. The Grimnyr looked like a blazing comet, swathed in layers of shining wards, her staff held out like a spear.

'Charge teams, back to our main position.' Myrtun didn't want to have to wait any longer than necessary when the drillers broke through. The heavier ping on the scanners indicated Fyrtor's breaching craft were not far off. The only variable that remained was the accuracy of the mining laser. It was a tool, an improvised weapon more suited to blasting apart asteroids than performing gargantuan surgery on an alien bioship.

The node lord was caught between the two offensives, driven back by the grenades of the Hearthkyn and Fyrtor's volkanite disintegrator, trapped against the ward shield flung forward by Jôrdiki. Scintillating beams criss-crossed its carapace, sending chunks sliding away into the darkness.

Scanners howled for several heartbeats before the first drill-ship punched through the outer wall, its spinning nose flinging gobbets of ground, melta-charred flesh in all directions. Shards of bone scythed outwards into the onrushing horde, cutting bloody paths through their mass. More drillers broke into sight, their red-hot tips spearing into the aliens, lines of centipede-like crawling limbs coming to a standstill when they met no further resistance.

'Stay as close to the drillers as you can.' Lutar's warning was barely audible over the shallow but overlapping vibrations running back and forth through the chamber's thin atmosphere, causing distortion effects to ring across the comm-channel.

The aliens barely flinched from the blow that had been struck, thrown forwards by the implacable intent of the node lord. The creature moved via swipes of its chitin-bladed whip-tail, propelling itself suddenly towards Fyrtor's counter-attack. Ichor spilled in gobbets from several wounds and one of its arms was missing. Even so, a cloud of instinctual terror accompanied the beast.

A flurry of disintegrator beams and bolts converged on the onrushing monstrosity, but it pushed on. A moment later everything went white.

Though her visor had darkened to protect against the blinding glare, spots danced across Myrtun's vision. She blinked hard, her warning to Fyrtor dying on her lips, unneeded. Still her sight wouldn't return; all she could make out was blackness and small flickers of light.

Myrtun realised she was looking upon the naked void, the whole flank of the bioship sheared away in front of her. Turning her gaze upwards she saw the silvery glitter and plasma-blue drives of the *Grand Endeavour*. Looking past her feet, a building-sized mass of bone, flesh and chitin floated away towards the system's star, slowly spinning around its centre like a monstrous rotisserie.

Turning, Myrtun saw that the last of the enemy, those not annihilated by the mining laser's beam, were caught between two forces. Beyond them, the Hernkyn Pioneers who had laid the charges came tumbling out of the upper opening like barrels in a waterfall, firing their shotguns and bolt revolvers back at a cloud of winged constructs in pursuit.

'Anyone still alive down there?' Lutar's voice was edged with worry.

'The shot was bang o–' began Myrtun.

'Never mind that,' interrupted Fyrtor, jetting across the void directly towards her. 'We'll finish the clean-up in a moment.'

He drifted to a halt in front of Myrtun and presented a golden holo-sigil – the seal of the Hearthspake of the Eternal Starforge Kindred.

'What's this message, then?' the old Prospect leader demanded. 'What's so bloody important?'

'Myrtun Dammergot, voidmaiden, et cetera, et cetera,' began Fyrtor, turning off the holo. Myrtun met his gaze through their visors, and his eyes were moist with emotion. Her gut writhed, but she focused on every word. 'I bear the sad tidings of the demise of the great High Kâhl Orthônar, fallen in battle against the ancient ork menace.'

If she hadn't already been floating in the void, Myrtun would have thought the ground had disappeared from under her. The last time she had returned to the Hold ship was for Orthônar's Ceremony of Elevation. It was almost impossible to think about. She had lived through the reigns of two High Kâhls already. Now a third.

Some measure of reason returned.

'That is certainly grim news, and I wish I had agreed to meet under better conditions, but it wasn't worth your life to deliver.'

'I'm not done yet.' There was something in Fyrtor's manner, the look in his eye, that tightened a knot in Myrtun's gut more than the thought of losing the High Kâhl.

'The orks? They came to the Hold ship? What happened?'

'The Hold ship is fine, or was when I left,' Fyrtor said. 'Stay your tongue and I'll bloody finish.' He waited to see if she had anything else to say, but Myrtun kept quiet.

'By full triumvirate commendation of the Votann of the Trans-Hyperian Alliance,' he continued, 'and binding vote of the Votannic Council – the invitations to which you ignored, by the way – the successor to position of High Kâhl of the Eternal Starforge Kindred is named as Myrtun Dammergot.'

CHAPTER THREE

Welcome Diversions

From the high bridge of the reclamation scow, the bioship looked a lot smaller. In part that was because the sub-ships of the scow were closing in from all of the cardinal angles, moving in to ensnare the colossal, half-dead beast with anterior, posterior, left, right, dorsal and ventral platforms. Knowing that the huge creature would soon be surrounded by scaffolding and high-torsion anchor cables made it feel less threatening. The reality was that parts of it were very much alive, living off independent circulatory and nervous systems. On top of that, bio-constructs were still in plentiful supply to defend its innards from interlopers, and Myrtun didn't envy the heavily armoured crews from the Third Ice that would have to eliminate them.

Myrtun gripped a plain ceramic mug tight in both hands, wisps of steam bringing the earthy scent of brü. There was moisture in the air from a great brass urn squatting on a plain table in the middle of the chamber, the only source of heat. The platform had been extended up to its highest point and in every direction stretched space, seen through transparent view panels that encased the structure in a faceted globe. There was a strange disconnect between the vastness of open void reaching out to nothing and the feeling of closeness created by the relatively small, steamy space. It felt as though the universe had mass that was pressing down on Myrtun, crushing her like deep-sea pressure.

Or perhaps that was just the weight of Fyrtor's message settling more heavily on her shoulders. She tried to push the thought from her mind and concentrate on the operation unfolding in front of her.

Like the scow, the sub-ships were mostly plain metal and ceramic – only a section of hull was given over to the contrasting light and dark green of the Urani-Surtr Regulates. Three icicle-like triangles of white against the green signified that these vessels belonged to the Third Ice Kindred. It was into their territory that Myrtun had ventured, and whose kâhl for reclamation operations now stood next to her.

Grimdâr Jôrundil was taller than Myrtun by some margin, and looked as though she had been carved out of solid red granite. Her brows were ridged and knobbled beneath the ruddy skin of her face, her flat nose and cheeks giving the impression that she had been pressed up against the inside of her cubicle as she had been wrought by the Embyr of her Kindred. There was no softness about her at all, nor any of the Kin that worked the controls of the scow and commanded the sub-ships, the clone-skeins of their Kindred skewed towards physical hardiness more than anything else.

Myrtun knew that the Kindreds of URSR existed in a parlous state between survival and extinction for every day of their lives. Threatened from nearly all sides, they put their faith in producing more and more Kin, to expand their territories and replace their constant losses. Everything from rations to furnishings was kept to a bare minimum to devote as much resources as possible to the Crucibles. A haul like the bioship was a huge deal for Grimdâr's Kindred and the Regulates as a whole, and the speed with which they had sprung into action spoke testament to the area they occupied between subsistence and comfort.

'One might say you have done the easy part, really,' Grimdâr said to Myrtun, and to Fyrtor, who was standing to her left with his gaze directed just past the front of his feet, watching the first of the boarding gantries extending out from the main hull of the scow.

'This one was harder,' Myrtun reminded the kâhl. 'New type, with new biology.'

'Worth more,' added Fyrtor, not looking up.

'Which will be reflected in final market prices,' replied Grimdâr. 'I can't dictate that now, or be held to future fluctuations. That offer I've given you is standard recompense by any measure.'

'Maybe your measures are a little smaller than everyone else's,' said Fyrtor, though there was no rancour in his voice.

'Perhaps some Kindreds have spoiled themselves with too much of what there isn't enough of,' Grimdâr said in a matter-of-fact way. She knew this was business, which was serious, but none of it was personal.

'There're opportunity costs to be covered,' said Myrtun. 'We had to divert from a journey back to the Hold ship to come here.'

Fyrtor spluttered and coughed as he choked on his brü.

'Plus all the usual depreciation, expenditure of consumables,' Myrtun continued, ignoring the indignant noises coming from the other Prospect commander.

'I'll be deducting the cost of the brü if you carry on like this,' grumbled Grimdâr, before downing the remaining contents of her mug in one mouthful. She let out an explosive breath of satisfaction and extended her other hand, using her thumb to twist a ring on her middle finger so that its gem pointed upwards. A hologram of the URSR icon gleamed above her palm. 'Two per cent share on market valuation on disposal.'

'What about me?' Fyrtor exclaimed, thumping his mug down on a nearby console.

'Sub-contract, nothing to do with me,' said Grimdâr. 'Sort yourselves out.'

'Two point five, then,' countered Myrtun.

'I'm getting half of that,' insisted Fyrtor, stepping up to put himself between Myrtun and Grimdâr.

'Two point two-five. That's more'n I should offer, given you cut half of the bloody thing off.'

'It's barely a scratch,' said Myrtun. She looked at Fyrtor. 'You get a third.'

'Nope.' He shook his head. 'Nothing less than two-fifths.'

'Two-fifths, *after* fees are processed.'

The three of them looked at each other for a while, waiting to see if there was any further shift. When it was clear the terms had been agreed, Myrtun and Fyrtor both activated the gems on their chains of office, projecting slowly rotating images of the Trans-Hyperian Alliance logo. Chimes sounded as the three mercagrams touched, sealing the deal.

A short Ironkin clerk that had been standing behind Grimdâr stepped forward with a digiplate and showed them the screen. The deal was displayed with the attached seals.

'Usual wording.' The clerk switched off the rectangular device. 'Copies will be provided to everyone's register.'

Myrtun drifted away to watch the continuing operation. Drill-hooks had been fired into the outer layer of carapace, securing the reclamation scow to the side of the bioship. Salvage teams drove along the gantry in open-topped six-wheeled rigs, their hefty lascutters ready, towering mechanical retractors looming over them on booms affixed to their transports.

A weird thought occurred to Myrtun as she watched the first incisions being made and the retractors peeling apart a layer of skin as thick as she was tall. The bioship would be claimed, piece by piece, every component down to the last drop of ichor and grain of bone dust. That matter would become part of the Third Ice Kindred's supplies, and from them it would disseminate across the URSR and then into other Leagues. Eventually some of that material, indirectly, would end up with the Embyr and feed the crucibles of another generation of Kin. They would grow, live and die, and in turn their constituent matter would be reclaimed and nothing of the Bane would be left behind.

Just as they did to others.

The difference, Myrtun decided, was that her experience of this, her memory and thoughts that surrounded the bioship and the encounter with it, would be preserved in the Votann. The Bane took everything but kept nothing, whereas the Kin were a means for gathering not just material but information. By serving the Votann as observers, they were witness to the processes of the universe.

She found that comforting. She did not have to concern herself with the question of why she existed. The fact that she existed gave meaning to everything else.

'Too bloody long, gadding about all over the place,' muttered Jôrdiki as she busied herself around the Fane of the *Grand Endeavour*. She was garbed in robes of black and orange, and around her neck hung a necklace of runic amulets, each studded with a coloured gem that caught the light flickering from the banks of the Votannic conduits. She wore her golden hair in half a dozen plaits, her skin pale but mottled with darker patches. Bands engraved with more runes adorned her wrists. These were not merely ornamentation, but keys to the Fane that allowed her to commune with the distant power of the Trans-Hyperian Alliance's triumvirate Votann. Though she held the esteemed position of

Grimnyr, she was the youngest of the Prospect Council, just entering her middle years by the count of the Kin.

She gestured with the runic bands now, moving from outlet to input to receiver, activating the systems of the Fane so that it could interface with the Votannic repository on the Regulates' reclamation platform. She muttered mnemonic lines as she half-danced through the protocols, the clunky lyrics a verbal instruction manual to herself. She had tried her best to write it all down for that inevitable time when another Grimnyr would take her place, but words on the screen failed to convey the rhythm and tempo of the connection sequence.

Finally pirouetting to a stop in front of her main terminal – the last manoeuvre purely a flourish for her own amusement – Jôrdiki stabbed a finger at the interlocution rune. With a hum and a series of ascending beeps, the Fane started working. Invisible Votannic waves reached out to the dormant vault account on the platform, opening it like a Brôkhyr might lift the panel of a malfunctioning data console.

Jôrdiki felt the moment of connection ripple around the systems, and then for a few heartbeats, the two were as one, exchanging data like binary stars swapping stellar atmosphere. More lights blazed into life as databanks filled, while from the offload terminals a green glow confirmed that the messages and announcements carried on the *Grand Endeavour* had transferred across, ready for any ship that followed after.

It had been quite a while since last contact, and there were several thousand discrete data packets to catalogue, decipher and interpret. Jôrdiki rubbed her hands and grinned at the thought.

Myrtun wore a heavy, loose-fitting robe of black, embroidered in the distinctive orange of the Trans-Hyperian Alliance with a variety of Kin designs. Her left hand, resting upon the arm of her chair, was a mechanical facsimile of gleaming silver, its internal workings concealed behind polished segmented metal. Her right hand absent-mindedly stroked a cloak of pale fur spotted with burgundy markings – the pelt of a Thoristan lancefang she had once domesticated as a pet.

On their own grand seats, stretched along the long table to either side, were her Prospect Council, the Kindred of the Eternal Starforge's governance as far as the Dammergothi Prospect was concerned. Rarely was her Prospect arrayed in full, as now – the council chamber doubled as the Hernkyn commissary for most of the time, since space was always at a premium on a ship – but even so, it was Myrtun's presence that commanded the full attention of the hundreds of assembled Kin.

'We're heading back to the Hold ship,' Myrtun announced to the folk present. Only the background hum of the *Grand Endeavour*'s engines, the whirr of air filtration units, and the occasional belch or cough broke the rapt stillness. Myrtun swept her gaze over her Kindred. 'I am to be High Kâhl.'

She didn't expect any reaction to this, and there was none. These were both facts that had been known since she had returned from the bioship. Nobody was sure what it meant for the Prospect, and so congratulations and commiserations were both held back until the future became clearer.

Myrtun reached out and gripped the gilded handle of a great mug fashioned from the skull of an aeldari pirate captain she had slain many orbits earlier. A patina stained the old bone, and brü froth slopped over its rim as Myrtun stood and raised the mug of alcoholic stimulant for a toast. Chairs and benches scraped, bionics rasped and whined as the Kin followed suit across the chamber, their tankards, cups, and goblets catching the light from dozens of ruddy lanterns hanging from the rivetted beams of the vaulted ceiling.

'Until then, once more to opportunity,' Myrtun said quietly.

'Opportunity!' The lusty roar of the Kin shook the room and raised an appreciative smile from Myrtun.

The contents of the drinking vessels were downed in swift gulps. On the high table, Iyrdin Cabb suffered a brief choking fit before finishing her drink.

'Sabotage,' she spluttered. Her crest of blue hair, braided into a long ponytail, whipped back and forth over her leather jacket as she glared around the table, a tattooed finger thrust accusingly. 'Someone's tampered with me brü.'

'Don't talk grit,' laughed Myrtun, cutting off her companions before any chose to take the accusation literally. 'You poured it yourself, like we all did.'

Nearly all of the Kin who ventured under the command of Myrtun were there, spread across scores of well-worn tables. Some still wore void suits of orange and black; others had worker coveralls, while many were dressed in thick trousers, heavy shirts and sleeveless jerkins. Leather jackets with fur-lined collars and heavy duster coats had been thrown over benches and tables. Many sported piercings or tattoos of some nature, and hair both facial and on the scalp ranged from clean-shaven to outlandish, with every manner of crest, cut, moustache, and beard on display in a rainbow of colours. No few sported broad-brimmed hats or bandanas.

'We've got some sour business to attend to,' Myrtun announced to the Kin of the Prospect, her voice resounding along the length and breadth of the hall by cunning design. 'Due to the damage we did to the bioship, and giving Fyrtor his fair cut of the proceeds, I find that the bio-salvage isn't going to cover what was left outstanding on the expedition sponsorship.'

The news was greeted with a rumble of discontent.

'We got word that there's trouble brewing and some folks will pay for good warriors. I hope you've rested your axe arms and recharged your energy packs, because we've got another fight ahead.'

She let this settle in and took a breath. Though the shortfall hung like a cloud over Myrtun's thoughts, it provided her with good reason not to head back to the Hold ship just yet, allowing her to postpone an approaching life of drear conformity.

'It's mercenary work for an Imperial commander,' she continued, 'out towards the Ariel Sound. Since the warp storms broke, there've been more and more attacks on the Imperial systems out that way. Seems their own haven't been very alert in responding.'

Some calls of support thundered back, but many took the news with quiet, grim nods. Myrtun could tell that her people were fatigued after relentless adventures, but she knew they were good for at least one more expedition. They just needed the right incentive.

'And I've heard,' she said with a look at her table companions, 'that their coffers have been filling steady this past generation. We can be certain of suitable recompense for our efforts. Rules of supply and demand. We supply the kill count and demand the best pay!'

'Or salvage rights if we're too late!' someone shouted from across the hall, to a mix of jeers and laughs.

Talk settled down as drinking vessels were refilled.

'Happen it's always uncertain, dealing with Imperial folk,' said Jôrdiki when the mugs were steaming with brü once more. From within the shadow of her hood she looked at Myrtun with mismatched eyes – one green and one brown, a mark that the Kindred had taken as a sign of the Votann's intent for her to become Grimnyr.

'You mentioned that there was a signal?' said Lutar. The Ironkin sat on Myrtun's left-hand side, an empty mug and plate in front of him. The light caught a small imperfection in the dome of his head, a scar-like scratch on the top.

'A distress call, you said,' added the dock chief, Greta.

'It's not all that clear,' Jôrdiki reminded them. 'When I downloaded the data-locker from the Regulates' outpost, there was some other traffic among the standard notifications. Most of it is just noise that the systems try to interpret. A lot of folk trying to sell stuff or their services. Happen the Kindred of Liminus Crag have a new ion drive design they're offering to any interested Brôkhyr, and there's a surplus of sonic drills being offloaded by the Cthonic Guild at Barsum... And these Imperial signals are all over the place, warp-bent and everything. Anyways, I have to unpick all that. What I actually said was there seemed to be a cluster of references and echoes from the Ariel Sound and the area around it, as well as that open offer for war work. It's not *my* decision to head there.'

'We can't go back to the Hold ship empty-handed, Jôrdiki,' said Myrtun. Her skull cup was halfway to her mouth, paused for this declaration. 'Especially now. How would that work? Would I owe myself?'

'You misunderstand, I ain't arguing against taking the work.' The Grimnyr glanced at the other councillors, as though voicing something that others had not said but had thought. 'It's just... *now* you want to listen to what the Fane has been trying to tell you? Have a mind to why you've been dodging all other messages. Is it just the debt? Happen we all know that only the direct order of the Votann would dissuade you once your mind is set.'

The skull cup thudded back to the table.

'What is your point?' The question was asked quietly, but all at the table knew what that portended.

'From what Fyrtor says, turns out it's the Votann that the

council are speaking for,' Jôrdiki continued, wiping her top lip with the back of a hand. 'If it goes badly at Ariel Sound, the Kindred need to know what we've been about, to make sure the Trans-Hyperian Alliance knows too. You're High Kâhl now. If the Imperials cross us, it's the whole Kindred they're crossing. If we don't come back, someone will have to settle the account.'

Myrtun weighed up the words as carefully as a Brôkhyr assayed a new circuit link, looking for the faults. Jôrdiki was often speaking against Myrtun's adventures. She didn't seem cut out for the life of Hernkyn at all, but that couldn't be helped. They needed a Grimnyr and Jôrdiki was it. This time she seemed to be agreeing with Myrtun, but in a backwards way.

The kâhl gave an almost imperceptible nod to show that her assessment was complete and the Grimnyr had been found satisfactory, at this time.

'I reckon you should probably tell the Hold ship where we're going then,' she said. 'So that everyone knows. Guess it's not just my business any more.'

Jôrdiki necked the rest of her brü, stood up, and turned her mug upside down to indicate that she was finished. 'I'll do that, then.'

When the Grimnyr was gone, the conversation washed over Myrtun. She responded unconsciously to others, her mind occupied with thoughts of the Imperials and what she might find when she actually got back to the Hold ship.

The corridor was plain metal bulkheads and rockcrete flooring, the former painted a bluish off-white as across much of the *Grand Endeavour*, the latter a pale green to indicate the zone of the ship – the personal quarters of the council and officers. The space rang with the footfalls of Lutar and Myrtun as they returned to their chambers. A couple of the other councillors had gone before them, wanting to keep their heads fresh for the coming warp journey. A few, along with many of the lower ranks, remained in the hall enjoying their carousing.

It was one of the few occasions that Lutar felt apart from his flesh-and-blood kin. The enjoyment of eating and drinking – particularly the imbibing of the stimulant-alcohol known generally as brü – was an element of Kin society in which he could not partake and would never be able to emulate, no matter how sophisticated his neural computational network. There were some Ironkin who had found simulated substitutes that, when paired with semi-random subroutines, could induce something akin to the unpredictability and loss of restraint associated with insobriety. In Lutar's experience, though, these were almost invariably bores when 'drunk' – his fellow Ironkin were not particularly broad in their interests or experiences.

Instead, Lutar derived some pleasure from observing his kin in their various states of inebriation and then recollecting the most humorous parts to them at inopportune moments. Sometimes he did the voices too.

Myrtun was often amongst the last to leave, being both of a constitution that could outlast most of her underlings, and of stubborn pride to demonstrate this when possible. Tonight's quiet demeanour and early exit were a sign that not all was well with the Prospect's kâhl.

Usually he would wait for her to confide in him when she felt the time was right. Almost invariably she did, perhaps a day or two later, when she had reached a resolution for herself. With a somewhat risky jump into the fringe systems between the Leagues and the Imperium, Lutar thought it better not to allow her concerns to brew any longer than necessary.

As they reached Myrtun's cabin and she laid a hand upon the broad lockwheel jutting from the metal, Lutar placed his hand on her arm. It took a moment for her to respond to the touch, her head turning and eyes moving slowly towards him as though confused.

Lutar knew well what she saw. In stature he was similar to any other Kin, as though armoured in a void suit, and even most Kin observers would be hard-pressed to notice any difference from a distance – perhaps a slightly odd precision to his gait, a distinctive stillness when not moving.

'Jôrdi's analysis was accurate but unwelcome,' he ventured, the tip of conversation inserted like the point of a shuck used to prise open the clams grown in moisture beds on the lower levels of the ship.

'She don't like being called that,' Myrtun answered, which was an obvious deflection. Lutar said nothing, knowing well how this would play out – they had gone through this script with each other hundreds of times, on varying topics and fears. This time Myrtun surprised him with a deep sigh, looking directly at his dome, where a face would have been.

'Something to do with becoming High Kâhl, I suppose,' she admitted, bottom lip protruding in thought. The line of her gaze moved up towards the strip lumens hanging from the ceiling, and thus having severed the moment of contact, she was able to admit the weakness she was so loath to share. A hesitant silver hand touched the scratch on Lutar's dome and then drew back. Myrtun's voice cracked as she spoke. 'I don't want it! I don't want to go back. I'm not High Kâhl material. My place is out here, not sitting on the Votannic Council voting on bean allocations and sweat-filter reclamation regimes.'

Lutar waited, knowing that she wasn't finished.

'But it's my duty, right? Forget the council, the Votann decreed this. That's not an opinion I'll debate. So I've got to go.' She let out a breath that she had been holding too long, coming as a soft wheeze. Myrtun held out a hand and he took it, her artificial fingers on top of his. She met his implied gaze and smiled softly. 'Let's be honest, I'll not be warming the chair long, not at my age. But that's even more the point. Why pick me, at this time of my life? This spin with the Imperials is my last adventure. My final chance to do something.'

'And you don't trust yourself, do you?' His fingers tightened just enough to comfort. She wiped moisture from her eye, failing to hide the gesture by flicking back her hair at the same time.

'Just keeping going, never looking back. It would be easy. Always another catastrophe, another peril, one more mystery to unearth. I would keep chasing dreams till I dreamt no more. I have to tie myself down to stop falling.'

She let go of his hand.

'It's done now,' she said to herself as well as Lutar.

Myrtun straightened her shoulders and marched to her door without a backward glance.

The soft clunk of the door shutting heralded a long sigh from Myrtun. She hadn't lied to Lutar – she could never do that – but she had withheld some of the truth. Resting her back against the cool metal for a moment, fingers seeking comfort from the fur of her mantle, the kâhl allowed herself to relax into the familiarity of her chamber. For a lifetime of adventure, it was sparsely furnished. She had given most of her trophies and souvenirs away, either in trade, or as gifts, or to be added to the High Kâhl's vast repositories on the Hold ship. Collecting such mementos had lost its appeal, her room taking on the look of a museum more than a personal space. A shrine to her own life that spoke of something far greater than she felt.

The chamber was actually a suite of three rooms joined by scrollworked square archways. This was her bedroom, the walls clean of clutter and freshly painted with a coat of light grey. The bed itself filled most of the space, a broad swathe of mattress and brightly coloured blankets. Her greatest treasure, though Myrtun was forced to admit that her ageing bones and aching joints were making it more of a necessity than a luxury with each passing anniversary of her creation.

To the left was the arch to the tiled washroom, a swirl of sea-like greens and blues. The archway to her right beckoned her with the dimness of the unlit room beyond, and she pushed away from the door, unclasping her cloak to drape it over the foot of the bed as she passed. The lanterns within flickered to life, revealing a study-workshop double the size of the two other rooms combined.

It was impossible to tell exactly where the workbenches with their scattered tools and projects finished and the books and desks of the office began. There was a general demarcation between the oil stains and ink stains, but books and papers littered the metal benches just as gears, bundles of wire, and callipers dotted the deep-red wood tables of the other half. It was the opposite of the ordered, neat workspace of Thôrdi, her chief Brôkhyr. She was no artisan, but a lifetime acquaintance with guns and machines and armour left its mark. A 'tinker-fool' Thôrdi would call her now and then, with a wry smile as he handed over some spanner or screwdriver he knew he would never see again despite Myrtun's assurances, or when casting an appraising eye over her amateur creations.

Of all the works of the Brôkhyr, it was automata that captured Myrtun's fascination. Not the semi-intelligent E-COGs or the Votann-created Ironkin, but genuine automata powered by clockwork or battery, acting out a pre-determined sequence of actions in imitation of actual life. Mostly the Brôkhyr made them as practice pieces while apprenticed, showing they could master the intertwined disciplines of mechanics, robotics and control circuitry. They built automata that had purpose, such as filing down gear teeth straight out of a mould, or hammering data rivets into circuit boards. But Myrtun's constructions served a different purpose. She had learned that not all value in life was calculated in profit or pure utility. There was more than scratching a survival out of the galaxy, like the Urani-Surtr Regulates. A star could be both a source of bountiful harvest and a subject of awe and beauty.

Her automata danced – singly, or in pairs, and once in an entire six-strong rondel that saw them take turns to spin around each other arm in arm. They were a way of making sense of everything, a means to turn the disorder of wire and cog into planned motion, comforting in their predictability.

She picked up one of half a dozen pairs of lenses left on different surfaces around the room, perched them on her nose, and moved to inspect her latest project. It was a short, slender figure, mostly legs and a head, with tiny arms, that would be able to do high kicks. That was the plan. So far she couldn't even get it to stand up.

Myrtun's fingers found a screwdriver and she started loosening the case of the main mechanism. Her thoughts went back to the exchange with Lutar. She hadn't told him about an increasing morbidity to her dreams, and her increasing preoccupation with death.

Not her own. That had been true. But she thought of those of her companions, her followers, who had lost their lives. Life in a Hernkyn Prospect was not for the faint-hearted, and it was not guilt for the dead as much as a discomfort at the lack of accounting. When possible they had been returned to the Votann, by their thoughtprints via the Fane of the Hold ship or another vessel.

Most, but not all.

Some had been lost, impossible to recover, or their physical bodies blasted into irreconcilable particles or bloody slurry. With them their memories, their experiences, the core of who they had become were gone. They had played their part in the great weaving of the Votann tale but in the end had been written out of it completely. She remembered them, and that lent a greater emphasis to her own mortality. If she died without returning to the Votann, would anybody else recall their names? Would the lost dead cease to exist, except as some potential recorded in a gene archive somewhere back at the Hold ship? She was the guardian of their legacy. Was it reckless to endanger herself even more?

As she pulled off the back of the automaton and looked at its insides, she knew that she could act no differently than she was doing. Lutar with his learning network and synalgorithms had more chance of escaping a destiny laid down by the Votann than Myrtun. Her experiences had shaped her, honed the rough clay of genetics into the person she was today, but her life's direction had been set a course long ago.

And the Votann had made her with a disposition for adventure. She could no more give it up than the automata, once completed, could decide to stop dancing.

The bridge of the *Grand Endeavour* was a scene of quiet, scrupulous activity around Lutar as he began the last of his pre-plunge checks. Kin sat at each station on sturdy stools, some accompanied by floating E-COG assistants, attending to their duties at blocky consoles made of brushed metal. The terminals were arranged in an arc, with Myrtun's command chair forming the centre of the radius, navigation and helm to her left, engines and weapons to her right, scanners directly in front. The faces of the crew were lit by displays showing schematics of energy systems, scan returns, and scrolling lines of runes and numerals, their fingers poised at runepads and trackwheels, touchscreens and numbered dials. Gauge needles bobbed back and forth as systems powered up and down, and the background hum of the engines and ventilators created a steady aural static that Lutar had come to know well since coming aboard. The warp-space team were at their platform directly beneath the main screen, which took up the greater part of the curving front wall, monitoring the systems needed to hurl several thousand megatons of starship through the barrier between dimensions. Everything was in order when the doors rumbled open at the arrival of their commander.

'You should have replaced Gurthin Dourdinr,' Lutar said to Myrtun as she took up her position on the bridge of the *Grand Endeavour*, in the broad throne-like seat at the heart of operations. Sub-displays and internal comm-controls were set into the arms, and heavy impact harnessing hung from its back.

'Nonsense. Between the two of us, we know more than any Voidmaster. This isn't our first time.'

'No, it is not,' he said, his tone suggesting that he wished it was their last. Lutar was a construct of routine, and the lack of a dedicated Voidmaster ran counter to his protocols despite an intellectual agreement with Myrtun's assessment.

As Wayfinder, it was Lutar's role to use measurements from the warp resonators to model the local warp-space flow and, via the calculus, plot the trajectory of the ship through it until they emerged from the other side of their 'plunge' ten or so light years closer to their destination. Two such plunges were required to reach the nearest system, claimed by the Imperials, though as yet uninhabited by them.

The pre-plunge routine settled Lutar's processors, even though the orders came from Myrtun and not a Voidmaster; the call-and-response rhythm was slightly changed when the Voidmaster did not have to interact with a separate ship commander. Despite this irregularity, the Ironkin's fresh neural paths were growing accustomed to the new pace. With some small surprise, a quick check of his memory banks revealed that it had been six orbits since Gurthin had lost his life at the hands of a depraved aeldari raiding party in the ruins of an abandoned pre-Imperial settlement.

Something disturbed the sequence, and he detected Myrtun rising from the command chair and advancing a few paces to stand beside him. He realised she was looking at the main display, where the swirl of a nebula and scattered stars swept from the bottom left to the top right.

'Ariel Sound is the edge of the Trans-Hyperian Alliance,' she said quietly.

Lutar knew this, and Myrtun was aware that his internal star charts covered the area, so he realised the statement was rhetorical and stayed silent, awaiting the rest of her thought.

'Beyond the Midjagr Vortex is Far-space.'

The term conjured a plethora of thoughts and images, but from her intonation there was a single word brought to the fore: freedom.

Lutar looked at the purple-and-blue bruise on the huge screen, trying to decipher its lure. To him it was the chance to extend his knowledge, to push back the frontier of Votann ignorance. Currents not yet calculated, star systems to be recatalogued or discovered. It pleased him to think of this, fulfilling an imperative given to him by the Votann. But he knew that was nothing compared to the excitement it engendered in Myrtun.

'We have pierced Far-space five times previously, for extended periods,' he said.

'But not *here*...'

Myrtun spent several more heartbeats looking at the display, lost in thought. With a blink and a half-smile directed towards Lutar, she seemed to return to the present, and stepped back to the command seat. She didn't sit down though, instead laying a hand on its sturdy back as she continued to issue check commands.

It was only from the long-range scanning data that it was possible to tell the *Grand Endeavour* was moving at all, at incredible speed in fact, having been accelerating to the required velocity for the past three days. The deck rumbled with the constant fire of the engines and schematics flickered with representations of the void ship's systems, but they paled when compared to the reality of captive miniature stars filling circuits with life, bursting forth from the engines to drive them onwards.

In moments like this, as the countdown began for the plunge, Lutar knew that had he possessed a heart, it would now be beating faster.

As usual, Jôrdiki spent the period transiting back into realspace in the Fane of the *Grand Endeavour*. While the command bridge was the temporal centre of the ship, here was its spiritual heart, if such a thing was possible. It was unusual for a ship like the *Grand Endeavour* to even have a Fane, and its existence was owed to the longevity of Myrtun's occupation and the continuing presence of Jôrdiki. It was something of a privilege to have the freedom to roam with the Hernkyn whilst honing her skills in prognostication and ward-forging. Jôrdiki had to remind herself of this fact every time she crashed up against the buttresses of Myrtun's towering personality. Better here, among the stars, in charge of her small Fane than a lowly attendant to one of the Grimnyr on the Hold ship.

As she polished the brass tubes that carried bundles of cabling between the newest Mainfane cores and the Interpreter digilectern, Jôrdiki marvelled at how much a simple Votannic communications station had changed into this semi-sentient technological miracle. It had evolved with her, growing over the years as she learned the ways of the Grimnyr and adapted the machine to suit her needs. In return, the maturing intelligence within the Fane had made its own requests: access to different wavelengths and scanners, connections to Crucible data records, Brôkhyr schematics of other Fanes. The two of them were like a single entity in some ways, part organic and part mechanical. They complemented each other, existing to fit together like a hand and tailored glove.

'Breaking to realspace. Countdown beginning.'

Jôrdiki barely registered Lutar's announcement. It was the fifth such transition since they had left Volungar and the small but grateful contingent of Cthonian miners from the Kindred of the Third Ice. There had been hundreds since she started her journeys with Myrtun.

Thinking about what would happen next sent Jôrdiki's feelings slightly adrift. It was confusing to think of the old Pioneer as High Kâhl, and more vexing for the Grimnyr to think of continuing expeditions on the *Grand Endeavour* without her.

Perhaps she would leave the Hernkyn. Maybe it was time to study properly at the great Fane of the Eternal Starforge. She had learned much from treatises and self-teaching, but working again with one of the older Grimnyr might raise Jôrdiki to her full potential.

Circuits hummed into life in the depths of the Fane, sending Jôrdiki a sudden sensation of discontent. She waited to see if anything would appear on the Interpreter, but the screen remained blank. The Grimnyr wondered if she had imagined the reaction.

'Jôrdiki, come to the command bridge.'

Myrtun's summons was as unexpected as it was abrupt. Stowing polish and cloth, Jôrdiki took up her staff and headed towards the travel tube that connected the Fane with the bridge. A single car that could seat four Kin waited by the monorail platform, its canopy hinged upwards. Jôrdiki stepped across the small gap and dropped into one of the front seats, the display in front of her illuminating at her arrival. She keyed the rune for the bridge. The car started forwards as the canopy lowered, the entire compartment sealed before it reached the end of the platform and the waiting darkness of the tunnel beyond.

There was a momentary feeling of pressure as the suspensors kicked in, lifting the car fully into the gravitic fields. The glow of magna-coils shone from the smooth walls, the feeling of movement growing stronger with every passing moment. Inside the car, inertial dampeners compensated for an acceleration that would have snapped even the hardy spine of a Kin. They passed no other stations, following a direct line between Fane and command level.

The deceleration of the second half of the journey was equally buffered, easing Jôrdiki slightly forward in the seat but no worse. The sudden brightness of the bridge terminal dazzled her for a moment, but her sight had recovered by the time the car had come to a stop and the canopy raised. She stepped onto a checked pattern of orange and black tiles, electro-lanterns hanging from brackets above and on the walls. Steel handrails led down several steps to the main concourse: a nexus of five different lines linking the bridge to the engines, council hall, private quarters, cargo hold, and the Fane. A few dozen other Kin were moving through from one station to another as their roles changed between warp space and realspace. Heavy emergency doors were held over the archways, allowing the whole terminus to be locked down in seconds in case of disaster or attack, while individual transport lines could be opened and closed, either to baulk attackers or to ferry warriors around the ship.

Fortunately, only twice in her time with Myrtun had Jôrdiki ever felt the *Grand Endeavour* under such threat. But, she reminded herself as she headed to the doors leading directly to the bridge, there was always a chance of a third time.

The doors parted to reveal a scene of serenity: Myrtun stood next to her chair, everyone else at their positions. Jôrdiki felt the jolt of transition like a fizz of electricity from her staff, just as she stepped across the threshold. A momentary dizziness swept through her – a combination of psychic feedback and its disorientating confluence with her moving from one place to another, as though a single pace had taken her from warp space to realspace.

That's why I stay in the Fane, she reminded herself, a hand on the corner of a set of engine status panels to regain her equilibrium. The residual effects of transition swirled through her gut and head, after-echoes that slowly diminished. While she recovered, Jôrdiki made her way across the bridge to take up a spot to Myrtun's left.

Ahead of them the main display flickered into life, showing a view of the Ariel Sound. It was a binary star system, its twin suns little more than bluish dots at this distance. Data scrolled over the view, pinpointing the orbital paths of the major planetary bodies and other celestial phenomena. The worlds and asteroids themselves were not yet showing up, the *Grand Endeavour*'s scanners sending ever-increasing pulses out into the void to map out their locale.

'Not much on the readings,' grunted Myrtun. 'There was a starbase last time we came through.'

A splash of kaleidoscopic colour from the left, originating off-screen, alerted them to the transition of the *Canny Wanderer* even as sirens wailed the warning and the Kin at the scanning desk called out. It was only a few moments before the comm-operator spoke up with a request from Fyrtor to establish a link. Myrtun gave a brief nod and returned her gaze to the display.

'There's war around these parts,' said Myrtun. 'Been on and off for more than my lifetime. A lot more recently, from what Jôrdiki's been saying. Imperials and warp-mad renegades going back and forth. What was that posting, Jôrdiki?'

'The station commander offered a standing bounty for destroying enemy ships,' the Grimnyr replied. 'On evidence provided, of course.'

'Sounds suspiciously like a plan. We make a couple of plunges and find some trouble, enough to be worth something.'

'That doesn't sound like a plan,' Lutar pointed out. 'Having a plan involves an objective, and steps, and… planning. When was that bounty report issued?'

'A while back,' admitted Myrtun.

'Fifty-three orbits ago,' said Jôrdiki. 'Nearly a human lifetime.'

'Which is probably why the readings are as they are,' said Lutar. 'No sign of a space station here.'

'What's that?' asked Jôrdiki.

'It was never rescinded!' declared Myrtun. 'The contract is still legitimate.'

'We've arrived,' came Fyrtor's voice over the speakers. *'What now?'*

'Just figuring that out,' Myrtun replied quickly. She looked at Lutar and then focused on Jôrdiki. 'There were some readings, though. Might have been ship wash in warp space from just before we arrived.'

'Other ships?'

'Maybe.' Myrtun didn't want to commit, that was obvious.

'They didn't break warp into the system here, but the trail did fade around this system.' Lutar studied a map on his screen. 'Renegade ships often translate closer to the system centre than we do.' The Ironkin spoke without much conviction.

'We need to wait for the scans,' Jôrdiki said to fill the space. A lot of the noise she had picked up had been far more recent.

'Warp wash, you say? My Wayfinder said she thought she saw some odd patterning in the swell. Figured it might have been you or another one of the flotilla.'

'I don't think our Pioneer ships overtook us on the way,' said Lutar. 'It was only a short plunge from Nierderhel.'

'I concur with that assessment,' said an unfamiliar voice, presumably the *Canny Wanderer*'s Wayfinder.

'So we go and find the station,' Myrtun declared. 'Just because we haven't seen anything yet doesn't mean it's not here.'

'You mean we might have come this way for nothing?'

'It might be worth going further in,' suggested Jôrdiki. 'There's been scattered, oblique references to this area from the Fane for quite some time. Maybe trying to draw our attention to something.'

'The further we go in, the further back out, and the longer until we can make the next plunge towards the Hold ship.' Fyrtor's tone made it plain that he disapproved of any delay. *'And it's just as likely that if anything happened here, then we've missed it.'*

'What about the warp wash?' asked Myrtun.

'You know warp space. Could've been made yesterday, could've been an age ago.'

'A few days to look around, that's all,' offered Jôrdiki. 'We need to trust the Fane.'

It was clear to Jôrdiki that the High Kâhl-to-be wanted to avoid becoming High Kâhl for as long as she could, and would latch on to any reason to stay. The Grimnyr knew that this place was important; she couldn't accept that the Fane had made an error. Even though no communication was certain, her instincts told her that this wasn't one of her occasional misinterpretations. She was very conscious of the self-built nature of the *Grand Endeavour*'s Fane. If there were any doubts about why they were there, it would likely mean she had misinterpreted the slightly cryptic warning. Either way, she didn't want anyone to lose trust in her or the Fane.

'We have to return to the Hold ship, Myrtun.'

'We do.' The next High Kâhl folded her arms and walked closer to the scanning display, as if to peer deeper into the Ariel Sound. Then she spun on her heel, as though she had made a decision. She looked at Lutar, but before she could speak Jôrdiki stepped forward, her staff thudding onto the hard deck.

'I'm no tame rover to be dragged all over the place with twitches on my leash,' Fyrtor continued. *'I had plans to venture round the Cerulean Belt before the council sent me after you.'*

Myrtun listened, nodding slightly in agreement. Her gaze settled on Jôrdiki once more, enquiring. The Grimnyr was expected to argue her case.

'The Council chose you as their messenger, Fyrtor,' Jôrdiki explained slowly, gathering her thoughts. 'Maybe not because you were the closest or fastest. They thought you were the right Kin for the job, whatever it entailed. And you helped Myrtun in that bioship. There's others, rightly so, that wouldn't have set foot on that monster. But you did what needed to be done. You never thought of pulling back and returning to the Hold ship, freed of your oath because it looked impossible. I have that same feeling. It ain't fate, it ain't magic, but our Fane read something in the warp waves, or picked up a signal that needed a response, even if it couldn't wholly translate it. We're here to find out what it is. If we're not going to look for a job, what was the bloody point of coming here anyway?'

Jôrdiki inhaled sharply, amazed by her own passion. She waited with the next breath caught in her throat.

'Fair enough. Maybe there's something in what you say. We're here now, we could have a sniff about for something worthwhile.'

'I agree,' Myrtun said curtly, gesturing to Kildi at the drive controls to make ready. 'We'll wait for the scout ships to join us, and then go have a look. Five days?'

'Seems long enough.'

'Five days and then if we haven't found anything, it's back to the plunge point and direct route to the Hold ship. I *promise*.'

Fyrtor gave his assent and cut the comm-link. Myrtun's expression grew serious as she looked at Jôrdiki.

'Remember, it's always my reputation too, yes? I believe in you, so let's hope we don't all look like fools.'

The frigate's engines exploded first, sending out long plumes of burning gas, a yellow-flamed overture to the full symphony of the reactor detonation. A perfect sphere of blue plasma engulfed the renegade vessel, turning it into scattered particles in an instant. The reactor overload temporarily blotted out the view of the ongoing battle beyond, its brightness obscuring the criss-crossed las-beams, missile wash and speeding plasma stars of duelling cruisers.

A cheer went up from the bridge crew, and Lutar could imagine the same echoing along gunnery decks and inside laser battery turrets. He noticed Myrtun give a satisfied smile, but she kept her calm demeanour.

'That's just the small one,' she cautioned. 'We've still got the big one to deal with.'

The big one was a behemoth of a vessel, larger than the *Grand Endeavour*. It looked as much like a carved idol as a battleship, a nightmarish dragon-shaped creation of fused rock and metal, with a gaping, gleaming maw that trailed a slick of impossible fire, and eyes alight with baleful warp glow. A hybrid daemonship, forged from a mortal vessel and the power of the empyrean. Scans showed life signs aboard, but whether they were willing servants of the warp gods or pitiful slaves was impossible to know.

'Ready for the next one?' Fyrtor sounded buoyant, the peril of battle insignificant compared to the potential salvage of the enemy vessels, a worthy reward for venturing to the Ariel Sound.

Two days and nothing had shown on the scans, but day three had revealed plasma traces from a starship. Recent enough to warrant more time, Myrtun had decided. And then debris and more plasma. A battle. Curiosity had vied with efficiency of effort for the Kindred, but after some debate and more impassioned words from the Grimnyr, both Hernkyn leaders had agreed to follow the sporadic trail.

That had proven fortunate for the beleaguered Imperial ship now battling for its life in a magnified portion of the main display.

'Most of the firepower seems to be to the front, but we can't let it get between us.'

'Agreed. I'll come to you. Stay on that heading.'

Lutar felt it necessary to intervene.

'If we do not manoeuvre,' he pointed out, 'we're going to push ourselves straight into the teeth of their guns.'

'We've not taken a scratch yet. Our shields will hold, but they can't take the punishment from our whole flotilla. They'd be touched in the head to take us on without their escort.'

'Minions of the Cursed Powers rarely display sanity, Myrtun.'

'Their friend has had enough, look.'

On the sub-display the other human renegade vessel – a drab-looking cruiser in a livery of grey and red – was breaking off from its exchange of broadsides. It was ascending from the battle plane, while the Imperial heavy cruiser started to turn and rotate so its guns would continue to bear.

On a screen next to Lutar's console, a group of three runes

surged ahead of the two Pioneer vessels: Fyrtor's heavy scout ships. A torpedo streaked from each, leaving an after-image trail across the scanner, the dense magna-coil cores at the hearts of their warheads spinning up to incredible speed.

Turrets along the scaled spine of the dragonship opened fire, a blistering fusillade of energy pulses to greet the incoming torpedoes. The timing was off and the detonations caught only a single torpedo, shredding its engines in a fountain of red-and-purple fire.

The daemonship tried to evade the remaining pair, its eyes becoming bright bursts of fire as arrestor thrusters blazed into life. Cumbersome and long, it had only turned a fraction of the arc needed when the torpedoes hit, one striking it in the face, another midships.

Magna-coil vortices erupted from the warheads, tearing at the surrounding structure. Part of the jaw and side of the face disappeared into a whirl of dust and splintering metal. Several gun decks buckled outwards, hurling debris and bodies into the void as if they were blood and bone from an exit wound.

The hits were solid but not critical.

Lutar watched intently and could see Myrtun's fingers were tight on the arm of her chair. Her gaze hadn't moved from the display since the torpedoes had launched. The bridge crew had fallen silent, glancing at the main screen when they could spare a moment from their stations.

Scarred and spilling more air and crew, the daemonship continued its ponderous turn, changing course away from the Kin vessels and Imperial ship. The latter fired a parting salvo of explosive shells at its retreating foe, and then the enemy cruiser was out of effective range. Plasma jets burning at maximum, the two surviving renegade vessels headed into the void.

* * *

Myrtun allowed herself a small amount of smugness before snapping out her next order.

'Helm, adjust course to follow, full speed.' She caught Lutar's expression, which conveyed a combination of relief and incredulity. 'Did you think I'd be wrong?'

'I thought the odds of your gamble were not in our favour,' the Wayfinder replied. 'I'm pleased that the outcome you predicted came to pass.'

'And now it's time to finish them off.'

Lutar directed her gaze to the strategic display. 'The *Canny Wanderer* is maintaining course and bringing back the escorts. If we pursue alone, the renegades will turn on us.'

'Fyrtor? What are you playing at? Get your scout ships to loop around in front of them, torpedoes ready. We need to herd them back in this direction, or we'll never catch them.'

'And if they decide to keep going? Right through my Kin? We've beaten them back. There's the wreckage of the first ship, plus plenty of other debris. It's enough.'

'You'll let that prize slip away?'

'We are too slow. We cannot catch them. So then you'll say we need to look for them, and we'll start a hunt. System by system. And then we'll run into some other foe or danger, and it'll never end. We're done here. It's time to honour that oath and return to the Hold ship.'

'Honour my...' Myrtun looked at Lutar and wondered if he was thinking the same thing. 'This isn't about becoming High Kâhl. We can't just let them...'

Her argument petered into silence, leaving Myrtun stewing in a mix of indignation and confusion. Was Fyrtor right?

Before she could answer her own question, a call from the comm-station introduced another problem.

'We are receiving transmissions from the Imperials. Do you want to talk to them?'

'Leave them be. We saved them, now they can go on their merry way. Just make sure you get them to agree to witnessing that kill for the bounty.'

'They're still outnumbered if we desert them,' said Lutar. 'They are not safe yet.'

'Then they best use the head start we've already given them.'

'We need to stay to pick up the salvage,' Myrtun added. 'Maybe we'll get a bonus if we stick around and watch their back.'

'I think they have some kind of problem with their engines,' said Lutar. 'Look.'

Through the magnified view, Myrtun could see that nearly half of their thruster tubes were dim when the others were bright with plasma plumes. There was severe damage to their aft decks.

'Ask them if they can fix it soon,' Myrtun said to the comms attendant.

'Why does it matter? This used to be Leagues space. The Imperials have no right to be here. They're lucky we don't blow them out of the stars next.'

'Leagues space? Not for ten lifetimes has there been any permanent Kin presence here.' Lutar shook his head. 'Not much of a claim.'

'Start a war with the Imperials?' Myrtun said with a grimace. 'That's your plan? Just straight-out pirates now, are we? And when things escalate, how many thousands of our Kin are worth the pay-out?'

'I'm not serious. But how would anyone know? They'd think it was the Warped Ones.'

'Stop just thinking about raw loot for once. There's more to be earned than metal and rockcrete and bounty. This is on the edge of our space and we've got enemies in good supply already. The Kindred need to be making allies in these hard times, not blowing them up. If that ship gets destroyed so close to our territory, what's to say the Imperials wouldn't assume the worst? And the space station offer seems to be a bust. Leastways, if we steer this lot on their way, they can take word to their higher-ups that the Kindred of the Eternal Starforge are open to fight for the right price. A bit of thought now can pay much bigger dividends in the future.'

Fyrtor's silence spoke of his lack of argument, and Myrtun bit back an urge to keep on at him. She realised how much that had sounded like something a High Kâhl would say, and partly it annoyed her. There was a time she would have agreed with Fyrtor. Still, it had been said now, and there was no sense belabouring her point and risking alienating the Pioneer.

The comms attendant spoke up again.

'As far as I can tell, they have reactors on half-power to prevent further damage, and if we would escort them to the system boundary they'll affect repairs on the way.'

'Tell them they can stick close while we tidy up here, if they want.'

'I know there's no point offering to send over our Brôkhyr. Shame, because there'd be good profit in that. Stupid Imperials never want our folks helping with their technology, waffling on about their Machine God and whatnot.'

'We should always be alert to any call of opportunity,' Lutar said, looking thoughtfully at the human vessel on the screen. 'All news from beyond the Leagues has to be of some worth.'

'Are you suggesting we talk *to them? You know half of them think we're just as worthy of extermination as orks and other filth?'*

Myrtun sat down in her command chair, feeling the energy of the battle beginning to drain away. Her knees hurt and the soles of her feet were sore.

'Lutar is right, we should make the most of this,' she said. She scrunched her toes inside her boots, trying to ease the discomfort.

'The Fane guided us here, perhaps to learn something useful. And I'm sure these Imperials are feeling well-disposed towards us already.'

'Some kind of comm-conference?'

'Nothing says "trust" like a face-to-face meeting.' Myrtun ignored the groan that sounded across the comm-link. 'I'll host. Why don't you bring along some companions and a favourite keg?'

'I don't really think this is necessary,' Lutar complained. 'I could simply not attend the feast.'

'Nonsense,' replied Myrtun. She absently ran a finger along the small crack in his helm. 'You've got your mirror filter so that they won't see you haven't got a face inside that dome of yours.'

Lutar's quarters were small but well furnished. A compact bunk nestled in one corner, not for sleeping as such, but he liked to lie or sit there while he read. A considerable number of books filled the bookcase that took up the entirety of the opposite wall. It was more of an exchange library than a personal collection, with volumes constantly borrowed or lent to others depending on desire or need in return for other books, favours or such that were deemed a good exchange. A digibook reader sat on a small bedside table with a number of storage crystals laid in a neat line next to it, under the frilly-edged shade of a dumpy lamp. Both table and lamp had been gifts from Myrtun so that he could read without the main lanterns on. Opposite the door, on a shorter wall, was Lutar's chart desk. It was a hobby rather than part of his duties – actual star charts were stored in the datacores, where they could be retrieved, analysed and updated digitally. The hand-drawn maps neatly rolled up on a shelf above the desk, a work in progress held down by three pots of variously coloured inks, were to pass the time. For every shift spent in combat or some other adventure, there were sixty of travelling between places without much happening. He also told himself that should some cataclysm ever befall the datacore, he would be prepared…

'Imperials are highly suspicious of technology. It would be better if I stayed away altogether, to be on the safe side.'

'Stop trying to get out of it. This was your idea, anyway.'

'It was not!' said Lutar indignantly. 'I said we might learn something from the Imperials, I didn't suggest inviting them all over to dinner!'

Myrtun placed a hand on the side of the dome, as though she were touching his face.

'I need you there. You're the clever, reasonable one.'

'I am to add ambassador to my list of roles, am I?'

Myrtun used her hand to brush down his armoured shoulders, though whatever debris she saw there was likely imaginary – he had taken a sterilising oil bath just before she arrived.

'No, I'm not having that. Ambassadors get sent places. I'm keeping you right here.'

Lutar initially railed against the idea of being referred to as a possession, but as he processed further, it gave him a welcome sensation of belonging. No Kin belonged to any other Kin, whether Iron or not. It was one of the First Truths passed on by the Ancestors. Yet the thought of Myrtun owning him in some way, or being singled out for a kind of unique attention, was pleasant. However, it prompted questions he was reluctant to ask.

'And when you become High Kâhl?' he said, trying to be casual. 'The Hold ship has a sizeable and esteemed bridge crew. There is no need of another Wayfinder, and three Voidmasters take shifts as commanders. Perhaps *here* is where I should stay.'

Myrtun said nothing, but continued to fuss over non-existent discrepancies in his appearance. For her part, the Prospect commander looked immaculate in her full regalia of heavy robe and lancefang mantle. She even had on the Prospector's Chain, a thick iron-wrought necklace with a green gem shaped as a four-pointed star. She must have noticed him looking at it, as she lifted the jewel in her hand.

'Stupid thing, too awkward to wear. And I always found it a bit ugly, truth be told. But it is my badge of rank and right. I bet these Imperials will have all sorts of medals and whatnot. They take that sort of thing very seriously, I hear.'

The comm buzzed. It was Gubrin Fastblade, her freshly appointed master of ceremony. Another Ironkin, one of the Brôkhyr, his nimble fingers and creative streak meant that he doubled as her personal chef on occasion. His name came not from any fighting prowess, though he was fearsome with a plasma sword, but his skill at chopping ingredients.

'Fyrtor and the Imperials are both on their way. Greta has everything ready for their arrival in bay four. Do you think Imperials have the palate for hotroot?'

'Don't see why not,' replied Myrtun.

'Perhaps make it a side dish and they can help themselves?' suggested Lutar. 'Just in case.'

'Good idea! I'll begin the final preparations.'

'What were we talking about?' said Lutar when the comm-link went dead, knowing well that Myrtun was dodging the issue of her forthcoming change of circumstances.

'Nothing I want to discuss tonight,' she told him firmly. 'The Imperials have fixed their ship, and we're at the system boundary. We'll be in the warp first thing on morning shift and heading to the Hold ship. Plenty of time to work things out once we get there. Let's just enjoy this freedom while we have it.'

Lutar gestured for Myrtun to precede him to the door of his quarters. She waggled her fingers at his face, and he realised he hadn't activated the glare filter. His dome darkened slightly from his point of view, but to Myrtun and everyone else on the outside it became mirrored.

Myrtun stood on tiptoe and peered close at him, pulling a variety of faces. She was looking at the distorted reflection, not him. He regarded his books with the thought that some philosophical tracts he had read attested that all anyone ever saw was distorted reflections. Guiding Myrtun to the door with a hand at her back, Lutar wondered what the Imperials would see.

Fyrtor had suggested to Myrtun that he land first and they both meet the human delegation together. It had seemed a good way to present a united front, but now that she waited in the Pioneers' common hall – hastily refurbished to be more suitable for an impromptu summit – Myrtun wondered if the other Hernkyn leader had wanted to avoid appearing to be her subordinate.

The kâhl of the *Canny Wanderer* had spared no effort on his appearance or that of the small entourage he had brought with him. She could see the freshly sewn seams on his padded jerkin and heavy trousers, the glint of new rivets on his companions' void armour. Like Myrtun he had a chain of office, though ornamented with a comet fashioned out of red marble and gold. Standing at her side, he might almost be mistaken for her equal.

Which he was, she reminded herself.

Sort of.

If you ignored all of her earned titles, seniority, and the fact that she was going to become the next High Kâhl. Aside from all that, they were just two Hernkyn Pioneer commanders getting together to parley with some Imperials.

Lutar was looking at their surrounds, his body arching back as he stared up into the rafters, though Myrtun could only see herself and the warped view of the hall reflected from his domed helm. Everything had been stripped back to burnished metal and varnished wood, broken up here and there by shelves of knick-knacks culled from the stores and various personal collections. Myrtun had donated a couple of automata to the cause – her earlier ones that she didn't find very entertaining any more. There were books and small sculptures and hand-painted icons on scraps of armour taken from enemies, while over the great plasma hearth there hung a massive picture of the Nêrn Straits – twin pillar nebulae that Myrtun had been the first to explore during one of her earliest forays into Far-space. She had named them after the Hernkyn kâhl that she had first joined on leaving her crucible. He'd seemed so old and wise at the time, but now she realised Nêrn Dammergot had been half her current age when orks tortured him to death in front of her. She suppressed a shudder at the memory. It was better to focus on now, not the distant past.

'The Pioneers won't recognise this place,' remarked the Wayfinder. 'That's the first time those lantern panes have been washed in a quarter of a lifetime. I can actually see the grain in the tabletops! Which means somebody has scraped out all the grime from the grain in the tabletops.'

'Reckoned I could sell that grime as high-quality chewin' resin,' said Gubrin Fastblade. The master of ceremony wore his thick Brôkhyr coverall over a dirty white shirt, a combination he had 'livened up' with a flower-embroidered jerkin he'd bought off a ratling seamstress many years earlier. Myrtun knew this because he had explained his 'ensemble' at length on the walk up from the monorail. The tan coveralls protected his legs and torso, and also doubled as his cooking apron, which was why it was dirty with not only lubricant and iron filings, but also some streaks of what was hopefully gravy, and an unidentifiable blob of something bright red at exactly the spot his belly button would be. He turned slightly, the slant of his domed head – mirrored like

Lutar's – giving the impression that he was glaring at Myrtun. 'But I wasn't allowed to keep it.'

'The Votann built us hardy, but I've no urge to test their genius,' Myrtun replied amiably. She was nervous and excited at the same time, which was the best kind of feeling to have. She tapped Gubrin on the arm. 'How long…?'

'Nearly here,' he replied patiently. It was, after all, only the fourth or fifth time she had asked him since he bustled in ahead of the party making its way from the transit platform that served the Hernkyn quarters.

'Why is that here?'

Lutar's question had all eyes turning towards him. It was hard to follow the exact line of his gaze, but he was looking at something amid the trophies that had been rehung over the side door leading to the commissary and kitchens. Myrtun saw gold but couldn't make out more than the vague shape among the other items.

'It's the bird thing,' said Gubrin, sounding pleased with himself. 'Imperials love it. Pictures and sculpts of it everywhere. A type of pigeon, isn't it?'

'Ark-will-arse,' said Fyrtor with a knowledgeable air. 'They pray to it sometimes, the daft numpties.'

'Aye, and I've seen 'em make a flappy gesture over their chests when they mention their Emperor,' added Jôrdiki. 'Happen it's a holy gesture for them, like a salute.'

'Do you reckon they'd mind if we flapped the ark-will-arse at them when they get here?' asked Gubrin.

'Never mind that,' Lutar said, cutting across the chatter. He thrust a finger at the crudely carved and gilded effigy hammered to the lintel of the door. 'What will they think when they see that?'

'Maybe, "Oh look, they've got the Holy Pigeon, they must be decent folks," or somethin'?' suggested Gubrin.

Myrtun groaned, coming to the same conclusion that Lutar had.

'They might ask where we got it,' she said. 'And does anyone remember where we got it?'

'Don't rightly recall,' lied Gubrin.

Behind him, Iyrdin raised her hand. 'I know! Jurda-Jor brought it back from the wreck of an Imperials ship. A destroyer or something, wasn't it?'

'It wasn't a wreck when it approached us,' Myrtun had to point out. 'We turned it into a wreck.'

'They did ignore your warning to stay clear of our salvage operation,' Lutar reminded her. 'They insisted we were in *their* territory, and kept on coming.'

'Borders are tricky things, especially in the void,' said Myrtun, gesturing for somebody to go and pull the avian insignia down. 'They only count if both sides have drawn them. Those ruins didn't look at all Imperial to me.'

Lutar and Gubrin headed to the door and pulled up stools to reach the ornamental bird. At that moment there was a thudding on the main portal: three slow, resounding crashes of something heavy against the metal.

'I told them to do that,' Gubrin called across the hall. 'Makes it seem all official and that.'

'This thing's screwed tighter than a...' Lutar trailed off, unable or unwilling to finish the simile. 'It's tight. Got anything on you to loosen these bolts, Gubrin?'

The Brôkhyr fished into his pockets and produced a spoon and a whisk with an apologetic shrug.

The three knocks echoed across the hall again, slightly quicker and more impatient. Myrtun felt her shoulders tensing.

'Oh, bloody hell. Fyrtor, you come with me, we'll stall them at the door. You lot, find something to pull that thing off or cover it up, right now.'

The other Hernkyn leader offered no objection and followed her closely down the central aisle between the benches.

'Just some folks come over for supper,' he muttered. 'Nothing to worry about.'

The pistons of the main portal pulled the doors apart with the quiet exhalation of recently overhauled hydraulics. The massive doors settled in place along the wall with barely a clank or clink, nestling against newly replenished quilted padding. Myrtun reminded herself that they'd have to give the *Grand Endeavour* a thorough clean and polish on the journey back to the Hold ship. She didn't want to hand a broken old trash bin to the next Prospect leader to command the ship.

Her first sight was of the 'Guard of Honour' pulled together by Gubrin, and she was impressed. A hundred Hearthkyn and fifty Pioneers in full void armour, drawn up in squads two ranks deep on either side of the corridor, guns held across their chests.

'They've been practising,' murmured Jôrdiki. 'But it came oddly natural once they started. They say a Kindred thinks as one, don't they?'

A contingent of off-duty bridge crew approached, followed by the much taller Imperials. As gunnery, navigational and comms attendants peeled apart, the Imperial ship's contingent were left standing a few paces in front of Myrtun.

She assumed the captain was the one draped in the most gold: a dark blue uniform chased with gold thread, epaulettes with loops of golden cord heavy on his shoulders, a triangular-brimmed hat with more gold, and a tassel of gold that hung to his right shoulder – and that was before the sparkle of actual gold and gems that covered his left breast with medals. A person of means, which was reassuring.

He wore a waistcoat and white shirt beneath, and tight leggings that tucked into boots just below the knee. Gold buckles too, Myrtun noted. She had seen a few humans in her long life and judged this one to be broader than most, and a little taller. He certainly dominated his contingent with his presence.

She also noticed something else, which gave her some hope. Amidst all the finery, the captain had a plain, one might even say battered, scabbard holding a sword with a hand-worn leather hilt and plain steel basket on a black hanger. His pistol and holster at the other hip were likewise heavy and workmanlike. There were small scars across his face, and he was missing most of his left ear. Myrtun stopped her hand moving towards the bionic of her own ruined ear and pretended to adjust her chain of office instead.

The captain bowed slightly and raised his hands to cross them over his chest with fingers splayed, making an approximation of the wings of a bird. Ignoring an uncharacteristic squeal of delight behind her, presumably from Jôrdiki, Myrtun noticed his left index finger was missing its tip.

A fighter. Not a man to lead from the back.

'Keptin Argrave Lorzentine.' He straightened. 'His Emperial Huly Marjesty's heevy krozer *Bringar ov Wur*.'

Taking a moment to wonder what the captain had said, Myrtun smiled and nodded her head in a return gesture. Before she could say anything, Gubrin appeared at her shoulder.

'Myrtun Dammergot of the Kindred of the Eternal Starforge,' he announced, speaking with stiff, formal enunciation. 'Scion of the Trans-Hyperian Alliance, Gatemistress of the Ebon Channel, Voidmaiden of the Nêrn Straits, Leader of the Dammergothi Prospect, commander of the *Grand Endeavour*.'

They'd agreed in advance that there was no need to share that she was High Kâhl Elect. Such news was not for outsiders any more than chatter about the Votann.

'If I might take your cloak, commander,' he added almost at a whisper, reaching for the clasp of her mantle. She pushed his fingers away as he stepped in front of her, his back to the Imperials. With some strange bodily jerks towards the Imperials, and questing fingers, he indicated an urgent need to take her cloak.

'Of course,' she said, trying not to look confused. She unfastened the cloak and handed it to him. Gubrin disappeared as softly as he'd arrived. Myrtun met Captain Lorzentine's enquiring look with a mock expression of exasperation. 'My master of ceremony... Everything has to be done proper, yes?'

Lorzentine said nothing, his face a picture of thought. Myrtun concluded that he was trying to decipher what she had said.

'Yars.' The captain's tone was slow and deliberate. 'Meen owen preest is nonsweervng een fulluweeng the huly ritchools.'

Lorzentine turned and indicated a man to his right, of not much greater height than the Kin, though skeletal thin rather than stout. He wore a dark brown robe of plain material, and a white tabard over it, embroidered around the edges with gold thread. A cowl covered his head, upon which was affixed a heavy badge shaped as a golden bird not dissimilar to the one the Kin were attempting to conceal within the hall. The priest – as such she figured from his garb and the captain's words – had dark, heavily lined skin, with bloodshot eyes and thin lips. He looked at her with bare hostility, those miserly lips pursed in distaste.

Myrtun introduced the council members attending her, speaking slowly and carefully. The Imperials introduced themselves, some with equal care, others with an air of barely tolerant disdain. One struck Myrtun as particularly judgemental: the second-in-command, who named herself 'Furst Leeftenant Oiliviar Aardrustos'. She had skimmed a condescending look along the line of Kin, and then returned her gaze to a neutral spot somewhere behind Myrtun's right shoulder.

While Fyrtor had his turn at cross-cultural embassy, Myrtun took the opportunity to withdraw a couple of steps to glance back towards the commissary door. She saw Gubrin standing on Lutar's steady shoulders, hanging Myrtun's cloak over the offending trophy. Now instead of a looted shrine relic, all she had to explain was why the Kin hung their coats over doors…

Hearing her name from the lips of Fyrtor, she returned her attention to the delegation. There were about twenty Imperials, of whom a handful accompanied her to the top table with a few select members of the council and Fyrtor's advisors. The rest of the Imperials and Kin kept to separate tables, Myrtun's insistence overriding Gubrin's assertion that 'after a few drinks everyone will be getting along fine'.

It took some time for everyone to get sorted and the food to start coming out. In proper Kin tradition, everything was brought out to the table, and all parties were invited by Myrtun to get stuck in. Table talk was halting and difficult, and at first pertained to matter-of-fact discussions such as the condition of the *Bringer of War* and the generally unhealthy state of events across the galaxy. Captain Lorzentine seemed to settle well enough. He gave reassurances that he would convey the need for payment to his superiors for the work undertaken by Myrtun, and the request for future gainful employment. As best could be arranged, stellar coordinates and travel routes were exchanged, though Myrtun was careful not to reveal the location of the Hold ship itself, but to direct the Imperials to a Trans-Hyperian Alliance trade post in the Yattir System that had been created for such external interactions. While Lorzentine spoke haltingly and ate sparingly, his lieutenant and the priest sat in stony-faced silence and didn't even take a slice of bread for themselves.

Tongues began to loosen a little as appetite and thirst were addressed. Stilted bursts of conversation emanated from other tables, the higher pitch of the Imperials not quite making a harmony with deeper Kin voices.

Talk at the high table moved cautiously onto the battle, but terminology proved a difficult obstacle.

'I hope that you did not suffer too many dead,' said Lutar. 'It looked to me that you took serious damage.'

'Tha *Bringar ov Wur* iz a tuff uld besterd,' Lorzentine replied with a smile. 'Bin surveng tha Empurar fur feev tharsund yeers un moar. Tuff rarteengs tu, tha beckburn uv tha sheep.'

'Un deesurpleen tu,' added First Lieutenant Oiliviar Aardrustos. 'Thay nu uf dey stipped firreeng, a gud florggeeng wuz fur tha suvirvurs. Tha gut to geev tham a feer ov yu moar tharn tha eeneemee.' She turned to look over her shoulder at the Kin eating a few tables over. Her displeasure was obvious when she looked back at Myrtun. 'Eendoolgens maks thaym sawft.'

While Myrtun mulled this over, trying to decipher the words and decide if it was a genuine insult or simply bad manners, she noticed a terrible flaw in Gubrin's seating plan – or rather that part of the plan had been overlooked in the confusion of getting everybody seated.

There was one among the Imperials whom the Kin knew very well. Not the individual but their organisation – one of the Martian cultists, a machine worshipper, dressed in a robe of scarlet patterned with black mathematical devices. Their face was a mess of pipes and lenses beneath a cowl, and both their hands, which picked tremulously at small morsels and fed them into a narrow, flexible tube protruding from a slit in the robe, were like knots of metallic worms. A smell of harsh incense clung to the cloth, not quite concealing a tang of oil and urine. And next to the tech-priest, at the far end of the table opposite Myrtun rather than two stools from her left-hand side, was Brôkhyr Thôrdi.

The tech-priest, as far as Myrtun could tell, was quite animated, gesturing with their finger-worms at the lanterns, the door, a sweeping gesture that might have meant the *Grand Endeavour* or the whole universe. Thôrdi was leaning forward, listening attentively, eyes half closed in concentration. He leaned back suddenly, an uproarious laugh erupting from the Brôkhyr.

'You tell magnificent stories, Elphurexdeshfur!' He slapped a heavily beringed hand on the machine cultist's shoulder, almost knocking them to the ground. Myrtun relaxed. She had been worried that the tech-priest's strange beliefs might annoy the Brôkhyr, who knew very well that there was no all-powerful deity that gave animus to machines and circuitry. It looked like Thôrdi was enjoying himself.

The flicker of metallic worms became more agitated than animated, and the pipes of the tech-priest's face bulged alarmingly. Myrtun could just about hear a few sibilant noises over the general din of the other tables, which had the Brôkhyr leaning closer again, his face twisted with mirth.

'Oh yes, I know,' he said. He made the shape of a great sphere with his hands and nodded. 'All of it, yes. Nothing to do with the basic dynamics of the universe. No, a magic space person makes *all* the machines work.'

This time the machine cultist's words carried the full length of the table with a drawn-out hiss.

'Thise blarspheemies argainst thee Marchine Gud ere whey yar currussed arnsessturs sheeps tok theem tu thise eel-reegurdid ne'erheels arn ars stinted lettul trulls ye gruw.'

'I think we've just been called trolls,' barked Thôrdi, brow furrowing. 'Trolls? Us?'

Iyrdin laughed. 'Ridiculous, we're far too short to be trolls. They're as big as a spoil heap and twice as full of grit.'

'"*Little* trolls", he said,' Thôrdi explained, his volume rising along with his incredulity. 'Can you credit that?'

His voice was loud enough to carry to the other tables, and an ominous silence descended on the Kin while the Imperials started chattering excitedly among themselves.

'Thes plarse stenks leek ar arblurshun blurk,' sneered First Lieutenant Oiliviar Aardrustos. 'Thise unkurth, fithlerss roonts kinnut e'en sirve ar prupar dinar. Luk, dissart orn thee tarbell twext fush ant sup! Ar plarse ov nay sorls, pritchar, ey wud see.'

'Sorlless ant bund fur thee arbess, fur soor.' The captain's priest made a fluttering gesture across his chest and abdomen, though whether as a prayer or to ward off evil, Myrtun couldn't tell. Arguments broke out across the table's length and angry calls came from the other Kin.

'Lefteenant!' The captain's growl cut across his subordinate's next words, and Myrtun could see her Kin falling silent, looking expectantly in her direction.

'I'll say this once, and carefully for you,' she said, laying down knife and spoon. She stood up, fists leaning on the tabletop, and looked along the rows to either side. 'Shame on you.'

Some of her crew looked away, not able to meet her gaze, but her words were not for them. Her stare fell on the Imperial captain and moved along the line of humans.

'We save your lives. Risk our own doing it, too. We stay with you, so your enemies don't come back and finish the job. We invite you to feast with us, to celebrate a brief alliance. Not once have you offered to cover our expense or effort. We may not be perfect hosts, but you are *terrible* guests.'

The lieutenant rose to her feet, a finger pointing in accusation.

'Yu skavvenjing raats theenk yu shud bee pad fer commun desensey?'

Before she could utter further insult the human captain stood also, hand raised to silence her. He flexed his shoulders, straightened his coat and turned to face Myrtun, one hand on the hilt of his sword.

Stools scuffed across the tiled floor as some of Myrtun's people took to their feet, a bass rumble of discontent accompanying them. Lorzentine remained very still, watching Myrtun carefully but without obvious malice. A few tense heartbeats passed. The captain lifted his hand away from his sword to his chest and gave the slightest of bows. After a stare from their captain, the other Imperials stood and followed likewise, except for the tech-priest, who was hissing and crackling to themselves, hood drawn far forward to obscure their face.

'Wee sharl live yo noo.' Lorzentine was about to say something else, but Myrtun held up a hand to stop him.

'I need your apologies as much as your judgement, which is to say not at all.' She folded her arms. 'May the warp tides be kinder than this parting.'

Again the captain paused, and there was a glimmer of something sharper in his eyes. He swallowed, jaw clenched. For a moment his gaze lost focus, moving past Myrtun's left shoulder. His lips moved silently, perhaps in prayer to his God-Emperor. Then, visibly relaxing, Lorzentine looked at her again.

'Sarf trarvells tu yo, Merton Demmergut.' The captain stood to attention and gave the bird-hand salute once more, before leaving with a stiff gait, his crew trailing after him like admonished apprentices.

CHAPTER FOUR

A Long-delayed Return

Every vessel on the Hold ship had turned out to welcome the returning High Kâhl Elect. From the bridge of the guildship *Sparkfly*, Iron-Master Lekki Gûlrundr had one of the best views, stationed not far above the approach lane to the primary docking area. The main viewscreen displayed twinkling sunlight reflected from the hulls of more than a hundred ships, arranged in artificial constellations made up of Hernkyn Prospects, Cthonian mining expeditions, Hearthkyn Kinthrong transports and a variety of support craft, as well as over a dozen other visiting vessels from guilds and other nearby Kindreds.

On another display he could see the Hold ship below the *Sparkfly*. To call it a ship was an understatement. The nomadic base of the Eternal Starforge Kindred was a behemoth of a vessel, as much in common with a dwarf planet as a starship. It was in basic shape a truncated triangle from above, a shallow rhomboid in cross-section from front to back and side to side, so that most of its mass was in the aft third. Banks of engines that could burn with the fury of a star now glowed dully, idling while the Kin awaited their incoming leader. The superstructure housing the majority of the Kindred rose above the engineering decks like a mesa from a desert: a keep of metal and rockcrete complete with turrets and towers housing batteries of cannons that had broken moons and annihilated squadrons of lesser vessels with their overwhelming salvos. From the surrounding plain jutted pylons and outworkings containing subsystems, point defences, and Lekki's speciality, barrier tech. Though usually referred to among the Eternal Starforge Kin as the Hold ship, the vessel's true name was well deserved: *Unbreakable Giant*.

'She's here.' The dull voice of his companion drew Lekki's attention back to the main screen. An Ironkin armoured in dark grey plate also watched the proceedings, unmoving. A huge plasma hammer hung from a strap across her back, and twin holstered bolt pistols weighed heavy on the belt at her waist. Erkund was formidable as a bodyguard but left much to be desired as a conversationalist. Given that Lekki was alone on the *Sparkfly* with her and a few dozen E-COGs, the nine-plunge journey from Svallindrim, home of the Enduring Guild of Master Runewrights, had been a quiet one.

On the screen, the *Grand Endeavour* was coming into view. Plasma launchers lining the near side of the Hold ship opened fire in salute, reactor feeds turned to minimal so that their bright display posed no danger to the nearby fleet. Flights of Steelfist void-attack craft and Thundercrown seismic bombers gathered in escort while the smaller vessels of the fleet fell in behind the arriving starship.

'I'm glad this mess will soon be over,' Lekki remarked, to himself more than Erkund. To his surprise, the Ironkin responded.

'Maybe not. She is new.'

'Which means she'll want to make a good impression on the Guild. Set the standard for the relationship.'

'Your optimism is without basis.'

Lekki grunted disparagingly. 'If she knows what's best for her and her Kindred, she'll not cause any problems.'

'It appears you have not read the latest biographical data.'

'That she's stubborn, antagonistic and headstrong? None of that matters. She isn't ignorant or inexperienced.'

'It is unfortunate that Orthônar perished.' Lekki glanced at the Ironkin, surprised by the sudden display of sentiment, but his shock dissipated as she continued. 'It has complicated the situation.'

'A stroke of bad luck, but that doesn't change things. What's owed is owed, and that's why the Guild sent me.'

'This is your first assignment. Beware of overconfidence.'

'The Guild trust me to do this. A "nice, easy job to break you in", Wardwright Stannak said.'

'That was before we learnt of Orthônar's death. What if the new High Kâhl refuses to accept her predecessor's burden?'

'Then the Guild's support will be withdrawn, as agreed. There is no negotiation in this matter. My instructions were specific.' Lekki returned to his seat behind the control console and kicked his feet up onto the panel, hands behind his head as the chair reclined with a wheeze. 'Besides, Myrtun will agree. She has no choice.'

Myrtun had thought that now she was High Kâhl, she would be done with waiting for other people. The truth seemed to be the exact opposite, she decided, tapping her fingers on the rail that edged the ramp down to the main bay doors of the *Grand Endeavour*. Her Prospect Council were with her, while Dock Chief Greta stood at the door controls in anticipation of receiving the signal that the boarding gantry was locked in place – a simple procedure in its own right that, given the *Grand Endeavour* was first into the huge primary dock of the Hold ship, should have meant a rapid exit.

The problem came from the host of Kindred dignitaries, not

least the members of the Hearthspake, who had been on ships watching Myrtun's arrival but now needed to welcome her officially to the Hold ship. This left her waiting for them to dock, get off their vessels, and arrange themselves in the bay before she could disembark.

'Before you get annoyed, remember that this is in your honour,' Lutar reminded her quietly, his brass limbs and barrel-like torso polished to a near-blinding gleam for the occasion. Although a Wayfinder was not particularly close to the unofficial hierarchy of the Kindred – a hierarchy that the Hearthspake insisted did not exist on account of all Kin being created and treated equally – Myrtun had insisted that he was at her side when she was welcomed by her people.

Eventually Greta gave the thumbs-up and pulled the long lever that activated the hydraulics of the main doors. After a brief siren warning, the immense portal unlocked, allowing a crack of light to shine through, throwing a line of pale yellow across Myrtun. The line widened to a ribbon, and then she was bathed in the glow of the Hold ship's immense dock lanterns, which lit a space that could comfortably accommodate twenty ships the size of the *Grand Endeavour*, and was currently doing so.

She advanced at the head of her companions, Lutar a step behind and to her left, the others in two lines behind. As her leading foot crossed the threshold onto the docking spar, the first few notes of *Call of the Hearth* echoed out across the vastness of the bay from somewhere to her right, hauntingly played on a single naroflute. Quite unexpectedly, a lump snarled Myrtun's throat and a tear came to her eye on hearing the familiar notes in this special place. She'd tried so hard not to come here, had spent a life away from it, and yet it was the Hold, the foundation that had always been strong beneath her even when she had been so far away.

She stopped to listen, eyes closed, long-suppressed emotion churning in her gut. Not the worry of becoming High Kâhl, but the sensation of returning to a place like no other she had found in all her travels – coming *home*. She was Hernkyn, drawn to the stars, but here was her Kindred. Countless orbits spent around foreign stars could not sever that bond.

Save for the naroflute, not a sound disturbed the still vastness of the bay, the overlapping notes resounding back from ships' hulls and docking quays to create its own harmonies. It was melancholy writ in music, its grip tight around Myrtun's old heart.

As the last vibration of the echo faded away, Myrtun opened her eyes.

The last third of the docking ramp was lined with dignitaries in all the splendour of robes and void suits, the gilded crests of their institutions held by bearers at their sides. The dockside itself was filled with Kin, from those newly out of their crucibles to hoary veterans as venerable as Myrtun. Though of one Kindred, their cloneskeins were as varied as the stars in the galactic core. Faces dark or pale, grey-skinned or ruddy, some metal Ironkin, others craggy like rock, with beards, sideburns, moustaches, topknots, crests, and a thousand other styles. Many had knobbly brows or chins, cheekbones like armoured slabs, taller and shorter, broader and narrower. Though cloned, the Kin were as diverse a people as any Myrtun had encountered on her travels.

The music started again, the flautist joined by a whole band of skirlpipers, rundorganists, pendrummers and more. They played *Call of the Hearth* again, but this time the melody and beat were rousing. After the introductory notes, despite never having even thought of the song for a quarter of a lifetime, Myrtun found herself mouthing the words, then murmuring a verse, until she couldn't help but burst into full song along with the other assembled Kin as they reached the chorus. Thousands of bass voices, some mechanical, filled the space with glorious sound.

Come the time and come the need
Come the peril and the darkness
We have come to hearken
Our Hearthland's call

From the four far corners of the void

Hearthland, Hearthland!
Together standing strong
One Kin as One Kin
We'll hearken the Hearth's call

From the mighty gleam of Forges
From the distant halls of Votann
From the care of Crucible
And Council place

From the four far corners of the void

Hearthland, Hearthland!
Together standing strong
One Kin as One Kin
We'll hearken the Hearth's call

Hearts of stone
And fists unbreaking
Vowing always to be as one
We will fight, until
We can fight no more

From the four far corners of the void

Hearthland, Hearthland!
Together standing strong
One Kin as One Kin
We'll hearken the Hearth's call.

A rousing cheer rocked Myrtun as the last strains of the song dwindled away.

A voice boomed out.

'Hail the High Kâhl!'

She turned, realising it had come from Lutar, but before she could say anything a wordless roar of approval deafened her again.

'To opportunity!' the Wayfarer followed, mechanical fist raised high.

'Opportunity!' the throaty response crashed back.

Myrtun made her way across the dock. The crowd parted as she neared, clearing a path across the primary quay to the pedestrian doors. A large-wheeled Sagitaur transport with its roof removed had been decked out in flags and runestaves, hull freshly painted a glistening orange and black, attended by a driver in shining armour. Two nearby Hekaton Land Fortresses were available for the Hearthspake. As all clambered aboard, twenty Hernkyn Pioneers on magna-coil bikes skimmed down from the *Grand Endeavour* and took up escort positions in front and behind the short convoy.

'You've been colluding,' Myrtun said to Lutar as he pulled himself into the back of the modified Sagitaur, followed by Jôrdiki and Iyrdin. Gubrin clambered into the front, alongside the driver.

'Merely establishing the protocols,' Lutar replied. 'I know you wouldn't want more fuss than necessary, but...'

'Nonsense,' Myrtun said, laughing. 'I'm High Kâhl now. The

one compensation I've been looking forward to is being lauded across the Kindred.'

'You were already famous and honoured,' Gubrin reminded her. 'Your exploits are hearthside legends on the Hold ship.'

'But not on my own ship?'

Iyrdin chuckled. 'Well, we was there when most of them legends was made. I expect the stories told here have a fair degree of embellishment to them.'

The motors of the bikes to the front whined into greater life, their magna-coils becoming rings of energy that lifted higher from the deck. As one, they moved off, gathering speed gently. The Sagitaur's motor purred louder as the driver accelerated after them, the deeper rumble of the two Hekatons following behind, accompanied by another round of cheers.

The tall gates cranked apart, opening the way to the main thoroughfare of the Hold ship – a huge arched corridor that ran for nearly a third of its length, front to back, branching off to a hundred halls and chambers. Along the roof ran the elevated carriage system, though for the moment the clattering cars were silent, halted in long lines along the rails so that their occupants could gaze down at the activity below.

And there was much activity. A second band in an open-backed wagon struck up another Kindred favourite – *The Forge of my Ancestors Gleams Brightly* – accompanied by crowds of Kin lining the hallway to either side. Though her Prospect had not been small, Myrtun felt overwhelmed by the sheer press of people. She was giddy for a few moments, buffeted by the noise and spectacle, emotionally unbalanced by conflicting feelings. To have such raw sentiment displayed for her lifted Myrtun's spirits to the high rails overhead, but weighing them down was the future to come, and the knowledge that her wild life of roaming and adventure was coming to an end.

She was glad the Sagitaur was open-topped – a canopy could have made her feel imprisoned and claustrophobic right then. Looking at the cheering crowds she realised that something was expected of her in return. Standing, her bionic hand gripping Lutar's shoulder for support, Myrtun raised a fist, pumping it now and then as she looked out at her appreciative Kindred.

It was the first of many such appearances and duties she would have to make. She was leader of the Kindred of the Eternal Starforge, but she was no longer in control of her own destiny.

The Hearthspake of the Kindred of the Eternal Starforge had twenty-three members, not including the High Kâhl whom they advised. Lutar could see the relief soften Myrtun's face as the doors to the chamber were closed behind her, sealing off the last of the throng that had turned out to welcome her to her new post. The Wayfinder was only present in the capacity of 'transition liaison'. His task was supposedly to allow Myrtun to adjust to being High Kâhl, to act as conduit from council to leader when not in session, but he anticipated that his job would be more inclined to helping the council get used to Myrtun.

The council chamber was positioned equidistant from the command bridge near the summit of the Hold ship's superstructure and the Votannic chambers at its heart, somewhere near the core of the original vessel that had set out in the lost history of the Kin. It was a place for discussion and deliberation away from public gaze, carpeted and wood-panelled to give it a feel of natural softness and calm, large enough for the round council table and seats, and three desks for the council secretaries. A brü urn sat steaming gently in the corner. A relaxed space, unlike the grand petition hall next door, where Myrtun would be making her first official appearance as High Kâhl.

The council comprised a mix of Kindred alongside a few

representatives of long-established allied institutions. Though none approached Myrtun in span, most were heading towards what was known as 'venerability'. The youngest was the Cthonian Mining Guild ambassador, Pyûk Rânsa, a middle-aged Kin with fiery fronds of hair that swayed as she nodded her head in agreement with herself. Sitting between the white-whiskered Surni Weldwright, the Brôkhyr Forge-master, and the totally bald High Grimnyr Vultan Vossko, she reminded Lutar of a lively flame. Most he knew only by reputation, but one he was acquainted with personally: Kyr Starbound.

Created even before Lutar, Starbound was the oldest entity on the Hold ship, if one did not count the semi-sentient link to the Votann maintained by the Grimnyr. The ancient Ironkin had been a Wayfinder, a Voidmaster and a Prospect leader before finally taking day-to-day command of the Hold ship; if Myrtun had civil authority, Kyr possessed operational authority. The relationship between them was likely to be the toughest challenge for both, as Myrtun was not used to sitting back while somebody else ran the ship, and Kyr had not previously served with a former Hernkyn as High Kâhl. The Chief Voidmaster was a bulky gold-and-ebon figure. Fingers that could bend steel nimbly toyed with a set of interlocked dials used by Wayfinders to calculate prevailing warp currents. Lutar watched the movements for a moment, thinking Kyr was working on the Hold ship's next journey, but quickly came to the conclusion that the venerable Ironkin was merely fidgeting.

First Myrtun was to make any appointments as needed and, when they were ratified, swear her oaths to the council. Lutar announced that the incoming High Kâhl had no plans to change the Hearthspake at this time but would, for a time, also make use of her Prospect Council as an advisory board. They would have no official capacity but would give her peace of mind while she adjusted to the needs of her new role. A few craggy eyebrows were raised, but since there was a tradition of having personal advisors for each council member, there were no grounds for objections. The unchanged council was ratified with a quick, unanimous show of hands, and a dignified toast was raised to the High Kâhl. Glasses clinked and murmurs of 'Honour to the High Kâhl, Glory to the Eternal Starforge' rippled around the table.

'I'm told that the council have continued to hear petitions and appeals in the absence of High Kâhl,' said Myrtun. 'I hope that means I just have to approve and seal a few things to clear the backlog.'

'Mostly, *ur-kâhl*,' replied Gurtha, chamberlain of the council secretariat, who was overseer of the council's operations and, by unspoken consent, also acted as chair of its meetings. 'There are some that insist on judgement from the High Kâhl in person, and they will be amongst the first of your audience today.'

'All right.'

Lutar could tell that Myrtun was about to stand up, thinking the meeting was at an end. He stepped forward before she could do so and addressed Gurtha.

'I believe the High Kâhl would like to be briefed on Orthônar's last edicts, so that she may continue his good governance and consider your next agenda.'

Without missing a beat, Myrtun adjusted herself in her seat, as if her cloak had been falling awkwardly, and nodded to Lutar and then Gurtha.

'Yes. What was the last business of the council for Orthônar?'

'It should have been a straightforward matter,' replied High Grimnyr Vossko, her scalp gleaming in the lantern light. 'We were due to move the Hearthfleet to the Bilskyrnun Tides, to begin new gravitic dredging on the boundary of a black hole the Guldurthing Prospect found there. As we made the relevant preparations,

I passed on a communication from the Votann of the Alliance. Orthônar took it as a personal command and had a Hearthguard expedition formed immediately. He took the *Stormblaze* ahead of the main fleet, but we lost contact when he entered the Well of Yrdu. The ship returned with only a single member of the expedition, and he refused to speak to anybody but the next High Kâhl. He is one of your petitioners today.'

'Then I need to speak to him.' Myrtun pushed to her feet, throwing a glare at the council members. 'Why are we sitting here chattering like idle dock workers?'

'You were not High Kâhl until our confirmation,' Gurtha said quietly.

'There's also the matter of being stuck here awaiting the final word to go to the Bilskyrnun Tides,' added Vukasin, kâhl for void operations. He was shorter and broader than any other Kin at the table, his head more of a bump on his shoulders than a separate appendage. Jet-black hair covered his head in unruly curls, framing a dark-skinned face. 'It's in Trans-Hyperian Alliance space – at the edge admittedly, but we're losing time. Other Kindreds will be investigating the gravitic disturbance and the dredging grounds will all get snapped up before we arrive.'

'What do you want from me?' Myrtun snapped. Lutar assumed she had thought the council would leap into action, spurred by her declaration. She should have known better. The rest of the council looked at her with a mixture of patience and irritation. The High Kâhl sat down again, shoulders hunched. 'Let's get on with it.'

'Am I moving the Hearthfleet? Yes or no?' Kyr Starbound's voice was soft but determined, perfectly inflected through their vocalisers.

'Oh.' Myrtun looked at the Chief Voidmaster, taken aback by the direct question. 'Yes. Yes, we are moving to the Bilskyrnun Tides.'

'Despite the warp storms?' asked Lutar, knowing that Myrtun had forgotten her celestography in the confusion of the situation. 'It is rather a risky proposition.'

'Yes, Orthônar was right,' declared Myrtun. She looked straight at Kyr Starbound. 'This black hole presents too good an opportunity to pass up. Make ready to move the Hearthfleet as soon as it's practical.'

'We have been ready for some time,' the Chief Voidmaster replied, without audible rancour. 'Now that the… disruption of your arrival has been dealt with, we can make the first plunge to the Skoll System at the end of High Watch.'

'Good.' Myrtun looked at Gurtha, an impatient look in her eye, almost halfway to her feet. 'Can we get on with these petitions? Is there any other business to attend to?'

'Quite a bit, ur-kâhl.' The chamberlain laid a hand on a pile of flexi prints in front of her and glanced around the table at the other council members. 'With the council's indulgence, perhaps we shall postpone the usual process and reconvene *after* petitions have been heard?'

A chorus of 'ayes' approved the suggestion, some delayed with obvious reluctance.

'Let us adjourn to the petition hall,' said Lutar.

The council stood and filed out through the adjoining door to begin the session. Lutar lingered a moment with Myrtun.

'It all seems to be going well enough,' she said, patting him on the arm. She smiled, but Lutar could tell it was slightly forced. 'It's not so bad after all, is it?'

The last time Myrtun had walked into the audience hall of the Hold ship, it had been as a young petitioner wracked with anguish and a burning need for bloody revenge. Durnir the Skyhammer had been High Kâhl back then. Peeking through the curtains that covered the doorway from the council chamber, she remembered how big and grand Durnir had seemed, sitting on the great chair on the stage at one end of the hall, surrounded by image-capturing equipment so that the proceedings could be broadcast across the Hold ship, indeed to anyone in the Kindred. The black stone of the High Kâhl's seat had looked like the lightless gulf between stars. Sitting atop it, Skyhammer resembled something printed in one of the oldest texts, her expression one of calm patience. Myrtun doubted she could master that, expecting it would likely come off as cold indifference. 'Interested and engaged' would be more natural, she had decided, while pondering this moment on the last plunge back, spending far too long in front of a mirrorfield trying various dignified expressions.

The hall was used to greet outside dignitaries too, some of them with sizeable entourages, and that required a grand venue, unlike the homely chamber behind her. Expectations had to be met. Here were put to use some of those fancier minerals and alloys that lent themselves more to display than engineering. There was no point using fine marble or beautifully carved granite where nobody would see it, after all. The hall was not just a testament to the industry and artisanship of the Kindred, but also a display of Profit – its flagrant ostentation a declaration that the Kindred of the Eternal Starforge had prospered beyond the bounds of simple survival and necessity. Broad slabs of white stone veined through with pale blues and greys made up the floors and ceiling, with large multi-paned windows along the top offering a view to the void tinged blue by the gleam of protective fields. The walls and columns in between were a deep blue speckled with white and green, like an impression of clear sea in starlight. The stepped viewing areas to either side of the main concourse were made of a cloudy diamond-like gemstone that, it was believed, the earliest Kin of the Eternal Starforge had fashioned in the rays of a supernova. When Myrtun had petitioned Skyhammer, the lacquered wooden benches that lined the steps had been bare but for a few dedicated court chroniclers, but now they were teeming with Kin, all eager to witness her first public petitioning – to be able to say in their old age that they had been there, more importantly. Myrtun had spent her life making herself a legend – not entirely by chance – but now she was officially part of history. As generations were inducted into the limitless minds of the Votann, she would become something greater than she was before, recurring over and over in the memories of her Kindred, each one a tiny slice of perspective.

A troubling thought occurred to her as the noise of the audience died down into hushed anticipation of her arrival. The experience of thousands of Kin within the Votann would vastly outnumber her own. When she was gone, all that would remain would be the impressions left upon those around her. Would her recollections, her own perspective and feelings about events and herself, be washed away by the deluge of others' views of her?

A series of bells sounded, announcing that the petitioning was about to begin. Taking a deep breath, Myrtun pushed through the heavy curtain and walked purposefully to the great chair. She pictured herself as Durnir, trying to keep her aching shoulders back, her spine straight, her gaze moving serenely across the gathered mass of people.

Sitting down, the words of Durnir came back to her, though she had not thought about them in a lifetime. Unbidden they arrived on her lips and spoke themselves.

'Those in want and need, those desiring wisdom or judgement, let them offer up their petitions, arguments, and defences before the chair of the High Kâhl. In doing so, be aware that you are bound to abide by all decisions announced herein and ratified by my Votannic Council.' She paused, feeling posterity pushing down on her from every direction. As Prospect commander she had made decisions that meant life or death for her Kin, but the weight of the responsibility now placed in her hands rivalled the ultra-dense core of a neutron star. 'Approach and make yourself known, petitioner.'

When the audience hall had been built, the custom had been for petitioners to enter via the gilded gates at the far end, making their way along an impressive grand processional between the steps, to come before the High Kâhl on the raised platform. Guests of the High Kâhl in the earliest time of the Leagues – as the first Leagues were actually forming through such meetings – arrived and presented themselves with much pomp and suitably impressive entourages. Over the generations, as visitations from other Kin became more familiar, such grandiosity seemed out of place. Only the highest-honoured guests were treated to such ceremony, and a secondary entrance had been created halfway along the hall, a gap in the steps to Myrtun's left leading to a high-pillared archway. Through this arch the dignitaries of the Kindred and others arrived in far less formal state. Even so, walking half the length of the hall proved rather time-consuming when the High Kâhls began to give audience to more mundane matters than those discussed between Kindreds and Leagues. The so-called 'Ambassadorial Arch' had fallen out of common use, and regular petitioners now gathered in a separate stand of plain benches in the right-hand bank of steps, within a few dozen strides of the stage on which Myrtun's chair was set.

Twenty or so Kin waited there now, sitting on the front two rows of benches. Even as the echo of her invitation reverberated into quiet, the first petitioner was up and pushing past the Hearthkyn warden stationed beside the small opening.

If the audience hall had once played host to grand embassies adorned in the liveries of the most powerful Leagues, their strength and splendour personified, the small deputation making its way up the steps was at the other extreme. The Kin that led the party advanced encased in an ornate war-rig of black and chrome, two rune-crests jutting from the back denoting his allegiance, which Myrtun identified as one of the Brôkhyr guilds. His exo-frame was of the type usually reserved for Thunderkyn, the elite warriors dedicated to protecting the Brôkhyr and their forges, but the pilot seemed ungainly in its embrace, lurching forwards on stilt-like legs, swaying hard from side to side. A fist encased in armoured plates was raised in greeting, but Myrtun was so bemused by the sight that she forgot to acknowledge the courtesy.

Behind the guild emissary floated a trio of E-COGs, as unlike the ornate wargear of the Brôkhyr as it was possible to imagine. They looked little more than hovering boxes with circular scan plates on their fronts and crane-like appendages extending from underneath. A range of different field emitters stuck out at ungainly angles from their tops and sides. One had a pronounced shudder and another had a mess of rivets around the scanner plate, as though the fixing ring had been reattached many times.

Bringing up the rear of the embassy was a far more impressive construct – an Ironkin every bit as tall as the war-rig, their segmented shoulder plates extending either side of a bullet-shaped head with a rune-crest extending over the top from the spine. In the Kindred, the Ironkin would have passed for one of the elite Einhyr, or even a kâhl; here it was obviously a bodyguard. Myrtun could see no weapons, but there was a sheen to the Ironkin's fists that spoke of internal field generators or perhaps a concealed plasma lance.

The emissary halted in front of the throne, his elevated position within the exo-frame bringing him almost to eye level, though he stopped a score of paces away at the bottom of the steps. From here Myrtun could see his face inside the armoured cage, and she had to quell her reaction. The Brôkhyr had a high forehead and fleshy jowls, with thin, lifeless hair and a meagre scrape of beard across cheeks and chin. What she had first taken as pebble-like growths – not uncommon among some Kindreds – were in fact boils or sores of some kind, or the red scars of some former ague. Given the Kin's cloneskeins made them virtually immune to most infections, seeing such obvious signs of disease was instantly repellent. There was a strange cast about the herald's eyes, which were slightly askew and heavily bloodshot, almost red around the dull brown centres.

'My particulars,' the Brôkhyr said with a touch of nasal whine, exo-frame wheezing softly as he gestured to the Ironkin. The bodyguard stepped up and produced a golden rune-shaped amulet fitted with a red gem, from which sprang a hologram of the same guild symbol and a datacore code.

'Brôkhyr Iron-Master Lekki Gûlrundr, emissary of the Enduring Guild of Master Runewrights,' the Ironkin intoned with a lilting female voice, sounding bored more than anything else.

'Welcome Br–'

A sudden disturbance from the petitioners' benches interrupted Myrtun. Bastium alloy clattered across the floor as the gate warden was hurled backwards, propelled by a savage-looking figure who advanced with purpose. He was clad in full Eternal Starforge exo-armour that had been much abused, scars of combat covering every plate, some of its mechanics exposed where parts had been shorn away. The warrior wore no helm upon his stubbled scalp, and his face was as much scar tissue as normal skin, with thick black sideburns and goatee. Stapled wounds marked his brow and one cheek, his nose just a rough blob with nostrils. The yellow of fading bruises ringed both eyes.

Several nearby Hearthkyn started forwards, shock staves brought to bear. The Einhyr – his rank was obvious – carried no armaments that Myrtun could see.

'I bear urgent news!' snarled the newcomer.

'Wait!' commanded Myrtun, holding up a hand. The Hearthkyn slowed but did not lower their weapons. 'You're the survivor from Orthônar's expedition?'

'Aye, that's me. Dori Hûltvan.' He stepped around Lekki's bodyguard and presented himself with a short bow.

'The one called Ironhelm. Champion of the Eternal Starforge Kindred.'

'Orthônar called me such, yes. I don't take the titles myself, not now.'

Myrtun was about to reply when the Brôkhyr emissary took a pace forward with a clunking tread, putting himself closer than Ironhelm.

'I believe my petition has priority, High Kâhl. I have been waiting a considerable time for Orthônar's return, on behalf of the Guild, only to find he will not be here. My oath to the Guild means that I must treat with you before I can return.'

'It's news of Orthônar that I bring, you ignoramus,' growled Ironhelm, stomping forward. 'Get back or I'll put you on your arse, war-rig and all.'

Myrtun glanced at the Ironkin bodyguard, but she betrayed no interest in what was happening, standing with arms crossed amid the trio of poorly built E-COGs.

'You look like you'd fall over if I breathed on you,' the Brôkhyr sneered back.

'With your breath stench, I might just,' Ironhelm scoffed.

'I'll have you both tossed in the gaol until you learn some manners,' barked Myrtun, who had settled more than a few fights in her time. She thrust a finger at Lekki. 'You! Maybe you've been waiting longer, but I wager what the champion has to say is more pressing.'

The emissary opened his mouth, but on seeing Myrtun's grim expression decided wisely to leave her threat untested. The High Kâhl gave him a nod of gratitude and turned her attention to Ironhelm.

'High Kâhl Orthônar is really dead?' she asked quietly. 'You saw him fall?'

'I did not,' admitted the champion. 'But he cannot have survived, and I had intended to die with him. But he swore me to my word to return with this tale for whosoever came after.'

'Then now it is time to relate that tale, Ironhelm.' Myrtun could hear footsteps and muted chattering from the audience benches, and she looked around. Word had quickly spread of what was occurring and more and more Kin were making their way into the hall. They were filling the steps already, all room on the benches taken.

'Gurtha!' Myrtun called. The chamberlain hurried up the steps to answer her summons. 'Would it be possible to open the main gates and redirect onlookers to fill the concourse instead? Let's not have anyone crushed by the sudden interest.'

'Insightful, ur-kâhl,' Gurtha agreed with a nod. She headed back to the main floor and consulted with the kâhl of guards. Armoured figures started to move up onto the steps to steer the newcomers.

'Tell us, Ironhelm, what took Orthônar into the warp-raddled systems to the south, past the Bilskyrnun Tides?'

'I don't know, is the truth,' admitted Ironhelm. He sagged a little, perhaps relieved to finally fulfil his oath, or simply exhausted beyond even a Kin's endurance. 'He never told nobody what he saw in that Votannic message he got. Something that had to be found. A quest, he said, from the ancient times. A real-life legend, he said we were creating.'

'If I could interject…?' said Lekki, half-raising a hand.

'You shall not,' growled Myrtun, signalling for Ironhelm to continue.

'I served Orthônar a long time, most my life as Einhyr and then as his champion, and he was as dear to me as any Kin,' Dori began.

Seeing that he would get no time to speak soon, the guild emissary muttered something under his breath and returned with his entourage to the petitioners' area. No sooner was he out of sight than he was out of Dori's thoughts.

'I'd have given my life for him even had he been just a victualler's clerk,' he went on. 'There was a ways about him that I saw in nobody else, a cloneskein of charm and bravery. Tactful, if he needed to be, but forthright when necessary. Anyways, suffice it to say, it weren't just the oath of the Einhyr that bound me to his side.

'And in all that time, I never seen him act as strange as when he received that message from the Votann that sent us away. Even when we was on our way, there was times me or some other would come upon him looking at his wristslate, lost in thought, and we knew he was reading the missive again. He must have memorised it by then. But maybe he thought that poring over the words, seeing them with his own eyes, might reveal something he hadn't seen afore.'

'He never showed it to you?' asked the new High Kâhl. She was quick to the point like Orthônar, which Dori liked, but he sensed a wilder quality in her too, which he did not.

Dori shook his head. 'No, never showed it, nor shared a word of it with me or anyone else, unless he swore them to secrecy and so they never told.' He looked across Myrtun to the benches where the Hearthspake sat, opposite the area set aside for petitioners. He caught the eye of the High Grimnyr, Vossko. 'If there's any that know what the Votann sent him, I reckon it would be them that tends the Fane.'

Vossko rose, hands clasped to her chest as she bowed her head in greeting. Her scalp was mottled a slightly darker brown, almost unseen in the glare of the thousand lanterns that hung from the ceiling.

'I do not know whether to say I am glad to see you returned to us, Ironhelm,' she said, speaking as though she spent time thinking about every word that left her lips. 'I am personally glad at your return, but I cannot help but feel it does not bode well for the Kindred. To come back to us alone bearing news of Orthônar's death.'

Dori thought he heard a whisper around the chamber, just at the edge of hearing. Was there accusation there? Or just inside his head? A flush of guilt brought red to his cheeks, and he shifted his weight in agitation.

'I'll not have had it that way either, but we're getting ahead of the story.'

'As to your question, Ironhelm,' the High Grimnyr continued, 'the message was marked for the High Kâhl alone, and such it remains. It was placed upon a ciphered runekey and given him by my hand, but not a word of it did he make known to me.'

'I'm High Kâhl now, you can show the message to me,' declared Myrtun.

'Alas not,' said Vossko, her face as sad as when Dori had delivered his terrible news. 'The message was marked for Orthônar by name, and not just for his title. Usually such communications come from another High Kâhl, perhaps a guild chancellor, but there was no signatory made known to me.'

'Whatever was in that message put him in a queer mood, for sure,' Dori told the assembly. The hint of whispering subsided as he spoke, silenced by his relating of the tale. 'We made ready and headed off as soon as was possible. Just a few hundred of us, so I don't think he was expecting much of a fight, if any at all. It was my insistence that the Einhyr accompanied him, for they were mine to command, not his. A decision I don't know whether to regret or not, for that was a hundred brave Kin that died beside him that would've been here... But then perhaps we wouldn't know at all what became of him.'

'Where did you go?' asked Myrtun. 'I'm told that contact was lost after you passed the Well of Yrdu. Where were you headed after that?'

'We didn't know at the time. In fact, I can't say for sure that even Orthônar knew where we was going. After each plunge he would consult with the Voidmaster and they'd look at the charts, and Orthônar would say something like, "No, it's not here," or, "This cannot be the right place," and he would look at the maps again and pick a new destination.'

Dori took a moment to recover his breath. The bruises and cuts were healing, but he knew that he was hurt inside too. Not just bones and organs, but something in his mind. The longer since he had left Orthônar, the greater his unease had grown. Sleep was fitful, waking was like a half-dream haunted by distant sounds of battle and his last sight of the Kinhost in the flickering light of war, holding against the enemy onslaught.

He must have given some outward sign of his discomfort because the High Kâhl suddenly looked at him sharply.

'Your injuries do not look well tended to me. Have you not yet consulted the Embyr?'

'My wounds are my business, if you please,' growled Dori.

'It does not please, but I cannot force you to have treatment,' Myrtun admitted. 'Perhaps I can at least make this more bearable.' She looked at her councillors. 'This seems more like a deposition than a petition – perhaps we should move it to the chamber?'

'No!' snapped Dori. He looked around the packed audience hall, suddenly seeing the masses of Kin that now filled the floor too, hanging on his words. Their presence settled his troubled thoughts and replenished his failing stamina. 'I came to tell the story of how Orthônar died. It should not be told behind closed doors. I'll not have hearsay and rumour spread when the truth can be heard from my lips.'

Myrtun considered him with a level gaze for several heartbeats, her mechanical hand tapping the black stone of the chair.

'Well, that seems fair enough,' she said at last. 'Lutar, have a chair and some brü brought out. At least the noble champion should be able to sit while he speaks to me.'

An Ironkin that had been standing to one side of the council benches bowed and departed before Dori could raise any objection.

'You can continue while we wait,' Myrtun prompted, adjusting her fur cloak to sit more easily on her shoulders. 'What happened after the Well of Yrdu?'

'We got lost,' Dori said. A ripple of comments flowed around the great hall, and he turned to address the rest of his audience. 'Aye, lost! Not a little off course. Not falling short of a destination. Proper lost. And what's even queerer than that, Orthônar intended it!'

This caused even more of a reaction – some shock, much of it calls of denial. Out of the corner of his eye he saw a gaggle of Voidmasters getting to their feet, exclaiming their incredulity. Dori focused his attention on them.

'Crazy, eh? We all know the Well enough, right? Come at it properly and it'll turn your course but give you a fair boost onward.'

'Stokor Wisefellow was Voidmaster on the *Stormblaze*, Ironhelm, as well you know,' shouted one of the ship commanders. 'She didn't get her name for nothing!'

'You're right, and Stokor argued strong against Orthônar, she did. Said the High Kâhl's intent would kill every one of us, and all but refused to carry out his orders.'

The Ironkin returned, forcing a pause in proceedings as a couple of attendants set up a metal bench broad enough to accommodate Dori's armour. A steaming pot of brü was placed on a table nearby and a mug handed to the High Kâhl. The Ironkin Wayfinder poured another and offered it to her petitioner with an air of quiet insistence. Dori had been denying himself any luxuries since his return – and more than luxury with his refusal to visit the Embyr to have his wounds treated – but the nutty, earthy aroma that carried to his nostrils spoke of a fine blend. He relented in his abstinence, nodding to the Ironkin with a half-smile of appreciation.

He blew the steam off the mug, but in a flash of memory he saw not a nourishing drink but a pool of Kin blood steaming into the air – Kendrik Forgesson lying on the deck next to it, his head blown off by an ork's energy blast.

'Are you well?' asked the Ironkin. 'Are you sure you will not accept assistance?'

'I'm fine,' snapped Dori, turning his attention back to the High Kâhl. 'I've an oath to fulfil and I'll not be steered from it till it's done.'

'What did Wisefellow almost refuse to do?' asked Myrtun, leaning forward, her mug cupped in her hands, one shrivelled and spotted with age, the other shining with metallic artificial skin.

'Going down the Well, of course,' Dori replied.

Shouts echoed across the hall, most of them from the Voidmasters.

'Preposterous!'

'Madness!'

'Lies!'

At this last one, Myrtun stood up and rounded on them, and a hush fell over the entire hall like a chill wind.

'Mind your tongues!' She thrust a finger at one Voidmaster in particular. 'You! Dare you accuse Champion Ironhelm of untruths? Or do you withdraw what you said and humbly ask for forgiveness for your slander?'

The Voidmaster – Dori recognised her as Ymmâ – looked as though the High Kâhl had just suggested she take a bath in one of the plasma reactor sluices. She clasped her hands to her chest and looked directly at Dori, giving a small bow.

'Humbly do I offer apology, champion. My shock was so great at the story you suggest that I could think of no other explanation. As heinous as my accusation was, it seemed better that than to accept that Orthônar had taken leave of his senses so grievously.'

'It did seem a grievous mistake, it's true, and your apology is accepted,' Dori said. When he was sure that no more interruptions were forthcoming, he continued. 'Orthônar would brook no argument, and said that any as was not of a mind to follow were free to take one of the cutters and wait for the Hearthfleet to show up. There was a few that thought hard about it and maybe fore the end regretted their choice to stay, as there would've been no shame in leaving. What Orthônar proposed *was* madness, and yet he looked at us and said, "Trust the Votann and fate," and there was such a surety about his mood that we thought he must have some special knowledge from that message of his. And so that's what we did. We trusted to the Votann, and we put our lives into the hands of fate, and we steered direct into the Well of Yrdu.'

Lutar believed Ironhelm's account; at least Ironhelm certainly betrayed no sense that he was lying. As incredible as the story seemed to be – and the reaction of many in the audience demonstrated much incredulity – the champion was earnest, addressing his tale to Myrtun and the wider Kin in equal measure. He behaved quite erratically during the narration, displaying several physical tics as he spoke, but his words were clear and his tale seemed lucid despite its strange path and the champion's sometimes performative tone.

Yet it made no sense. The Well of Yrdu was a warp storm of the greatest ferocity, unpassable except at its very edges, where the warp currents were whipped so fast that one could travel parsecs in hours.

'I have a question,' Lutar said, approaching Myrtun's throne. 'If you'll forgive my interruption.'

'I'm betting that question is how we did it?' replied Ironhelm. 'A ship'd break apart afore it even got through the outer storm, you're thinking, eh?'

'Before today I would have thought it impossible to cross the Well of Yrdu. However, according to your testimony you have done so. Twice, given that you must also have performed this miracle on your return journey too.'

'Aye, well, that's because you think we crossed it, edge to edge, like going from one side of a plate to another.' Ironhelm looked at Lutar and then past him to the Voidmasters and other Wayfinders. 'But we didn't go across it, we went *through* it. Into the maw, so to speak.'

With his left hand, Ironhelm made a circular motion, and with the index finger of his right hand he pointed down into the middle from the top.

'But why?' asked Lutar, more confused than ever. 'Even if you survived you would simply be a parsec or two away from where you started.'

'You'd think so, eh? But it's not so. Don't ask me the hows or whys, but the eye of the storm, the Well itself, so to speak, isn't a hole – it's a bridge of sorts. We went in, Voidmaster cursing, instruments all over the place, spinning like the grinder blade of a Cthonian's rock-cleaver. The warp barriers were straining, alarms blaring, the hull about to pull itself apart.

'"Stay on it," Orthônar yells at the helm. And to the warp engines controls he shouts, "Don't you disengage until you have my order, or I'll end you myself." It seemed like an age, thrown about like you wouldn't believe, and just when it was at its worst, Orthônar says to disengage the warp engines and end the plunge.'

Lutar felt himself leaning forward, eager to learn what happened next. There was not an eye in the whole hall that wasn't locked to Ironhelm. At times, it appeared as though the champion wasn't speaking to anyone in particular, his gaze impossibly distant and out of focus. He seemed to take no enjoyment from the telling of the tale, though he was a natural orator. His dramatic pauses might have been simply to catch his breath and marshal his thoughts, or perhaps to drag himself back to the present.

'We comes out of the warp with the crew hollering and cussing, the ship twisting and turning like something down the flusher, and helm is firing the thrusters to slow us afore we smash into a planet or something. And then there we are, on the other end of the Well, in a star system no less, a bit shaken up but otherwise none the worse for wear.'

The hall was as still as a hydronics pool.

'Did you get a reading on your location?' asked Myrtun, almost breathless. Lutar recognised the glimmer in her eyes, the flush to her face – of excitement at discovering the unknown. Her fingers were gripping the arms of the chair tight, her eyes wide. 'Where did you come out?'

'Beyond the storms, Myrtun. Beyond the great barrier that stretches for dozens of parsecs to either side of the Well of Yrdu.'

Ironhelm necked the last dregs of his brü and threw a pointed look at the urn. Lutar obliged, filling the mug almost to the brim with the dark, hot beverage.

'Fair hits the spot that does,' said the champion. He still looked unwell, but some colour was returning to his lips and cheeks. He sipped at the scalding-hot drink, nodding to himself, and then looked at Myrtun. 'Not only past the Utgard Wall, but beyond the Celestial Stair, as deep into Far-space as anyone's ventured in that direction. More than three hundred light years beyond the Utgard Wall, as close as Wisefellow could reckon it.'

Lutar could picture the bare stretch of chart. He looked up as Myrtun eased herself forward.

'Further than any Hernkyn have ever gone,' she said with rapt expression.

'Well, I'll be getting to that later, don't worry,' said Ironhelm, wagging an armoured finger. 'But we had a more immediate problem. *Orks*. There was proof of them everywhere. An old presence, it seemed. Broken remains of rock forts floating in the periphery. Almost mistook them just for asteroids but for their strange orbits. No plasma residue, nothing to say there'd been a battle. We put down on a barren microworld just inside the biospheric range. Spores. Low forms of orkoid life, like a mould on some fruit you'd left out. Nothing bigger than your fist, and vicious with it.'

'How old do you mean?' Myrtun was intense, listening to every word with eyes fixed on the champion.

'As old as the Leagues,' Ironhelm replied in a hushed tone, leaning forward. 'The *first* Leagues.'

Lutar brimmed with questions but knew it was not his place to speak them. The assembled Kin were likewise silent, enraptured by Ironhelm's story and content to keep their curiosity in check for the time being to avoid the whole audience becoming a chaotic mess.

'And you found more?' asked Myrtun, who suffered no such restriction. 'On other worlds?'

'Here and there. It didn't seem like the orks had been all that thorough when they'd been there. Some places we found evidence of them staying some time. Ruins, what we could make out of them. Old landing strips and pads.'

'We should consult the Votann,' said High Grimnyr Vossko from the council bench. 'There are old records of an ork empire that used to stretch from the Perfidious Spiral all the way to Ordyn's Trap. Perhaps they got as far as the Celestial Stair, which is just a few more parsecs to the east.'

'The Leagues crushed that empire twenty generations ago and more,' said Kyr Starbound. The Ironkin turned from Vossko to Ironhelm. 'You're saying these ruins were older than that?'

'If you let me continue, you'll see that it isn't really the big question.' Ironhelm took a gulp of his brü, brows knotted in annoyance. His frown broke a scab and a drop of blood oozed out, beading on a grey eyebrow.

'Please continue, champion,' Myrtun said with a sweep of her hand.

'And perhaps focus on the most pertinent details first?' suggested Lutar, trying to be helpful.

'I'm telling it as it happened, so as nobody makes any mistakes,' snapped the aged warrior. He grimaced at Lutar, and it was clear he would say nothing more until the Ironkin gave a bow of apology.

'Right. So the real queer thing wasn't the orks. You can find them all over these parts, or at least where they used to be. But there were other ruins. Just as old. And they were much easier to identify, on account of them having been built by Kin.'

Among the Kin, members of the Trans-Hyperian Alliance were thought overly enamoured of the Ancestors and the ancient days, but even Dori was stunned by the outcry that shook the hall at his announcement. The Kindred's reaction was more explosive than a bolt shell, equal parts shock, exasperation and delight. The last was most evident on Myrtun's face, even as she rose from her chair, a wordless exclamation adding to the cacophony of surprise. She marched down the few steps towards Dori and he rose to meet her, not sure if she was going to hug him or assault him, such were the warring emotions in her expression.

'You discovered an outpost of the Leagues?' demanded Vossko, banging the butt of her runestaff on the floor for quiet, head sheened with sweat.

'Why did you not furnish us with this information at the outset?' asked the Wayfinder that was acting as Myrtun's aide.

'Where are they now?' cried others.

'Which League?'

'What about the orks?'

'Did you meet any of them?'

It took some time for the Hearthkyn attendants to restore order among the crowd, while the chamberlain, Gurtha, likewise tried to restrain the members of the Votannic Council. When relative calm finally descended again, it was Myrtun's voice that broke it first, returned to a quiet yet firm tone.

'What happened to Orthônar?' There was an edge to the question that hinted at her guessing something of what was to come, having considered the matter during the uproar.

'I said we found ruins, not any folk, and not of the Leagues. I said Kin. We saw no League sign I ever recognised, though perhaps the esteemed Grimnyr Vossko might discover something in the oldest memories of the Votann, should she be able to delve that far. We detected the ork sign first. Spectrum analysis clutter and radio waves. Nothing intentional, just clamour from noisy filth. The second world of the system was the source. And when we came there, we found a mess in orbit – defence satellite remnants and ork wrecks. But not a functional vessel was to be seen.'

Dori remembered his own amazement, standing at Orthônar's side as they watched the view on the big screen, every moment bringing a revelation more wondrous or terrible than the last.

'The scanners picked up this ork presence easily enough, but there was something else,' he continued. 'The surface was stripped near bare by winds and silicate storms. Old mine workings pocked the rounded hills, going deep into the belly of the planet. And that's where the orks were to be found, still living in a captured Kin Hold.'

'You are sure of this?' Vossko asked hesitantly, looking as though she might collapse on the spot if the story turned out to be an elaborate fraud. 'You went down?'

'I was all for coming back and bringing more forces, as were others,' Dori told them, recalling the taut argument with his High Kâhl. 'Of course, just as at the Well of Yrdu, Orthônar was adamant that we needed to go in. It seemed the Hold wasn't what he was after. Least, not in itself. Something or somewhere inside. Maybe he thought if we left we might not get back? Whatever it was that had possessed him to go on this escapade, he was convinced it was in that Hold. And never mind that a thousand, perhaps ten thousand, orks might be living there now.'

'So Orthônar led the expedition into the Hold?' asked Myrtun, trembling and eager.

He nodded slowly. 'The orks were all over the planet, living under the surface in the Hold and its outlying settlements. But we found a keep of sorts. A tower that had withstood much of the erosion of twenty lifetimes. If there was anything of value left, Orthônar figured it would be there. So we made landing close by and crossed to the tower. It turned out to be just a bastion, a gateway into the underways, but there was an energy source close at hand. The signals, they looked like they might be from datacores of some kind. Something the orks hadn't found or touched for some reason.

'We thought this part uninhabited. Even after all this time the environment systems were still working, and we reasoned maybe the orks shunned it or the defenders had driven them out before succumbing to their losses over the years – victims of a wider siege, bottled up in their vault while their foes roamed wide. Such was our supposition, none of us knew for sure. There had been fighting long before, that much was obvious, but of any living creature there was nothing. Or so we thought.

'Orthônar wanted to press on, as he had done since the outset. We couldn't see anything of value, though. Place had been stripped over the ages.' Sighs and grumbles echoed around the hall at this revelation. Dori understood their disappointment. The excitement of finding an old fortress lost a lot of its shine if there weren't great riches and ancient treasures to be found within.

'He had us activate some of the auxiliary power systems,' he said, 'that drew on the heart of the world itself. Magma furnaces came to life, and so did the Hold.' The spectacle, or the memory of it, made him pause in contemplation. He looked around the hall, at the great lanterns and windows, and was transported back to a place far away, deep underground rather than floating in the void.

'It was magnificent,' he whispered. His next words choked him. He had to force them out as the memories became more painful again. 'But we had made a terrible mistake. One that cost Orthônar his life. One that cost us much more than that.'

Ironhelm fell silent. Myrtun had been patient. She had let him relate events his way, but now that he was getting to the point, it felt as though he was deliberately dragging out the tale.

'The orks hadn't left, had they? They attacked, and Orthônar was killed.'

The champion looked at her suddenly, as though he had forgotten she was there. Slowly, he nodded, his expression the grimmest it had been since he started.

'We were almost at the datavault, moving along a grand processional. They came from in front and behind.' He stopped again, a trembling hand raised to the wound on his brow. 'We fought them off that time. And the time after. But there was only one way in and out. Orthônar had to make a choice.'

Eyes downcast, Ironhelm looked like he might faint, occasionally twitching as though reacting to something unpleasant, but then he raised his head and stared Myrtun right in the eye, almost making her flinch. She wasn't sure what she saw in that gaze. A mix of hate and fear and utter desolation. She had never seen it before in the eyes of a Kin.

'He made me...' Ironhelm shook his head, fists clenched. 'I had to swear...'

'He sent you back here to tell his tale, and you have done so,' Myrtun said gently, resting a hand on his armoured shoulder. 'You fulfilled your oath.'

At that, a wild look appeared in Ironhelm's eye.

'Fulfilled my oath? My oath? Like I just had the one? I was champion!' He pushed her hand away and turned towards the audience. 'I was Orthônar's hand! Everyone here knows that. And at the end, when he knew he was going to die, he made me his oathkeeper. I carry his honour now, but I can't hold it any longer.'

The manic champion swung back to Myrtun, almost delirious.

'You understand?' He grabbed her cloak in gauntlets whose fingers were still stained with old, dried blood. 'Orthônar's oath. He passed it to me. Maybe he thought I would be High Kâhl, but I ain't. I can't fulfil a High Kâhl's oath, can I? Only you can do that.'

'What are you talking about?' Myrtun fought the urge to pry his dirty fingers away from her mantle.

'His *oath*!' Ironhelm roared. 'He swore to the Votann afore he left here. Whatever it was the Votann sent him there for, he gave an oath to do it. And he sent me back to tell you that he'd failed.'

'His oath died with him,' Vossko assured Ironhelm, approaching closer. 'It does not burden you any longer.'

'Oh, it does, and it will until it's been passed on properly,' the champion argued. His eye roved for a few heartbeats, looking at something only he could see, before fixing on the Grimnyr. 'Whatever it was that you gave him, it cost his life and the life of his Einhyr and many good Hearthkyn. And the Votann haven't got what they wanted yet.'

Myrtun could feel the attention in the hall turning to her. Out of the corner of her eye she caught the guild emissary approaching again. She shot a glance in his direction.

'Now is not the time for distractions,' she rasped at Lekki.

'By the power of the Guild, I speak to differ,' he replied, coming on. 'It is of Orthônar and oaths that I must talk. A High Kâhl's word is their bond, and my guild is bonded to this Kindred through Orthônar and now through you.'

'It can wait!' snapped Myrtun. 'Have you no decency? No sense of what we've just learned?'

'The Guild helped Orthônar!' growled Lekki. 'There are debts, sworn by oath.'

'Debts?' Myrtun's voice dropped to a cold whisper. 'You come to me now of all times to speak of debts? Get out of my sight, you grubbing little… Leave, before you are made to.'

'Wait, this really isn't a good…' Lekki's argument died in the face of Myrtun's implacable stare. A squad of Hearthkyn came closer, eyeing the bodyguard carefully. The Ironkin seemed nonchalant. Lekki shook his head, frowning. 'Tomorrow, we *must* discuss the terms. For all our sakes.'

'Go.'

Myrtun turned back to Ironhelm, who was gripped in a fit of quivering indignation and anguish. Her gaze moved to Vossko, then to the Voidmasters and others. As her eye roamed, she saw Lutar standing to one side. He motioned a slight shake of the head. She ignored him and looked out across the thousands gathered in the hall.

'We have all heard Ironhelm's account, and we can see the cost he has borne to bring it to us. It is clear that as High Kâhl I inherit not just the position and privilege enjoyed by my predecessors, but also their duties and responsibilities. An oath has been sworn by Orthônar, a contract sealed, and it seems that it is only right that I honour that contract as his replacement. More than a contract, an opportunity! A Hold from the oldest times, with something so valuable that Orthônar was willing to dare warp storms and ork hordes for it. Something that is still there, unclaimed for the Votann.'

'The Ancestors praise you, Myrtun,' said Ironhelm, bowing his head with a fist to his chest in salute.

There was a far more mixed reaction around the hall, with many unsure what the declaration actually meant. A glance to the council bench showed a row of disapproving faces.

'Given the import of this occasion, and that perhaps we cannot waste a moment of this opportunity, I must regretfully offer my apologies to the remaining petitioners.' Myrtun gazed around the hall. 'This audience must come to an end so that I and the Hearthspake can work out what is to be done.'

She turned away from the renewed clamour and headed back to the curtained doorway. At a gesture from her, Lutar fell in on her right side, clanking along in step.

'You had to say it out loud, didn't you?' he said, his remonstration unconcealed for a change. 'This isn't just another adventure, Myrtun. This is the future of our Kindred now.'

'You're exactly right,' she replied, turning her head towards him. The council members were filing after them from their bench, and she kept her voice low. 'Orthônar knew what he was about. There's the greatest opportunity of my long life waiting. For all of us! If I can't take on his contract, what's the point of being High Kâhl?'

'You don't even know what he swore to do!' It was rare for Lutar to show his exasperation, but Myrtun knew he meant well.

'No, but we can find out.'

Lekki almost pulled his shoulder dragging himself out of the war-rig, catching his arm in the bindings as the quiet rage that had filled him since he had approached Myrtun erupted into voluble expression.

'Piss of the Undershrikes! The Guild won't stand for it, Erkund! The humiliation! It's an insult to the chancellors and every member!'

Struggling out of the leg braces, he almost fell face-first onto the deck. His Ironkin companion steadied him with an extended hand.

'Oh, now you decide to help?' he snarled.

'I prevented you from being hurt.'

'And earlier, when those Hearthkyn brutes were threatening me?'

His protective E-COGs clustered around him, buzzing and whistling, their primitive minds unable to interpret his anger-fuelled behaviour.

'There was no intent to harm.'

'What about the reputation of the Guild? What about the harm there? And my personal reputation as their representative? Stood waiting like a wet-faced apprentice straight out of the crucible, still waiting to be rubbed down by the Embyr. It's an affront!'

'I am present to ensure no physical harm comes to you. Injury to your ego, whether temporary or permanent, isn't my concern.'

'No, I suppose not.' Lekki opened one of the lockers in the arming chamber and pulled out a thick towel. He rubbed his face, clearing off the sweat that had accumulated while encased in the armoured suit. There was a reason he preferred field wards. Far less claustrophobic.

'She better not fob me off tomorrow, or that's it.'

'It is not your place to unilaterally cease communications.'

'If she's not listening, it's not me that's ceasing, is it?'

He stripped off as he ranted and moved to the sonic shower. The hum of cleansing vibrational waves blotted out his continuing tirade, until he stepped out of the cubicle.

'...lucky I don't gather the members now and have them vote on immediate censorious action. I'm sure some will be in contact to offer their support after seeing how I was treated today.'

'They are preoccupied with Kindred matters.'

Lekki pulled out a new undersuit and robe while two of the ship's E-COG attendants removed his dirty laundry. They would be back in the locker, cleaned and pressed, by the time he woke. He wasn't even sure which part of the ship housed the laundry.

The *Sparkfly* was more than just a starship, it was an extension of Guild property. Even within the vastness of the *Unbreakable Giant*, a small vessel among many, it was territory of which he was complete master. The Kindred of the Eternal Starforge membership was not large enough to warrant a permanent guildhall on the Hold ship, so for the time being the vessel continued to be his headquarters, embassy and chambers. To stay elsewhere would invite expenses that would require redress later, and Lekki desired no entanglements of that nature. As it was, the docking fee was exorbitant, and having been forced to stay here far longer than originally intended and now kept waiting by another High

Kâhl, he was considering adding some reimbursement of those payments to the outstanding debt.

Moving from the arming chamber to his personal quarters – the largest of several suites available, usually reserved for a full diplomatic mission – Lekki helped himself to a variety of foodstuffs offered by E-COGs guiding suspensor trays. He also took a goblet of amber wine and lowered himself onto a long couch, where he sat brooding for some time, nibbling at hard crackers and sipping his drink.

'There in't no way to find out,' Jôrdiki quietly told Myrtun as the two of them stood shoulder to shoulder next to the brü urn. 'I had a quick look at the datacore archives, and even from the Fane itself I in't able to gain access. And as I told you earlier, when you asked, it'd be against my honour to fetch out something like that. You heard what Vossko said – it was addressed to Orthônar, not the High Kâhl.'

'It's bloody stupid, is what it is,' muttered the new High Kâhl.

Not a member of the council, Jôrdiki moved back to the wall, keeping away from the High Grimnyr while Myrtun stayed on her feet, pacing slowly around the chamber with a cup of brü in one hand and a half-eaten sweet treat in the other. A thread of syrup ran from the pastry across her wrinkled knuckles.

'I've heard your arguments, and I know it makes sense to you all, but I can't agree,' she told the councillors, not looking at them, her gaze moving from point to point along the panelled wall on the opposite side of the room. 'What would it say to other Kindreds when it gets out that your High Kâhl isn't as good as her word?'

'Not *her* word,' Vossko pointed out, for the fourth or fifth time. 'Ironhelm's wrong. It isn't on you to fulfil Orthônar's oath. The missive was for him, personally, and so his oath was his, not the office of High Kâhl's.'

'We told him exactly what we're telling you,' added Kâhl Vukasin. 'You can't take the Hold ship and the whole fleet into the storms. It's reckless. I know you think there's Profit there, but this isn't a Hernkyn matter you're talking about. The potential loss is far too risky despite the possible gains.'

'Especially with what we know now,' added Kyr Starbound. 'If we followed Orthônar, we'd all be destroyed in the Well of Yrdu.'

'But Orthônar made it through,' said Myrtun, turning to the Ironkin councillor. Jôrdiki watched the High Kâhl closely, knowing her moods well. She was invigorated by the confrontation, showing no signs of her age or that it was getting late into the evening on a day that had started early and been filled with incident. The harder life pushed Myrtun, the stronger she got. Which did not bode well for anyone hoping the meeting might come to a conclusion soon. The councillors seemed intent on making their own points, but there was no agreement on what was to be done, never mind how to inform the Kindred of that.

Vossko slapped a hand to the table in annoyance, the sharp noise alien in the quiet of the council chamber.

'The Votann would not have commanded the whole Kindred to risk itself trying to navigate a warp storm.'

'Thank you!' said Myrtun, crossing the room to stand by the High Grimnyr's chair. Vossko looked nonplussed and glanced at Jôrdiki. 'That's why Orthônar didn't take the whole Kindred.'

'And that's also why he did not come back,' added Lutar. 'If you intend to succeed where Orthônar failed, you must commit greater resources to the effort.'

Myrtun did not reply, perhaps taken aback by her closest companion's words. Jôrdiki took the momentary silence as an opportunity to speak, though she had been brought to the chamber purely on a technicality.

'If the Votann wish for the new High Kâhl to follow Orthônar, they will make it known to us,' she declared.

'It is not that simple, Jôrdiki,' Vossko replied, her tone free of condescension. 'The Votann can only act upon what they know. We have previously passed on that Orthônar did not return, and our Kin completed a communication earlier that related what we have learned from Ironhelm. However, without the memories of Orthônar himself, perhaps they cannot calculate the course of action required next.'

Gurtha, unusually, spoke next.

'We have lost one High Kâhl recently and these are not times for instability,' the chamberlain told the assembly. 'Uncertainty causes delays, inefficiencies. Costs. Today's events demonstrate the need for leadership from this chamber. To lose another High Kâhl so soon after Orthônar would be disastrous for our Kindred. With a precedent set, who else would fall to this curse of an oath? Would anyone agree to be High Kâhl, knowing that they would either have to sacrifice themselves or be seen as an oathbreaker? Better now that we agree that Orthônar alone was responsible for what occurred.'

'It is too late to decide,' Myrtun announced suddenly. 'All sensible folk are in their bunks now. Tired heads make bad decisions, and any announcement can wait for at least a sleep watch. And, as Jôrdiki says, who can say what may come to pass? Are we agreed to reconvene at next work watch?'

Assents rumbled around the room until only Vossko remained to make her agreement known. She looked at Jôrdiki and then Myrtun, pondering something.

'Aye,' she said eventually. 'On the morrow.'

Jôrdiki stood with the others but remained when the council were led out by Gurtha. Lutar also stayed behind.

'The council will never vote to take the Hearthfleet across the Celestial Stair,' the Grimnyr warned.

'I'm not suggesting they do,' Myrtun replied with a shrug. 'But we can go back with more troops than Orthônar had, can't we?'

'More Hearthkyn won't guarantee a ship can get through the Well of Yrdu,' Lutar said.

'You're both right,' said Myrtun, stroking at the fur of her cloak with her living hand. 'It's like I thought it'd be. Everyone else tells the High Kâhl what to say and do.'

'You are not a tyrant, Myrtun,' Lutar reminded her softly. 'For a first day on the job, I think you've handled everything as best you could.'

Myrtun smiled at the carefully crafted compliment, but said nothing. A small hatch in the ceiling opened and a handful of E-COGs floated into the chamber, carrying trays and cloths.

'I believe that is our cue to go,' said Lutar.

Myrtun nodded, set her brü mug on the table, and gestured for the two Kin to precede her to the door. They gathered as a trio just outside the chamber, the door wardens still at their posts behind them. They stood there in silence for a few moments, nobody sure what to say.

'I'm off to my bed,' said Myrtun, but her yawn was obviously feigned.

'I need to update my charts,' Lutar informed them.

'I in't tired,' said Jôrdiki. 'Happen I'll head to the Fane and have a shifty at the archives of the last while. Happen the Votann have made their will known already, but nobody's been looking for it. But that's all I'm doing. Vossko already thinks I'm up to nowt good there.'

Again they waited, until Myrtun grunted a goodbye and headed off.

'Your quarters are this way, ur-kâhl!' one of the guards shouted out, pointing down the corridor with her plasma stave.

'Maybe tomorrow,' Myrtun called back, not turning around. 'I want one more night on the *Grand Endeavour*.'

Jôrdiki shared a knowing look with Lutar.

'On the morrow, then?' said the Wayfarer.

'Aye, on the morrow,' Jôrdiki replied. They parted, heading their separate ways.

CHAPTER FIVE

Swift Departures

The whirr and click of automata helped fill the silence around Myrtun. The *Grand Endeavour* was empty but for a few Brôkhyr and their crews making repairs and handling normal maintenance, and they were asleep. Only her creations and the gentle hiss of the environmental systems kept her company.

Myrtun picked up another and started to wind the mechanism. She had the lanterns dimmed, hoping to lull herself into sleep, but it wasn't helping. The orange gleam from the brass bodies of her automata caught her eye and reminded her of distant suns.

A Hold, with the potential to send the Kindred into the higher echelons of the Trans-Hyperian Alliance, and nobody was interested.

She put the automaton down and released the catch, sending it spinning back and forth, a skirt of wires and plasthene lifting to become a disc and then falling again as centripetal force did its work. Her thoughts followed the motion, spinning, spinning, spinning.

Nothing made sense. She had harboured low expectations on learning that she was High Kâhl. Gone were the ancient days when that would have meant absolute authority. Like Lutar said, she was no tyrant, but rule by consent was not always the answer. The council would always be conservative, preferring to sustain the status quo than risk anything. They weren't Hernkyn. They were good at making the most of opportunity, but they couldn't sniff it out if it was a mug of brü right under their noses.

Which made it all the more galling for Myrtun, because she knew that's exactly what was needed from the council. Steady hands on the helm, as much literally as figuratively. A High Kâhl who was ready to go chasing off after an adventure at the slightest sniff of excitement was no good to the Kindred. Disruption caused confusion and delays. They were better off putting all their effort into the gravitic dredging. Myrtun had lived long enough to know that opportunity was a fickle prey, but even if missed, it would eventually come about again. Maybe she was wrong about this.

She sighed, wondering why the Votann had put her name before the council.

Whirr. Click. Whirr. Click.

How easy for her little machine folk to carry on, ignorant of what else they might have been. Each did its thing without distraction, as was intended – well, almost as intended in a few cases, especially those she had made first. But she couldn't treat Kin like automata. She had to lead and they followed, but they couldn't be forced anywhere they didn't want to go. And even if they would follow, given the choice, she didn't have the right to ask it of them. She had to be responsible. There was more than just her Prospect at stake.

She carried on activating the mechanisms until the table was full of small metal dancers. At first, she hadn't had any plan beyond making something to keep herself amused. And then she had added a second, a third. By the sixth, she realised there was a pattern. Now, if she arranged them a certain way, they could all dance together, some doing their pirouettes, others swaying forward and back, or skipping up and down. Each in its place, creating a mesmerising picture of the whole. She could see the path the next one could take, going round in a circle between the others.

The implied choreography made it all the more obvious that Myrtun didn't know where she was meant to fit any more. The Kindred was a thing far vaster than her collection, but it had its own arrangement and traditions and ways of doing things that meant folks didn't bump into each other. Not too much.

She pushed her hand into the midst of the dancing, not angrily but with another resigned sigh. Her intervention caused an automaton to bounce off her hand and topple backwards, which sent another careening into a coupled pair. In turn they spun out of control, and by cascade effect soon the table was full of fallen automata waving arms and legs, some writhing as though in a fit.

'The Ancestors are watching,' she muttered.

Her eye was drawn to the most recent quartet she had built. They had somehow escaped the carnage and were still merrily dancing off to one side, safe from the others.

Seeing them gave Myrtun an idea.

The Hall of Stars was partly a repository and partly an astronarium. Digital vaults made up the bottom part of the circular wall, banks of datacores broken regularly by index and access screens. Above, from about twice Lutar's height, the hall became a faceted dome studded with projectors. Only a dim deep-blue glow from the displays lit the chamber, leaving the highest part of the dome only to be guessed at in the shadows.

Lutar crossed to a panel and keyed in the Hold ship's current location. He entered the activate command and walked to a golden circle at the centre of the floor, the eighteen cardinal directions marked with the appropriate runes. He stood on the central plate and faced towards the galactic centre. The dome was plunged into total darkness. Lutar looked up, again filled with the sensation of holding his breath though he possessed no lungs. One by one the projectors glimmered into life like stars in the firmament, but soon they were lost amongst hundreds of holographic stars hanging in the air around the Wayfinder.

When non-Ironkin came here they would wear special goggles that allowed the Hall of Stars to track their head and eye movements, but Lutar, like all Wayfinders, was connected to the system over an etheric link. As he imagined himself turning his head, the display shifted. If he focused on a constellation or individual star, it burned brighter and would magnify in front of him. System details passed directly into his neural network, updating the data stored there.

But he hadn't come here simply to upload the latest survey sweeps from the Astro Corps. He turned his attention towards the pile of nebulae and black holes known as the Celestial Stair. Swathes of the scene suddenly pitched into darkness, the areas of space they represented yet to be mapped, or so old that they were no longer retrievable except by specific interrogation of the Votannic datacores.

Lutar pulled back the view, allowing more stars to return to the hall. A lot of them blinked in and out of existence, their exact positions undetermined even by the sophisticated triangulation runs of the Astro Corps survey flotillas. Standing inside the swirl of the Gylfargap Nebula and looking north-east, Lutar could not focus on the area around the Well of Yrdu.

The Wayfinder detected the presence of another entering: Kyr Starbound.

'The Hall of Stars cannot mesh together the inconsistent data readings of the Well and its environs,' the ancient Voidmaster announced. Their communication came as a direct transmission rather than vocalisation as they entered the golden circle. At their influence the view shifted, becoming a much sketchier schematic with pure white pinpoints rather than the representations of real stars. 'This is a computed rendition using averages of all data points.'

'Which is a false reality,' Lutar replied. 'It bears no relation to the true positions of the systems. Any navigation based on it could be out by several light years.'

'Yes. But it doesn't matter. That's not the view you're after, is it?'

'No.' Lutar sent a command to the hall's faculty and the view changed, transforming from the outside inwards in response to the Wayfinder's demand. The pinpricks of stars vanished and were replaced with ribbons of orange and red and yellow. They slowly undulated and weaved around each other, creating a stream of constant movement around Lutar.

'Warp forecasts are even less useful than the commonality schema,' said Starbound. 'At least, where you are intending to go.'

The view spun and expanded; the rivers of warp currents morphed into tributaries and mainfares, pooling, creating swirls and lakes, sometimes looping back on themselves like the coronal ejections from a star. At their centre, amid a bewildering mess of lines of different hues, a blackness swallowed everything. Not a literal black hole – such celestial features were far easier to find and trace than the phenomenon being displayed here.

The Well of Yrdu.

It might have been considered the eye of a hurricane were it a planetary phenomenon, except that the Well was not *part* of any warp storm, but rather a centre around which other raging giants slowly circled. Starbound gestured, tracing a plunge route that ran around the edges of the tempestuous cluster, moving from one storm to the next in the direction of their flow like a void ship using gravity wells to slingshot itself across a star system.

Lutar moved the display so that they were looking at the warp currents from an angle above the main galactic ecliptic plane, rather than looking directly down into the Well.

'See?' He pointed, and a golden shimmering thread traced the line of his index finger. He circled his finger slowly to draw a line around the top of the Well. In places it looked like the warp streams did not circumnavigate the Well, but went down into it, forming a rough edge or lip, like water plunging down a cataract.

'An artefact of the Hall of Stars, not a true representation.' Starbound magnified the view by fifty per cent and the resolution started to fray, leaving the top of the Well nothing more than a rough oval of dissipating particles.

'More importantly…' Lutar flipped the image, experiencing a momentary sense of vertigo as the galaxy turned upside down. From the underside, the Well of Yrdu disappeared, becoming an almost perfectly circular disc. 'These are the latest readings from the plunges made by the *Stormblaze*?'

'Unfortunately, Champion Ironhelm did not return in the *Stormblaze*. As the sole Kin aboard, and close to succumbing to his wounds, he launched the ship's autocutter. The internal systems just about retraced the route of the *Stormblaze*, but its sensors were very poor compared to the readings of the parent vessel.'

The warpscape faded back to the starfield and pulled away, expanding Lutar's view. A red light blinked in the darkness on the periphery of the display.

'As best we can tell, that is where Orthônar took the *Stormblaze*. A system more than three hundred light years away from anything else in the datacores. I have taken the liberty of naming the system Oathstar.'

Lutar looked at Starbound, surprised by the lyricism of the name.

'I like it,' he said. 'Better than Orthônar's Folly.'

'Or Myrtun's Folly?' Starbound's suggestion irritated Lutar, but he did not respond immediately. The Voidmaster continued.

'That is why you are here? To see if a route can be plotted to follow Orthônar?'

'No, that isn't why I'm here.' Lutar shut down the hall's systems and the gleam of stars faded to nothing, replaced by the humdrum glow of datascreens. 'It was clear from Ironhelm's testimony that celestial navigation would not solve this mystery. We either "trust to fate" and enter the Well of Yrdu, or we do not. Orthônar looked for another way past and found none.'

'You think she should take us there?'

'Of course not. It would be foolhardy to risk the Hold ship and fleet with such scant data.'

'But?'

Lutar looked at the other Ironkin and exchanged a sensation of wry mirth.

'You and I are both Hernkyn Wayfinders by the will of the Votann. Are you not also intrigued by what lies in the spaces of a map? We do not have to risk the whole Kindred to take a look…'

When she had come to the Fane to see what had become of the message to Orthônar, Jôrdiki had visited only the outer datacore cells. It had been almost a quarter of her lifetime since she had last entered the Fane proper of the Hold ship, and she stood in the corridor for some time preparing herself. She was used to the self-made Fane that had built itself aboard the *Grand Endeavour*, and the second-hand communiques that she exchanged through it. Jôrdiki wasn't sure if she really remembered what it was like to work with a fully functioning Votannic conduit.

The main hall lay behind a small, armoured door built into a thick bulkhead designed to withstand any blast or assault. Layers of alloys, ballistic weave, ceramics, and self-repair systems encased the whole Fane in a near-indestructible cage. The doorway itself was plainly decorated so as not to draw attention to its contents should the Hold ship ever be invaded. It deserved a far grander entrance – carvings, mosaics, murals. Instead a simple reference had been acid-etched into the outer steel layer of the door, marking its place as the one hundred and thirty-second chamber of D-deck (south). *D-132(s)*. Jôrdiki might have thought it an E-COG vault or tool storage had she not known better.

The invincibility of her surroundings was, perversely, matched by an equally effective self-destruction mechanism inside. Within seconds, plasma from the reactors could flood the whole chamber, turning lifetimes of data and communications into unusable slag. There could never be a danger of the Fane being overrun, never a risk of any knowledge of the Votann being discovered or – and the thought made Jôrdiki shudder – an enemy controlling a means to access them. It was a last resort, and thankfully one that few Holds had ever been forced to use. This was just for a primary conduit; the Votann themselves were hidden deep in vaults somewhere within the Trans-Hyperian Alliance's territory, surrounded by defences that equalled any fortress across the galactic core and beyond.

The door opened with a hiss to reveal High Grimnyr Vossko silhouetted against the rainbow gleam of the interior.

'Don't stand there gawping like a freshly propagated novice, I've a bed waiting for me.'

'Sorry, *ur-grimnyr*, happen I ain't rightly sure what I'm doing here.' Jôrdiki walked forward as Vossko beckoned her to enter, stepping gingerly across the threshold. 'It's been a long time.'

No two Fanes were alike, even within the Kindred, but they all shared similarities. Jôrdiki relived the impressions of her first visit so long before, when Vossko had not been High Grimnyr but simply one of the Votannic attendants, and Jôrdiki had not been out of her crucible for more than ten watches.

First was the chill. Deep within the heart of the Fane immense empyric processors churned data at a rate that generated enough heat to melt steel. Added to that there were the plasma bypass tubes that made up the failsafe defence system. Thousands of liquid supercoolant pipes and fans connected to the Brôkhyr foundries above kept the entire edifice at functional temperatures, and their presence affected the whole space.

Second was the noise. Jôrdiki thought of it as the Whispering Voices, while others called it a hum, a buzz, or the Votannic Murmur. The data flow of the deep systems was audible, sometimes forming syllable-like pulses as different rhythms and harmonies formed from a trillion data gates opening and closing. Jôrdiki had heard Astronyr Voidmasters say that the background radiation of two hundred billion stars was the music of the galaxy. To her, the noise of the multidimensional quantum algorithms used by the Fane were the lyrics.

Third, and for Jôrdiki the longest-lingering memory, was the smell of the Fane. The cleanness of ozone emanating from the coil arrays competed with the lived-in aura of up to a dozen Grimnyr at a time, who spent watch after watch in this place monitoring the Fane, sending and receiving messages from the Votann. Another addition to the miasma of sterility came up along the cabling from the transduction apse directly below. Jôrdiki knew that the end of a Kin's life was as normal as the beginning, that transducing their essence into the Fane was no less a physical process than rendering down their bodily constituents, but the mortuary-like atmosphere reminded her too much of her first confused moments in her crucible.

'Old memories, best left behind,' said Vossko, breaking Jôrdiki's train of thought.

'What's that?'

'Your scowl, the distant gaze, I see it on the face of many a Grimnyr. This place is awash with memories, and the conjuring of recollection.'

'Inevitable, happen as like. So much of the past is layered here – generations born and died have passed along these cables, into these empyric circuits.'

'The future too, though,' countered the High Grimnyr. 'From here sprout destinies unknown, lives unwinding, paths yet to be trodden. You always fixate on the endings, not the beginnings, Found-daughter.'

The sobriquet was archaic, and Vossko had always used it affectionately rather than in judgement, but it had been a long time since Jôrdiki had heard it – a reminder that she had not originally been of the Eternal Starforge. The way she spoke, the way she thought, the way she acted – it was all just a bit different to those created by the Embyr of the Kindred. Her body had been spun into existence within the crucibles not far from the Fane, but the cloneskein, the genetic template that she had been based on, had come from somewhere very different. At least, she assumed so. Nothing had been left as evidence of the Kindred from which her crucible wreckage had come, and nothing in the Votannic datacores suggested who might once have laid claim to their cloneskein.

'Happen it's no wonder, when I and my five Kindred-Kin are the only ones left of us?' Jôrdiki replied, sombre. 'Our origins lost, we in't got no beginning, only an ending. When we're gone, happen nothing of our original Kindred remains. We go to the Votann of the Trans-Hyperian Alliance, but we were not created at their instigation.'

'Hush, you are not gone yet. You've half a life left to you. You've been with Myrtun too long, bottled up on that ship on your own. You've forgotten that something greater than all of us spreads out from this place.'

'Perhaps you're right.' Jôrdiki looked around. Aside from Vossko, who was there at Jôrdiki's request, two other Grimnyr were in attendance, sitting on stools as they studied a piece of intricate runework on a length of transparent datatape spooling from one of the deep-core access ports.

'I've set in a recall search for the transmissions that nominated Myrtun to the position of High Kâhl, but don't get your hopes high,' Vossko continued. 'It's mostly administrative buffer. As for the other thing you asked for, incoming missives around the time that Orthônar's mystery message arrived, that's a lot easier to access.' She waved to one of a line of lectern-like standing desks along one wall. They had datascreens and small shelves so that a combination of digital and physical copies could be analysed simultaneously. One in particular was laden with documentation.

'I've been doing a fair bit of work on that already,' Vossko said. 'I've even asked the Votann if they would unseal the message for us, though there's been no reply to that yet.'

'Nothing?' Jôrdiki hadn't realised how her hopes had risen when the High Grimnyr had agreed to meet her at this unusual watch. 'No reason why Myrtun was chosen? Nothing about Orthônar's oath?'

'There were three different messages, one from each Votann,' Vossko explained, leading Jôrdiki to the desk. Three separate datacards had been affixed to the frame of the lectern screen, each mostly filled with transmissions data, followed by a single sentence. 'See for yourself.'

Jôrdiki glanced at Vossko's translations, surprised at their curtness for such a moment of import.

'This is it? Everything? Not a summary?'

The High Grimnyr nodded. 'Sometimes one can be erudite without loquacity. This is the essence of the Votann's will.'

Reading them again, Jôrdiki was also surprised that each communication seemed its own conclusion rather than a consensus opinion.

> URD-0r: *The High Kâhl Has Travelled The Greater World More Than Most.*
> VeRD-4n: *The High Kâhl Has The Wisdom of a Life Longer Than Most.*
> Sk-43L: *The High Kâhl Has The Strength Of Will To Make Their Own Fate More Than Most.*

'Do they often communicate like this?' she asked. 'Each Votann giving an answer?'

Jôrdiki had expected something more cryptic, but Vossko was High Grimnyr and had to be trusted to interpret such signals properly. Most of the communications Jôrdiki had received on the *Grand Endeavour* had already been interpreted and passed on, but when she had been honoured with a direct Votannic communique, they had always been three variations of similar intent, yet a lot vaguer than the three clear statements attached to Vossko's workstation.

'Moreso in latter times,' admitted Vossko. 'Now and then we receive a dissenting opinion from one of them, but I believe in this case it is a coordinated response rather than a disagreement. Why they did so in this format, I cannot say. Perhaps each thought their condition was a priority.'

Jôrdiki examined the messages again. There was certainly no effort to gainsay or contradict each other, simply bald statements about three different requirements.

'That certainly seems to fit Myrtun,' she admitted with a long sigh. 'But it doesn't say her by name. Happen the council misjudged the intent of the Votann? Which other candidates were considered?'

'Trust me, we deliberated long and hard, though the answer initially came to us swiftly,' Vossko assured her, leaning past to activate the screen. 'Some Kindred call their ancient Grimnyr

"Living Ancestors" because of their knowledge and wisdom. For the Eternal Starforge, that title is best appended to Myrtun. She is a legend, but also her idiosyncrasies are well known to every member of the council. She has grown more hot-headed and stubborn as she has aged, unlike most folks.'

Jôrdiki looked at the screen as the High Grimnyr keyed in a code and brought up several archive addresses. Vossko opened one, revealing a picture of Myrtun – shockingly young, without the facial scars and replacement arm. There was an eagerness in her face that Jôrdiki knew but realised she had not seen for some time. The youthful Hernkyn was sat astride a magna-coil bike, the deployed boarding ramp of a small scout ship behind her. Jôrdiki felt her heart palpitate briefly when she understood what she was looking at.

'This was just before her encounter with the orks!'

'Yes. Her very first time with a Prospect. Only the memories of the Votann and the Ironkin stretch back that far. Forty-four rotes later, Lutar was dragging her near dead from an escape pod. The first thing she did when she got a new ear and arm was to sign up to the next Prospect leaving the Hearthfleet.'

'She is fearless, that much I know.'

'To run towards doom is a different sort of fear, Found-daughter. A fear of living. Of being. Myrtun has spent her life throwing herself out into the darkness. At first she wanted to find the orks that tortured and killed that first crew in front of her. Vengeance it would seem, but I think it was something else. Something that still drives her.'

'What is that?'

'To follow her first crewmates to the Votann. She chases after the fate she thinks she should not have escaped. That is what the message of Votann tells us. The same is true when she tells us that she intends to go after Orthônar.'

'You really believe she will?'

'You do, that's why you are here, isn't it? Not to dig up an excuse for Myrtun, but to find something to persuade her not to go after him?'

Jôrdiki considered this, looking at the young Kin on the screen while picturing the force-of-nature Myrtun in her head. Vossko's words made too much sense. Jôrdiki had known Myrtun was not the glory-or-death person she seemed to be – she regarded her fame within and beyond the Kindred as a matter of interest rather than pride. To be a doom-seeker... In the traditional sense, of course. Not looking for death in itself, that was not in Myrtun's character, but to charge headlong after a *meaningful* fate after surviving that traumatic encounter with the orks?

'She cannot drag the Kindred into her reckless life,' Jôrdiki told the High Grimnyr.

'If she insists on bringing this before the council, she will be voted down. Orthônar was wise enough not to share what later drove him to madness, but kept only his own counsel. Myrtun may well force a divide between High Kâhl and Votannic Council at a time when we can least afford a crisis. Opportunity abounds at the Bilskyrnun Tides, but we have foes growing in number and daring too.'

'Myrtun has faults, but disloyalty and selfishness are not among them,' Jôrdiki tried to assure Vossko. 'When faced with the decision of the council, I'm sure she will act for the best of the Kindred.'

'In considering what is best for the Kindred of the Eternal Starforge I have decided that the Votannic Council cannot be embroiled in any mad schemes and adventures I might drag them into,' announced Myrtun from the stage in the audience hall. It was as packed as the day before and hundreds more Kin were gathered in the halls nearby, watching proceedings on viewers hastily erected to ease the pressure on the door wardens.

Since declaring she would make a special announcement at the start of the watch, another thousand of her Kin had made their way to the centre of the Hold ship, wanting to be part of the historic events that were unfolding – only those whose duties prevented them from attending remained in other parts of the Hold ship. Instead, they listened in on the comm-network or watched on personal screens, as did thousands of others on other ships in the Hearthfleet, and doubtless over the coming watches and rotes.

Myrtun had only occasionally felt an imitation of so much expectation in one place, when all her Prospect had been gathered to a single purpose, each unconsciously sharing bonds that made them a single entity more than a collection of individuals. Now, with the whole Kindred setting their mind upon her, she could feel it almost like a physical pressure.

Only now did Myrtun have a real inkling of what it meant to be High Kâhl, at the centre of the Kindred of the Eternal Starforge, the head of an interconnected community that thought with ten thousand brains but spoke with one voice. Had it been the same for Orthônar, as he had stood in this same spot? And why had he not shared the messages of the Votann? Had they demanded silence, or was the import of his mission such that he did not want to raise hopes – or fears – in his Kindred? And before him, a dozen and more High Kâhls had made pronouncements that altered the course of Kindred history in a way that no other Kin was able.

How would this moment be remembered in the datacores of the Votann?

The Eternal Starforge gathered not because they wanted to boast of attendance in later times – though many would – but because they could not help but be drawn to each other, to find commonality of purpose and action. It was how the Votann had created them.

The High Kâhl heard some murmurs of approval, a few sighs of relief coming from the council bench. She glanced at them and then to Lutar, who stood to one side of the official council members. He had no more idea of what she was about to say than the council. Myrtun had called the audience without consulting or confiding in him or them. It was better, quicker this way.

Even so, her gut writhed at the thought of what she had to say. She had considered telling the council first, but realised they would have ended up in the same position as the rote before, arguing around and around, getting nowhere. This way, in view of the whole Kindred – her words going out to others in the Trans-Hyperian Alliance – Myrtun knew that her decision would bind the council. Convention, tradition, and expectation were hers to wield now that she was High Kâhl, and that had its uses.

'There will be many here pleased to know that it is my wish that the Hold ship continues with its planned journey to the Bilskyrnun Tides for gravitic harvesting,' she continued. This time she caught nods out of the corner of her eye from the councillors. They would not last. 'But on the other hand, we cannot ignore both the meaning and substance of Orthônar's oath and disappearance. The meaning is clear. Oaths were sworn by the High Kâhl to the Votann, and those oaths have not been fulfilled. It is a debt unpaid that hangs over us.

'In substance, the reasoning is even clearer. Orthônar wasn't mad, or stupid. Neither are the Votann. His intent to deliver on that promise to the Votann was based on not just pride and honour, but a material benefit as determined by the Votann themselves. We are not a people prone to vainglory or random acts of indulgence. Though we do not yet know what was asked of Orthônar, that it was asked at all, and that he went to extraordinary lengths in his efforts to fulfil his oath, demonstrate to me that it was something of value to the Votann, and therefore of incredible value to the Kindred of the Eternal Starforge. We cannot pretend otherwise.'

She stopped to look squarely at the council, who were now stiff of pose and expression, a few of them looking downright annoyed. Myrtun spared a glance to Lutar before addressing the council members.

'I am High Kâhl, and in that role I have respected the wishes of the Hearthspake. But I am also still kâhl of a Hernkyn Prospect, and commander of the *Grand Endeavour*. It is within that capacity that I have chosen to investigate the disappearance of High Kâhl Orthônar.'

Surrounded by cheers and cries of dismay, along with no shortage of shouted questions, Myrtun turned around to find Ironhelm on the petitioner benches. She raised her hands for the audience to settle, which took some time.

'With the champion to guide us,' she continued once the noise had abated, 'we shall dare the Well of Yrdu and find the lost Kinhold where Orthônar was last seen. If he is dead, as we fear, we shall reclaim him for the Votann, and as many others as possible. And then we shall claim what else is there to be claimed, for which so many have given their lives already. No matter how hard we debate, we can't find answers here for what happened or why he went. And while we can't answer that question, we can say that we do the Votann's work.'

Council members were on their feet, as were a great many others across the hall. None tested the patience of the wardens though, choosing to give support or argument from the stands and the floor. Once again Myrtun gestured for the clamour to be quietened. It took longer the second time. Lutar had joined her by the time she could make herself heard.

'This isn't a one-way trip.' She wasn't sure if the words were for him or everybody else. 'I fully intend to come back and continue as High Kâhl, but until I do, the Hearthspake has my full blessing and its chamberlain has my authority to act as regent in all matters.'

'The *Grand Endeavour* has no Voidmaster,' announced Kyr Starbound as they advanced from the council benches. Vossko and a handful of others trailed behind as an unofficial delegation.

'Lutar and me have done a good enough job till now,' replied Myrtun.

'Not for where you're going,' the old Ironkin replied. 'If you make a mistake going down the Well, nobody's coming back to tell of it.'

Someone else was coming forward from the other side. Myrtun thought it was Ironhelm but was confronted by the Brôkhyr Lekki, this time out of his ill-suited battle armour. His bodyguard and jittering E-COGs still accompanied him.

'There's still the Guild matter to be discussed!' barked the Brôkhyr.

'I can only talk to one of you at a time,' Myrtun snapped back, seeing that Ironhelm was indeed making his way over too, along with a couple of other petitioners who had yet to be seen.

'I'm coming with you,' declared Starbound.

Their announcement created a sudden silence around Myrtun.

'What about the Hold ship?' demanded Gurtha, the chamberlain. She looked more worried than angry. 'The Bilskyrnun Tides are no pleasure jaunt.'

'And you have more than enough experienced Voidmasters to handle the difficult parts,' replied Starbound, their metal hand gesturing to encompass others on the benches beside the throne.

'I'm not going to miss this opportunity to travel the Well of Yrdu, and I'm sure there's a few others that'll be happy to go too.'

'I really need–' Lekki's protest was cut off by a shout from further along the hall.

'You're a massive pain in the arse, Myrtun, but the *Canny Wanderer* will be at your side,' called Fyrtor, standing amid a sizeable gang from his Prospect. 'And if there's any salvage to be had from that old Hold, you'll need some help, aye?'

Other Hernkyn Prospectors shouted out their support too, forcing Myrtun to silence them for a third time.

'I'm happy for the assistance, but we can't all up and leave the Hold ship without eyes and ears. Fyrtor spoke first, so he's coming. Anyone else, we'll hold a lottery. Two more Prospects and that's it. The more that goes, the more chances of losing someone along the way. There'll be plenty of opportunity to make good at the Bilskyrnun Tides, and we need fast ships to get there and claim the best harvesting fields around that black hole.'

Lots more questions were raised, a barrage of noise that sent Myrtun retreating to the council chamber leaving councillors and petitioners in her wake. Lutar slipped through the curtained doorway after her, moving to the brü urn as other council members started to enter.

'No time for that,' Myrtun said as she grabbed his arm. 'We've got to prepare for a trip. Gurtha! You can handle all the arrangements. I'm heading to the *Grand Endeavour* and I am not to be disturbed for anything less than actual calamity.'

She glared at the chamberlain, who nodded meekly and set her data tablet down at her spot on the table. The others that had followed were equally cowed, even Vossko.

'Look,' said Myrtun. 'You know this is for the best. The council rules in my name, and you all know that things will be smoother for it. I've given permission to harvest the gravitic tides, and handed official authority to the chamberlain. It's not like when Orthônar left. You know where I'm going. And I really do plan to come back.'

'So did Orthônar,' Vossko said quietly. 'But perhaps you are right. Some time without… disruption may be in order.'

With the High Grimnyr echoing the High Kâhl, the other councillors acquiesced with a few frowns but no verbal arguments. Myrtun took the opportunity to leave before their mood changed, Lutar in tow.

'I feared you would–' began the Wayfinder.

'Feared?' Myrtun almost stumbled, taken aback by his words. 'You think I'm doing the wrong thing?'

'"Wrong" is too broad a term, my jewel-star. There are many applicable reasons for why you should do this. But also some that are not. Motive in this case is important. If you are just trying to avoid the crushing responsibilities–'

'I'm not.'

'–or this is in some way related to your history with orks–'

'It isn't.'

'–then that's settled, isn't it?'

'High Kâhl Myrtun!' The shout from behind was recognisable as having come from Lekki without them having to turn around. There was something about his voice that put Myrtun on edge, even when he was just saying her name. A sense of entitlement touched with indignation?

'I can't,' she said.

'I'll see you back at the *Grand Endeavour*,' said Lutar, stopping and turning.

'Later, my star-guide.'

As she heard him raise his voice, intercepting the guild ambassador, Myrtun's thoughts were fixed on Lutar's phrasing. *Back* at the *Grand Endeavour*, he had said. Returning to their proper place. The Prospect ship was where they were meant to be – the last couple of days had been the expedition.

As soon as he saw the Wayfinder turning back towards him, Lekki knew that Myrtun was brushing him off again.

'Really?' he muttered, to himself more than his silent companion. 'The insult deepens.'

'I'm sorry,' Lutar began, but Lekki wasn't interested in any excuses.

'I have tried,' the Brôkhyr snarled. 'The patience of the Guild is not endless. I have brought the ore to the smelting, but still it doesn't know the flames. Unless the smelting comes to the ore, there'll be grave repercussions, mark my words.'

'An oath? Or a threat, Master Lekki?' asked the Wayfinder. His tone was polite, but there was a steely edge to the question. 'Both are hazardous it seems.'

'Funny, I wonder the same,' interjected Erkund.

Lekki bridled at both of them, unsure how he had earned such disrespect.

'Tell Myrtun that I shall be on the *Sparkfly* if she wishes to resolve this issue amicably.' He gestured to Erkund. 'My hands are shackled. I will contact the Enduring Guild of Master Runewrights to see if they will offer any leniency. Until I hear any word to the contrary, or offered agreement from Myrtun herself, consider the contract annulled.'

Holding his head up with as much self-respect as he could muster, Lekki turned on his heel and marched away, ignoring the Wayfinder's questions that followed him down the corridor.

Jôrdiki was surprised to discover High Grimnyr Vossko waiting on the dockside near the berth of the *Grand Endeavour*. The ship was launching at the end of the watch and awaited her arrival. Dock Chief Greta stood at the top of the ramp, silhouetted against the main bay lights.

'Running a little late?' Vossko asked, rubbing a hand over her bald head. 'Myrtun seems precipitously eager to leave.'

'Aye, that's no surprise. She hates waiting about once a decision's been made. And before a decision's been made, happen to think on it.' Jôrdiki stopped with one foot on the rampway. Her belongings had been moved back aboard from her briefly occupied quarters on the Hold ship, but she held a bundle of books and transparencies under one arm, borrowed from the Mainfane. 'You're not volunteering to come too, are you, like Starbound?'

Vossko's expression of shock was answer enough, but she replied anyway.

'By the Ancestors, no! I see your relief, but take no offence. Gurtha is all well and good running things, *managing*, but somebody needs to stay and *lead* the Kindred. You must be pleased, though. Back as head of your own Fane, nobody else to whom you must answer.'

'Except Myrtun. And happen, this wouldn't have been my choice at all if I'd been consulted.' Jôrdiki took a step back onto the quayside, leaning closer to confide in the High Grimnyr. 'I could learn so much more with you and the others, about the Votann and the First Truths, and of the warding-ways.'

'Then why are you going?' Vossko took Jôrdiki's spare hand in both of hers. 'I would be happy to resume the teaching, Found-daughter.'

Jôrdiki looked at her hand and then at Vossko and couldn't find an answer. Not one she really wanted to articulate, about debt and duty, and a bunch of other things that would feel hollow if she said them out loud. The whole situation was stupid, and she felt like an idiot continuing to be part of it. And yet she had known the Prospect more than anything else in her life, and did not have that Kindred connection to the rest of the Eternal Starforge.

A fleeting look of pity clouded Vossko's features, annoying Jôrdiki more than any thought of being separated from the Mainfane. She realised the High Grimnyr didn't rate her self-built Fane at all, though really it was a remarkable achievement. Not wanting to show how much the unconscious condescension smarted her pride, Jôrdiki carefully pulled her hand back and gave a nod of respect.

'Happen I had best be going. We'll send messages, when we can. Reckon you won't hear from us on the other side of the Well though, like with Orthônar, but you never know.'

Not waiting for a reply, Jôrdiki turned and stomped up into the ship. At the top she paused next to Greta, who seemed to read her thoughts.

'High Kâhl's already aboard, you're the last.'

'Everyone came back?' Jôrdiki was surprised that there weren't some Hernkyn staying on the Hold ship.

'And about three dozen newcomers. We've filled out all the quarters.' The dock chief slammed her hand against the control that started the withdrawal of the ramp, the door wheezing shut at the same time. The bright gleam of the lanterns was shut out, but Jôrdiki could see just as well by the dimmer light of the bay lamps. The shapes of covered magna-coil bikes, Sagitaur transports and other vehicles filled the space, the air thick with fresh oil and ozone. 'I'll let the High Kâhl know you're here and we can get going.'

'Aye, do that.'

Jôrdiki hefted up her books and threaded a path through the Prospect's vehicles. She turned left out of the doors, heading towards her Fane, and then stopped, realising just how familiar it all felt. For a moment it seemed as if someone else was in her body, steering her path. Shaking off the feeling, she started forward again.

CHAPTER SIX

Following the Trail

Not for the first time since departing the Hold ship, Lutar had to stop himself from turning to look at Myrtun in the command chair. Instead, he forced his gaze in the other direction, towards Kyr Starbound, standing at the Voidmaster's position to the left and just behind the helm and navigational stations, the latter of which was occupied by the Wayfinder.

'Countercyclic forming ahead,' warned Lutar, calmly voicing his analysis of the data continuously streaming in from the warp surveyors. Lines of numerals and runes filled his screen like isobars on a meteorological display, except that these represented the density of warp energy through four dimensions, none of which actually *existed* within warp space. Covered in a layer of reality generated by the warp fields, the *Grand Endeavour* sensed its surroundings by measuring the amount of ward energy required to keep the barrier intact, and thereby the corresponding amount of empyric pressure trying to break through. 'Magnitude three point two, for a drift average of three per cent.'

He and Starbound could have communicated digitally as they had done in the astronarium, but although it would have been quicker it excluded the rest of the bridge crew, and in particular their commander. It was to Myrtun that the Voidmaster directed their following words.

'That's just about on our exit point for the Thriga System, ur-kâhl,' explained Starbound. They shrugged void-armoured shoulders with a creak of theseum alloy joints. 'We could drop the plunge short and add a few rotes to our travel in-system, but I think that a shear like that shouldn't trouble the *Grand Endeavour*'s warp barriers.'

Lutar stopped himself from remarking, but not before his speakers emitted a strained grunt of disapproval. Starbound kept their attention on Myrtun.

'Our Wayfinder, who is of a cautious disposition, seems to think that plan imprudent.'

'Our Wayfinder is held in the highest regard by this command,' replied Myrtun, smiling at Lutar. She returned her gaze to Starbound. 'It has helped to balance out the overconfidence of the former Voidmaster.'

'Thank you,' said Lutar, but the High Kâhl continued as though he hadn't spoken.

'But in this case, I welcome the appraisal of my new Voidmaster, whose experience in these situations is even greater. Take us through the planned drop.'

'Understood, ur-kâhl.'

Suppressing the rebellious temptation to begin calculating the necessary route immediately, Lutar waited for Starbound to pass the order before the Wayfinder attended to his navigational station. He quickly devised the vector that would propel them most swiftly through the cyclics they had to negotiate, slipping around the edge of one to bounce off the rim of the other.

'Passing course to helm,' he reported, double-checking the numbers.

As he was about to send over the data, he noticed some fluctuation in the eye of the countercyclic. It was probably nothing. He was still smarting from the unspoken accusation that he was timid, and so activated the transmit and sent the course across to Fillia at the steering controls. He watched her screen while she translated the vector into course adjustments, each a subtle manipulation of the warp barrier to push the ship across the streaming empyric energy, or to be more exact, allow it to be pushed into position by the pressure on the opposite side.

'Helm laid in, correcting course now,' Fillia told Starbound. The Voidmaster looked across to their commander.

'Prep warp anchors for drop,' Myrtun announced. 'All stations, set for realspace drop. Ready energy relay from warp barrier to sensors and weapons.'

A series of affirmatives rippled back from the different stations.

Lutar had only been looking away for a few moments, but when he returned his gaze to his display he immediately saw that the countercyclic had doubled in strength.

'Commander, one hundred and thirteen per cent increase in countercyclic growth. We'll hit the negative current too hard, we have to abort the drop.'

'All navigation reports through my station,' barked Starbound, cutting off Myrtun as she rose to her feet. 'Helm, decline prow by four points, increase lateral flow by five hundred. We can ride this one out.'

'Myrtun?' Lutar looked between the High Kâhl and Voidmaster.

'High Kâhl in command or not, this is my responsibility,' Starbound reminded them.

Fillia made the mistake of turning to Myrtun for confirmation. A shudder ran the length of the ship as shear forces rippled against the warp barrier.

'Helm!' Starbound stepped forward, shouldering Fillia out of the way as they leant towards the controls. 'Increasing lateral flow. Navigation update?'

Lutar checked his screen. 'Increasing still. Now at two hundred and twenty-two per cent original strength.'

'We'll do a power drop,' said Starbound. They straightened and prodded a finger towards the controls. 'Helm, keep us within five millitangents of the hold line or I'll make sure you never sit in that seat again. Navigation, provide regular updates.'

Affront at the Voidmaster's behaviour warred with Lutar's innate sense of obedience and duty. It seemed pure stubbornness on Starbound's part to push on despite the increasing dangers.

'What's a power drop?' demanded Myrtun, now at Starbound's side.

'Just as we open the realspace rift, we use the standard drives to punch out of the realspace envelope created around the ship,' Lutar replied before the Voidmaster could. 'It's a highly risky manoeuvre meant for only dire circumstances.'

'Seems like we're in that now,' said the High Kâhl.

'We can still drop normally,' Lutar pointed out. 'Countercyclic shrinking slightly, down three per cent.'

'And waste half a dozen rotes getting back to where we need to be for the next plunge?' Starbound turned towards Lutar. 'A power drop will mitigate the shearing effect of the two cyclics, making it less risky than a standard drop where we are. Ur-kâhl, I know what I am doing.'

'Go ahead,' said Myrtun.

Lutar knew better than to protest further, both in terms of Myrtun's mood and the diminishing window of opportunity. Starbound kept close to the helm station, passing on instructions as Lutar reported the changes in warp current status.

'We're riding the first cyclic,' the Voidmaster announced. 'All readings are normal.'

Lutar had never thought about the lack of physical sensation during regular warp travel. The reality sheet around the ship might be spinning, spiralling, hurtling precariously through the warp, but within its confines there was no movement or inertia to pass on that illusion of velocity. Given the precariousness of their current situation, it was anticlimactic to not feel the deck shuddering underfoot, the pull of forces as they lurched one way then another, beholden to the empyric whim of the warp. All he felt was the regular throb of the reactor network, half-aware of its electromagnetic residue more than any vibration.

'Countercyclic is magnitude five point eight, stable. It's drifting. Separation is forming a pressure gully, negative five magnitude.' It was too late to drop now without the aid of the engines – the moment they opened a rift between the warp and realspace, the *Grand Endeavour* would fall down into the vacuum created between the two drifting swirls. Lutar heard Starbound ordering the last course corrections before they hit the spot where the drop had to be made.

A sudden buzzing from his station alerted Lutar to a dramatic change in the readings coming from the warp barrier interface. A third whorl of energy was being birthed out of the widening gap between two existing cyclics.

'Storm-level swell directly ahead! Magnitude three and growing fast!'

'We have to go now,' replied Starbound, half-turning towards Myrtun. 'Open the breach and fire main engines. Helm, bring us hard to port, use the engine thrust to negate that new swell.'

'All engines full thrust!' Myrtun was out of her chair again, fists clenched. 'Initiate emergency breaching sequence now. Sound the full alert.'

A series of deep horn blasts resounded the length and breadth of the *Grand Endeavour*, sending Kin everywhere bolting for their emergency stations while others belted in to their positions or headed for safety harnesses. Myrtun sat down and strapped herself in as the rest of the bridge crew secured themselves. Starbound stayed where they were, a thrum of magna-coils coming from their feet as they clamped to the deck, armour locking down into a solid thesium statue. The Voidmaster's voice emulator emitted a strained growl of annoyance.

'Where's the damn breach?'

'It's being swallowed,' Lutar replied, shocked by what he was witnessing on his display. 'The storm is beyond magnitude ten, extending past our breach point. We're going to end up without our barrier but not break through!'

Now the console started to shake beneath Lutar's hands. He much preferred it when there wasn't any feedback to warn of the coming calamity.

'Cut the thrusters, all power to the breaching engines!' Starbound swivelled at the waist to shout at the drive attendants. 'Drop us now.'

The horns became an automatic wail as the ship's reactors went into overdrive and a pulse of energy tore at the empyric pressure holding them within warp space. A secondary chorus of alerts warned that the reality barrier had been lost, a moment before Lutar registered a sudden bang – not so much a noise as a soundless sensation modulated through his rudimentary empyric sensors. It came with a sensation of spinning vertically, his visual and balance systems thrown into disarray by contradictory signals.

Someone yelled. His auditory processors couldn't identify whom.

Routing power to his sensor circuits, he focused on the empyric readings. The screen was blank except for a zero marker in the middle.

'We're out.'

He didn't recognise his own voice, mechanical and bland.

Systems rebooted, both across the bridge and through his body. The kernel of self-awareness that was Lutar blossomed into personality again, and static hiss crackled from his speakers.

Aural feedback dampened out the clamour of competing sirens and bleeps, allowing him to hear properly again. Myrtun was speaking, quick but calm.

'…get us in a stable trajectory and then shut down drives. Damage teams to complete full sweep. Cool reactors to fifty per cent and start maintenance routines. Sensors and weapons on full.'

Lutar saw several numerals blinking on and off around the rune that designated the position of the starship.

'Commander, I suggest a full diagnostic of the empyric sensor array. I'm receiving feedback readings even though we are no longer in warp space.'

'Let me see that,' growled Starbound. Their armour extended and their feet mag-locks detached with an audible clunk. Stomping over to Lutar's position, the Voidmaster looked at the display. 'Your sensors are reading right enough. With your leave, commander, we should take a look outside.'

'External views on main screen,' Myrtun ordered, unbuckling her safety belt. 'What do you think we'll…' She drifted into silence as the main screen split into views around the *Grand Endeavour*. Above and behind, it was clear something was not right. The starfield was tinged with polychromatic flashes, a visible distortion wavering across the view. Here and there the void seemed to bulge, distant stars flaring into brightness as though seen through a lens.

'It's a warp interface,' said Lutar. 'The warp storm is breaking into realspace.'

'Aye,' added Starbound. 'If we don't leave now, we could be trapped here for Ancestors know how long.'

'We can't go back into that mess we just left, surely?' Myrtun looked from Voidmaster to Wayfinder and back again. Lutar moved his gaze to Starbound.

'If we move in-system, we'll fall prey to the stronger graviometrics,' the Voidmaster said. 'We can't plunge again if we're closer to the system core. This whole area is getting too volatile. The other ships could already be lost. We need to head direct for the Well now, while we still can.'

'You think you should still be Voidmaster after that near calamity?' Lutar could not think of anything as reckless as the Voidmaster's insistence on braving the storm.

'If we'd dropped like you wanted, we'd be half a light year back and behind that warp storm front. Then we'd really be down the disposal pipe without a mop. Neither of us knew those cyclics would blow up like that, but the region around the Well of Yrdu is riddled with nascent tempests since the storms increased. We can't predict them, so you have to know how to handle them.'

'I don't appreciate your tone or attitude,' Myrtun said. She crossed the deck and stood opposite the Voidmaster. 'I am commander of this vessel.'

Starbound replied softly but firmly.

'You'll not get through the Well without me. You can see that, yes? I make no apologies for my tone or for talking over you. You can issue the command, but I'll decide what needs doing to obey. Otherwise, you might as well head for the Bilskyrnun Tides right now, and drop me off back on the Hold ship.'

Starbound had pushed too far, and Lutar waited for Myrtun to put the cantankerous Ironkin back in their place.

Any moment.

'All right,' Myrtun agreed, sending a flash of confusion burning through Lutar's circuits. 'You are the Voidmaster.'

He recalibrated his aural sensors and checked the real-time log to ensure he had heard correctly. The disparity between expectation and reality rendered him mute.

'Good. Then we'll traverse realspace around the system perimeter and make a fresh plunge,' announced Starbound. They directed a short bow towards Myrtun. 'With your permission, of course, ur-kâhl.'

'You have bridge command, Kyr,' Myrtun told them quietly, before heading out of the main doors.

Lutar stared after her in dumb shock until Starbound's voice brought him back to focus.

'Wayfinder! The Thriga System is no good any more. Bring up the charts so we can see which way we need to go from here to reach the Well without getting sucked into a storm.'

Lutar considered it possible that he imagined the subtext of accusation within the Voidmaster's words, projected there by his own sense of failure in the recent disastrous episode. It didn't make him feel any better as he accessed the map datacore. It was time to focus again on his duties, something which had become more difficult of late.

'Yes, *ur-stellyr*.'

It was not just the Thriga System that was beset by the new influx of storm activity coming to the quadrant. The warp overlap birthed at Thriga spawned tempests that blocked many neighbouring systems as well, leaving only a slender route to the Well of Yrdu. With each plunge Myrtun became more anxious that the galaxy was trying to obliterate the path to Orthônar.

She said as much to her council as the *Grand Endeavour* waited in the Gelmir System for the *Canny Wanderer* and the *Hammer of Nithroggir*. The third vessel – *THA-C342* – had failed to make the last two rendezvous and Myrtun feared it had been lost. Jôrdiki had sent messages to the Hold ship to see if they had received any contact, but their reply had not yet been received, assuming the message had actually got through. Even with Votannic communication Jôrdiki was finding it hard to penetrate the storms, and it seemed certain that they would lose contact completely once they entered the Well.

'There are two ways to get to the Well from here,' explained Lutar, manipulating the controls of a holo-projector to bring up an image of the systems around Yrdu.

Myrtun and the other council members were gathered in an antechamber of the Fane so that Jôrdiki could attend whilst also monitoring the Votannic channels. It was a little cramped, allowing room for the projector and the three tables arranged around it, plus the obligatory brü trolley needed for any serious council business. Lutar was there, of course, the first time she had seen him in several watches except when duties on the bridge overlapped. And then he had been polite but perfunctory in his communications. There was certainly enough work for him dealing with all the data about the storms, but it still felt like he was avoiding spending time with her away from their official roles. She had never seen him like this, and if she had been thinking about any other Kin, she might have thought he was in a sulk.

'There's a safer route that takes three more plunges, through Geflir and the Jaddak Reach, to come at the Well from Hjelheim to the south.' The display rotated and highlighted the route, almost doubling back on the way they had come. It changed again at a tapped command from Lutar. 'Or we can plunge direct to Nifilhel and then down the Muspiral Neck into the heart of Yrdu.'

'I suppose you think the more roundabout route is best?' said Starbound. Though the Voidmaster was responsible for running the command bridge, the Wayfinder's choices on all navigational matters were meant to be supreme. Myrtun had always let her opinion be known to Lutar and had most often got her way, but it looked as though her Wayfinder was trying to be more resistant to the High Voidmaster's influence.

'On the contrary, ur-stellyr, I would recommend the Nifilhel option.'

'You would?' Myrtun couldn't hide her surprise, and instantly regretted it as a quiet but annoyed buzz emanated from Lutar. She tried to recover, but her words came out wrong. 'It is not like you to be incautious, Lutar.'

'I have made a reasonable assessment of the merits of each route,' the Ironkin told them, addressing everyone in the room.

'Happen I have something important here,' said Jôrdiki, standing up, a faint glimmer coming from some of her runes. 'I've been processing a weak signal we picked up a few dozen rotes ago. Happen it bears on our talks.'

Lutar waited for her to head into the adjoining chamber before continuing.

'The warp is too volatile to trust that the Jaddak Reach and Hjelheim will be navigable by the time we reach them. Our latest readings show the area becoming less and less stable with every passing rote. Whereas the Well itself becomes our ally if we travel via Nifilhel. It is a stable phenomenon, if any warp feature could be said to be, and its influence on Nifilhel falls within broadly predictable parameters. These new storms haven't the magnitude of the Well, so they can't influence the nearest currents either.'

'Sounds like a good choice,' said Iyrdin. 'Cut and dry.'

'From a purely navigational perspective, it is,' replied Lutar. 'But I have given the matter wider consideration. Firstly, as best we can piece together, Orthônar entered the Well from the west, not the east. Isn't that right, champion?'

Myrtun had not seen much of Ironhelm since they had left

the Hold ship, and he had been content to remain in his chambers for most of that time. He had agreed to spend a watch each day training with the ship's Hearthkyn, with the ultimate aim of forming the core of a new Einhyr company for the Kindred – all of his previous elite warriors had died with Orthônar. This seemed to weigh heavily on him, for he was sometimes seen muttering to himself, or lost concentration partway through a conversation, his eyes flicking to sights only he could see. He declined any social invitations, but Myrtun did not think it was good for him to spend all of his time alone and had given him watch duties along with the rest of the crew.

As they had approached the Well, Myrtun had insisted he join the council and act as guide, but the nearer they came to the source of his anguish, the more temperamental he had become.

'Aye, I'm sure we plunged from Rostorangir,' he replied gruffly. Ironhelm's injuries had healed, albeit with a few fresh scars, but he still did not look well. Cheeks sunken, eyes rimmed with darkness, it was clear he was not getting enough to eat and was sleeping poorly. Still, they had nobody else they could turn to in this situation, and despite a few idiosyncrasies he seemed reliable enough on watch. 'Like I told you. Do you really think it makes that much difference?'

Lutar did not have time to answer before Jôrdiki hurriedly re-entered, clutching a hard copy of a communication.

'I've not heard from the Hold ship, but the message going through the last processors came direct from the Votann.' She thrust the transparency at Myrtun and continued quietly. 'I think *THA-C342* is lost in the warp.'

Jôrdiki seemed unusually intense, her eyes not moving from Myrtun as she relayed this information. Then the Grimnyr's eyes flicked to the page and back. Myrtun read the message and a chill ran along her limbs, prickling her skin.

> URD-0r: *That Which Is Lost Cannot Be Found.*
> VeRD-4n: *That Which Is Lost Cannot Be Found.*
> Sk-43L: *Do Not Seek That Which Is Lost.*

The High Kâhl nodded casually and met Jôrdiki's gaze for just a moment, indicating her understanding.

'We can talk over this in detail when we're done here,' she said to the Grimnyr before returning her attention to Lutar. 'You were telling us about the Nifilhel route.'

Lutar picked up as Jôrdiki took her place again, rotating the display to look at it from above the galactic plane.

'You may recall that we passed relatively close to this area on our way back to the Hold ship. There are seven stable systems between the outer Well and the systems of Mordemerran, which leads into the Ariel Sound.'

'Where we met the Imperials?' Iyrdin said, looking at the other council members.

'Fyrtor told us not to go through Mordemerran because it was now storm wracked,' said Myrtun. She examined the holo-chart. 'But that's still a distance of three score parsecs. You think it's all the same storm belt?'

'What's this to do with navigation?' grunted Starbound. 'None of this is relevant to Nifilhel!'

'Bear with me just a little longer,' the Wayfinder replied, turning to Starbound for a moment, his returning gaze conveying that he was really addressing Myrtun alone. 'If storms are expanding from the Well and across Mordemerran, that leaves just a handful of systems to travel through safely between them, including Ariel Sound, where we encountered not just the Imperials but also the Cursed Ones that were attacking them. It was the opinion of our brief guest that the renegades were part of a greater fleet coming into the area, and it seems likely that they will know more about the warp turmoil than we do. This calm strait between the storms is most probably a fertile hunting ground for them, bridging what we know as our territory, systems identified as Far-space, and the outskirts of Imperial reach.'

A scattering of rune markers noted the position of possible attack sites around the Well and beyond.

'And we might encounter them coming through Nifilhel?' said Myrtun, seeing where their route crossed a cluster of the runes.

'It is a possibility, but in weighing the matter I think it better to travel the quicker route, utilising the expertise of our veteran Voidmaster' – Lutar nodded to Starbound – 'than to become trapped by the expanding storm activity and unable to go forward nor return to the Hold ship.'

Myrtun sat back, arms folded as she thought about this. The missive from the Votann preyed on her thoughts too, as did the fact that Jôrdiki had shown it to her but not shared it with the rest of the council. To equivocate too much would be disastrous now, inviting doubt when the expedition needed firm leadership.

'Does anyone else have any facts or thoughts to offer on this?' she asked the council, her gaze lingering on Jôrdiki for a heartbeat longer than the others, and finishing on Kyr Starbound. The Grimnyr said nothing, but Voidmaster Kyr spoke up.

'Commendable representation, Lutar, I fully agree with your assessment. As soon as the other ships arrive, we should make our way to Nifilhel and then the Well of Yrdu.'

'Good, then I also endorse the Wayfarer's course,' said Myrtun. 'We shall wait no more than five rotes for the rest of the expedition. We then meet at Nifilhel for the last leg into the Well itself.'

'We're almost there,' rumbled Ironhelm, standing up. It seemed as though he was addressing someone other than those in the room, his haunted gaze looking past the occupants. The veteran gained some focus as he looked at Myrtun. 'Bold hearts now, stay true to our oaths. The Ancestors are watching.'

Lutar shut down the projector while the other members of the council filed out. He lingered for a moment, and Myrtun knew he wanted some time with her alone, but she needed to speak with Jôrdiki more urgently. The Wayfarer deduced her reluctance to engage and left without saying anything. Myrtun told herself she would seek him out before they started the next warp plunge.

CHAPTER SEVEN

Difficult Choices

Carefully lifting a mag-bolt from the housing of the E-COG, Lekki pulled the inspection panel aside and placed it on the floor. A lamp held on a headband illuminated the interior of the construct, showing the Brôkhyr a mess of circuits and wires surrounding a small neuronic core.

So engrossed was he in his inspection that the clank of the workshop doors opening made him jolt with shock, almost spearing the tip of the magdriver into his eye.

'What do you want?' he demanded, spinning round to confront Erkund. 'I'm busy! And it would be polite to knock.'

'I am here for your protection, and my core functions are for efficiency, not manners,' the tall Ironkin replied. 'You could be choking to death on a poison administered by an assassin and I would be waiting patiently at the door for permission to enter.'

'Is that likely?' Lekki stood up to face Erkund.

'A non-zero probability.'

Lekki said nothing, waiting for Erkund to reveal why she had disturbed him, not wanting to be baited into a pointless argument.

'You have received a reply from the Guild to your missive. Do you wish me to relate it?'

'Yes! What did they say?'

Erkund assumed a stiffer pose, which meant that she was acting as a channel for the broadcast. It was odd to Lekki to hear the words of Wardwright Stannak in the voice of the Ironkin.

'What's this about being given the brush off, Lekki? If you want to get anywhere in the Enduring Guild of Master Runewrights then you need to learn how to deal with these lordly types. Orthônar, Myrtun, doesn't matter who it is. You need to demand they address our concerns right away. If not, you already know what is expected of you. The Guild placed a lot of faith in Orthônar and the Kindred of the Eternal Starforge. We entrusted something to them that is almost beyond value and we are owed our due in return for that. Get it done!'

Something about Erkund's intonation managed to conjure the face of Wardwright Stannak, his enormous sideburns flowing, jowls shaking as he delivered this indictment. Lekki felt a shudder of shame, the admonishment confirming his own fears about himself and his suitability for this duty.

'How will you extract agreement from Myrtun now that she has departed?' asked Erkund, her manner having returned to its usual offhand nature.

'Well, I'm not going after her, if that's what you're suggesting. I need to be here, where we have leverage.' Lekki placed the magdriver carefully on the countertop next to the dormant E-COG, rubbing his lip with a finger as he considered his position. 'I shouldn't have gone alone, that was the mistake. One voice is easy to ignore, even with the weight of the Guild behind it. Time to rouse the membership and show these Kin what they're dealing with.'

The chamber of the Hearthspake of the Eternal Starforge reminded Lekki a little of the guildquarters on Svalinndrim, the frost-encased moon that was home to the Leagues-spanning Guild. It was there that he had been examined by the chancellors and assigned the duty of emissary. There were no plaques on the wall bearing the names of the past chancellors, nor tapestries depicting the circuit diagrams of the Five Noble Grids, but the presence of real wood and the smell of brü were reminder enough.

Rather than be badgered by the whole council, Lekki had agreed to speak only with Gurtha, the appointed representative of the absent High Kâhl. They sat opposite each other at the large table, a steaming beverage in front of them both. The chamberlain regarded him over a pair of half-rimmed glasses, which Lekki believed she wore as a consequence of a very specific cloneskein characteristic that affected Guthra's short-range vision but enabled her to see in a broader spectrum than most Kin. He weathered her silent, hard stare for several heartbeats before finally speaking.

'Neither of us have the power to end this dispute,' he told her. She said nothing but watched carefully as he spooned sucretin into his brü, the chink of the spoon on the ceramic mug disproportionately loud. 'The Guild terms are clear, and despite whatever authority you have been granted, you are not the High Kâhl.'

'Myrtun was not the High Kâhl, either, when this deal was made,' replied Gurtha. She picked up her steaming drink and took a mouthful. Lekki suppressed a sympathetic wince at how hot the liquid still was, but Gurtha seemed unaffected. Taking a cautious sip of his drink, he added two more spoons of sweetening powder.

'Something wrong with the brü?' asked the council secretary, one eyebrow raised.

'What? Oh, not at all. I have a susceptibility to bitter tastes. It overpowers every other flavour of a thing. You know, do you have any milk? I find that works well.'

'We don't raise kine here, unfortunately. Why don't you just avoid drinking brü if you don't like it?'

'I need a stimulant buzz, but raw brü affects my digestion. So...' He lifted the cup to his mouth and wetted his lips again, wary of the liquid's scalding heat.

'Yours is a singular cloneskein, it seems,' said Gurtha.

'Aren't we all unique in the designs of the Votann?' He leaned forward, putting the cup down to rest his hands on the table. 'I know I look... unkempt. And not of traditional Kin constitution. But I am very intelligent, and more to the point, the only person who can negotiate new terms with the Guild. We are being inconvenienced here, but I think I can see a way forward for the moment. If you give me your assurance to recover what we have lost, I am sure the Guild will be reasonable.'

'Agree to lose another expedition in the Well of Urdu? Ridiculous. And just what is it that you are seeking?'

'A very special key. It belongs to the Guild but was given to Orthônar at the request of the Trans-Hyperian Alliance Votann. We complied only under strict contract with your former High Kâhl that it would be returned. No lesser undertaking from you will suffice.'

'This is coercion.' Gurtha downed the rest of her drink in two long gulps. 'And reckless. Unlike Myrtun, I won't risk lives needlessly, and the council won't agree to any contract that puts us further at your whim.'

'All disputes involve some kind of coercion. We want what is ours, and if you refuse to give it to us, the Guild will withdraw what it has given you. Do not act as though this is somehow *my* fault. It was entirely avoidable.'

'Myrtun doesn't even know there's a dispute.' She spread her hands as if to indicate there was nothing more to be done. Lekki realised this was true.

'We can talk in circles for a dozen watches and not resolve this.

If you find the means for me to speak to Myrtun, I will do so. If my Guildkin tell me to act, I will do so.' Lekki stood up and placed his hands on the table in what he hoped was a pose of resoluteness. 'Thank you for the brü.'

Gurtha muttered under her breath but made no other effort to broker an arrangement. With a curt nod, Lekki turned and left her to pass on the news to the rest of the Guild membership.

Jôrdiki fretted about the Fane, which had been both her workstation and quarters for several rotes now. Her CORVs bumbled around without much purpose, agitated but undirected. She had been kept busy with the transmission that had arrived during the council, but also with her work on some earlier messages, including those she had downloaded after the encounter with the bioship as well as data scripts she had brought with her from the Hold ship.

The Grimnyr turned to her lectern, brushing wayward bits of hair out of her face. A deep breath centred her thoughts. The CORVs settled into their contact alcoves again, like watchdogs returning to their kennels. Jôrdiki sat down upon her stool. Her hand touched the terminal as she did so, bringing the screen back to life. Several overlapped files filled the view, but she knew it wasn't these that were causing her so much anxiety.

She brought up the one that had been dogging her thoughts for the last rote and a half since she had re-examined her translation.

> *CORRECTIVE UPDATE. REVISED INTERPRETATION. AUTHOR: GRIMNYR JÔRDIKI. DO NOT RESEND. ARCHIVE ONLY.*
> *URD-0r: That Which Is Lost Can Be Found.*
> *VeRD-4n: That Which Is Lost Can Be Found.*
> *Sk-43L: Do Not Seek That Which Is Lost.*

She stared, two competing options creating a stasis of thought between them. A watch passed and she didn't move, mentally revisiting everything that she had done and said to Myrtun since leaving the Hold ship. Was this a betrayal? Was she wrong again and the first translation was right? Unless she could be certain, what was the point of disrupting Myrtun and the rest of the expedition?

And as she had done so for the last rote and a half, Jôrdiki finally broke out of her indecision by ignoring the problem, bringing up the nearly decoded transfer from Fyrtor that she had received.

With shoulders hunched she set to working on the last level of ciphers.

Lutar took a few paces along the corridor outside Myrtun's chamber, turned on his heel and paced back again. He did this several more times, out of habit rather than nervous energy, which he did not possess. He knew Myrtun better than anyone else, and recognised the sudden strain in her when Jôrdiki had passed on the message from the Votann. It had been more than a reaction to news that a starship was likely lost – as commander of a Prospect fleet Myrtun knew the risks of warp travel, and the *THA-C342* had already been missing for a considerable time. That meant that either the message went beyond simply announcing the expected loss, or that the loss itself was more significant to Myrtun than she had let on.

Either way, Lutar knew he had been too occupied with his duties, and that he had been giving Myrtun space to think without his interference. Too much time it seemed, as they headed onwards into the roiling warp without a plan. Now was the time to be more direct again. But several rotes had passed without a chance to speak to her, which was why he was now doorstepping her at the start of the first watch.

He paced a little more, counting ten steps one way, twenty the other, then ten back to where he started. As he did so he examined the corridor in detail, using all of his senses to familiarise himself with the stretch he traversed, as if he hadn't walked along it over a thousand times since coming aboard the *Grand Endeavour*. The floor underfoot was of a glossy, yielding plastek-fabric weave, dark blue with faint speckles of lighter blue and green. The walls were flat bulkheads joined by riveted studs, plastered and painted a soft grey, the wrought metal joins a darker grey. He looked at the ceiling, which he realised was not something he was wont to do often. It was made of transparent plastek sheeting with the gleam of lighting filaments behind.

The buzz of electric circuitry alerted him to the activating door before it hissed open. Myrtun hurried out and almost collided with Lutar as he tried to assume a casual pose. She looked up at the Ironkin, shock becoming annoyance.

'What are you–'

'I want to talk with you,' Lutar said hurriedly. He stepped back, hoping that the physical act of giving her space would also be appreciated in the metaphorical sense too. 'About what we're going to do.'

'Plan seems good to me,' rasped the old Kin. 'And Starbound approves.' She stepped past him and started down the corridor.

'Are you sure you want to press on?' Lutar asked, keeping pace with her. 'Fyrtor is overdue and there's no sign of the *Hammer of Nithroggir*. We set out with more than three times as many warriors as Orthônar, and now we have fewer.'

Myrtun stopped but didn't look at him. Her shoulders sagged. She simply stood there, saying nothing, leaving Lutar unsure what to do or say. He had never seen her like this at all. She'd been downhearted before, sometimes pessimistic. Now she looked… beaten?

'I'm sorry, my jewel-star. I didn't–'

'It's not you.' Myrtun drew in a shuddering breath and let out a sigh, seeming to sag even more. She turned and looked at Lutar. He knew that the physiological changes that had affected her over the years they had been together were gradual, but at that moment he hated that he was just now realising how old she looked. The lines in her dark face were like crevasses in a broken moonscape and her eyes had nothing of the lively glint he expected to see.

'There's something… Something that I should tell you, my star-guide. I need to tell everyone, but you first.'

'Ur-kâhl!' Jôrdiki's shout caused Myrtun to flinch, which struck Lutar as very peculiar. He turned to see the Grimnyr coming down the corridor at a brisk walk. 'Myrtun! The message from Fyrtor. I've extracted and translated it.'

'There was a message from Fyrtor?' Lutar looked at Myrtun, wondering if this was what she had wanted to share. 'The *Canny Wanderer* is still with us?'

'I've just finished decoding it,' continued Jôrdiki, gesticulating with agitation. 'Yes, the *Canny Wanderer*'s not destroyed and the *Hammer of Nithroggir* is with them. They both arrived before us and conditions worsened, so they made the plunge to Nifilhel.'

'Great news!' declared Myrtun, and suddenly it was as if half a lifetime had been shed from her.

'Not all of it,' the Grimnyr answered. 'A Cursed Ones ship found them and slipped away before they could destroy it. A scout, Fyrtor thinks.'

'We need to get there before the Cursed Ones,' said Lutar. He stepped away and then turned back. 'With your permission, we'll ready for the plunge immediately.'

'Of course,' snapped Myrtun. 'Stop dilly-dallying!'

Lutar broke into a slow run, activating his internal comm-unit. His voice blared out of the address speakers across the ship.

'All crew to battle stations. Prepare for emergency warp plunge.'

* * *

Looking at the scanner returns on the main display, Myrtun almost felt a sense of relief. Almost. Both the *Canny Wanderer* and the *Hammer of Nithroggir* were still intact, each with a flotilla of smaller support ships like moons around a gas giant. But bearing down on them were a similar number of unknown vessels, some of which were large enough to be battleships. The cumbersome *Great Endeavour* would not reach them until after the battle had started, though it would certainly swing the fight in favour of the Kin if Fyrtor and his fellow captain, Holgir Landsfinder, could avoid taking too much damage in the interim.

'Establish three-way contact with the *Wanderer* and the *Hammer*,' Myrtun ordered, then turned her attention to the Kin at the engines and reactor panels. 'Push reactors to one hundred and twenty per cent, all power to engines.'

The watch senior at the controls, Lutti, turned in her seat, confusion written across her features.

'What about weapons and shields?'

'Don't need them yet,' replied Myrtun. 'Let's hope the sight of us coming is enough to make the Cursed Ones break off. If fortune favours us the survivors of our last encounter have spread the word.'

The internal comm crackled into life, bringing the voice of Brôkhyr Hruthar. Her tone was tinged with doubt.

'Myrtun, if we run reactors past full for too long, we won't have overpower for the shields and weapons if we need it.'

'My orders stand.'

'Yes, Myrtun.'

'Aye, ur-kâhl.' Lutti turned back to her station, fingers moving dexterously across the projected holorunes.

'I trust you'll keep me informed, *ur-brôkhyr*,' Myrtun told her curtly.

The High Kâhl knew that these questions were only her crew

doing their duty, but it was hard not to feel that they were doubting her commands. Before becoming High Kâhl she wouldn't have thought such a thing possible, but now with Starbound on board and Jôrdiki acting strangely, Myrtun was feeling less secure in her leadership.

'Grand Endeavour, *this is Landsfinder on the* Hammer *of Nithroggir. We are redirecting to your position.*'

'*Hammer*, don't do that! You'll be presenting your backsides as targets to the enemy.'

'*Myrtun, this is Fyrtor. We cannot hold here. There are more enemies coming from in-system. We drove them off just a couple of rotes ago, but now their reinforcements have arrived, they'll come back.*'

Myrtun saw the glances in her direction from across the deck, and a longer, more meaningful look from Lutar.

'The Cursed Ones will soon be in torpedo range of the *Hammer*,' reported Yhêl Ûnas, supervisor of the scanning team. 'The *Canny Wanderer* is burning manoeuvre thrusters and turning in our direction.'

Fyrtor had decided not to wait.

'*Where are you going,* Wanderer?' demanded Landsfinder. '*Don't you dare leave me here!*'

'*We can't stay, Holgir. If you don't turn now, you'll be an easy target for their torpedoes when you do.*'

Myrtun looked again at the strategic display. If the *Grand Endeavour* carried on as she was, they would cruise past the other two ships and end up either facing the Cursed Ones alone and waiting for the *Hammer* and the *Wanderer* to come about again, or they would have to make their own hard turn in the face of the enemy. Neither was a desirable scenario.

'Fyrtor, Holgir, you need to reverse burn and heel around hard to come alongside us. We'll present a full front against the enemy.'

Both ships had completed their manoeuvres and were now

heading directly towards the *Grand Endeavour*, nearer the edge of the system.

'*If we slow down at all, those ships will be all over us like skitmice in a grain hold,*' said Holgir.

'If you don't, they'll chase us all the way to the system edge and beyond.'

There was no word from Fyrtor, but the hiss of the doors opening announced a new arrival on the bridge deck. Myrtun swivelled the command chair to see who it was, and was surprised to see Ironhelm in his battered void armour.

One experienced glance at the strategic display told Dori all he needed about the situation.

'It's never wise to pick a fight that you're not sure of winning,' he told Myrtun, crossing the bridge deck. 'I heard the talk from the other ships over the comm. Thought you might need a reminder about why we're here.'

The look from the new High Kâhl would've chilled the blood of any lesser Kin, but Dori had looked death itself in the face more than half a dozen times. Rather than meet her stare, which might have been taken as a contest of wills, he looked around the bridge, nodding with satisfaction at what he saw.

'Good crew you have here. Good ship too.'

'What do you mean, a "reminder"?' growled Myrtun, swinging her chair to follow Dori as he walked past and looked over the shoulders of the Kin at the drive controls.

'What we've come here to do,' he said, turning around, arms folded across his chest. He suppressed a shiver of agitation as he caught sight of himself reflected in a screen. Ghostly, he would have said. 'Because I don't recall anyone announcing that we were here to take on a fleet of Cursed Ones. There're more than enough battles ahead yet, against the orks.'

Myrtun's displeasure somehow deepened, which was impressive considering how sour her expression had been before. Dori didn't flinch. He had heard a great many stories about Myrtun Dammergot, and harboured hopes that she might even deliver on her oath, but at that moment she seemed more involved with doing her own thing than fulfilling the quest.

'There's not a battle won without risking everything,' Dori continued. 'Even when the odds are massively in your favour, there's always a cost. Maybe casualties, often just time. Orthônar was the most honourable and bravest Kin I've ever met, but he always said to me, "Never have a fight without purpose," and that applied from a brawl in the common room to taking the whole Kindred to war.'

'If we just run...' Myrtun fell silent, perhaps examining her reasons for seeking the confrontation. Dori saw the Wayfinder, Lutar, and Voidmaster Starbound conferring at the navigational display. On the main screen the markers for the other two Kin flotillas were closing fast, the ships of the Cursed Ones gathering in their wake.

'Ur-kâhl, we have a suggestion,' announced Starbound.

Myrtun continued to look at Dori for a couple more heartbeats and then turned to her Voidmaster.

'Suggestion?'

'Aye,' the Voidmaster replied. 'Fyrtor, Holgir, are you receiving our strategic assessment onscreen?'

Both captains signalled the affirmative. Lutar manipulated the controls while Starbound continued. The display showed projected routes, with the Cursed Ones reaching the ships of the Kin before they made it to the outskirts of the Nifilhel System, and their torpedoes in range even before then.

'If we try to run all the way to the system boundary for an unobstructed warp plunge, we'll be overhauled before we get there.'

Starbound signalled to Lutar and the display changed again, this time showing all three Kin flotillas becoming surrounded by the end of the watch. 'If we turn and face them all, we will lose any chance of breaking out should the battle turn against us.'

'That's why I wanted to engage earlier,' snapped Myrtun.

'We couldn't stay, either of us could have been isolated and overwhelmed,' Holgir argued. *'What's your suggestion, memnyr?'*

Once more the display altered, now showing the Kin ships turning their course slightly, moving away from the gravitic influence of the nearest system bodies. Away, but not completely free of them.

'A warp plunge from in-system?' Fyrtor sounded as if the Ironkin had proposed jumping out of the airlocks to board the Cursed Ones' ships. *'So we just risk getting pulled apart or flung wildly into the storm-tossed warp instead?'*

Dori was struck by the memory of Orthônar arguing with his own subordinates about daring the Well of Yrdu. For several moments, voices from the past overlapped with those of the present. The former champion had backed Orthônar as was only proper – loyalty to the High Kâhl had been more important than any opinion he might form by himself. Would he feel the same if Myrtun decided to stay and fight, risking the whole expedition? Dori knew that to some it would look as though the whole quest was just an empty vanity, and his oath to a dead lord redundant, but they had not looked into Orthônar's eyes and seen the insistence there.

Between fever dreams from his injuries and more lucid moments on the journey back, and since arriving at the Hold ship, Dori had given that moment a lot of thought. It occupied his waking mind and troubled his dreams, as much as the dead voices that he couldn't quite hear.

'I'd rather fight a foe that I can see,' declared Myrtun. 'Warp tides are servant to nobody, but even Cursed Ones can know fear. The way I see it–'

Dori cut across the High Kâhl's oration, pitching his voice not just to her but the whole bridge crew and those on the other ships.

'Why did Orthônar send me back? Why? His words were clear enough. Etched into my memory like acid on steel. "Take my oath back to the Kindred." His oath. Not to take word of his death, not to go for help that he knew would never arrive in time. "It is your burden until you die or you pass it to another," he commanded me. Well, Myrtun Dammergot, I've passed it to you. There's nothing else I can say except that in your hands you keep the oath of Orthônar alive. If we die here, it isn't my failure, it's yours. If we win but we don't have enough warriors to defeat the orks, that's on you as well. Don't seem fair, does it? Well, it ain't. Fair don't count for nothing. All I know is that one High Kâhl thought what he was doing was important enough to die fighting for it. And it was *that* I was given. The one task, to pass on that burden to you.'

Dori watched Myrtun's attention move from him to her navigator, to the main screen, and back to him, and then complete the same circuit again as she considered what to do. Rather than looking resigned to capitulation, the old Hernkyn's expression became more determined, her jaw set, eyes hard.

'So you'd have me throw us into the warp, hostage to fortune and the whims of the Dark Powers?' She advanced a step and then another, but Dori held his ground, arms crossed tight, shoulders squared.

'We've got to dare the Well of Yrdu, anyways,' he said. 'Ain't nothing certain. But you've got the best Voidmaster in the whole Kindred with you saying to do that, and if I was a High Kâhl that's the sort of advice I'd want to be hearing.'

'*Myrtun,*' said Fyrtor across the comm-link. '*I'm leaving. I'm not giving you a choice.*'

'I am your High Kâhl, Fyrtor Hernkendersson, and if I command you to stay, you'll bloody well stay!' Myrtun's angry gaze swept the bridge, seeking further dissent.

'Our opportunity for escape is diminishing,' Lutar added, directing their attention to the screen with a waved hand. If the *Grand Endeavour* was going to slow and alter course to the new plunge point, it would have to do so now. Dori noticed Myrtun twitch at the mention of 'escape'.

A war was being waged inside the High Kâhl, and Dori read the assaults and counter-charges through Myrtun's subtle shifts of expression and stance. Her hands clenched into fists and she gritted her teeth.

'Steadfastness is a virtue till it becomes stubbornness,' he told her. 'That's a First Truth to me.'

His argument could come back to bite him: calling her out might force Myrtun to dig her heels in even more. Though he had said the burden was passed to Myrtun, the former champion did not really feel as though he'd been freed from its weight. Somehow, whatever it took, he would get through the Well again and fulfil Orthônar's quest or die trying. The voices were demanding it, even if he couldn't understand any specific words. That urge – that need to return – had been eating at him since he had left, and it had to be more than just guilt and a sense of duty. That would be the only way to find peace. He tried to keep his growing desperation hidden as he watched Myrtun.

Dori saw her mouth a word, half-formed, soundless, but recognisable all the same.

Opportunity.

She turned to address the crew.

'Voidmaster, lay in a course for the closest optimal point for warp plunge. Fyrtor, Holgir, bring your ships in close for mutual defence. Have as many of your attendant flotilla as possible load crews onto the main ship and default to E-COG command. We'll have them slow up the Cursed Ones to give us the best chance of making the plunge unhindered.' She paused, taking a shallow breath, moving her gaze from Starbound to Lutar. 'It's on you now. Get us through the Well.'

She rounded on Dori, who expected to see resentment written across the face of the High Kâhl. Instead, Myrtun looked more relaxed than at any time since he had come aboard. She approached and spoke quietly, and despite her casual manner there was steel in her tone.

'Orthônar chose his oathkeeper well,' she said. Dori felt uncomfortable with the compliment, but she was not done. 'He's dead now, oath or not. I don't need a broken veteran, punishing himself for no failure at all. I need the High Kâhl's champion. I need Ironhelm.'

'Ironhelm fell along with his Einhyr,' Dori said with a shake of the head. He walked past her to the main doors, pausing as they clanked open. 'But you can have what's left.'

With the doors closed behind Ironhelm, Myrtun felt as though a haunting presence had left the bridge. The warrior carried a doom that shadowed everything around him. She had been compared to a Living Ancestor on more than one occasion, but standing before Ironhelm now felt like being scrutinised by Orthônar himself, as if the former High Kâhl's demanding spirit lived on in his champion's body. Perhaps it did, Myrtun considered as she attended to the tasks required of her, easing herself back into the command chair, barking orders as easily as she drew breath, and with as much conscious effort. In pledging herself to uphold Orthônar's cause she had joined Ironhelm in becoming a bearer of her predecessor's will. Had she not mused on the nature of returning Orthônar to the Votann? When she died, the job of delivering her would be someone else's burden, a task that no Kin could fulfil for themselves. The Ancestors were dead, but through the First Truths their legacy continued.

And though their eyes had shut long ago, indeed the Ancestors were watching – not with a gaze from aeons gone, but with the eyes of every living Kin. Each generation was the embodiment of the Ancestors cast anew by the Votann. The galaxy changed. Stars died, planets were destroyed, and civilisations fell. But as long as the Votann endured, the Ancestors still lived.

His work complete until they made the warp plunge, Lutar excused himself from Starbound and came over to the com-mand chair. He never seemed tired, frustrated, scared. Was he even capable of those things? Or did he, as it seemed to Myrtun, embody only positive emotions and sentiments of Kin life?

'It will be a watch and a half until we are ready to make the next plunge,' he said. 'I wish to be excused bridge duties for that period. In order to prepare for what will doubtless be a difficult journey out of Nifilhel and into – I mean through – the Well of Yrdu.'

'Prepare? What do you mean?'

Lutar hesitated but could not avoid replying.

'I asked Jôrdiki to use the datacores of the Mainfane to construct a model of the forces within the Well, based on records from the *Stormblaze* and our recent readings. I have been using it to simulate the plunge, but now I must make adjustments to account for our less-than-ideal entry point.'

'You've been spending all your off-watch time practising,' replied Myrtun. Lutar looked surprised that she knew. 'Jôrdiki told me what you have been up to. A couple more watches won't make much difference, will it? Use the time to do something else.'

'I do not need to rest.'

'You know that if you think about something too much, you can end up forgetting how you do something. You get in your own way.'

'I am not sure that applies in my case. My neural network doesn't have the equivalent of conscious, subconscious and unconscious modes.'

'You have subroutines – that's sort of the same thing, isn't it? You don't deliberately engage them.'

The subroutines pretending to be emotional reactions made small tweaks to his posture and appearance just as a living Kin's would. He had been created to experience Kin emotional and social behaviour but didn't realise how successful he had become at mimicking it over his long existence.

'I need to practise,' he said, his tone more sombre. 'I made a mistake at Thriga. Two, if Starbound was correct in their assessment. Where we are going, into the mayhem of the Well, every decision I make has to be right. There will be no second chances. If I get it wrong, we will all die. None of us will return to the Votann.'

Myrtun wanted to say something upbeat, to encourage him or cheer him up. The options all seemed hollow. Instead she found a sentiment she could share wholeheartedly.

'I trust you. You are my star-guide.'

Lutar smiled and laid a hand on her arm. 'If I find my way through darkness, it is because I can always follow the light of my jewel-star.'

The words made Myrtun feel melancholy for some reason, but she forced a smile all the same. She watched him leave the bridge deck, remembering the messages from the Votann, wondering if she was worthy of Lutar's faith.

If they all died on this quest it would not be by act or omission of Lutar, or anyone else. The responsibility lay with Myrtun and her alone. As did the choice of whether to ignore the Votann and make the plunge through the Well.

She had one and a half watches to decide.

The assembled members of the Enduring Guild of Master Runewrights numbered twenty-four full Brôkhyr and thirty assistants, all of whom were crammed into the upper control room of the *Unbreakable Giant*. The chamber was the heart of a comprehensive, complex weave of barrier wards built across the gigantic starship. There was an unofficial Guild motto written on a wipeboard over the master monitoring station.

We are the Fifth Pillar.

Kin tradition taught that four 'pillars' held up their society: Hearth, which meant the reactors that powered everything; Forge, where everything was made; Crucible, where Kin were created; Fane, which connected them to the Votann.

But all of it was held together by fields of many different purposes: structural integrity, defence, clearing local navigational debris, guiding small vessels to the port berths, even containing the raging power of the Hearth itself. Banks of dials and displays lined the walls from which the power inputs and function of every shield, from the largest to the smallest, could be monitored. A team of five Brôkhyr and the same number of E-COGs usually stood duty here, and all the Guild members were artisans responsible for building and maintaining the ship's systems as well as the mobile field generators found in shuttles, E-COGs, and the protective crests incorporated into high-specification void suits.

'Come on,' said Krynn Tranna, the Kindred of the Eternal Starforge's local chief. He was eldest of those present, far more experienced than Lekki, with grizzled features and hands much callused from labour, his tattooed forearms spotted with scars from flash-sparks. 'There's got to be some other way. Myrtun's new, but she's a fine Kin, of the best you'll see.'

'She had her chance,' Lekki said firmly. 'You saw, I expect. I was there, in the hall, waiting for my audience. All she had to do was give me a moment of time. I tried to tell her it was important. She wouldn't listen. Takes the Guild for granted. Takes *you* for granted, all the same.'

This conjured a few disquieted mutterings from the crowd.

'Why can't this wait till she comes back?' a higher-pitched voice called from near the back. Lekki strained to see over the heads of the engineers, and saw one of the newer members standing on tiptoe, looking back at him. Her hair was a deep purple, swept back with a plain band of brassy metal, revealing a forehead knobbled with tiny growths that made her skin look like coarse sandpaper, a peculiarity of her cloneskein. 'What's it we're actually getting?'

Lekki was not entirely sure he had the answer to that question. The Guild would inform him, he had been told, when everything was in order, or he would know because Orthônar would return the special artefact that had been entrusted to him.

'It's Piya Fyrgrite, isn't it?'

'Yes, that's me,' she replied, pleased that he knew her name.

Lekki was no fool. He'd revised the details of all the membership before coming, using the same prodigious powers of recall that had seen him pass his Guild tests without a single reference volume, a feat that had catapulted him into the esteem of the Masters and set him on his path to Guild representative. He knew the worth of the personal touch – Wardwright Stannak had emphasised how much Kindred members valued their independence. Nobody wanted to be pushed around by some outsider from guildquarters.

'So, Piya, you swore your Guild oaths not long ago. I don't

need to remind you of them, do I?' he said, trying to act as friendly as he was able. He far preferred the company of E-COGs even to other Brôkhyr. It was much easier to work out why E-COGs weren't doing what you wanted them to. However, he'd taken Stannak's schooling to heart, not wanting to fail the Guild because of his lack of charisma and antisocial proclivities. 'The bonds of the Guild are like the ward-walls we create – invisible, but giving us the strength to endure. No matter how small an issue, we must remain resolute and united, interlocking just as the threshold frequency of an interstitial generative format layer incorporates an entrocyclic reductive epicentre loop.'

He waggled his fingers and then knotted them together with a chuckle, but his joke elicited little reaction from the others. With a self-conscious cough, he continued.

'Why do we have five to a watch shift?' he asked.

'Guild regulations,' replied Krynn.

'Why do we have one vibro-lathe for every three Brôkhyr?'

'Guild regulations,' Krynn said with a nod of understanding.

'I could go on,' said Lekki.

'Please don't,' said another of the members, a grey-skinned Brôkhyr by the name of Heykha the Stoic. She crossed her arms, creasing the thick material of her work apron. 'How come we don't get a say in this?'

'Orthônar dealt with the Masters, it isn't a local issue.' Lekki stepped towards the primary control kiosk, separated from the bulk of the chamber on a small stage of its own, behind the master monitoring station. The Brôkhyr parted awkwardly before him, with barely room to move out of the way. 'I'll pass on any dispute or message you want to raise, but this is from the highest level.'

Pulling himself up the couple of steps to the control panels, Lekki produced a key-talisman shaped in the rune of the Guild. He held it up for the others to see.

'This Master Key has been entrusted to me as a duly appointed emissary of the Enduring Guild of Master Runewrights. It represents the authority of the Guild and the will of its membership.' Lekki placed the emblem onto a scanreader near the centre of the main board. Detectors within the console picked up the unique coded combination of nanofields enveloping the decorative projector. Green lights glimmered into life at stations all around the chamber. 'As emissary I give my oath that the favour of the Enduring Guild of Master Runewrights is hereby withdrawn from High Kâhl Myrtun Dammergot and the Kindred of the Eternal Starforge. Representative Krynn, please enact the declaration of the Guild as I have explained it to you.'

Krynn reluctantly joined Lekki at the main controls while three other Brôkhyr moved to substations in other parts of the crammed space.

'Not the reactor, I take it?' he said, his hand hovering over a large dial.

'No,' Lekki replied impatiently. 'Nor any atmospheric containment fields. I don't intend to kill everybody...'

'Right enough,' grunted Krynn. He gave a nod to the other Brôkhyr and twisted the dial. He turned down several others while amber lights flashed warnings, the other members flicking switches and pulling circuit breakers. Automated voices crackled warnings from speakers across the Hold ship.

One by one, the defence fields of the *Unbreakable Giant* shut down.

Even in ideal circumstances, a multi-ship plunge was a complex and dangerous affair. The most basic difficulty was one of spacing. If the ships were too close when they opened the warp breaches – a fraught process at the best of times that involved tearing the veil between realspace and warp space to create a rift of unpredictable size – the resultant holes in reality could overlap with catastrophic consequences. Similarly, a poorly timed breach might create gravitic wave effects that could cause disaster for the other vessels. If the plunging ships were too far apart, they risked ending up in different warp currents on the other side of the breaches, dragged into different paths and scattered from the moment they entered. The chances of regrouping in warp space and manoeuvring together after that were reliably non-existent. In fact, navigating into, through, and out of warp space as a coherent squadron was just about one of the hardest things a crew could attempt. Lutar had been in four such operations, none of which had ended in total disaster, but only one had actually succeeded in bringing the ships involved together through the warp. Usually it was far better to nominate a rendezvous system and leave each vessel to make its own way there, which had been the prior arrangement for Myrtun's expedition.

That previous occurrence had been necessitated by exploration into Far-space on the border of Imperial territory. At least, Far-space close enough to Imperial control that any of the Emperor's vessels encountered would treat the presence of Kin as an attack. That had merely been a precaution; this time it was essential that the *Grand Endeavour*, *Canny Wanderer* and *Hammer of Nithroggir* operate together. The most pressing reason was the Well of Yrdu itself. One ship following another in warp space was difficult; three of them trying to thread the same route through an active warp storm verged on impossible. It would be actually impossible if they did not enter at the same time, in close proximity to each other. At the other end of the journey, assuming successful navigation of the Well – which was a large assumption – there was no telling if Orthônar's expedition had stirred up the orks or what sort of void ships might have been mobilised to protect the system. Ships arriving one by one were always vulnerable to being outnumbered and taken out by a prepared defence.

And in this particular case, leaving the Nifilhel System was not at all straightforward. They were inside the gravitic boundary, for a start, but even more problematic was the presence of foes. The ships of the Cursed Ones had been kept at bay by a rearguard of smaller Kin ships controlled by E-COGs and directed from the *Grand Endeavour*. The enemy had been slowed, not only by timely counter-attacks that had cost four ships so far, but also by the uncertain odds. The Kin mainships were bigger and had more firepower than the grand cruisers they faced, but their enemies were more numerous. Up to now, their commanders had been cautious in their pursuit, waiting for an opportune moment to strike. As soon as one of the larger Kin vessels breached the warp, the Cursed Ones would press in on the remaining ships, making their escape even more hazardous.

So it had to be all together, at the same time.

Lutar had shared his simulation with the Wayfinders of the other ships and Starbound, and for a full watch they had trained over an inter-ship link to make the procedure as seamless as possible. Once through the breach, it was then down to individual skill and a generous amount of fortune.

'Once the Cursed Ones detect the warp breaches forming, they'll launch torpedoes,' Fyrtor said over the fleet-wide comm-link. *'We can't evade them during final breach approach. You know the danger of a cascade event – just one detonation at the wrong time could implode the breach and take out the whole flotilla.'*

The sterile display on the main screen of the *Grand Endeavour* showed the last of the smaller Kin-crewed ships docking with the larger vessels. Some were not warp-capable, and three ships plunging simultaneously was risky enough as it was without a handful of escorts trying to breach at the same time. Lutar watched a close-range schematic on a sub-display as the last six escorts and scouts of the Herndammergot Prospect slipped into the *Grand Endeavour*'s open bays.

'E-COG ships are being despatched as a screen during breach,' Myrtun announced. 'They'll intercept any incoming torpedoes or attack craft. Just be sure you stick to your speeds and headings. We can't afford to change anything at this stage.'

Lutar saw a flicker across his station screen, like a reset only too slow. For a fraction of a moment there had been readings in the top right corner. Not long ago he would have dismissed it as a glitch, but the warp funnel that had formed around them at Thriga had taught him that perfectly calibrated sensors didn't glitch.

'To all jump commands, we are bringing the plunge clock to zero,' he announced. 'Prepare to activate breaching engine.'

'What are you doing?' demanded Myrtun. Starbound came striding across the bridge to investigate.

'Scanners are detecting incoming torpedoes,' declared Yhêl at the scanning station. Her attention didn't move from her screen. 'Multiple launches, converging angles.'

'There are Cursed One ships ahead of us.' Lutar's display was blank now, with no evidence of the flicker he had seen, but he was sure he had witnessed something. 'We're being herded into an ambush.'

'Void ahead is clear to the breaching point,' argued Yhêl. 'All scans are negative.'

'There was a brief warp overlap, fore and to starboard. A perfect angle for a crossfire,' Lutar insisted.

The navigational comm-network that had been set up to allow the Way-finders to coordinate directly crackled with enquiries from Lutar's counterparts on the other ships, demanding to know what was happening.

'Where are these Cursed Ones?' asked Starbound. Lutar ignored them, confident in what he had seen.

'Initiating plunge sequence. Coordinate countdown on my word.'

'We're still taking on ships!' protested Holgir over the main link. *'We need more time to get them aboard.'*

'So are we,' Myrtun announced. 'Hold plunge sequence.'

'We do not have time,' said Lutar. On the main display, the incoming torpedoes had crossed a quarter of the distance to the nearest Kin ship, the *Canny Wanderer*. Some of the E-COG vessels were still out of position, caught by the early launches. At least two torpedoes looked as though they would miss the escort screen.

'All reactors, prepare for breach,' Lutar continued, overriding Myrtun's order from his station. If Kyr could run the bridge in an emergency, so could he. A glance at the Voidmaster showed the Ironkin dividing their attention between the scanning displays and the helmkin. The reactors spiked in power, ready to punch a hole in reality ahead of the *Grand Endeavour*. Lutar's display stuttered again, phantom readings appearing for an instant where they had been before.

'Lutar!'

He turned at Myrtun's shout.

'There are enemy vessels holding in warp space ahead of our position,' he told her, keeping his voice slow and steady. 'I do not know how they are doing it. Some kind of sorcery their kind often wield. When we change course to avoid the torpedoes, they are going to breach into realspace and catch us on our flank even as their other ships come at us from behind. Their warp rifts will interfere with ours, making any plunge extremely hazardous. We must jump now.'

'We need to alter course,' barked Fyrtor. The torpedoes were halfway to his ship. *'We have all our crews back aboard.'*

'Stay on course!' Myrtun and Lutar answered together. The Wayfinder added, 'We'll plunge before they reach you.'

'We give the landings as much time as we can,' Myrtun said softly, but her expression was as hard as her will.

'You're risking all of us, the whole quest, if we delay.' Lutar saw no change in Myrtun and he readied himself to disobey her. He was about to issue the breach command to the Wayfinders when the internal comm came to life.

'All remaining crewed flotilla vessels aboard,' Greta announced. *'We haven't closed dock gates yet, though!'*

Lutar looked at his commander.

'It's no good, our turrets aren't enough to keep those torpedoes away,' said Fyrtor.

'Good enough,' Myrtun said with a nod. 'All ships, breach to warp.'

'Breaching to warp,' echoed Lutar, fingers tapping at the command runes.

Yhêl at the sensor banks suddenly gave a shout.

'Detecting massive energy surge ahead.' She spun on her stool to face Lutar. 'Just where you said it'd be.'

The breaching drives thrummed into life, throwing forward a pulse of interdimensional energies, their course like a knife along a flexi, the two parted sides peeling away. Ahead and behind, the other two ships activated their drives and the external view became an anarchic kaleidoscope of colours and images, all of them whirling with impossible motion, turning the starfield into a blur of movement.

'Reality barrier activating.' Myrtun could not keep the relief wholly out of her voice.

'Enemy vessels detected,' Yhêl confirmed.

Lutar saw the massive increase in warp energy where he expected it, the pulses of the Cursed Ones' arrival rippling outwards.

Sudden alerts bleeped from every station to signal the transition to warp space. At the same moment, Fyrtor's voice crackled over the diminishing comm-link.

'We're in trouble. The closest torpedo detonated, and our warp wake

pulled in more than a dozen warheads. We've taken hits across the aft decks. I'm not sure we hit the breach on the right course.'

Lutar examined his readings, creating a picture of what they signified. The peaks and troughs of warp waves intersected with the reality barriers of the other two ships, creating small crosscurrents and rippling bow waves. A cluster of slightly higher numbers where the *Canny Wanderer* should be was diverging from the blips of the *Hammer of Nithroggir*.

'Thelgin of the *Canny Wanderer*, bring yourself up thirty points to resume optimal course.'

'We're bleeding air into the warp barrier. Need to correct for resultant drift.'

Lutar muted the navigational channel and left his station to speak with Myrtun. He gestured for Starbound to join them as he made his way back along the command deck. When they had gathered, Lutar spoke quickly but quietly.

'We do not have long until we hit the Well's outer limits. Once we are there, we must commit wholly.'

'Yes, I know that,' said Myrtun.

'You think the Canny Wanderer can't make it?' guessed Starbound.

'If they are listing in any way, all course adjustments we make as we thread the eye of the Well will be compromised for them. It would be better if they turned away now.'

'Give up a third of our force?' Myrtun clenched her jaw, brow puckered. 'Is it really that bad?'

'We don't have time for them to properly measure the amount of drift and calculate the compensating factors. It is almost certain they will go astray if they enter the Well in current fashion.'

Myrtun drew in a long breath and nodded.

'Fyrtor, can you hear me?'

'Aye, Myrtun. Just about.'

'You can't come in with that damage. You'll be broken up or cast adrift.'

'Nonsense! My crew's as good as yours, we can get through the Well.'

'You are drifting without precise measurement, Fyrtor,' explained Lutar. 'By the time you have measured how much you are off course, it will be too late to adjust. It is not a matter of quality, simply reaction time.'

'I'm not giving up now, right when we're getting to the important part. It's my decision, not yours, Myrtun.'

'There's no point throwing away good Kin lives for this,' the High Kâhl responded. 'You don't have to prove anything.'

'Prove…? You know you're not the only Hernkyn in the Kindred, you wicked old stone-faced hag. Doing what's never been done, going to places never seen, it ain't just for you. Don't it occur to you that perhaps seeing an ancient Kin Hold is just the sort of thing that makes me sleep sound? And what do you think you'll achieve, without my tunnellers and fighters? You're as dead as the others without me, and you know it.'

Myrtun laughed.

'"Stone-faced hag" is getting better, young kin.' She looked at Starbound and Lutar, eyebrows raised. 'Is there really nothing we can do?'

Lutar turned to look at his station, checking the distance to the start of the Well's disturbance.

'Helm, are you steady?' he asked Fillia.

'Swell is minimal, Memnyr. Heading maintained.'

'Too late for a tow,' mused Starbound. 'Besides, ain't no cables in existence could handle the strain of going through the Well of Yrdu.'

Lutar continued to look at his screen, sure that the subtly changing numbers meant something, that there was a kernel of a plan hidden there that he couldn't quite articulate.

'Maybe not a physical tow...' he murmured.

'What's that?' asked Myrtun. 'Speak up.'

'What if we acted as a sounding rod for the *Canny Wanderer*?' the Wayfinder suggested.

'How do you mean?' said Starbound.

'When miners find existing caves and tunnels, they send out E-COGs called sounders to explore ahead of them. Gas harvesters do the same to measure atmospheric pressure, locate rich cloud seams and storms. It means they can see the topography and know where to go.'

'How's that help here?' Myrtun asked, her own agitation starting to show as their time to the Well drew short.

'I can hear you talking. What are you on about, Lutar?'

'*Grand Endeavour* will have to go ahead of the *Canny Wanderer* and feed our readings directly to you so that your Wayfinder has extra time to adjust course to account for the drift. You would be steering off our warp readings.'

'They'd have to be really close to get that level of signal clarity, right up our engines pretty much,' said Starbound. 'No room for error at all. A small mistake and we all end up off course, and getting lost in the Well means never getting out. And would that even give us enough time?'

Lutar directed his digital gaze at Myrtun.

'I think I know how to give us the extra edge we need, with the help of Jôrdiki,' he told her. 'But there's no time to test the theory. What do you want to do?'

CHAPTER EIGHT

Decisions and Consequences

Warp plunges had never made Myrtun uncomfortable in the same way they affected some other Kin. Neither physically nor mentally did the prospect of hurtling through a dimension of pure psychic energy discommode her, which she accounted to the cloneskein wrought for her by the Votann. Another sign, she had always said, that she was meant to be void-bound Hernkyn. Some Kin were not so fortunate, and though they all had very little in the way of psychic connection, a handful of her crew suffered nightmares, nausea, waking dreams and other phenomena.

More common were the superstitions, worries and fears that manifested. Hernkyn were prone to story-telling to fill the long voyages, and all manner of dread tales of the warp circulated through the flotilla and from fleet to fleet like an infection, whether true, half-true or fully fictional. The reality was intimidating enough: an unreal dimension populated by sentient psychic entities that preyed on mortal creatures' emotions. Exposure to warp space, even for the psychically stunted Kin, was an invitation to insanity. There were no external links; the main screen showed a facsimile of the reality barrier's interface, rendering the impossible into waves and troughs, splashes of colour amid a monochrome of red and black.

There was no physical sensation, but if one stared at the screen for too long it was possible to trick the mind into imagining the rocking of a ship at sea, the rising and falling prow breaking crests, the stomach-churning roll over swells of nothingness.

Myrtun dragged her eyes away, realising that she was becoming ensnared in the hypnotic swirls.

Lutar was at the navigational desk with Jôrdiki at his side, her CORVs hovering just behind, while Starbound had taken direct control of the helm station. The two Ironkin communicated using soundless waves, the situation requiring that the usual vocal convention be forgotten.

It had been decided that keeping closest proximity with all three ships was the best way to navigate the Well. On the screen below the main display was a schematic of the relative locations of the *Grand Endeavour* and *Canny Wanderer*, followed nearly as closely by the *Hammer of Nithroggir*, almost nose to tail like caravan beasts. Lutar relayed warp readings back to Fyrtor's ship while Holgir Landsfinder's crew were able to double-check the *Canny Wanderer*'s attitude and course relative to the other ships and warn if they were deviating too far.

'First flow of the Well is just ahead,' warned Lutar, turning briefly to Myrtun. 'This is the final chance to manoeuvre out of its pull.'

'No,' said Myrtun without hesitation. 'We're not stopping now.'

The movements rendered onto the big screen increased in speed, and started to shift direction, going from mainly vertical lines to diagonal, to cross-currents. Myrtun felt a shudder.

'What was that?' she demanded. Everyone was already braced or strapped in following normal protocol, but Myrtun hadn't expected to feel anything.

'The Well is an overlap, it seems,' replied Starbound. 'There's some realspace leaking in. That means actual physics like gravity and inertia. It shouldn't get too bumpy.'

'Thank you for letting me know,' grumbled Myrtun.

'We didn't know,' said Lutar. 'There was nothing to suggest the Well was anything other than a storm. This is good news! It's more like a funnel, channelling down through warp space into reality. That backs up what Ironhelm has been saying.'

'We need to break through the current and into the eye,' Starbound reminded them. 'Begin manoeuvres. Grimnyr? Are you ready?'

'Ready,' said Jôrdiki. Myrtun saw the two CORVs shudder slightly, reacting in sympathy to their Grimnyr's nervous mood. The High Kâhl wanted to say some words of encouragement but thought it better not to disturb Jôrdiki's concentration. What she was about to do made the difference between success and failure, life and death.

'On my word,' said Starbound. 'Cutting across the streams in three...'

'Two... one...'

Time stretched as the Voidmaster counted down, while Jôrdiki connected her mind to the ward runes of her staff and CORVs, and via them to the great sea of warp space. She didn't need to hear the Ironkin announce the moment the *Grand Endeavour* moved from the relative peace of the warp current to the pull that was the Well of Yrdu – the sudden wrench she felt was warning enough.

Jôrdiki staggered, not just from the psychic lurch but from the motion of the vessel too. Shouts and calls of dismay sounded from other members of the bridge crew. Now that they had entered the storm, the real-warp overlap was even more severe. Jôrdiki could feel the starship bucking and yawing like a reluctant steed, while Starbound worked at the steering controls to bring the vessel in line with the current.

She pushed thoughts of the ship, of her body on the ship, out of mind. She was a signal, a waveform transmitted through the sensors of the CORVs, oscillating along the ward barrier intersection with warp space. She became the encapsulating bubble, the protector of the *Grand Endeavour*, and she felt the lapping of unreal waves against her flanks, the dragging flow of empyric energy that slowed her headway and wanted to rip her sideways. Jôrdiki resisted, aware that her ward runes were glowing hot, her staff like a torch, her many bangles and talismans glinting with redirected energy. The CORVs were two indistinct winged shapes either side of her, guiding, keeping watch with eyes like silver flares, linking back to her physical form.

It was then that she sensed a state of *flow*. It came as a tactile feeling, but that was just the part of her brain currently being used to interpret the impossibility. A keening noise accompanied it as another group of synapses responded, and then the illusion of light and movement, as though Jôrdiki were a fish in a swell or a bird in a wind.

Something buffeted her left side and she focused her thoughts there, sensing growing pressure. As though extending a hand, feeling grains of emotion pouring between her fingers, she seeped further and further from the metal shell of her CORVs, her view expanding deeper into a space that had no dimensions, its emptiness now becoming her.

The slenderest of silver threads dangled from her tailfin-feathers-feet. She was a mote of burning light with the fury of a turning galaxy, exploding inwards with a great outpouring of energy, imploding from her innermost space to become one without herself and inside herself, and looking upon herself as the eye that was a light. She felt teeth looking into her while their gaze bit apart her essence as swirls of energy teased her particles into conscious loops and holes of reality gnawed at her nothingscape.

* * *

Lutar looked in fascination as tiny snowflakes started to form in the air around Jôrdiki. The Grimnyr had not moved for several heartbeats, though he could detect the life pulsing within her, and her CORVs floated around her, moving slightly to one side or the other even as she swayed with the motion of the starship.

The numbers on his display started to change, splitting and multiplying, the runes shrinking as the range of the barrier ward's sensors pushed out into warp space, channelled and boosted by Jôrdiki.

'It's working,' he said quietly. He relayed the data to Starbound and the other Wayfinders, including the *Canny Wanderer*'s navigator. The runes around the *Grand Endeavour* shifted as the reality barrier moved them inwards, skipping across virtual wavetops, every peak and trough accompanied by disturbed murmurs and unquiet moans from the ship's structure. Other runes changed in their wake, silhouetting Fyrtor's ship against a backdrop of rushing energy. The *Canny Wanderer* manoeuvred harder, working against their drift, keeping station between the other two vessels.

'It's working,' he said, loud enough for his voice to carry to Myrtun.

'Well done,' said the High Kâhl. 'Let's–'

Her words were lost as the Well of Yrdu opened, becoming a vacuum of nothing that somehow seethed with crashing energies, dragging the *Grand Endeavour* into its depths with a clamour of twisting metal and a shattering of screens like thunderclaps and lightning shrieks.

Lutar was shouting and though Myrtun couldn't make out the words, his intent was obvious: they needed to engage the breach drive and break back into realspace.

The High Kâhl looked around the bridge as sparks flew from ruptured consoles and her crew clung to their stations while everything rumbled and rattled and juddered so much that Myrtun thought her insides would be liquidated.

Starbound stood at the helm, locked in place, fingers moving over the steering controls.

'The ship will break apart!' Lutar's voice arrived via Myrtun's bionic ear receiver.

Her heart raced, though whether in dread or excitement was impossible to discern. Sensation washed around and through the High Kâhl, and she didn't know whether to laugh or scream. The simulation on the main screen whirled and whirled as though the *Grand Endeavour* was a leaf caught in a tornado. If they tried to disengage, there was no telling where they might be flung, nor what would happen to the two other ships.

And she would never know. Even if they survived the drop, if she quit now there would be no coming back. Orthônar's voyage would be dismissed as a miraculous one-off. Perhaps in another generation or two, another Hernkyn Prospect would stumble upon the ancient Hold and drive out the orks and be confronted with the riddle of the dead High Kâhl.

'No.' She spoke across the transmitter, feeling a cold calmness in her core, riding out the barrage of biochemicals as the ship rode out the warp tempest. 'No, we're not giving up. Attend your post. Bring me through the storm, my star-guide.'

There was a slight delay before he replied.

'I always will, my jewel-star.'

Thunder.

Thunder that becomes the boom of gunfire. Gunfire that becomes roaring laughter. Tortured metal that becomes guttural cries – screams – that Myrtun never knew could be wrested from a living creature.

Burning and smoke, not of wires and circuits but sinew and fat, stirred into greasy eddies by the air circulation systems. Grime. Coughing. More thunder-laughter, more metal-screams.

A beast of dark green flesh, leering, snarling, casually pulling an arm from a shoulder, tearing at fabric and flesh with equal ease.

Blades digging into flesh, fangs cracking bone, and the stench of blood and smoke, death and dying. Moans, screams. Inside the head, outside, bloody handprints on walls and spattered on screens now marked permanently with hot brands in her memory, burning again as though fresh, recollection ripped from the depths of her nightmares.

She is in front of the beast of her dark dreams. Its mouth opening, jaw distended like a serpent's. Wider than the Well, its gullet like a black hole to swallow her up.

A fist. Her fist. Blazing. The fire within consuming hand and arm, her own shrapnel-bone lacerating ear and flesh.

She recalls the hardness of the grenade in the heartbeat before it detonates, taking her arm and the ork warlord at the same time.

Stunned silence.

More raucous laughter. The monsters laugh at their leader's demise, at her bloodied stump. She runs. No breath for screaming. Runs. Pad of feet, thud of boots, always behind, keeping pace, not trying to catch. Into the hatchway, slamming the door shut. Punching rune-buttons. More blood pitter-patters on runekeys and the grey seat.

Now they realise what she's doing. Bullets ricochet off metal and reinforced glass. Blades scrape and fists hammer.

Burn them.

Fire of expulsion, one-handedly trying to control an artificial comet searing into the void.

Fire and smoke in her nostrils. A burning ship. And then silence once more.

* * *

Laughter.

Not cruel but joyous.

Myrtun opened her eyes.

Lutar stood over her like a protective statue. He turned to look down as she stirred.

'We've made it,' he said.

CHAPTER NINE

Oathstar

Standing just inside the main hatch of the lander, Dori was caught in a duality of thought: he both knew and did not know what to expect when the armoured door slid open.

The orks had not put any ships into orbit, nor had the landers encountered any ground-based weapons, just like last time. The green-skinned beasts were either too lax to feel the need to bolster their defences, or they were confident that they could overwhelm anyone who went below the surface.

Had they bothered to clear the bodies?

The last time he had passed this way, there had been corpses in his path. His had not been the first attempt to break back to the ships. Orthônar had dispatched a dozen warriors to ensure the landing site wasn't overrun. The orks had ambushed them not far from the entrance, and butchered or captured them all. It was only because he had gone alone that he had been able to slip past their guards, who had been too busy despoiling and looting corpses and captives.

Thrusters arrested their descent, sending a rumble through Dori that didn't quite mask the shudder he felt on recalling his departure from this place. He had wanted to avenge those dead, to save them from the brutality of their torturers. Only the oath had stopped him. It would have been a noble end, but an end all the same, and his promise to Orthônar had still been loud in his ears. To be caught would be a failure, and so he had crept like a coward past the smaller grots as they tore at void suits and plundered equipment, while their burly overseers made sport of desecrating the dead and living alike with bullet and blade.

'You'll know peace again,' Jôrdiki assured him, reading his face within the dome of his patched and riveted void suit. 'Your oath'll soon be settled.'

'And my memory?' he asked. 'What of my dreams, Grimnyr? Will they settle too?'

'Happen they will,' she replied firmly. 'When your unquiet is put to rest, all else will eventually calm too. Are you ready now?'

'I'm not,' he confessed, 'but I figure that's fine. There'd be something wrong with me if I thought I was.'

Jôrdiki smiled. There were more lines in her face than before the trials of the Well, but also she seemed slightly softer, as though the experience had taken something sharp away. She didn't seem as distant.

They had all experienced something. Few spoke about it yet, and many might take what they lived through back to the Votann alone. Ironhelm had been wracked with foreboding. Even now, he thought he saw shadows on the periphery of vision, and in the whirr of the air circulators and static hum of the electrics he heard saws on flesh and bone, the rasp of serrated teeth.

He felt the lander touch down, a few moments of extra weight, and then the springing back as hydraulics took the controlled impact. Dock Chief Greta had insisted on overseeing the stowage of the troops and gear aboard the lander, the only craft of this first foray to the surface. She stood at the controls a short distance away, awaiting the signal from the pilot.

'You've all looked at the maps I drew,' announced Dori. Long experience fuelled and informed his words as his mood of apprehension segued to anticipation. Soon his fears would be gone, either reality or just imagination. The closer he came to that moment, the quicker his heart beat. 'You know what's what and where's where for this first part. Main interface building should be dead ahead. We go in, secure that entry shaft and then hold it. Wave two comes next if we don't have any trouble.'

'Do you think the plan will work, Ironhelm?' Jôrdiki asked.

'It should,' he said, with as much confidence as he could muster. He saw a light on Greta's panel flash amber, and then another glowed green. He wondered why the hue that signified action, the signal to go, was the same as the skin of the Kin's most hated foes. 'We didn't have Fyrtor's tunnellers last time. If we do this right, we can get right into the vaults before the orks know what's happening. Let's just take this entrance quiet and see how we go.'

'Opening main door,' Greta announced.

Dori was first out into the starlit gloom. As he advanced warily down the steps, darkstar axe in one hand, bolt pistol in the other, the former champion was struck by the quiet. Last time he had arrived at the head of forty Einhyr, an army at their back. More troops were coming, but this time he had insisted that the High Kâhl was not in the first party. It had been a terse argument, won only by him refusing to leave the *Grand Endeavour* if Myrtun did not stay aboard. There was a very real possibility that this place would shortly claim a second High Kâhl, but Dori would not hasten Myrtun to her doom.

The air was still breathable, according to his suit, but he kept his helm on all the same. If the orks had allowed his Kin to moulder since his departure, the filters would spare him the stench.

The lander had come down almost exactly in the centre of the old starpad, itself situated on a mesa amid what might once have been a fertile plain but was now a great dustbowl stretching to the horizon, a smear of red and grey in every direction. At the lip of the landing field were three low buildings and the broken remains of a tall tower, its upper levels collapsed around the central stairwell and elevator shafts. Further to the left were the skeletal remains of gantries and loading quays that would have extended to sub-orbit originally, now torn down and mostly looted.

Taking a few paces across the cracked, gravel-strewn flatness of the landing pad, Dori looked back and up. Sparks of red hung high over the world – the hulls of the three mainships still reflecting the freshly set sun. Beyond, the stars looked like smears of colour, as though someone had spilled water on fresh canvas and then dragged fingers through it in a vague circle.

The Well of Yrdu.

A core of blackness marked its heart, and the route back to the Kindred.

The others, Jôrdiki among them, had stopped to look back too, gathering around and behind him. Gun turrets controlled by E-COGs whined back and forth atop the lander, watching for foes, reminding Dori that despite the quiet and stillness they were far from alone.

He opened one of the pouches at his belt and pulled free the ring that Orthônar had given him.

'What's that?' Jôrdiki asked.

'A key. It'll get us into the hold.'

He increased his pace, the whispers in his head growing louder.

'This way,' he said, pointing his axe towards the broken tower.

Every crunch of foot, jangle of metal, and scrape on wall made Jôrdiki's skin writhe as though dug through with worms. Each heartbeat brought the expectation of a muzzle flash and the bark of a shot, or perhaps just the sudden sensation of impact and then pain. She strained to hear booted feet or grunts from further down the shaft as the group of Kin lowered themselves into the dark on stout cables, their companions at the summit playing out more length from steady hands. Quieter than any mechanical winch, and just as dependable.

As stealthy as they tried to be – Ironhelm leading the descent with just an ambient glow from inside his helm to see by, a smudged beacon-light that drifted somewhere between Jôrdiki's feet – it was impossible not to sway and bang against the sides of the wall, or dislodge rust and stones with a stabilising boot tread. Each skitter of falling debris and creak of tensile steel was like an alarm blaring in her mind.

'Wait on,' she said over the comm, noticing that her CORVs had moved away slightly from the line of the drop and were playing their dulled lamps over a doorway just below and opposite her position.

Planting her feet more firmly against the wall, she turned around so that she was facing across the shaft. The door looked like the other seven they had already passed, but something had drawn the attention of the CORVs.

Or spooked them.

'Ironhelm?' As she called his name, the champion arrived, pulling himself up the shaft to her right, weapons thudding against his legs. Jôrdiki's wardstaff was strapped across her back, and she was acutely aware of how many times it had caught in her legs or tapped against the wall.

Without any further question or instruction, Ironhelm pushed out from the shaft's side and swung over to the door. Slit windows glittered in his lamp for a brief moment.

'Can't see anything,' he muttered. 'Least, nothing near the doors.'

Jôrdiki let herself commune with the ward runes linking her

to the CORVs. As she did so she felt a flicker of recognition, not from the circuitry of the floating rune-guardians but something a little further away.

'There's a circuit near here,' she said, excited by the revelation. 'Wardtech. Happen it's a Mainfane, or something like it.'

'Probably part of the landing array,' replied Ironhelm.

'I can open these doors,' said Jôrdiki.

'Wait!' snapped Ironhelm, but not before the Grimnyr had sent an access code through her CORVs and into the portal circuitry.

A lock clanked open, echoing ominously up and down the shaft. As the last sounds died away, gears crunched into activity, rusted over long years of neglect. Flakes of corroded metal showered down through the glimmer of lamplight like rust butterflies, accompanied by a drawn-out squeal of protest from the mechanism. Jôrdiki winced with every squeak and shriek while the doors cranked open awkwardly, stuttering along rails until they seized, leaving a gap just big enough for a void-armoured Kin.

Ironhelm looked at her, his displeasure obvious.

'Sorry,' was all that she could offer in return.

The champion pushed his way through the doors, Jôrdiki close behind. Her CORVs swept past, bobbing up and down eagerly a few paces ahead while the rest of the small scouting party joined them. The elevator shaft had opened into a broad lobby area, with three corridors running from it at right angles to one another. The CORVs seemed keen to go straight ahead, so they followed the runic engines out of the lobby.

Age had settled on everything with a patina of grime, but even through the dirt Jôrdiki could see that this was once a magnificent Hold. The floors were tiled with triangles and hexagons, each painted with a small runic symbol that created a kind of floral pattern over and over. She could not decipher the runes, not without some study and access to her library.

The walls had larger rectangular tiling, elongated checks of grey and dark green, while arches five or six times the height of a Kin, made of a glossy emerald-like material, held everything up. No doors or passages broke away from the main thoroughfare, and soon the beams of the CORVs were playing across a set of immense double doors set into the wall directly ahead. Through their circuits Jôrdiki could feel the presence of more wardtech, as though something was responding to their arrival.

'Can't see no sign of runepad or screen,' she said, passing her lamps back and forth over the door.

'Must be a ward-lock,' said Ironhelm. 'We ran into a few last time we was here. Had no Grimnyr with us that time. Can you open it?'

'Of course,' Jôrdiki said with a confidence she didn't feel. 'I am Grimnyr, after all.'

Without knowing which Kindred had built the Hold, or even which League they had been part of, it was hard to formulate an approach. Some ward-locks worked on sophisticated ciphers, others needed particular sequences of contact.

She extended her empyric sense into the CORVs, and from them passed a portion of awareness into the circuitry around the lock. She had to be very careful; if the defences were anything like those of the Fane on the *Grand Endeavour*, she could end up obliterating the device within and potentially killing everyone standing outside.

The circuits linked to the plasma conduits, as she had expected, but also to a coolant system for a large piece of machinery on the level above. There were blind ends and redundant loops, and a profusion of switching circuits connected to a runic sequence. As far as she could ascertain there were no external traps, which just left the self-destruction mechanism to disable. But tampering with that could, on its own, trigger the entire defence system.

'Problem?' said Ironhelm as the Grimnyr withdrew from her contact with a sigh.

'No,' she replied, a little too quickly. 'Not a problem, as such. I just need to think.'

'The second wave is waiting on our word,' the champion reminded her. 'And that disturbance in the shaft could be rousing our enemies right now.'

'I know, I know!' Jôrdiki walked away from him, trying to focus. All that occurred to her was that Vossko would have been a far better person to bring on this expedition. She paced away from the doors so that she could see them in full, using an empyric command for the CORVs to illuminate with full beams.

It was an impressive gateway, with a relief design running over both doors of two Kin facing each other. One was armed with an axe; the other was clearly holding a wardstaff. The runic inscription that joined them on a long band of scrollwork was just about decipherable. It was a First Truth, one that usually featured in any Fane or site of prominent wardtech.

'"United in strength, only fear will part us,"' she read aloud.

'Not that helpful,' grumbled Ironhelm.

Jôrdiki looked at the doors again, seeking inspiration. The runes were familiar enough on the outside, but the circuitry inside bore little relation to them. They were more like the system used on the floor.

'Why would they use a different rune system?' she asked nobody in particular. 'These are written in an ancient form of the empyric runes. But they've used their own writing system *inside* the lock.'

'I think we need to keep scouting,' said Ironhelm, turning away. 'I can't spare warriors to guard you here, though.'

'I need a bit more time,' said Jôrdiki, reading the door again and then once more.

'We don't have time.'

'Enough of your chatter!' rasped Jôrdiki, turning on the champion, surprising herself with the vehemence of her command. 'Some of us are trying to use their heads. Unless happen you intended to batter your way inside using *your* head? Let a Grimnyr do her work!'

Stunned by this outburst, Ironhelm backed away a couple of steps, saying nothing.

Jôrdiki read the inscription slowly, examining the runeshapes. They had changed little despite the antiquity of the place, unlike the Kindred runeset used elsewhere. It was as if it was a message from Grimnyr to Grimnyr, rather than for the local Kin to read.

'No…' Jôrdiki stared wide-eyed, stunned by the simplicity of the thought that had occurred to her.

She stepped forward, wardstaff raised before her, its runes shining with icy light. The runes on the door glittered in response. Jôrdiki took empyric control of the emanating energy and focused on one of the words. She sent the runeforms into the lock mechanism one at a time, and as she did so, the corresponding word gleamed red in the door.

F.E.A.R.

For a fraction of a heartbeat nothing happened – an eternity in the timeless world of empyric wards – and Jôrdiki thought she had made a mistake. Then she felt a surge of ward energy lapping at her, suddenly cut off like a forge door closing on heat as the protective circuits of the CORVs snapped into action.

With a gentle hiss, the seal between the doors broke. The portal swung outwards, forcing them back down the corridor, and as the doors parted, a faint gleam within the hall beyond struck into a bright light. Lamps by the hundred came to life, bathing not only the hall within but also the corridor in yellow as the ceiling itself glowed like plates of gold.

The hall was broad rather than long, but directly opposite was an immense machine that they all instantly recognised.

'It *is* a Fane...' whispered Ironhelm.

'A complete conduit,' replied Jôrdiki. 'Direct to a Votann, I would say. More powerful than anything we have on the ships. Perhaps we can contact the Hold ship, even through the Well.'

Jôrdiki stepped forward, but Ironhelm stopped her with a hand on her arm.

'What was all that business about "fear" then?'

Jôrdiki chuckled. 'It was just a riddle, that's all. Happen those words were meant for others not of the Kindred. Other Grimnyr, in fact. "*Fear* will part us," it says, plain as anything. Meaning the doors, of course.'

Ironhelm looked around, frowning.

'Never mind clattering about in that shaft, this is going to rouse some attention, mark my words. We best get the second wave down now and start making plans.'

'I'm no expert with this Fane, but I can probably contact the *Grand Endeavour* from here. Happen it'll be quicker than going back up to normal comm range.'

Ironhelm eyed her dubiously for a few moments, perhaps suspecting rightly that she just wanted a reason to activate the Fane.

'Fine,' he said. 'You're probably right.'

The CORVs were already heading into the Fane hall, their curved bodies reflecting gold and silver from the magnificent machine within. As soon as Jôrdiki crossed the threshold, the Fane tapped at her empyric presence, latching on to her ward runes directly. A hum emanated from all around them and she felt empyric circuits glowing into life, coursing with energy for the first time in many, many generations.

There were several panels that gleamed into full displays, projecting holographic runepads and more complex interfaces. A convex central display, taller than Jôrdiki, shimmered with energy and formed a three-dimensional representation of a Kin head formed of green light, angular and stern, bald, with heavy rocky brows and a narrow jawline. Its beard was like jagged icicles.

The Fane was inert for the moment. Jôrdiki sent an empyric link command, ordering the device to use its receivers to detect any nearby Votannic signals, hoping to latch on to the standard positional emanations of the Mainfane aboard the *Grand Endeavour*. She yelped as the eyes of the projected face opened, but they did not seem fixed upon her. This was not a Votann, only a conduit, and the representation looked back and forth as though seeking something, looking through her, lips pursed in concentration.

Jôrdiki felt growing concern – not her own but a feeling that seeped from the circuits of the Fane. Absence was more accurate. The Fane was missing something, trying to find something that had been lost. She sent the command again to link with the *Grand Endeavour*.

Jôrdiki stumbled backwards when the Fane spoke, its voice a deep rumble that came from the machines and, somewhat unsettlingly, a split moment later, from the CORVs.

'Signal received. Strongest modulation locked. Link established. Origination: Kindred of the Eternal Starforge vessel *Unbreakable Giant*. Uncyphered address, flat broadcast. Message contents: *This is a general call for aid. Our Hold ship has been discovered by Cursed Ones and we expect their fleet to attack soon. Position attached. Recalling all Kindred vessels to our defence. We are making a plunge to the Aegirsund to try to evade the enemy. All allies welcome. Repeat, our Kindred is under attack, all help required.*'

CHAPTER TEN

The Weight of Responsibility

Myrtun was not disposed to believe in gods or fate, nor 'luck' insofar as it went beyond interpretations and expectations of probability. She was prone to occasional slips of reason, like all Kin, in particular in her adherence to routine, which sometimes bordered on ritual. Despite a varied and long life in which she had encountered many strange things, including the manifestations of the warp that Imperials called daemons, she had never thought it possible for a being to be divinely blessed or sorcerously cursed – outlandish but explicable psychic powers of the warp notwithstanding.

Yet as she reviewed the events that had overtaken her since her decision to leave the Hold ship and pursue Orthônar, it was hard not to think that she had offended a vengeful omnipotence in some fashion. *Dogged by misfortune* would have been a generous interpretation. *Doomed by hubris* seemed far closer to the mark, she thought bitterly.

Had Jôrdiki not activated the Fane on the world below, they would have been in total ignorance of the Hold ship's plight. As it was, the *Grand Endeavour*'s relays still had not picked up any signals directly. It was fortunate that the messages were open transmission, rather than cryptic, ciphered utterances of the Votann that required study and interpretation.

That the series of missives being transmitted from up to a score or more rotes ago were coming through in haphazard fashion meant it was likely to be some time before there was any acknowledgement, if any, from the Hold ship. The picture that had formed was not encouraging. A Cursed Ones fleet was gathering for an attack against the Kindred.

Myrtun was in a desperate bind. On the one hand was her contract to recover Orthônar and find what could be exploited in the Hold; on the other was the need for her to return to the Kindred Hold ship and lead its defence. Her personal reputation and honour – and by extension that of the Eternal Starforge – were staked against the potential survival of the Kindred. If it had just been that, perhaps her decision would have been easier. All she had left of her life was the legacy she would leave, and if her honour had to be forfeit for the salvation of the Eternal Starforge Kindred, it was a simple, if hard, sacrifice to make.

But more was afoot than she could define. It seemed that Lekki's talk of debt was personal – or rather the High Kâhl's – and pertained to whatever Orthônar had been doing here. There had been broken messages from Gurtha asking Myrtun to return the Guild's treasure. Presumably it was something in the deeps of the hold. But they wouldn't find anything unless they could recover some clue or other from Orthônar's body – assuming it could be retrieved. It was all confused, but the insistence of Ironhelm also nagged at her to continue on.

She looked at her assembled councillors and counsellors around the high table of the *Grand Endeavour*'s main hall. There was expectation in their expressions, each believing or hoping that she was going to do what they thought was for the best. Myrtun cleared her throat, started to say something, but stopped. This small lapse triggered murmurs and frowns, her companions' woes compounded by this out-of-character moment for their forthright leader.

Lutar intervened, doubtless thinking that he could ease what was obviously a difficult announcement for her.

'I am comfortable saying that we will support you and endeavour to serve you best, whichever course of action you choose, ur-kâhl.'

His use of her formal title was like a nail in her side, adding yet another wound to contend with. It was a reminder of the burden that had been forced upon her, and an unintentional challenge. The content of his words, the sentiment he had expressed, was precisely the problem that she faced. It did, however, give her the means to say what she needed to say.

'That's the problem, isn't it?' she told them quietly. 'I trust that everyone here, every Kin on this and the other ships, will give their hardest. And their lives, if need be. But I haven't earned that. As Hernkyn I knew what I was about, what was right and wrong. There was lives in the balance, yes, but never someone I didn't know by name and face – it was those I knew had chosen to stick with me even though they knew what I was about, and what might happen if they followed me on those foolish ventures.'

The thought brought a smile as she remembered terrible situations that had been life and death at the time, but willingly confronted by the great promise: opportunity.

'Now there're thousands of Kin, tens of thousands, whose futures depend on what I say and do next. Not just our Kindred, but others whose lives might be affected by what's happening here and with the Hold ship. My instinct isn't any use here. Pressing on regardless, never mind the consequences, doesn't work for matters like this.

'So I have made a choice. One I never made before, though perhaps I should've. I can't decide such a big thing on my own. I'm commanding this council to Weigh the Decision.'

The greatest reaction to this announcement amid much surprise came from Heliga, who had counted Warden of the Weights among several titles for most of her life. She looked more shocked than pleased that she would have to carry out her duties in respect of that position.

'Have we time?' asked Iyrdin Cabb. 'Weighing a Decision is not a quick process.'

'Better to be right than fast,' answered Myrtun, remembering the words of Ironhelm.

'With respect, Myrtun, I am surprised there is any debate at all,' said Starbound. 'Surely the Hold ship's defence takes priority over anything else?'

'Hold that for the session,' said Myrtun. 'You're Voidmaster of this ship, you'll be able to Weigh In just like everyone else at this table. That includes those folks from the *Wanderer* and the *Hammer* who've joined us. Heliga, make sure as they get their share as if they was our crew.'

The Warden nodded her understanding and departed. Not long after, several Hernkyn arrived to rearrange the tables, creating an open square on three sides with all the councillors looking inwards. Four of the heftiest crew arrived carrying a dark wood and bronze-reinforced strongbox on poles, followed by Heliga, who had donned the robe of office for Warden of the Weights – a floor-length habit and hood with a tabard stitched with the runes for Reason and Burden, the shoulders ornamented with epaulette-like decorations in the shape of old scales.

The crew set down their box and Heliga opened the lid with great ceremony, revealing the parts of the Scale of Decision and matching weights. Her attendants lifted the scales from the case and set them in the centre of the space between the tables. They were almost the height of a Kin, and the arms, when placed, were as wide as the scales were tall. Hanging on chains of silver, two golden platters were hooked on, one to each arm. Then

Heliga, consulting her book on the conduct of the Weighing, circled the council members and to each was allotted one or more weights from the box, shaped in facsimiles of the Kindred rune for wisdom, each of varying alloy and therefore mass. The number and type of weight was determined for each based on position and experience, as a means to quantify wisdom.

The whole Weighing of a Decision was a method by which some Kindreds tried to make a physical measure out of the intangible. Certain High Kâhls and councils weighed all but the most mundane matters, whereas others, and Myrtun's Prospect had been among this number until now, had never seen them out of storage. It was remembered by the Votann that the original measuring of the scales had been a practical endeavour: when the founder ships left ancient Earth, those aboard encountered many worlds with different strengths of gravity, as well as their own artificial grav-tech. By combining literal weights with archived digital measures, it was possible to ensure accurate accounting of masses and gravitic strength in a variety of environments, including the warp. From those original sets of scales and weights, duplicates had been painstakingly replicated by hand, matching exact composition and dimensions.

'As instigator of the Weighing of the Decision, Hernkâhl Myrtun is to set out the opposing options,' Heliga intoned solemnly, making the most of her rare moment of council authority. Her other duties revolved around the kitchens and breweries, which gave her great popularity and respect but little business with the council beyond acting as quartermaster.

'Not as High Kâhl?' asked Starbound.

'This is the Prospect Council, not the Votannic Council,' explained Heliga. 'Her authority as High Kâhl is not relevant here. You have the weights of a Prospect Voidmaster, not for being ur-memnyr.'

'Any other questions?' Myrtun asked, standing up. She pointed to one side of the balance. Atop the arm was a figurine of an armoured kâhl in a crowned helm, hammer in hand. On the other was an effigy of a long-bearded Grimnyr, perfectly balanced in mass, holding aloft a wardstaff. Myrtun had never thought about the symbolism of this before, but it now struck her that it appeared she and the Votann were at odds.

'The kâhl represents battle,' she said, picking her words carefully. The ritual wasn't important, but phrasing the choices in as neutral a fashion as possible was. 'It is Orthônar. It is to stay and fight here. The Grimnyr stands for the Votann. For the Fane where we communicate with them. For returning to protect the Hold ship.'

'As is customary, the lesser weights begin the debate.' Heliga brought out a timer the size of a large beer stein, the bulbs decorated with star motifs and held inside a gilded cage shaped like a basic orrery, the ecliptic plane the same whichever way up the timer was placed. The grains within were darkish brown-red, meant to represent the red dwarf star of the system where the Kindred of the Eternal Starforge had been founded.

'Each voter has a turn of the timer to speak their mind,' Heliga continued her instruction. She turned a page of the book and glanced down. 'There are to be no interruptions whilst a voter has their time. All members must be present during the declarations of every other voter.'

She ran a finger down the page, quickly mouthing words to herself.

'There's a bunch of stuff about using the privy, drinks, and eating and whatnot. I'll skip it for now, but if anyone needs a break, let me know between timer turns. You'll be pleased to know I've arranged provisioners to make food and drink available throughout. There're also a lot of rules about language, like not referencing each other by name or title but only addressing the substance of arguments. Basically, keep it polite. Once everyone has had their turn to talk, voting proceeds in the same order. Those of you with multiple weights are free to distribute them between the balances as best suits your disposition of thought.'

Heliga carried the timer over to Durdan Cloakmaster, who had taken his council title as his name. The lowest officer that qualified for a place on the Prospect Council, he was in charge of procuring, taking care of, and storing the official garments of the council, including his own outfit, which he always wore to council meetings on principle: a dark leather kilt and an elaborately brocaded jerkin. He cleared his throat, looked at the other council members, and turned the timer.

'First of all, let me say that I'm disappointed that I didn't get more notice that this was going to be a special occasion,' he began. 'If I'd known, I'd have made sure you all had your ceremonial garb on. It's a bit of an omen when half of us are just in our everyday coveralls, isn't it? Anyway, about this whole thing. I loved Orthônar, but I think maybe it's time we had a good think about what we can achieve here…'

'That is… Yes, I can see…' Lekki found he had nothing to say. He looked at the glowing dots on the screen of the *Unbreakable Giant*'s main scanner array. 'Seven ships, you say?'

'So far,' replied Kâhl Vukasin. The commander wore an armoured void suit in the Kindred colours, a long-barrelled pistol at his hip. The many lights of the chamber shone multicoloured glints from his numerous facial piercings, bright against his dark brown skin like stars on the navigational display. 'We have ships on the system periphery reporting a mass disturbance in warp space that can only be more vessels. At least twenty.'

The guild emissary looked around, impressed by his surrounds. The strategic command tower of the *Unbreakable Giant* was almost as big as the whole upper deck of Lekki's vessel, with a quarterdeck rising at the rear to house the main tactical stations. Overhead was a high vaulted space illuminated by three immense lanterns shaped like symbolic suns, lighting a bewildering number of screens, holo-displays, dials and runepads. Lekki had no idea what any but a few of the systems did, nor the duties of the small throng of Kin who operated them. His eye was drawn to a display to his left, filled with static-ridden images, the view heavily pixelated from maximum magnification.

'That's a feed sent by the *Greyhorn*, our closest ship to the enemy fleet, from the Dankrusa Prospect,' explained Vukasin.

The enemy flotilla was made up of three larger vessels – battleships or grand cruisers by class – and four cruiser-sized ships. There was no mistaking them for Imperials: their hulls were painted in dark reds and blacks, splashed with crude icons of their chosen powers, their prows broad rather than tapered and armoured. One in particular stood out, more resembling a dragon than a ship. Even with the grainy data-feed, it was obvious that it was no ordinary vessel. Its engines churned the void rather than glowed with plasma; its gun decks gleamed with unnatural energy. A daemonship made of physical materials but infused with the intangible, corrupting energy of warp space.

'What are you going to do?' asked Lekki.

'What am I going to do?' Vukasin asked incredulously. 'I'm going to wait for you to restore all of our shield systems, and then I'm going to order a full attack on the ships that are here, before they are reinforced. They've tracked us across one warp plunge, there's no reason to think they can't do it again. If we can't get away, we have to fight.'

'I understand. You will have your systems restored as soon as I can get to the main controls.'

'You can't do it from here?'

Lekki held up his Master Key amulet. 'This has to unlock the panel first. Without this, nothing will happen.'

'On you trot, then,' growled Vukasin.

Lekki hesitated, aggrieved at being dismissed like an apprentice. They still didn't take him seriously. If this drama was not enough to persuade Gurtha or Myrtun to treat with him when the danger had passed, nothing would. He had half a mind to refuse and demand an apology, but another look at Vukasin's gathering frown persuaded him that a confrontation was the last thing he actually desired at that time.

When the current situation was over there would be time for repercussions, and possibly recriminations. All available communications channels were currently employed asking for assistance and warning of the danger, but he would get a message through to the Guild explaining what had occurred when he had re-established their sanctions.

He took two elevators and a small electric wagon to reach the control room, where he found Erkund, Krynn, and many others already waiting for him.

'We turning it all back on?' asked the Eternal Starforge representative, throwing a strange look towards the Guild Ironkin standing in the control kiosk.

'For now,' said Lekki, brandishing his amulet like a talisman as he strode across the chamber. 'But when we are safe again, we will be reimplementing the shutdown. Myrtun can't use every little attack and distraction as a way of wriggling out of her responsibilities.'

'This one wouldn't let us try to reactivate the primary circuits,' added Krynn, pointing at Erkund.

'By order of the Enduring Guild of Master Runewrights, this system desk is disabled,' said the Ironkin. She stood poised with arms and legs slightly apart, braced and ready.

'It's all right now, I will override the lockdown and we can restore the defence systems,' said Lekki, trying to step past her. Erkund kept her body between him and the reader on the panel.

'The dispute has not ended,' she said.

'It can be paused,' insisted Lekki, trying to step forward. She held him back with a metal hand on his shoulder.

'There has been no instruction from the Guild to lift sanctions.'

'We're going into battle, you grit-headed dolt,' snarled one of the attendants, lunging at Erkund. She easily parried his fist, and the Guild member wheeled away with a pained shout, clutching at an obviously broken arm. The distraction was enough to let Lekki slip past, and he slapped his amulet onto the reader disc.

Nothing happened. He waved the amulet back and forth, turned it over and tried again, all to no response.

Metal fingers closed carefully around his wrist and lifted his hand away.

'There has been no instruction from the Guild to lift sanctions,' Erkund said again.

'What did you do?' croaked Lekki, knowing that with just a simple twist the Ironkin could take his arm off, or snap his wrist with a comparatively small increase in pressure.

'I have done nothing,' Erkund told him. 'Your Master Key has not been initiated for unlock.'

Lekki looked at it, feeling betrayed by the Guild chancellors.

'You are a messenger, not a negotiator, Lekki,' the Ironkin explained. 'The chancellors will transmit the unlock cipher when they receive word that Myrtun has held up her part of the bargain.'

'We could all die!' Lekki pulled his hand carefully away from Erkund's grip. 'We need to contact the Guild.'

'You can use the transmitter on the *Sparkfly* to pass on that information, if you wish,' she replied, stepping back so that he could get past. 'I am aware of no communication embargo.'

'Don't worry,' Lekki told the other Brôkhyr nearby, though he was failing miserably to heed his own advice. He thrust his thumbs into the belt of his robe so that nobody could see his hands shaking. He took a breath, steadying his voice. 'I'm going to get this all cleared up.'

Dust billowed out from landing thrusters as more craft arrived from the *Canny Wanderer*, choking the night air with clouds cut through by the orange of plasma plumes and wavering beams of blue and white. Dori saw brighter patches spill out into the gloom from hull lanterns as ramps opened to disgorge tracked carriers, a transport tunneller secured on the back of each. Brôkhyr-led teams of drill experts hurried from the holds to prepare their machines while Hernkyn on magna-coil bikes sped out from the landing site to secure the area. It looked more like a survey for rare minerals than a build-up to battle.

A figure approached from the gloom, resolving into Fyrtor, helmless but hooded, a rebreather covering mouth and nose, his void suit replaced with a fur-lined long coat. He pulled up thick goggles and extended a hand, which Dori shook. The Hernkyn's grip was strong, the movement vigorous, but Dori could see the quick movement in Fyrtor's gaze, the edginess in his step that betrayed nerves.

'The great Ironhelm,' chuckled Fyrtor, clapping his hands together as though chilled. 'Wish we'd met under better circumstances.'

'I was champion,' Dori replied. 'Unless you had business with the High Kâhl, battle's the only way you'd be at my side.'

'Yes, right,' replied Fyrtor. He made a show of looking around. 'No sign of the orks yet, I assume?'

'Not that we've detected.' A nagging, unfocused insistence gnawed at the back of his thoughts, making it hard to concentrate on the Hernkâhl's words, like picking a voice out of communicator static. 'Any more luck with the ship survey?'

'Nope,' Fyrtor replied with a shake of the head. 'The Ancestors built this place well. Shielded against anything but general mass probing. Near as we can make out, there's an anti-spectral refraction alloy used in the walls.'

Fyrtor moved away from the dropsite as another lander roared down.

'We can't tunnel blind,' he said, pulling his goggles back into place as another tide of disturbed grit swept over them. 'I've got four survey digs prepared. They'll show us what's going on and, with a bit of luck, where the orks are concentrated. We'll take a look at the results and see if anything jogs your memory about where Orthônar was last seen.'

'Do you really think it'll be that easy?' Dori looked around at the activity, certain that such industry could not go unnoticed for long, even if the orks had confined themselves to the deeps and vaults. 'Just dig in, grab our dead and then go?'

'If I was a pessimist I'd never leave the Hold ship,' laughed Fyrtor. He led Dori up the steps of an adapted Sagitaur crawler. Inside, the cargo compartment had been fitted out with dozens of screens and comm-relays. It was crewed by several Kin with Mining Guild badges sewn on top of their Kindred colours. A three-dimensional projector dominated the centre, currently inert. 'Here, Brôkhyr Hari Stampesson is our drill leader.'

The Brôkhyr turned at the mention of his name. He was dressed in a thick coverall suit with extra plating across the shoulders and chest, his hair hanging in long braids of dyed blue over the orange material. A toolbelt heavy with equipment sat low on his hips, and he had an elongating screwdriver in one hand, which he waved like a baton.

'Ah, Fyrtor, there you is.' Hari moved to the projector and switched it on. Sketchy, static-broken images flickered in the air until Hari administered a sharp kick to the projector podium.

The display settled to show the landing pad, nearby buildings, and the ground beneath them to a considerable depth. There were vague outlines of corridors and chambers not far below the surface, but beneath them was just a mess of lines and fractures with patches of darkness.

'We can guess a little of the Hold's layout, at least in this area, by analysing where our surveyor beams were *unable* to penetrate the material. A sort of negative, if you will. The denser the refraction, the more likely there is to be structures. Over here' – the screwdriver indicated the cluster of broken ruins and a small but complex network of chambers beneath, dominated by the central elevator shaft – 'we have readings from the scouting party. I wonder, to focus our efforts, as it were, if you would be able to recount anything of your journey down and return from the hall where you last saw Orthônar.'

Dori examined the display closely, picturing where he had just been with Jôrdiki, trying to remember the first time he had come. He started to explain the route they had taken, poking a finger into the projection where needed, sometimes his guesses coinciding with a blob of what might be a hall or vault. Walking around the podium, he retraced imaginary steps, keeping his directions brief, not wanting to get dragged into remembering the fighting that marked a stairwell or landing, the deaths that had occurred at a junction or doorway.

'Somewhere here, I think,' he concluded, pushing his hand into the image to indicate where he meant.

'That is good, thank you,' said the Brôkhyr. 'We'll triangulate our efforts on that position.'

Hari left them looking at the image to marshal the drillers, while his subordinates communicated the survey sites to the outriders and other Sagitaur crews.

'This might take a while,' said Fyrtor, indicating with a nod of the head that they should leave. He followed Dori back down the steps and reached into his coat. Pulling out a gloved hand, he proffered a flask. It was black ceramic decorated with a silver skull and runes that read: *Contents Dangerous*. 'Something to pass the time?'

'Brü?'

'Of a sort,' the Hernkyn replied coyly, uncapping the flask. He gave it a sniff, blinked hard and passed it over.

Dori activated his helm controls and the transparent alloy dome juddered back into his pack, the motor whining and erratic from battle damage. He let the aroma of the brü drift up his nostrils, appreciating the bitter-sweetness of it. He looked at Fyrtor, who smiled and winked, and then he took a mouthful.

The brü was the perfect temperature and the roasted taste flowed into his mouth first, comforting and familiar. Just as he was taking that in, a harsh, sweeter spike of alcohol speared his tongue and burned down into his throat. He almost choked and thrust the flask back to Fyrtor.

'Ancestor's Beards, what was that?' croaked Dori, sure he could feel blisters forming on his gums and tongue.

'A distillation of my own devising I like to call plasma water,' Fyrtor declared proudly. He took a gulp, winced, and then broke into a coughing fit. When he had recovered his breath, he eyed the flask admiringly. 'My best yet, if I say so myself,' he wheezed.

Dori closed his helm, the wind picking up, spraying more dirt. He looked skywards at the orbiting ships, not sure which gleaming star was which.

'I'd have thought you would have been up there, with Myrtun, deciding what to do,' Dori said.

'You mean the council? No point having a debate about whether to stay or go unless we know what we're in for.'

'I'm surprised Myrtun hasn't just turned back for the Hold ship. That must be her first duty.'

'If we leave now, there's no saying whether we'll ever get back here again. She's got Jôrdiki trying to contact Vossko to get a better idea of what's happening.'

'What's the point in recovering Orthônar and the others if there's no Kindred to go back to?' countered Dori. Flutters of formless anger disturbed his thoughts even as he said the words.

'You sound like you think we should pack up and leave,' said Fyrtor, surprised. 'I would've thought that's the last thing you'd want to do.'

'What I want and what should be decided ain't the same. Still, I ain't part of the council, so I don't have a vote. I figure I'm not leaving here, one way or the other.'

'You can't fight the orks on your own. You wouldn't stand a chance.'

'Like I said, I don't figure I'll be leaving.'

Fyrtor fell silent, clearly disturbed by this chain of thought. The quiet did not last long before it was broken by Hari coming out of the Sagitaur at a hurried pace.

'Quick, quick, look at this,' he said, beckoning them to follow him back inside. Dori went after Fyrtor.

'We've only done an initial reading,' Hari said as they entered the transport, 'nothing too useful yet, but look at this. It's the preliminary thermal scan from the surface.'

There was only a vague amount of colour where the scouting party had ventured, but a distance down, around and lower than where he had thought Orthônar had fought his last battle, a reddish gleam illuminated numerous tunnels, shafts and chambers, almost as if they had been mapped by hand.

'I don't get it,' said Fyrtor. 'How can we see that clearly already?'

'Spores. Growths. Orks.' Hari waved a hand through the red maze. 'Heat from life. That's generated by the orks and their fungus farming.'

Fyrtor glanced at Dori, eyebrows raised.

'There must be thousands here,' said the Hernkyn. 'No wonder Orthônar never stood a chance. Neither will we, for that matter. We need to pass this to Myrtun, let the council see what's going on.'

'Wait,' said Dori, placing his hand on the Brôkhyr's at the controls. 'We can still drill in from above, yes?'

Hari nodded. 'There appear to be few orks above this layer,' he said, drawing across the display with his screwdriver. It left a blue line that cut almost directly through the dark mass where Dori thought he had left Orthônar.

'Then we put a force down here' – Dori jabbed a finger between the darkness and the red rash of aliens – 'and the rest go straight in. Fight as a rearguard from the outset.'

'Perhaps you should come to the council, after all,' suggested Fyrtor. 'It sounds like they should hear this from you.'

Dori stared at the schematic, its glowing lines and bright colours nothing like the dark halls and tunnels they represented. Now that the Hold ship was under attack, was it really worth risking another High Kâhl and so many warriors?

A wave of unspoken protests throbbed across his mind, almost staggering in their vehemence. It was not fully formed words, just a feeling of frustration and suffering. It seemed to be stronger than ever, and the fact that he was so close to the Hold couldn't be coincidence.

If Myrtun asked him flat out what he thought she should do, could he really lead her to her possible doom? What was an oath worth?

He had the flight back to the *Grand Endeavour* to think about it.

Lutar divided his attention between the ongoing speeches of the council and the comm-feed that had been established to Jôrdiki in the Hold's Fane, via the Mainfane on the *Grand Endeavour*. The proximity of the Well of Yrdu interfered with Votannic traffic back to the Hold ship while, according to Jôrdiki's account, the ancient Fane on the planet below could operate as a receiver and transmitter but barely anything else – seemingly everything had been lost from its datacores or, she had speculated, deliberately erased. With the boost to the Mainfane secured, the Grimnyr was making her way back to orbit with Ironhelm and Fyrtor so that they could participate in the Weighing of the Decision.

The setup was better than normal comm-links for keeping in touch with the party on the surface. Brôkhyr Hari from the *Canny Wanderer* was still examining the mineral readings from the scans to determine the best launch sites for the tunnellers, while Kâhl Enryk Gunnar of the *Hammer of Nithroggir* – Holgir was attending the council by way of a comm-screen – mustered the growing number of Hearthkyn and Hernkyn from her ship and the *Grand Endeavour*.

For the most part the council had repeated the same principles: that the first and overriding duty of any Kin was to their Kindred and their Hold. Nobody had argued against that yet, but Iyrdin Cabb was now speaking, and she was in favour of remaining.

'The Hold ship has been under threat before,' she explained, standing with fists leaning on the table, occasionally running a hand through the stiff comb of blue hair that bisected her scalp, or tugging at the braid of the same hanging over her left shoulder. She wore her void suit but for the helm, and had grunted and huffed impatiently through the other speeches, obviously unhappy at not being with her warriors on the surface. 'There's more ships gathered in the Hearthfleet for the journey to the Tides than usual. Three understrength Prospect flotillas arriving late aren't going to do too much.'

The Hernkâhl took a gulp of water and licked her lips, a sign of nerves perhaps. Battle was inevitable whatever the council decided, but how soon was it coming?

'Imagine we get back to the Hold ship and it's all been a fuss over nothing? Would we ever be able to come back here? I think we know the Votannic Council wouldn't allow it. There's no way they'd let the High Kâhl – our Myrtun – get out from under them again. They weren't all that keen this time, that's a fact.'

She continued as the sand drained, repeating herself a lot, which had been a common occurrence thus far. Nobody wanted to simply sit in silence and watch the grains run if there was time left to keep talking. Lutar turned his attention to the comm-links.

Jôrdiki had deciphered several more messages in a similar theme to the first, asking for available Kindred vessels to meet the Hold ship in the Throjar System. Lutar consulted his internal charts and found Throjar nearly a thousand light years away from their estimated position, by conventional means. He was due to speak soon and logged that piece of data for his argument.

Iyrdin had a short time left and finally changed tack to make a more impassioned plea than her previous attempts at reasoning.

'What we have here is something remarkable!' she insisted, rapping armoured knuckles on the table. 'We've already dared the Well of Yrdu and found a lost Hold. What other secrets, what other bounty might we uncover here if we stay? This is just the beginning, not the end. To leave now would be to abandon the thread of the story that brought us here. It is not the role of Hernkyn to scurry back at any sign of danger, but to grip opportunity with both hands.'

Lutar spared a glance at Myrtun. She had sat in silence, appearing to be absorbed by the speeches of everyone, but had shown no reaction that might betray whether she had yet settled on a course for herself. If she was of a mind to stay, she needed allies, and was last to speak. Her weights amounted to considerable influence, but those on the council who had already spoken in favour of return were probably enough to keep the subject in balance.

Lutar again returned to what his position would be and what he would say, knowing that although his quantified influence in regard to his weights was not so great, his words as a staunch ally of Myrtun might carry far more sway.

Myrtun listened to another member of her council tell her where her duty lay, what the responsibility of being High Kâhl was about, and how the Ancients had valued the Four Pillars that held up Kin society: Hearth, Forge, Fane, and Crucible. All were on the Hold ship and without them there was no Kindred of the Eternal Starforge.

She had known all along what she *should* do, but it was at odds with what she wanted to do, and that meant she didn't know what the right course of action was. She had been genuine in calling for the Weighing of the Decision, because it had been clear she could not hope to go against the council as she had with the Votannic assembly on the Hold ship. She had hoped that enough of them would be in favour that it literally tipped the balance to staying and seeking Orthônar, but that seemed unlikely now. Even with Iyrdin Cabb's and Lutar's support, and possibly that of Fyrtor and Holgir, there still wasn't enough weight in her favour against Starbound and the others. If Jôrdiki chose to reveal everything about the Votann's message then the decision was as good as made, given that the Grimnyr's vote was not far short of Myrtun's own.

All her reluctance had achieved was delaying the inevitable. She knew that they would go back to the Hold ship, and sense told her that was the right thing. But there hadn't been a single argument like Iyrdin's in favour of staying that made Myrtun feel like it was the good choice. Kin prided themselves on reason – such as the Weighing process itself – but Myrtun had been around long enough to know that reason only went so far. Loyalty could be corrupted by reason if treachery was more profitable. Reason was cautious, but opportunity demanded fears be overcome. A principle based on evidence and reason wasn't a principle of choice; it was a quantified fact that carried no particular moral weight.

Glancing at Starbound and Lutar, whose neurotronic circuits allowed them to make thousands of reasoned decisions simultaneously, Myrtun considered that if the Votann wished for the Kin to be ruled by reason alone, they would have created them all as Ironkin. As it was, though Kin benefited from a multitude of different cloneskeins, they were all subject, at some level, to the same biological flaws and benefits as other living creatures. They also, it was worth noting, had souls: though their warp presence was almost zero, it was not *actually* zero.

All of that was right for Myrtun, Hernkâhl of the Dammergothi Prospect, which was meant to be the basis of this debate, yet nobody had been able to ignore the fact that she was also High Kâhl, even if she had forsaken that role for the Weighing. Perhaps High Kâhls and their committees of counsellors were meant to put reason first so that other, more wayward members of the Kindred could follow dreams and snatch opportunity.

CHAPTER ELEVEN

Enemies Close In

Settling into a chair in front of the recording station in the comm-suite aboard the *Sparkfly*, Lekki arranged the fall of his robe to look less creased, and wiped a few crumbs from his lips and scraggly beard.

'What are you going to say?' asked Erkund, stopping just behind his left shoulder, her metallic body reflected in the dark glass of the screen.

It was the question that had been plaguing him since leaving the fields control centre. It seemed straightforward enough – the *Unbreakable Giant* was under attack and he needed to restore their defensive shields. It was not an unreasonable request. In fact it was very practical. The trick was in conveying that need without suggesting he was somehow culpable for the predicament. It would be easy for someone else to look at the situation and decide that he had acted importunely or precipitously when he shut down the defence screens in the first place.

'I'll just explain what's happened and get the Guild to transmit the unlock cipher for the Master Key,' he eventually replied, flicking on the recording screen. 'Move out of my frame.'

Erkund stepped to one side while the screen came to life, a mirror image of Lekki at its centre, the rest of the chamber slightly out of focus behind. The Brôkhyr turned to his Ironkin bodyguard.

'Do you think I should attach some scan data, to prove the level of threat?'

'If you do not think the word of a guild emissary is to be trusted, then certainly do that.'

Lekki wanted to say something in rebuke but couldn't argue with Erkund's reasoning. If he said that the Kindred of the Eternal Starforge were in danger – and they had already broadcast their own request for help – that should be sufficient.

'Right,' he said, tapping the runes to activate the recording session. A small icon appeared in the corner of the screen to indicate that it was live.

'This is Iron-Master Lekki Gûlrundr, emissary to th–'

'They will know who the transmission is from. It will carry your dataseal.'

'Don't interrupt! I have to start over.' Lekki erased the recording, reset himself on the chair, and pressed the recording rune.

'This is Iron-Master Lekki Gûlrundr, em–'

'You understand that this will take some time, even if you are successful?'

'What did I just say about interrupting?' Lekki spun round to jab a finger at the Ironkin. 'You're doing this on purpose.'

'Yes, but not to annoy you. Kâhl Vukasin is currently manoeuvring the *Unbreakable Giant* and its fleet to confront the enemy in the belief that you are restoring the field systems.'

'Yes?'

'You are currently *not* restoring the field systems, and even if the Guild replies as soon as they receive this message, it will have taken some considerable time for our transmission to reach them and theirs to get back to us.'

'By which point we'll be in a fight with no shields…' groaned

Lekki. He buried his head in one hand, rubbing his forehead to ease the sudden pain behind his eyes. 'Could this get any worse?'

'Yes. It will rapidly worsen if you do not inform Kâhl Vukasin of your inability to restore the field systems.'

Lekki let out a wordless growl and hauled himself from the seat. He took a couple of paces and then stopped, torn between two courses of action.

'Shouldn't I contact the Guild first, and *then* I can say to Vukasin that everything is in motion? Better that than saying I haven't done anything yet?'

'We are currently accelerating towards the enemy fleet without defensive shields.' Erkund moved to one of the sub-panels and tapped at the runeboard. The screen came on with a view of the escalating hostilities. Smaller Kin ships had moved out to screen the larger vessels in the fleet, firing salvoes of torpedoes to stop the enemy ships from closing formation – such close proximity limited their ability to avoid the guided projectiles. Flights of attack craft were disgorging from an enemy carrier vessel, squadrons of void fighters intent on intercepting the torpedoes, the larger craft behind them likely laden with anti-ship weaponry in the form of missiles and bombs, or perhaps carrying boarding parties to conduct hit-and-run attacks.

The unnatural dragonship had remained directly on course for the *Unbreakable Giant*, flanked by two cruisers. It looked as though they intended to invade the Hold ship itself.

'By the eyes of Grilbyr!' cursed Lekki, storming out of the comm-suite and into the piloting chamber. He activated a ship-to-ship channel. '*Unbreakable Giant*, this is Iron-Master Lekki on the *Sparkfly*. I have an urgent message for Vukasin. Put me through to him immediately.'

He sat down in the piloting chair and started activating the ship controls set into the arm. Half a dozen E-COGs emerged from their recharge niches and moved to stations around the chamber, plugging themselves directly into the systems.

'Why are you powering up?' asked Erkund.

Lekki ignored her, waiting for Vukasin to answer. It took only a couple of moments, and by his tone the kâhl of void operations was not in a good mood.

'Where are my shields, Iron-master? I need them now.'

'Yes, about that…' Lekki was again reminded of being admonished as an apprentice, but this time it really wasn't his fault things had gone awry. 'The Master Key needs a new unlock cipher from the Guild, which I am in the process of getting for us.'

'You mean you can't give me my shields back?' There was a timbre to Vukasin's voice that made Lekki cringe.

'Not yet,' he replied. 'Perhaps a more circumspect battleplan is in order?'

'Circumspect?'

'Maybe leave this fight to the rest of the fleet?'

Lekki activated the reactor and engines and watched as red bars turned amber and then green on the power display.

'Are you intending to leave?' asked Erkund.

'What's that?' said Vukasin, picking up the Ironkin's words.

'I am taking the *Sparkfly* and joining the rest of the fleet,' lied Lekki.

'Are you really?' Disbelief dripped from every word out of the comm-speaker.

Erkund strode past and started tapping controls on the drive station, pushing aside the E-COG with a foot. Power levels started to drop.

'Now what are you doing?' demanded Vukasin.

'I-I…' stuttered Lekki. He scowled at Erkund. 'What *are* you doing? This is my ship!'

'It is the Guild's ship,' the Ironkin reminded him. 'I cannot allow you to abandon your duty to the Guild.'

The reactor levels reached idle again, the hum of power dropping back to a barely detectable vibration in the hull.

'Abandon...? Do you think so little of me that you would accuse me of running away?'

'I do, but that is not my primary concern.' Erkund took a step forward, arms crossed. 'The Master Key is needed to reactivate the shields. If you die, the Master Key is useless. Ergo, I must keep you alive to fulfil the duties of the Guild, and you must remain aboard.'

'One of you just tell me what in the Hundred Halls of Orasin is going on!' snarled Vukasin.

Lekki swallowed hard. He had no desire to be stuck on board the Hold ship while it was under attack, but Erkund was giving him no choice. He couldn't order the Ironkin to stand down and he had no way of overpowering her, not without risking serious injury to himself or damage to the *Sparkfly*.

Erkund raised a hand towards the door to the comm-suite, her meaning clear.

'Kâhl Vukasin, I am doing all I can to remedy the situation as swiftly as possible.' Lekki tried to sound authoritative, but his tone veered into pompous. 'I will restore the shields as soon as I can, but for all our sakes, don't place the *Unbreakable Giant* into more danger than we are in already.'

'I can't run, and I can't fight, and the Hold ship is the size of a large asteroid, so we're not hiding any time soon. The best we can do is try to stay out of trouble for as long as we can.'

The link severed with a loud click and left Lekki in the quiet of the dormant piloting chamber. His thoughts were whirling, but the sight of the Ironkin directing him to the comm-suite focused his attention. He needed to get a message to the Guild and then everything would sort itself out.

* * *

Lutar stood up and settled his shoulders as though relaxing. Physically this made no difference, but it did make his thought processes feel a little calmer.

'I bear bad news, which I must share as part of my testimony to the council. I have caught up with the transmissions from the Hold ship, which were sent out over the course of the last few rotes but, due to distortion by the Well of Yrdu, were undetectable by our ships' Votannic conduits.' He looked at Myrtun to ensure she understood his next words. 'We are fortunate that Jôrdiki activated the Fane in the hold below, or we would have been entirely ignorant of any threat to our Kindred. These last missives make it clear that the Hold ship is taking up a defensive position in the Throjar System. They fear that their pursuers possess the sorcerous capability to hunt them in warp space, and thus real-space provides a surer sanctuary than continuing to try to elude their hunters. By my calculations, in reference to the data collected during Ironhelm's return, navigating the Well of Yrdu in the reverse direction is not as hazardous as entering. The greatest difficulty is determining where we will exit and in which direction we will be heading, given that the warp currents will rapidly send us into the violent outskirts of the storm.

'*If* we can ride the Well correctly – and our successful prior navigation attests that we should be able to do so – then we can exit the Well in the Aegirsund. That leaves us just a single plunge of about five light years to reach Throjar.'

He paused, knowing the impact of his following words, though he ensured there was nothing in his intonation that could be taken as suggesting one course of action over another. He simply wanted to deliver the current facts.

'In roughly five watches' time,' he said, 'we could be back at the Hold ship.'

There was, against protocol, a babble of voices, until Heliga insisted on silence while the sands were still running. Indignant, she signalled for Lutar to continue.

'However, if we commit to the expedition to the surface, we cannot say how long that will take, or if extraction would indeed be possible if events turn against us.' He saw Myrtun studying him intently and paused once more so that he could arrange his next words in the best possible manner.

'I do not offer an opinion on these matters at this time. I will cast my vote according to any further news we receive.'

Jôrdiki hurried to the chamber of the Mainfane while the others that had come back from the surface made their way towards the council hall. She went directly to her desk-lectern and activated the screen. She typed in the directory numbers without thought, bringing up the datafile that had occupied her thoughts since it had arrived.

> *CORRECTIVE: REPLACE_ALL:*
> *URD-0r: That Which Is Lost Can Be Found.*
> *VeRD-4n: That Which Is Lost Can Be Found.*
> *Sk-43L: Do Not Seek That Which Is Lost.*

Activating a thorough scan of recent transmissions boosted by the Hold's Fane, she searched for any other updates on the message, perhaps something that would help her compose another corrective or reassert the previous interpretation. Nothing was revealed as having arrived while they had been cut off by the storms. Jôrdiki wasn't sure if that was a good thing or a bad thing.

Why wasn't it a unanimous message? Reading her translation again, Jôrdiki decided there was no contradiction between the sentiment of the two and the instruction of the one. Given the nature of her correction, the negative repurposed to the positive, she knew it wasn't a deciphering issue. That part wasn't her interpretation – the signal from the Votann had definitely been a tripartite split.

What did that mean?

A thing could be found, but the seeking of it might be injurious.

Had they not come to that point now? The affirmative of the mission – Orthônar could be found – was a direct reply to the enquiry made. Why had the third Votann opted for a warning in the reply? Or, perhaps more pertinently, why hadn't the other two offered a similar warning? Was it oversight or deliberate that the message was mixed, and why had there been the need for a corrective? Had there been agreement between the triumvirate?

Dealing with the Votann was all about phrasing questions in specific ways and interpreting the answers with a proper perspective, but all of these unknown factors dragged on Jôrdiki's thoughts. This was not a theoretical or historical issue, it was genuine life-or-death for many, many Kin.

If she had spent more time with the other Grimnyr, she would have been more confident about how to handle the situation. Had she grown into bad habits, here on the *Grand Endeavour* on her own?

Myrtun had decided to Weigh the Decision – why now of all the times? – and that meant Jôrdiki's opinion had solid value. No more arguments with the stubborn Prospect commander. Not only could she persuade with words, a Grimnyr's weights might also be enough to carry the vote one way or the other. As was right, given that she was the voice of the Votann. Her vote on top of a majority of the council, or combined with Myrtun's alone, was likely to decide the balance.

Which meant that the decision was as much hers as it was Myrtun's...

Her word and the placing of a few weights could see them

heading back to the Hold ship, abandoning this fruitless journey that she had opposed from the outset. Myrtun could not have failed to know that Jôrdiki had not been in favour. By calling for the Weighing, was the High Kâhl giving herself a way out of a bad decision?

Too many thoughts chased each other around her head. The result of the vote had implications beyond the fate of the Hold ship. Whether the Fane was really in danger or not, Myrtun had left the *Unbreakable Giant* to pursue her personal adventure. If it was then revealed that the bulk of her council and allies wanted to abandon it, her decision from the outset was shown to be wrong, her leadership perhaps brought into question. There were measures – processes – that could be brought into place to remove a High Kâhl, though usually such things were a formality if the incumbent was badly injured and unable to continue their duties, or otherwise rendered incapable of serving. Myrtun had not wanted the position in the first place; nobody had thought her suitable. Perhaps it was best for all that she was allowed to spend the final seasons of her life as Hernkâhl, as she had spent the rest of it, unencumbered by unnecessary responsibility.

One last adventure for Myrtun.

'Everything is ready for the attack,' Dori told the council, dropping his axe on the table. He sat down on the bench of a neighbouring table, declining the space that was offered to him. The nagging ache in his head had increased as he had journeyed back from the surface, rather than dissipating as he had hoped.

On the way back, via comm-link, Fyrtor had argued to stay, claiming that it was the Hernkyn who carried the will of the Votann into the places of darkness. There was a Fane and a Hold here, and though they lacked the means to retake it right now, surely it had been Orthônar's intent to lead the Kindred here in force in the future, to see what could be reclaimed for the Kindred and the League. Dori was almost convinced, but he knew that he heard everything through the bias of the oath he had sworn.

Jôrdiki was still in her Mainfane, and so the opportunity to speak passed to Myrtun. Dori watched her carefully, wondering where her mind had been set.

'I said at the start of this procedure that I wanted the council to decide, and also time is pressing,' the High Kâhl began. 'In that spirit, I set aside my time to speak. All that has been said, on both sides of the debate, has been laid out before us. I call on the Warden of the Weights to begin the voting.'

Heliga accepted the instruction with a solemn nod while other council members looked at each other in surprise and confusion.

'No more talking,' said Heliga as whispered conversations broke out. When the chatter had died down she turned to Durdan Cloakmaster. 'With no further debate, the first vote is yours.'

Heliga gestured for the council member to approach the scales. Being at the 'base' of the horseshoe, sitting equidistant from either end with the balance within the tables, Durdan had the furthest to walk of any of them, and took his time to appear stately and poised. Dori suppressed a growl, recalling that the Votann, in their wisdom, entertained a wondrous variety of cloneskeins and the Kin that grew from them. All had their part.

With a very deliberate movement, Durdan picked up his weight and placed it on the Grimnyr side of the scales. Such was the slight mass it barely moved the balance, but it was a signal. The next handful of committee members voted likewise, and the scales tipped further and further towards returning to the Hold ship with each one. Iyrdin Cabb was the first to vote against, and so did a few of the other members, though it was not sufficient to bring the balance back to its upright. The next votes went against staying again, until Holgir and Fyrtor placed their weights. The first distributed hers mostly for remaining, but had one placed on the side for departing. Fyrtor placed all of his to keep up the hunt for Orthônar, and the scales again swayed back towards the neutral but did not quite attain it.

The council members that were left, including Starbound, had several weights of substantial value, most of which tipped the balance in favour of defending the Hold ship, as Dori had expected. The Weight of the council's opinion was starting to show even more.

Lutar stood up and moved to the centre of the tables, turning to Myrtun for a moment before reaching for his weights. The first he placed on the side of the kâhl – to remain. The other three, with a regretful sigh, he set upon the Grimnyr's side of the scales.

Dori looked at Myrtun, and for an instant her facade of solidity broke – her lip trembled to see her oldest confidant, her literal saviour, seeming to break faith. The Ironkin sat down without comment and others followed, most splitting their weights, some evenly, others favouring one course or the other. Starbound placed three weights upon the Grimnyr scale, fourth in hand. Dori saw the Voidmaster glance at Lutar before giving their last vote to the 'remain' side of the balance. The balance was closer than Dori had expected, but still visibly weighted towards leaving the system to rejoin the Hold ship. It was impossible to tell if Myrtun's weights alone could shift the decision. The veteran wondered if she should. The Weighing was meant to give each individual a say equal to the value of their opinion, but as yet there was one who had not made their views known.

Jôrdiki had not yet joined them.

'What about the Grimnyr?' Dori asked. 'Do we wait for her?'

Heliga consulted the Tome of Weighing, running her finger down pages as she flipped back and forth through the slender volume.

'It is at the discretion of the council,' she said, though she frowned as she said it and did not sound entirely convincing. She closed the book and looked at Myrtun. 'Perhaps give her a turn of the glass to join us?'

The mood was tense. As it stood, Myrtun could weigh in and decide the vote right now. If she allowed Jôrdiki to vote against, it was certain they would be setting course for the Aegirsund regardless of Myrtun's feelings on the matter. Dori realised he was holding his breath.

CHAPTER TWELVE

Legacies of Past Actions

Myrtun paused. Jôrdiki's absence looked like opportunity but was in fact a trap for the unwary. Not a deliberate one, Myrtun decided, Jôrdiki was not the sort, but a hole that could swallow up the High Kâhl all the same. If she waited, Jôrdiki's vote was likely to be cast in the most direct interest of the Grimnyr and Votann – to protect the Fane of the Hold ship. Such was right and proper, and who was she to overturn that? If Myrtun went ahead with her vote and cut Jôrdiki out, there would always be questions about her authority. A 'loophole leader' some might say, with justification. She had already skipped on the Hearthspake; to use a procedural glitch in this circumstance created a pattern of unaccountability. If her voice was to be heard, if the position of High Kâhl was to mean anything, Myrtun could not bring herself to take advantage of the Grimnyr's lapse in time-keeping.

'Please remind her that she is expected,' Myrtun said to Heliga. 'We will wait for her to arrive.'

'Perhaps we should send someone to check on her?' suggested Kaila Broadstretch, from the Pioneers.

'Nowt wrong with me,' announced Jôrdiki, crossing the hall. She was red in the face and out of breath. The Grimnyr looked at Heliga and then at the book the Warden of the Weights was holding. 'Happen with permission of the council I'm allowed to make a special address?'

Heliga turned wordlessly towards Myrtun, mouth slightly open, eyes enquiring.

'Given there's only me and you to vote,' Jôrdiki said, approaching the High Kâhl, 'I don't see there's a problem. It ain't like I can convince anybody to change their mind.'

Myrtun couldn't work out what was happening. Was this an attempt by Jôrdiki to push her own standing, in preparation for rejoining the other Grimnyr, one among several rather than a power to herself? But, as she said, there was nobody left to convince anyway, so what did it matter?

'I'm happy to hear what you have to say,' Myrtun replied, before looking around the tables. 'With everyone else's agreement?'

A hasty chorus of affirmatives came back. Everyone was eager to hear Jôrdiki's deposition and then have the matter settled. Myrtun sat down and waved for the Grimnyr to take her place at the table on the opposite end of the arc. As Jôrdiki moved away, Myrtun noticed she was carrying a mini-projector in her hand. She placed it on the table and activated it. A faint blue light emanated from the top.

'With your indulgence, I'll share some messages that have come from the Votann in the recent past, to help you understand my thinking. It's not an easy question that Myrtun's put before us today. Happen as heart and head ain't in the same place for some of you, and even those of one mind, I figure the choices we've been given have a lot at stake either way.'

The Grimnyr tapped a rune on the projector and lines of message appeared. Myrtun clenched her jaw tighter as she read them.

> URD-0r: *That Which Is Lost Cannot Be Found.*
> VeRD-4n: *That Which Is Lost Cannot Be Found.*
> Sk-43L: *Do Not Seek That Which Is Lost.*

'Happen it's time the truth was known,' Jôrdiki continued, looking directly at Myrtun.

'You showed me this as proof that the *THA-C342* was lost in warp space,' said the High Kâhl.

'But we spoke after as how I thought it was about the greater questions, of whether the expedition should continue,' replied Jôrdiki. There seemed no malice in how she spoke, but if she was looking to heap grit on Myrtun's reputation, she was soiling her own too.

'You chose to share that view with me in confidence,' Myrtun growled. 'You could have spoken to the council at any time, including when we were discussing the *THA-C342*.'

There were discontented grumblings from some of the council members now.

'I trusted you to do the right thing,' Jôrdiki replied. 'Trust is important, between Kin, but especially between kâhl and Grimnyr.'

'This seems to put a different light on matters,' said Starbound.

'Hush, you,' said Jôrdiki, again without anger, more as an aside. 'You ain't been given permission to speak, and this ain't about anybody except Myrtun and me.'

The muttered complaints continued, though none was voiced too openly. Myrtun fought her rising temper. If Jôrdiki was trying to bait her into saying the wrong thing, she had to keep her head. She folded her hands into her lap and kept her voice level, eyes flicking back to the message from the Votann.

'I think this would have been more relevant before the debate began,' said the High Kâhl. 'This seems a little like you want the attention.'

'Sorry about that, I really am,' said Jôrdiki, and her expression matched her words. 'I had to be certain of what I was going to say, so I needed to run through it all properly afore I came.'

She pressed another rune on the projector and the holo flickered. It took a second look for Myrtun to notice what had changed.

> CORRECTIVE: REPLACE_ALL:
> URD-0r: *That Which Is Lost Can Be Found.*
> VeRD-4n: *That Which Is Lost Can Be Found.*
> Sk-43L: *Do Not Seek That Which Is Lost.*

'You kept this secret?' Myrtun's patience withered under the heat of her renewed anger. She rose to her feet and took a step. Lutar stood too, preparing to intervene.

Myrtun's voice was a cold snarl. 'Keep out of this, I'm not best pleased with you at present and I don't want things to get worse. My own Grimnyr has this all that time, hiding it. Warden, can we recount the votes?'

'Wait,' said Jôrdiki. 'You read what you want to read, Myrtun. To me, it still doesn't say that we should have sought Orthônar, only that it was possible to find him. Happen we know that's true. Now we are here. But that's not all, is it? There's another message, older, that's more relevant than any of this, and it's what has been giving me the most vexation to work out.'

'What do you mean?' Myrtun's ire was cooling, the forge of her anger somewhat doused by Jôrdiki's equanimity. She seemed neither afraid nor triumphant. In fact, there was no indication she considered she was in an argument at all.

'When Orthônar had been declared gone and the council needed to pick a new High Kâhl, this was the message the Grimnyr translated from the Votann.'

The words gleamed into life. Myrtun had not seen them before and studied them with care, brow creasing even more deeply with a rereading.

> *URD-0r: The High Kâhl Has Travelled The Greater World More Than Most.*
> *VeRD-4n: The High Kâhl Has The Wisdom of a Life Longer Than Most.*
> *Sk-43L: The High Kâhl Has The Strength Of Will To Make Their Own Fate More Than Most.*

'That's me?' she whispered. 'That's why the Hearthspake picked me, on that?'

Jôrdiki stepped closer, and now there was a look in her eye that Myrtun recognised: pride. The Grimnyr turned now to the council as Myrtun read the message a third time.

'The greatest traveller, the longest life, the strongest will,' recited Jôrdiki, her eyes moist. 'These were the qualities the Votann demanded of the next High Kâhl. The council considered *every* member of the Kindred. Happen that's thousands and thousands of Kin, and only one could be said to match all three demands. Just one. Myrtun Dammergot.'

Myrtun's composure broke completely, tears running down her cheeks. She watched Jôrdiki pick up the weights of her votes and place them carefully on the scales. When she was done, the Grimnyr stepped away. The two sides were almost equal, leaning ever so slightly towards the Grimnyr. Whatever Myrtun wanted to do, her votes would be enough to make it happen.

'You silly wench,' sobbed Myrtun, taking Jôrdiki in a fulsome hug. 'You put me right through the grinder there.'

The Grimnyr pulled herself away, wiping her own tear with a fingertip.

'I had to make you understand, Myrtun.'

'Understand what?'

'*You* are the choice of the Votann. *You* are the High Kâhl. They wanted someone exactly like you to be the one making decisions like this.' The Grimnyr spoke to Myrtun but then the council, looking from one to the other. 'The Votann are the only other ones that know why Orthônar came here. He failed, and so they directed the council to choose a successor. One that would go after Orthônar. One that would keep true to what the Votann had already asked. I know you don't think you're High Kâhl material, and that you ain't suited for this at all, but it ain't up to you to decide. The Votann gave you this power to use as you would use it, not as you think some other High Kâhl should.'

Myrtun nodded, accepting what the Grimnyr told her. With shaking hands she took up the first of her weights and approached the scales.

She looked at the council and saw belief in their faces – a willingness to follow where she would lead, which hadn't been there before. With another smile to Jôrdiki, Myrtun placed the first weight beneath the figurine of the kâhl, tipping the balance.

Lekki did not think about death much, but the scene playing out across the screens of the *Sparkfly* very much brought it to mind. What had started out as an offensive by the Kindred of the Eternal Starforge had turned into a running space battle, trying to keep the enemy ships as far from the *Unbreakable Giant* as possible whilst avoiding becoming embroiled in any longer engagements. A few more vessels from other Kindreds had arrived to help the defence, but the forces of the Dark Gods had swelled with recent arrivals too, and there were still signals suggesting other vessels in the warp.

The only real note of hope was that none of the attacking

ships had yet come close enough to test the defences of the Hold ship – the enemy were as yet unaware that their prey had no defensive shields. The monolithic vessel still sported considerable guns and torpedoes, as well as launch bays, and its overall bulk was defence against all but the strongest attacks. However, if the opposing commanders learnt that there was nothing protecting the engines, the weapons batteries, the command tower…

'No acknowledgement signal?' Lekki asked Erkund again. She shook her head. The Ironkin had established a direct link to the *Sparkfly*'s dedicated Guild comm-channel, but as yet there had been no confirmation that Lekki's broadcast had even passed whatever comms blockade the enemy might have created. The presence of so many Cursed Ones' ships was highly disruptive to warp-based transmissions on top of any deliberate attempts to isolate their prey's communications.

The dragonship had continued in its single-minded quest to bring its weapons to bear on the *Unbreakable Giant*. Just thinking of that name made Lekki want to weep. The giant was very much breakable now, thanks to his clumsy dealings with Myrtun and his rash decision to cut off the fields. Sitting in the piloting chair, watching ships explode on the screens, the criss-cross of plasma flares and laser beams, the trails of torpedoes and inter-ship rockets, the emissary had been forced to accept his mistakes. Kin were dying, many denied to the Votann forever. Void combat was brutal and unforgiving. Bodies were lost to the vacuum; the power of the weapons unleashed could break armoured hulls and left very little of the fleshy beings that existed within. Explosive decompression, slashing laser lances, the chill void itself meant that the dead outnumbered the wounded in any starship engagement.

'We're doomed,' he moaned, his head and shoulders sagging. 'My vanity has destroyed us.'

'And the Hold ship and most of the Eternal Starforge Kindred,' added Erkund.

Lekki glared at her. 'Why must you be like this? You barely speak to me, and when you do, it is with scorn and derision. What have I done to so offend you?'

'You are a disappointment in your lack of adherence to the ideals of the Kin,' Erkund said bluntly. 'You prize personal ambition higher than collegiate gain, ego over service, and blame your failures on others rather than accepting your own faults.'

'Didn't I just accept responsibility for this mess?' groaned Lekki, slouching out of the piloting chair. He waved a hand at the unfolding drama on the screen. 'But let's be honest, I didn't bring those ships here to attack us. Even if the shields were working, the situation would still be grim. Myrtun's at fault more than me! Talk about my ego? She couldn't bring herself to speak to me for a heartbeat. And then she flits off like a fly to chase after the Votann-only-know-what nonsense. And took three Prospects with her to do it. They'd be handy just about now, wouldn't they?'

'I believe it is all becoming academic,' said the Ironkin, directing Lekki's attention to the screen.

A knot of enemy ships, the dragonship at their head, had broken through the attempted cordon of smaller Kin vessels.

'They don't seem to be slowing down,' said the Brôkhyr.

'I believe they intend to board the *Unbreakable Giant*,' replied Erkund.

Both of them continued to watch as the trio of battleships and two cruisers arrowed directly for the Hold ship, engines blazing at full power. The remaining enemy fleet closed in behind them, forming a shield against attack.

'Strange,' said Lekki. 'Why don't they all close in? They don't need that many ships to fend off the rest of our vessels, surely?'

Erkund said nothing and remained focused on the screen.

Lekki sat down again, tense in every part of his body, mind racing in circles, trying to think of something to do. The other Runewrights were attempting to bypass the main controls, but Lekki knew the cipher had locked down the whole system. The only way to get anything worthwhile operational again was to rebuild the power feed systems and control circuits from scratch and reboot individual field generators. But that would take far longer than they had and would need the reactor running at a sufficiently low level, enough to render the ship's weapons powerless.

'They are not responding to *our* ships,' said Erkund, drawing a finger across the screen to leave a line of highlighted orange depicting the general arc of the enemy formation. Shells and lasers continued to illuminate the void and the burning wrecks of at least a handful of vessels.

'Maybe we should launch after all,' suggested Lekki. 'Not to escape! No, not that, it's too late now. But we've got some of the best shields in the fleet. Maybe we could intercept a salvo or two for the *Unbreakable Giant*. It's too late now. It's obvious the Guild didn't receive the message.'

'Wait…'

Lekki saw that the firefight was intensifying even more, but the runes depicting the positions of the Kin ships didn't correlate to angles of attack, and the fresh streak of torpedoes seemed to be coming from further out-system.

Erkund cocked her head to one side as though listening, then moved to the inter-ship comm-panel and switched on the speakers.

'*Arteenshon Keendred ov tha Eeternul Stirfurge, keen ov Merton Demmergut. Thees ees Keptin Argrave Lorzentine of His Emperial Huly Marjesty's heevy krozer* Bringar ov Wur *und thee Feeftinth Corwad Fleyt.*' Runes denoting half a dozen unknown vessels sprang into being on the other side of the Cursed Ones fleet, each cruiser size or heavier. '*We peeked ep yur deestriss corl und uffer oor full asseestance. We ur thees det to you urn beehaf uv Merton Demmergot.'*

'Well,' said Erkund, straightening.

'I'm not sure it's of great value,' said Lekki, gesturing to the nearest enemy ships. The *Sparkfly* suddenly shook with the vibration of the *Unbreakable Giant*'s main cannons firing. The dragonship was engulfed by impacts, its void shields gleaming bright blue. Emerging apparently unscathed through the expanding cloud of debris and quickly dissipating burning gas, the vessel fired back. Dorsal lance turrets speared beams of scarlet energy along the flanks of the Hold ship. The other two ships opened fire, turning broadside-on to rake more lance fire back and forth along the Kin stronghold. The *Sparkfly*'s comm-system picked up the breach alerts and alarms from the *Unbreakable Giant* even as closer-ranged batteries opened fire, filling the space around the attacking ships with detonations and plasma clouds.

Undeterred – perhaps exultant at the realisation that their target had no energy defences – the Cursed Ones closed quickly. Concentrated lance-fire speared into a narrow portion of the upper Hold ship, burrowing deep rather than slicing. The purpose of this focused attack became clear a few moments later.

Swarms of attack craft spewed from their hangars, heading directly for the *Unbreakable Giant*.

Leaving Jôrdiki and a group of Hearthkyn to protect the Fane, Dori found himself leading Myrtun and the *Grand Endeavour*'s warriors further down into the abandoned Hold. This time they did not use the elevator shaft but followed in the footsteps of Orthônar's delving. By way of ramps and stairwells, the High Kâhl's force, hundreds strong, descended the first levels quickly. These had already been cleared of debris by the advance team, but it was not long before they ventured further than the scouts, coming to the first of the grand galleries that marked the main levels.

The hall extended a considerable distance, and was high enough that the colonnades to either side disappeared into the gloom beyond their suit lights. Footsteps echoing in the vastness, the Kin advanced, the gleam of their weapons like nebulae and galaxies in a night sky.

'We fell back here after the first attack,' Dori told Myrtun and the Hearthkyn he had trained to be the new Einhyr. 'A regrouping point. We'd split into three, you see, to explore the depths. Each met its match somewhere below, and Orthônar called for the commanders to come back here and unite. The orks didn't follow and we figured that maybe they weren't so keen on facing us all together, like.'

'They were waiting?' said Iyrdin Cabb. 'Gathering their numbers as well?'

'Just so,' replied Dori.

Where once there had been buildings beneath the great vaulted ceiling, there were now only rough outlines of brick and rust. Though they could cut a straight line across the markings, Dori found himself keeping to the old streets, turning down roads between mounds of debris, following the ancient ways of the city. It was hard to picture what it must have been like – the Kindred of the Eternal Starforge had been void-born for many generations now. But Dori had visited a few other Holds, two on moons, another on a planet far more lush than this one. Perhaps that was a lie too, he thought. Maybe the surface had once teemed with life, scoured by the orks or possibly destroyed in the fighting between them and the Kin.

'I wonder what it was like,' whispered Myrtun. They all kept their voices low, more out of respect than stealth. The crunch of boots on grit and the hum of power packs seemed too loud in the mausoleum-like settlement. 'The last watches of those that had lived here. Did they run, to build new lives somewhere else? Did they die defending their homes?'

'I reckon I know a little about how some of them felt,' Dori replied grimly. Dull pain in his chest flared into something sharper. 'Leastways, if they decided to fight.'

They carried on.

Between the sounds of their traversal, Dori heard other noises. At first he thought it might be ork spies – the smaller ones, scampering about in the dark beyond the lamps. The scanner carried by Iyrdin backed up what the survey had discovered: the orks kept to the lower vaults. But he definitely heard footsteps. The sound of distant laughter, deep and hearty. Not an ork cackle, a Kin noise. A babble of voices, the scrape of tools, the rumble of vehicle engines. Music played faintly – a recording, not a band – the scatter of tossed dice, the yap of hounds.

Looking around, Dori saw half-glimpses of movement in the beams of light. More than just the drift of dust kicked up by boots. Silhouettes and shadows, figures and faces. None lasted more than an instant, but like ghosts the memories of this ancient place took form, echoing down alleys and across busy streets. Nobody else seemed to be affected, sweeping their lamps across piles of rubble, occasionally catching a glint of metal in the debris.

A Kin young enough to be fresh from the crucible, her braids slapping up and down as she ran, seemed to pass through Dori. He gasped, turning, but there was nothing behind him. Still he could not shake the illusion of grandiose buildings to either side, banners hanging on their plain rockcrete walls between tall, narrow windows. As though to catch an artificial sun.

He stared up into the dark and wondered if such a thing was true. Perhaps in the height of the ceiling there was some artifice that made an indoor sun. Maybe the surface had never been that habitable, but the Kin had done their best to replicate the world of Old Earth here in the depths.

Dori wondered why only he was seeing this. Then came the smell of cooking, of long-brewed beer and the ozone tang of electric motors. He knew it was a hallucination. His suit was sealed. None of it was real. Nothing more than an impression, a memory from someone else.

He'd experienced nothing like it the last time he had passed this way.

The visions of the dead wore on his temperament, bringing dark thoughts of whom and what they had decided to leave on the Hold ship. A sudden doubt crept into him, a thought of the *Unbreakable Giant* like this place, ruined and abandoned.

'Dead, all dead,' he muttered.

Myrtun glanced at Dori through the dome of her helm. 'Do you still believe you should have died down here with Orthônar?'

Dori didn't like the question, it brought too many conflicting thoughts.

'Still time for that,' he replied, shifting his grip on his axe.

'I mean, if Orthônar hadn't sent you back, none of this would be possible. No expedition, no chance to finish what he was doing.'

'And what was that?' Dori answered sharply.

Myrtun didn't speak for some time, until they were nearly at the far end of the gallery, standing beneath an immense arch that led into the next vast chamber.

'Maybe we'll find out when we get to him,' the High Kâhl said softly.

'Our readings are changing,' reported Brôkhyr Hari from the surface. *'We are detecting surges of heat across the lower levels, spreading upwards to your position. Accounting for the vibrations from the*

drilling, there is also increased sonaric activity. Both indications, I would say, that the orks are on the move, sooner than I had anticipated. Our forward force may find themselves embroiled in combat before they have established a proper defence line.'

Myrtun's contingent was passing down a broad spiral stair into a lower hall, and the scenario was becoming grimmer. Broken pieces of armour, discarded weapons, and a few bodies stripped of their void suits lay on the steps, cut down where they had tried to retreat. The orks had been arbitrary in their looting, taking some weapons but leaving a plasma hammer and a bolt pistol; the helm of an armoured suit sitting atop the mutilated body of its previous owner.

The other commanders were on the same comm-feed and didn't need to have the message relayed to them. Jôrdiki was also monitoring the link in the Hold's Fane, and it was the Grimnyr who replied first.

'I've been trying to access the Fane's most recent datacores to see if there is anything about the ork attack or Orthônar's expedition, but so far nearly every system except the Votannic channels is dead. There're a couple of strange internal broadcast systems operating that I can't figure out. Happen there's a receiver somewhere lower down that has activated, maybe because of us, maybe something else.'

'Do you think the orks know where the Fane is?' said Myrtun, worried that the Grimnyr did not have enough protection.

'What's this broadcast?' demanded Ironhelm. 'You mean a Votannic transmission?'

'Not too strong,' Jôrdiki replied, her voice becoming fainter as she moved away from the comm pickup. *'And no, we haven't had sight nor sound of the orks yet. I can only feel it because of the CORVs. Happen it's been activated by something.'*

'Us or the orks?' asked Myrtun. 'Hari, can you redirect the drillers to our position? Better to stand all together than get picked off in two separate battles.'

'We can't adjust the trajectory that severely, not now, but I can bring them in closer to your position and they can fall back to you on foot.'

'No, no, don't do that!' interrupted Fyrtor, from aboard one of the drillers that had been heading to the first position. *'That'll mean abandoning our best way out of here.'*

'I'll need to synchronise with the transmission to learn more about it, which means it could boost the signal and give away the Fane's location,' said Jôrdiki, as Myrtun tried to keep the various tracks of thought straight in her head.

'Fyrtor, Hari, is there somewhere you can reach that you can defend and then pull out? You don't need to stop the orks, just slow them down. Jôrdiki, I want you to come and join us. I don't think it's safe to stay at the Fane. If you can, try to trace the signal's destination.'

'Happen I can do that on my way,' the Grimnyr replied.

'More bodies,' Ironhelm reported grimly. Over a dozen dead Kin lay at the bottom of the steps, their void suits torn and battered, their helms dented and cracked. The walls were scarred with impact hits and the glassy slashes of plasma weapons as well as cruder hacks and cuts.

'Einhyr, with me!' ordered Ironhelm, the blade of his axe gleaming as he activated it. 'Form up for protection.'

The Hearthkyn pushed forward and created a screen in front of Myrtun as she exited the broad stairwell.

'Scout parties, full sweep,' she told her Hernkyn. The Pioneers took up their task, dozens of Kin dressed in a mix of coats and jackets, coveralls and void suits, an eclectic group compared to the more uniform appearance of the Hearthkyn. Myrtun smiled, seeing in them the embodiment of her previous life: independent, tough, always at the forefront of whatever was happening. Though no longer in their vehicles or on grav-coil bikes, they were still swift and sure as they advanced past the Einhyr, breaking into squads, their lamps illuminating their progress as they spread out into the vast hall beyond. In the distance, Myrtun could see piles of dead and the gleam of more armoured figures scattered around.

'Retrieval teams, start your work.' At Myrtun's word, groups of Hearthkyn followed behind the Hernkyn scouts, among them the two armoured, cowled figures of Denrir and Asan, agents of the Crucible and Fane that oversaw the birth and death of the Kin. Theirs was the painful task of assessing the dead: sorting those who might be returned to the Votann and those whose brains had been too damaged for the last transferral. Given the mutilation inflicted on the bodies already seen, Myrtun hoped that Orthônar had been spared such a fate. She watched the two Embyr sorting through the dead, shaking their heads, sifting corpses like Cthonian miners sorting ore. Of the many bodies there, only a few were carried back towards the stair by the Hearthkyn, increasing Myrtun's anxiety for the fate of her predecessor.

'We're going to hold them up in the vault below yours,' Fyrtor reported, evidently having conducted a private consultation with Brôkhyr Hari. *'We'll have the drillers withdraw once we're in and then fight as we fall back to you. The drillers will be able to come back for us on the level above you.'*

'So you come to us, then we go to them?' said Ironhelm. 'Not so easy with orks at your backs.'

'That's why we have the other tunnellers incoming,' said Fyrtor. *'Right, Holgir?'*

'Aye,' replied the other Hernkâhl. *'We're holding off, and when you have the chance to pull back we're going to push through and attack them from behind, hit and run. They'll have to turn and deal with us or risk getting caught between two forces. That's when you make your break for it.'*

'We need more light,' snapped Ironhelm. His demeanour had been worsening the deeper they had come, and now there was a fraught edge to his tone that worried Myrtun. The champion was with his squads, striding one way and then another, looking out into the gloom of the hall and muttering.

'What's wrong, Ironhelm?' she called. As she strode towards the champion, the Einhyr closed in on Myrtun, forming a protective barrier. 'What is up with you?'

'They use the darkness,' he said, turning, a haunted look on his face in the pale lights of his helm. 'The first time they came from the dark places. There're other ways into here, not just the great gates.'

'We have the Hernkyn, they'll spot anything trying to creep about.'

Ironhelm stared at her as if he didn't comprehend. Blinking hard he shook his head, eyes darting left and right, brow knotting with confusion.

'I ca... In my head, the shouting, the fighting.'

'That's to be expected,' said Myrtun, grabbing his shoulder in a firm grip. 'Leaving here was traumatic–'

'Not then, before,' Ironhelm snapped. His vision lost its focus and his voice became a murmur. 'When the orks came. Butchering, slashing down everyone. Warriors trying to make a stand, battered by cannons, ripped apart by clawed walkers.'

'I hear him,' said Jôrdiki. *'Happen as the Fane is doing it. It's murmuring to itself, sending out something – a last recording maybe? I don't know why Ironhelm is affected by it, but I can also tap into it with my CORVs. I'm just looking at it, witnessing it like I'm on the other side of a window. Ironhelm's feeling it. He's getting the whole memory dump into his head.'*

'We're in position now,' Fyrtor announced. *'Setting up squad placements and scanner parties deployed.'*

'Did you hear Jôrdiki?' Myrtun asked Ironhelm, giving him a slight shake. 'It's an empyric broadcast. No ghosts. Just a broken download that has latched on to your memories of being here before.'

'I can't…' Ironhelm pulled away and then gasped, eyes widening with surprise and relief. He looked around as though seeing his surroundings for the first time.

'I've managed to put a block on the transmission,' said Jôrdiki. *'It's using all the power of one of my CORVs to do it, though.'*

'Where are you?' asked Myrtun.

'Not far, at the other end of the galleries above you. We'll be with you soon.'

Though it wasn't exactly as Myrtun had envisaged, all her forces were nearly in place. But there was still something very important missing.

'Iyrdin Cabb, any sign of Orthônar among this mess?'

'Nowt yet.'

'Keep looking, he must be here somewhere,' growled Myrtun. She fought the urge to run around the hall, turning over bodies herself. She wasn't much for decorum, but seeing their leader fret like that would do no good at all for her Kin. It was hard to just wait.

'Hari? What are the orks doing now?'

While they had been talking, Myrtun, Ironhelm, and the core of the force had advanced about halfway along the hall. Broken columns and bloodied smears showed where the bombardments of the orks had taken its toll.

'Orthônar won't have just stood and waited to be pushed back,' said Ironhelm. He pointed ahead with his axe, where the massive gateway to the next level broke the wall, the lamp beams of two Hernkyn squads disappearing into the darkness beyond the fallen slabs of corroded metal. 'The orks were over that way, up from the deeps. Orthônar would have counter-attacked, trying to drive their front line back into the ones that were still arriving. Maybe even force them to the gate itself if he could.'

Brôkhyr Hari's voice came to her ear over the comm-frequency.

'Coming at you fast. The thermal image and sound profile suggests infantry wave ahead of anything bigger. Plumes and vibrations deeper down says to me that they're starting up war engines. They'll be some way behind the first attack.'

'They're impatient,' said Iyrdin Cabb. 'Good for us. Let them run straight into our guns.'

'Have you found Orthônar yet?' Myrtun wasn't sure where Cabb was among the Hernkyn squads. 'Check carefully by the gate.'

'I'll let you know, soon as we find anything,' the Hernkyn leader replied with a hint of reproach. Of course Iyrdin would, Myrtun thought. She was getting too anxious.

They continued, walking past teams setting up mole mortars and quad-barrelled field guns while E-COGs used their field generators to push rubble into low ramparts. Several Brôkhyr Iron-masters oversaw the work, each with a burly Ironkin assistant and a coterie of E-COGs to attend them. Thôrdi was one of them. The veteran of forge and battlefield alike strode over to talk to Myrtun as she and her bodyguards passed.

'We'll be a second line,' he said. His age-worn face looked even more creased inside the helm of his void suit, lit from below so that his wrinkles were like chasms. 'Don't do anything hasty, pull back behind us soon as you need. We can lose a few guns and E-COGs, we only got one of you.'

Myrtun thanked him and moved on. She stopped herself just as she was about to ask Iyrdin again if there was any sign of Orthônar.

'They're coming,' announced Fyrtor. *'Time to earn our share.'*

CHAPTER THIRTEEN

Inevitable Confrontations

Lutar heard Fyrtor's pronouncement and felt the closest an Ironkin could come to a flutter of fear: a rapid re-evaluation of the decision process that had led to him being here. Certainly he now regretted starting the decision cascade directly after parting with Myrtun. She had not spoken to him after the council, and despite the way things had turned out, was clearly not happy with him for his equivocation. In his current situation, he now gave less weight to the need – desire? – to alleviate some of his guilt-driven anger – assumed irrationality? – with a gesture intended to impress upon the High Kâhl how highly Lutar held her in regard, and the lengths he was willing to go to, the sacrifices he was prepared to make, to ensure she had the same regard for him.

Having already undermined the central thesis of his decision, it was inevitable that he now considered what came after as a series of mistakes based upon that single error. Leaving the *Grand Endeavour* amid the general deployment of the remaining troops to the surface had been easy enough. The ship was in safe hands with Starbound, even if minus a Wayfinder.

He was, with visor mirrored, indistinguishable from any other Kin. Making his way to one of the driller sites had been a formality. He did not want to fight *beside* Myrtun, that was too much. For her to know that he had risked himself in person to help her fulfil her oath was sufficient. Certainly if matters did not go well, he had no intention of leaving this place without Myrtun. He had seen first-hand the gloom that had possessed Ironhelm on being forced to part with Orthônar.

The initial misconception had then been compounded, he decided, by a navigational error on top of an alteration in operational status. It was, thereby, only partly his fault that he had ended up on one of the borers heading towards the vanguard of Fyrtor rather than one that was intended for the secondary, diversionary assault during the withdrawal.

The truly damning factor, Lutar realised, was in following through with his plan instead of aborting it when it had gone awry. Too many adventures with Myrtun had left their mark on his network, leading to a sense of commitment and stubbornness that ran counter to rational assessment.

Even now, he could still be safely ensconced on a driller heading back for the upper levels rather than carrying an L7 missile launcher in support of a unit of Hearthkyn from the *Canny Wanderer*. Once here, though, it would have been cowardice, not rationalisation. The Ancestors watched him just as closely as any other Kin.

Fyrtor had chosen a good spot for the defence. The area looked like an old series of workshops, complete with forge chimneys and furnace pits. It was a broad hall devoid of much cover, with a low ceiling and only three arched entrances – two in front of the vanguard and one behind the force, heading down a corridor to two massive stairwells that zigzagged up to the main gate of the hall where Myrtun was making her preparations.

Lutar started to think about the High Kâhl and had to refocus on what was around him, ahead of him. The weight of the missile launcher and the pack of ammunition mag-clamped to his back. The shimmer of plasma that made the shadows strobe across his pan-spectrum senses.

The tramp of approaching feet.

Guttural grunts.

Scraping metal.

'Hold fire,' commanded Fyrtor. 'You're steady, relaxed. This will be the best volley we fire today. We don't need forty bolters firing at ten orks! Wait for my order. Mark your sections and fire at targets there.'

Lutar knew his section precisely. Along with the squad next to him, he had been assigned a box in front of the right-hand gate, one in from the sector that ran to the wall. He had a small greenish cube visibly overlaid on the area to be sure.

Lights, swaying and erratic, lit the tunnels beyond the entrances. Ruddy, orange, broken occasionally by something white and flaring. A touch of blue, perhaps from some kind of powered weapon. The noise was growing louder. Lutar desired to see the data of Brôkhyr Hari's surveyors, something more quantified than impressions. Then he reconsidered. Better not to know, perhaps.

He lifted the L7 launcher and keyed his comm-feed into its sight link. His view merged with that of the weapon, creating a reticule-like display on the right side of his frontal sensory hemisphere. Lutar could see the heat plume that was so easily detected from the surface. It came as a gust before the ork advance, a mist overlaying everything else trying to crowd the Ironkin's senses.

It seemed that the entrances were empty one moment and then full of snarling green humanoid beasts. Red-eyed and raging, they boiled into the foundry like the molten metal that had once poured along the channels cut in the floor. Some started firing, bullets spanging off the floor and ceiling, their aim wild. Throaty roars accompanied the gunfire, perhaps celebrating it, the pounding of boots echoing across the hall as the orks surged forward on bandy legs. Long arms ended in brutal fists, which clasped cleaver-blades and crude guns. Bodies clad in padded armour, reinforced with haphazard pieces of plate and rings of metal. Heads within bowl helms, some with improbably large horns, others with stubby crests of spikes and manes of looted cabling.

Their faces drew Lutar's attention. Green skin, thick and warty, scarred, marked by algal growths and dry cracks like a sun-parched rock. Pug-nosed, jutting jaws, snaggled fangs, dark tongues, beetling brows. Eyes filled with the delight of murder and mayhem.

A few lucky rounds pinged about the squads of Kin, ricocheting with chips of stone from floor and walls. A warrior on the far left gave a cry and stumbled back, her helm visor cracked. She recovered and lifted her bolter, as did the rest of her squad Kin, ready to reply in kind.

'Hold…' warned Fyrtor. The orks had barely entered the hall, just a score or so from the horde pushing on.

Though he could fire the L7 with a digital command, Lutar slipped his finger into the trigger guard. Suddenly he felt more in contact with the weapon, taking reassurance from the increased sense of control. It was no longer a separate system, it was *his*. He started to process rapidly, anticipating the moment that had to be fast approaching.

Excited.

Yes, that was the word for it. It was exciting.

'Hold,' commanded Fyrtor again, with greater tension in his voice. The Hernkâhl had lifted his bolt revolver to the firing position. Others were aiming their weapons down the length of the forge hall.

Three score of orks were already barrelling across the broken floor towards them, their gun muzzles coughing fire and metal slugs to little effect, the roar of weapons strengthening. Lutar found that his risk-assessment algorithms were struggling to cope with the situation, and he had to override a reflex to pull the trigger of the L7. He found that odd. In terms of raw probability, there was a far higher chance of being destroyed in a warp breach event than here, and he had performed innumerable warp plunges.

Unfamiliarity bred fear, he concluded. His assessment here was raw, based on little data and virtually zero experience. Ship-to-ship combat was a different situation altogether.

Was this nerves?

As Dori had expected, a greater number of dead Kin were to be found on the approach to the main doors. It was strange that there were no orks here. Why had the aliens cleared away their own, but left the Kin? Picking through the heaps of bodies, the darkness slashed through with beams of light to reveal rictus faces, broken helms and shattered void suits, the former champion formed a picture of what had happened after he had been ordered to leave.

'We were at the ninth line of pillars when the ork cannons started the main attack,' he told Myrtun, jabbing a thumb over his shoulder at the great columns behind them. 'I remember hearing the boom as I ascended the steps, louder than the war shouts. And the regular thud of our heavy weapons. I think Orthônar ordered the counter-attack immediately, knowing he couldn't hold the whole of the hall.'

He moved forward, axe in hand as though he was still with his High Kâhl. 'I remember shouts and bolt-fire, but it was distant.'

The corpses made a rough 'V' shape arrowing towards the gate and then stopping between the pillars two rows in front of them.

'They pushed forward, almost got to the gates, but were surrounded,' Dori continued, deciphering the grisly scene, his voice becoming a hoarse whisper. By that point he would have been back in the lander, heading for the *Stormblaze*'s warp cutter that had brought him to the Hold ship. 'Look here, broken flagstones from the tread of the walkers. Burned bodies.'

Dori's chest throbbed with pain at the thought of the Kin lost that day. There would be nothing from these charred remains fit for the Votann. So many lives literally turned to ashes and smoke. Why had Orthônar come here? The question burned hotter than the ork flamers that had killed his companions. If Orthônar was amongst them, there'd be nothing left to recover. Dori's searching became even more urgent and he shouted for Denrir and Asan to concentrate their efforts around him.

'Scanners are picking up something new,' warned Iyrdin Cabb.

'Something?' snapped Myrtun. 'What something?'

'Heat and movement, on the right side of the hall. I'll have my–'

Sudden cries and the report of pistols echoed across the hall, accompanied by the flare of bolt projectiles from the direction mentioned by Iyrdin Cabb.

'Grots!' one of the Hernkyn scouts warned. 'Coming in through a duct!'

The rattle of cruder, lighter weapons joined the bark of bolt pistols as the firefight grew.

'I told you,' growled Dori. 'They know all the ways in and out of this place.'

'And I told you we have scouts and we'd handle it, which we are,' Myrtun replied sharply. 'Let's just find Orthônar, get Fyrtor's lot back here, and then we can pull out.'

'Aye, let's do that,' replied Dori, a cold pit in his stomach at the thought that the doom that had befallen Orthônar might overcome Myrtun too.

Watching the onrushing ork horde, it occurred to Lutar that he wasn't exactly sure what he was supposed to do. He knew the technical workings of the L7 missile launcher, but the inloaded manual had been long on technical aspects and silent on tactical application.

'What are the principles of support fire in this situation?' he asked, turning to the Kin next to him.

'What?' The Kin glanced at him, her Autoch-pattern bolter still aimed down the forge hall. 'What are you talking about?'

Lutar realised it was time to end his subterfuge and turned his mirror clear to show his artificial nature.

'My name is Lutar.'

'By the Three Wise Heads!' spluttered the Kin. 'What in all the Leagues are you doing here? Shouldn't you be on the *Grand Endeavour*?'

'I am… helping,' Lutar replied. He was precisely aware of the distance to the orks and the diminishing amount of time to find the answer to his problem. 'Or I wish to be. My L7 has two fire modes, and I have a variety of targets. How should I prioritise my options?'

'Prioritise…?' The Kin then understood, rolling her eyes. She smiled and nodded her head towards the aliens, who were almost at the distance marker Lutar had created for himself. 'I'm Theyn Gundr. When I was fresh out the crucible, my old theyn had one piece of advice – if in doubt as to what to do, always shoot the big ones first.'

'The big ones?' Lutar turned his attention back to the orks and saw that the aliens indeed clustered around the larger members of their mob, which had now doubled in size. 'My thanks, Theyn Gundr.'

'Great,' said the Kin with a laugh. 'Stick by me and we'll get you through this.'

Via the targeter of the L7, Lutar could see the different densities of the surging ork squads. He picked one that presented the most targets and selected 'burst' mode on the missile launcher.

Though they had nearly crossed half the distance to the line of Kin, the enemy showed no signs of fear or fatigue. If anything, their speed and ferocity were increasing as they grew in number and came closer to their foes. They were almost at the target line.

'Hold!' bellowed Fyrtor.

The green-skinned horde charged on, their sporadic shots no more useful at this range than when they had first entered; many simply fired wildly in the air in their battle joy. It was easy to think of them as comical, clownish almost, but millions of Kin had been slaughtered by beasts like these over many millennia, including Orthônar and his expedition, and the builders of the Hold.

Vengeance possessed a value of its own, quite apart from any tangible benefit of following Orthônar here. Every Kin fought with the knowledge that they would one day fall, and if they were fortunate, they would be returned to their Kindred and Votann. But they also knew that the Ancestors were watching, and so the memory of their death, the legacy of their sacrifice, would push later generations to acts of greatness. To honour the Ancestors, to bring value to their deaths, meant taking the lives of those that had killed them, whether individually or in the great cosmic balance.

For the last few moments as he waited for the order from Fyrtor, Lutar buoyed himself with the fact that his missiles might cut down those that had perpetrated the murder of the previous High Kâhl and the Kin who had fought alongside him.

'Open fire!'

Lutar, along with a greater part of the company, had been waiting for the order, and they all squeezed their triggers on the first syllable of the command. Plasma, bolts and missiles streamed along the hall, lighting it with trails of fire and propellant. Lutar followed the flurry of projectiles from his L7, just a little slower than the bolts of the Kin around him. Explosive rounds detonated across the ork mobs, ripping at armoured and padded vests, rupturing green flesh, breaking bone. Plasma turned aliens to half-charred lumps of blackened mess or seared-off limbs.

Then his missiles hit.

The taller of the orks he had targeted was struck directly by the first projectile, which exploded on impact, hurling the alien backwards amid a cloud of splintered metal and gobbets of ripped flesh. Lutar could not see what happened next through the flare of the subsequent detonations, but in the moments following, it was as if a great axe had swept into the mob of orks and cleaved across them at waist height. A literal tangle of limbs and innards splashed across the forge floor and covered the surviving beasts, many of whom were staggered by the shock waves and studded with pieces of metal and bone shrapnel.

Lutar had expected to feel elated at seeing his foes slain. Instead he was bemused by the foul mess he had created, watching as the following orks tripped and slipped on the blood and offal of their companions. Elsewhere, despite missing limbs, parts of bodies and even half a face in one case, the creatures piled onwards, oblivious to the decimation they had just suffered. The momentary revulsion Lutar had experienced on seeing the orks turned to pulp quickly subsided beneath a surge of disgust at the creatures that were so uncaring of life, so desirous of battle, that they lived only for the brutal work of war and such bloody scenes.

He felt an urgent, inescapable need to vocalise.

'Vengeance for Orthônar! The Ancestors are watching!'

Myrtun heard faint gunfire echoing out of the gateway and knew that the battle had begun, just as word from Fyrtor confirmed it. Other shots were far closer at hand. It was not just the smaller grots that had made their way into the grand hall by secret means; a dozen or so scrawny orks had followed them out of the vent duct and set upon the squad of Hernkyn as they had dealt with the smaller aliens in the first attack. Five Kin had been overwhelmed by their sudden assault, ripped apart by bullets or their heads smashed in with stone-edged clubs. The last few aliens were being hunted down before they reached their boltholes.

'I'll redeploy some squads to cover the right,' said Iyrdin Cabb.

Myrtun was about to agree when Ironhelm cut across her.

'No, we can't weaken our watch elsewhere. There'll be other ways in, mark what I say, and if we dash back and forth looking for them we'll be undone.'

Iyrdin Cabb said nothing, waiting for Myrtun to issue the order.

'One squad, to replace losses, and have the Hearthkyn move closer in for support,' she said. 'We can't afford to let them have free run behind us, not when Fyrtor will be arriving from in front.'

As she spoke, she continued to peer at the grim remains of the previous battle. It was an ugly scene, but one she had to confront if she was to take anything of value from this place.

'Here!' A call from one of her bodyguards drew their attention ahead and slightly to the left.

She hurried over, but Ironhelm reached the spot first, where he stood staring down, still as a statue. When Myrtun caught up with him, she saw what had fixed him so: the body of Orthônar. The slain High Kâhl was still held between two Einhyr, who had been cut down, their backs pocked with bullet and blade wounds, as they tried to drag their lord away from the fighting. Orthônar lay twisted between them, dead eyes staring up into the gloom-hidden vaults. His throat had been opened almost to the spine, and there were bloodless slashes across his body that had been made sometime after death.

Ironhelm sank to a knee beside his former lord. He placed a trembling hand on the ravaged chest, bowing forward. With a short hiss of escaping air, the champion released his helm visor, revealing a face tormented by emotion. Rage and despair vied with each other across the Kin's features.

He leaned closer and placed his forehead against that of Orthônar's. Slowly he stood, but he continued to stare at the corpse.

'No sign of his axe,' said Myrtun.

Ironhelm didn't respond.

'We'll take him back to the Hold ship. But first we need to see if there're any clues as to why he came here. Maybe look for that message?'

Still Ironhelm was lost, occasionally closing his eyes, perhaps seeing the face of Orthônar as it had been rather than the ravaged, sunken mess it was now.

'Dori? We're not done yet!'

Her voice snapped Ironhelm from his trance. He nodded slowly, catching up with what Myrtun had said.

'No axe.' He examined the body again, but now with a dispassionate expression, as if he were inspecting a gun or piece of armour. 'The orks must have taken it for a trophy. If the message was on him, it isn't there now. His pack's missing too, and his belt.'

'And his hand,' added the Hearthkyn who had found him, pointing to the severed end of the High Kâhl's left arm. 'Why that?'

Myrtun shook her head and looked at Ironhelm, who shrugged.

'Maybe he was holding the axe in it?' said the champion. A grim half-smile twisted his features. 'It'd be like Orthônar not to let go.'

'Happen you might be right,' said Jôrdiki, joining them with Asan at her side. The Embyr gestured to the Hearthkyn, and between them the two lifted the body and started back down the hall. Myrtun watched them go, feeling oddly deflated. She had thought that discovering the body of her predecessor would reveal his purpose here, but now she thought about it, how would that be possible?

'When he's returned to the Votann, happen they'll let us know what to do next,' said Jôrdiki, as though she saw Myrtun's thoughts.

'Are we done here?' Myrtun asked Ironhelm. 'Are we no longer oathsworn?'

The champion thought about it for a while, his eyes looking back into the darkness of the hall though he couldn't see Orthônar any longer.

'I reckon so,' he said uncertainly.

Myrtun held in a sigh. It would do no good to show that she was already good to quit this place. She had come for opportunity and all she had found was more death. Still, there was yet a little time left to make something of it.

'Fyrtor, we're done here,' she announced. 'Fall back when you can. Hari, have those drillers meet us ready at the top of the stair.'

'On our way,' Fyrtor assured her. *'Keep that line of retreat open.'*

As if to illustrate that they were far from in the clear, a fresh burst of shooting rattled out across the hall from somewhere behind Myrtun, to her left. She turned in time to see a second ragged volley, the light of muzzle flare betraying a score or more attackers. Bolts responded in number, burning across the gloom to catch the interlopers in a crossfire. Deafening grenades exploded, cutting down several more Kin as they closed around the orks to finish them. Howling their unintelligible cries, the creatures charged towards Myrtun, but a squad of Hernkyn intercepted them before they had covered more than a dozen paces. Bolt shotguns tearing them to pieces, the orks fell, snarling and gasping to the last.

* * *

All ships, evacuate primary dock immediately.

The message emblazoned every comm-screen, flashing red and orange, while a gruff voice spoke the words over the inter-ship audio channel, repeated after an interspersing of high-pitched chimes.

'We're in the primary dock,' gasped Lekki, his attention snapping from the panic-inducing runes across the screen to the close-range scanner display. Erkund was already monitoring the unfolding situation.

'An enemy destroyer has turned and is making an attack run directly for the port,' she advised. 'Everything inside will be turned to slag and debris if it is able to get a direct hit on the opening.'

'It's only atmospheric fields in place,' moaned Lekki as he pulled tufts of curled hairs out of his meagre beard in frustration. 'No proper shields!'

He strapped himself into the piloting chair and started the launch activation sequence. As the reactors built up, he darted a glare at his Ironkin companion.

'Are we allowed to leave this time? Do I have your permission?' he asked bitterly.

'To remain would be to invite destruction.'

'Well, thank you. Very much.'

Lekki watched the power level meters evening out at one hundred and ten per cent output. He prepped the engines, one eye on the display that showed the other craft around them powering up and moving away from their moorings. The *Sparkfly* was one of the most efficient ships in the port and was ready to leave almost immediately, but judging by the scan returns, some of the older vessels would still be getting up to launch power when the destroyer came into range.

'*Incoming torpedoes, brace for impact!*' warned the signaller from the control tower of the *Unbreakable Giant*.

Two missiles as long as the *Sparkfly* separated from the destroyer, arcing slightly towards the Hold ship as the launching vessel continued on a curving course to bring a full broadside to bear.

'Docking command, *Sparkfly* ready to depart.' Erkund spoke as though she was at the comm-panel, using her internal relay. 'Request immediate clearance for launch.'

'Destiny's Messenger *is leaving berth six ahead of you,* Sparkfly. *Await instruction.*'

'We can't wait,' snapped Lekki, disengaging the mooring brakes. Grav-lines released, leaving the *Sparkfly* to lift gently away from the quay.

'Sparkfly, *do not attempt to depart at this time.* Destiny's Messenger *is blocking your path.*'

'Just getting ready to go as soon as we can,' muttered Lekki to himself, easing the dock thrusters from idle to minimal power. The *Sparkfly* drifted forward at about walking speed. He nudged the controls to swing the nose around until he could see a rectangular starfield with the corners cut off – the void beyond the port entrance.

'Sparkfly, *remain at your berth!*'

Suddenly the defence turrets around the docking bay opened fire, slashing across the starfield with yellow laser blasts. Out across the vacuum a torpedo exploded, for an instant filling half the gap with brightness. The turrets continued spewing out beams, the course of the surviving torpedo traceable by the converging points of light.

Lekki saw blossoms of dark red as the torpedo separated into two dozen warheads, each powering forward on its own rocket engine. The E-COG-controlled turrets tried to track them all, beams flickering from one target to the next, but the smaller warheads were moving fast and almost undetectable.

The view was blocked as the *Destiny's Messenger* hove into the exit path, illuminating the dock with blazing thrusters.

'Are they insane?' Lekki watched with mounting fear as the

trader nosed forward, gathering speed to head out of the dock, directly towards the flight of warheads.

He watched incredulously as the merchant ship increased power, the engines switching to plasma drives, almost blinding in the confines of the dock. Overcoming inertia, the bulky ship surged forward faster and faster, passing through the filmy glimmer of the atmosphere screen. Lekki could see more of the void outside again, and watched in horror as the *Destiny's Messenger* turned *into* the oncoming missiles.

'We need to leave,' said Erkund, but Lekki sat stunned as first one then several more warheads struck the merchant vessel midships. Detonations rolled along the structure of the craft, igniting its air supplies and breaking power cables so that fire and sparks roiled along in the wake of the explosions.

Dull crumps sounded inside the *Sparkfly* as the remaining warheads hit the flank of the *Unbreakable Giant*. Plumes of shattered rockcrete and droplets of molten metal sprayed across the dock opening. Still burning, the *Destiny's Messenger* climbed and turned, and as it moved the glint of the incoming destroyer was brighter than any star.

'They took the hits to protect the dock,' gasped Lekki. He pushed the thrusters to full, accelerating hard away from the quayside. Other vessels were turning and following, forming a short line to exit the Hold ship. The gleaming dot that was the attacking destroyer grew bigger with every strained heartbeat.

'If we're in the way when they open fire...' Lekki couldn't bring himself to finish the thought.

'We cannot raise shields inside the bay, they will fry the systems of the other ships,' warned Erkund as Lekki started to reach for the field controls.

'Speed it is then,' he replied, activating the plasma drive on quarter power. The sudden acceleration pushed him into the piloting seat and sent several unsecured E-COGs flying across the chamber to clatter against the back wall.

The *Sparkfly* shot out of the dock like a round from a bolter, trailing plasma.

'We are clear of the dock,' announced Erkund, just as the spot of the enemy destroyer grew brighter still. An instant later, the red beam of a lance slashed over the *Sparkfly* and cut a deep furrow along the upper decks of the Hold ship. Where the lance touched, metal and rockcrete boiled away into the void.

'That was close.' Lekki started to accelerate away from the *Unbreakable Giant* and slid the shields' power to full. With a sigh of relief he watched the schematic of the guildship glow a comforting blue all around, its defensive screens fully operational.

The void battle was raging everywhere now, bombers dropping payloads across the upper decks of the *Unbreakable Giant* in preparation for the wave of attack boats closing in from the Cursed Ones' dragonship and its accompanying assault cruisers.

'The destroyer is powering up for another lance strike,' warned Erkund. 'They will have adjusted their targeting.'

Lekki switched one of the visual screens to a rear view, centred on the brightly lit primary dock. Two further ships had made it out, but the destroyer would be ready to fire before many more could exit. The scanner showed at least six more vessels inside – system craft for ferrying between larger ships for the most part, as any vessel with any serious offensive capacity was already out and fighting. They probably didn't even have shields.

'They'll be roasted like meatballs in an infra-oven,' groaned Lekki.

'Worse, the dock is a weak point into the Hold ship's interior,' said Erkund. 'A solid hit could split the hull open and provide easy ingress for those attack craft, direct to the inner halls. The Crucible, the Forge, the Heart, the Fane...'

Lekki glowered at the Ironkin with a heavy-lidded stare.

'You had to mention that, didn't you?'

With a growl he cut the drives to half-power and activated the retro thrusters. Its structure creaking, more damaged E-COGs sliding back across the floor, the *Sparkfly* turned hard, the strain tugging at Lekki's neck and shoulders as forces tried to prise him out of the safety harness. Even Erkund swayed a little, her feet magnetised to the deck.

'What is your intent?' she demanded, unable to move in case a single foot did not provide enough traction to keep her attached to the floor.

'Doing the bloody right thing for once,' Lekki said, and laughed, feeling quite delirious at the thought of impending death.

'This is not permitted by the Guild's protocols,' protested the Ironkin, but she was powerless to prevent Lekki from steering back towards the main bay.

As they settled on their new course and accelerated again, speeding along the flank of the *Unbreakable Giant*, Erkund was free to move. She took a step towards the drive controls.

'We can't fulfil our duty to the Guild if the Kindred are wiped out!' snapped Lekki. 'No Kindred, no bargain!'

The Ironkin paused, processing this argument. It didn't matter what conclusion she came to, as a moment later the Cursed Ones destroyer opened fire. Another spear of ruby energy connected the enemy ship to the *Unbreakable Giant*, cutting along its decks towards the primary dock.

Lekki altered course by a fraction and the *Sparkfly* curved into the lance beam, shields flaring yellow as they took the brunt of the energy. Sirens wailed as the reactor moved to critical load, red lamps brightening half the panels in the control chamber. The outer viewscreens turned to static, overloaded by the intensity of the plume surrounding the speeding ship as it plunged nose-first towards the destroyer.

And then the lance powered down, leaving the *Sparkfly* glowing like a lantern bulb but intact.

More Kin ships flew from the dock behind the guildship, but the danger was already past. Larger gun batteries flashed into raging life now that the destroyer was in range, pounding out volleys of huge shells to fill the void around the enemy ship with lethal debris and shock waves. Void shields coruscated red and purple for a short while and then collapsed, the following explosion yellow and red as part of the Cursed Ones vessel broke apart under the barrage.

'If we actually get the unlock signal from the Guild,' said Erkund, 'we shall need to have the Master Key at the field control chamber.'

Lekki saw on the scanner what she was referring to: flights of enemy attack craft landing on top of the *Unbreakable Giant*, close to the command tower where the fields chamber was located.

CHAPTER FOURTEEN

Battles in the Dark

Jôrdiki saw Myrtun and the others around her turning towards the din created by the ork sneak attack, but an instinct drew her attention in another direction, towards the main gate. She could feel something in the darkness – a presence her other senses could not detect. As she concentrated on the shadows beyond the twisted ruins of the great gate, another skirmish broke out, back on the right-hand side of the hall near to the exit, even more intense than the last one. She half-heard Iyrdin Cabb giving orders to redress the order of battle, and Ironhelm arguing against it. At the same time, Fyrtor was on the inter-host comm announcing that he was ready to start his withdrawal to the upper hall.

One of Jôrdiki's CORVs was occupied fully by holding back the rogue empyric transmission from the Fane several levels above. Through the other, she pushed her empyric sense into the shadows beyond the gate. There was resistance there. At first it felt like a growing mass of ork energy, as was known to happen when they were in sufficient numbers or especially belligerent mood. Given the battle erupting in the levels below, it was not impossible that some of the surge of alien power could be felt.

There were now three firefights in different parts of the hall. Though Jôrdiki was no expert, none of the attacks seemed especially dangerous. But they were drawing warriors out from the gate, a phenomenon that was not lost on Ironhelm. Yet despite the veteran's protestations, the orks could not simply be ignored lest they reach the Brôkhyr and their gun batteries, or Denrir, Asan, and the Hearthkyn tasked with retrieving Orthônar and as many of the other dead as they could.

All the while, Jôrdiki felt the building pressure of empyric energy in the gateway, trying to repulse her but simultaneously drawing her towards it. Her wards burned brighter as she channelled more power through the available CORV, sending the semi-autonomous assistant towards the gateway.

The Grimnyr flinched as she thought she heard a snarl close at hand, sending her staggering back several steps, almost tripping on one of the dead Kin. At the same time as she recovered her balance, she detected an increase in energy from the Fane through the other CORV. It felt as though she was trapped in a balance between two shifting weights, each trying to break Jôrdiki with the added burden. On the one hand was something shadowy and bestial, prowling the darkness of the real and the empyric. Steadfastness and ancient power opposed it, resistant, but tested like a gate barred against the crashing of a ram.

Jôrdiki realised that she could tip the scales, but to do so would mean releasing the CORV that was currently protecting Ironhelm from his Fane-broadcast visions.

'We're nearly at the stairways,' reported Fyrtor, meaning the steps that led up into the antechamber beyond the gate ahead of her. At the same time, the darkness thickened before her and in her mind. Her brain became sluggish – her mind was a wanderer lost in a bog, every thought a painful step wrenching free from the mire that wanted to drag her down.

As she floundered she also became more aware of what was happening. The dark swamp was filled with red eyes, hidden, waiting. In their midst a monstrous shadow spun forth a web of gloom, snaring thought and eyes alike.

While her mind's eye saw this, Jôrdiki saw a glint beyond the gates with her actual eyes. Instinctively she drew on the power of the Fane, releasing the CORV from its duty intercepting the broadcast. She heard a shout and a drawn-out moan from Ironhelm some distance behind, but all of Jôrdiki's attention was now focused on the gate. With empyric energy flowing to her from the Fane, both CORVs gleaming with ward power, she thrust forth her staff to illuminate the chamber beyond.

The glare of white light revealed at least fifty orks hiding there. They were more of the scrawny, feral type that had been clambering through the ducts, clad in scraps of armour, their green bodies painted with war markings, skin inked with glyphs and geometric patterns.

In the middle stood the ork psyker, still surrounded by an umbra of summoned darkness. It too held a staff, wrought of copper and hung with talismans and fetishes made from dead Kin, ancient and recent. Scalps and skulls swayed as the creature swung towards her, its eyes ablaze with hate and power, its ambush revealed.

Before she could shout a warning, the shaman gestured with its staff, sending arcs of green lightning streaking towards her. Reflexively she drew on her ward runes, the light of her staff becoming a barrier. Orks shrieked and stumbled back from the white fire while empyric lightning scattered across it like cracks in the air.

The ork psyker rasped an order, throwing another storm of energy against the barrier. More afraid of their leader than the piercing flamelight, the other creatures rose up and ran for the gate, heavy pistols and spears ready to kill.

Jôrdiki drew on the Fane, releasing all of the checks on the power trying to press in on her. Her visions flooded with nightmare scenes of the Hold being overrun, as though the Fane had kept that pain bottled up for millennia and was now letting it go. The CORV to her left exploded into molten shards, pieces of ward runes flying like shrapnel into the nearest foes.

Unbalanced by the sudden change in empyric flow, Jôrdiki could only resist the next chain of lightning with brute empyric force. The impact of the psychic assault earthed through the remaining CORV, causing sparks to erupt from its dissipater crest. Even with its protection Jôrdiki was hurled back by the blast, hitting the ground amid the part-decayed dismembered remains of Kin too defiled to be returned to the Votann.

While green electricity danced over their heads, the orks surged into the hall.

Placed between the gate and the Hernkyn, Dori was torn between moving to the aid of the Grimnyr or stemming the increasing attacks on the outskirts of the subterranean settlement. A sudden blaze of power drew his eye to the gates, a moment before a wave of nausea welled up from his guts. Stumbling to one side, head pounding, Dori felt the inrush of ghost voices, harder than anything he had experienced before. Buildings burned and bellows echoed from the cracked, tumbling walls of the settlement. There were enemies everywhere, cackling and grunting, falling upon the desperate defenders with howls of alien glee.

A sound that brought to mind a faulty reactor shrieked around the hall, accompanied by a flash of green light that drew Myrtun's attention back to the main gateway. She saw Jôrdiki clambering to her feet, staff outthrust, a nimbus of white flames forming a hemisphere around her. Myrtun's gaze followed the line of the Grimnyr's, and her chest shuddered to see a wave of orks surging through the gate, ready to pounce on Jôrdiki. Behind them, a larger alien hurled bolts of green energy. The dome of empyric force protecting the Grimnyr flared at every strike, seeming to grow dimmer. A burning CORV lay on the ground between the two psykers, the other madly bobbed back and forth, its crest almost blinding with empyric build-up.

'Cabb, support Jôrdiki! Fyrtor, there are orks at the gates and probably on the stair. You need to break back to us now! Ironhelm!'

The champion didn't respond to his name, but bellowed a war cry and charged towards the orks that had infiltrated the left side of the hall. Myrtun could guess what had happened: without the CORV to intercept the signal, the full force of the Fane's last broadcast was overwhelming Ironhelm. Myrtun had only the vaguest sense of it: panic and failure, the bestial glee of rampaging orks, and the desperation of trapped Kin. To Ironhelm it was real, as he swept his axe from side to side, striking at ghosts only he could see. Fortunately, in his rage he did not fire his pistol or he would have struck one of the Kin trying to contain the insurgent attacks.

'We'll pull back now, but they'll be on us like grease on a crank spindle,' said Fyrtor, his voice betraying just a hint of laboured breathing, the pickup of his comm catching an occasional crack of a bolt firing or the thud of a detonation. *'Holgir, are you ready for the diversionary attack?'*

'I'll meet you at the stair, Fyrtor,' said Myrtun, breaking into a run towards Jôrdiki, her bodyguards following, leaving Ironhelm. 'Better to hold there awhile than let you get stuck.'

'We're already on our way,' Holgir informed them. *'We should breach as Fyrtor reaches the stairs.'*

As she came closer to the gate, Myrtun realised there were more orks still there, hiding beyond the gleam of Jôrdiki's psychic fire. Iyrdin Cabb and several Hernkyn were firing bolt pistols and shotguns into the group of aliens that had burst into the hall, and were taking scattered fire in return. Between the two forces the Grimnyr stood unscathed, her wards bathing the surrounds with their intensity.

Several more Hearthkyn joined Myrtun's counter-attack as she came level with Jôrdiki and pressed on. Seeing the Kin bearing down, the ork psyker flinched, relenting in its attack on Jôrdiki. It turned its copper staff on the High Kâhl, gesturing wildly with its other hand, bracelets and charms spinning and swinging. A fresh halo of green energy coalesced around the alien, swiftly gathering power.

Myrtun opened fire, shouting the order for her Kin to do the same. Bolts flared into the gloom of the gateway, punching into green flesh, tearing at armour. Howling, the ork raised staff and splayed fingers, sparks erupting from both.

A jet of white fire left dancing runeshapes across Myrtun's vision, smashing into the ork. Its own empyric channelling flared out of control, jade licks of energy teasing from its open mouth, its emerald eyes blazing with rampant alien power. The brutes around the ork seemed not to notice, but came at the High Kâhl with guns blazing, the whine of bullets and crack of impacts engulfing the squads of Kin around Myrtun.

With a final piercing shriek of agony, the ork turned into a vortex of whirling green flames, setting alight a handful of the nearby alien warriors.

Suddenly realising their plight, the bolstering effect of their shaman removed, the remaining orks faltered. A few continued on with slowing strides, only to be cut down by the next ruthless volley of fire from the vengeful Kin. Most of them turned and routed, fleeing swiftly beyond the lamps and empyric gleam, back into the gloom that had concealed them.

'Enemies coming down to you,' Myrtun warned Fyrtor. She looked over her shoulder and saw only intermittent flashes of gunfire in the main hall. 'We are following up. Cabb?'

'Here, ur-kâhl,' the theyn reported, just to the right-hand side of the broken gates.

'Keep a lid on things here,' commanded Myrtun. Iyrdin Cabb raised her pistol across her chest to the opposite shoulder in salute. 'Hernkyn, remain here on watch. Hearthkyn with me. Right, Fyrtor. We'll see you soon.'

The precision of the Kin withdrawal from the forge hall pleased Lutar, having a sense of pattern and rhythm that seemed mechanical but actually owed far more to a fluid, organic sense of timing. The force had divided into several groups, each of which took turns as rearguard while the others fell back a short distance. A series of combined volleys would break the building impetus of the orks, forcing them into the scant cover of old partitions and the furnace pits that had been dug into the floor. The rearguard would then retreat past the nearest of the other forces, creating a new rearguard to face the swell of the next ork wave. Another section had been ordered to clear the way behind, to stop the orks fleeing from Myrtun before they arrived directly behind the retreat.

The purposeful but implacable withdrawal held the orks at bay but was costly in both time and ammunition. Gauging his own supplies, Lutar had started limiting himself to shooting only one volley in three. Other heavy weapons fire was also diminished, leaving the bolts and plasma of the other warriors to take the greater part of the burden. As effective as they were, the ork numbers were still noticeably increasing. And, in being slowed from their initial headlong charge, their gunfire had increased in intensity and a little in accuracy, taking an occasional toll from the squads pulling back. Those who fell to the aliens' volleys were taken by other Kin, both the wounded and dead, dragged along as the squads retreated, deposited on the floor when their bearers were required to open fire.

'Now's the hard part,' Fyrtor warned. 'We're nearly at the corridor, which means a narrow front. We can't bring many guns to bear. I want a parting salvo from all the remaining heavy weapons, and a sustained bolter burst. Then we fall back as quick as we can to the chamber where the corridor meets the stairways. Myrtun's waiting for us there and she'll give us covering fire.'

'That's you to the front then,' said Theyn Gundr.

'Thank you for your assistance,' replied Lutar, slamming his penultimate rack of missiles into the L7. 'I am sure we will swiftly be returning to orbit.'

'Aye, it's been an experience, but I'd soon as get back to the Hold ship for now,' replied the theyn. 'You can be proud, the Ancestors have seen a fine Kin today.'

Lutar projected a murmur of appreciation, amused at the notion of the theyn giving him approval. He was at least four, perhaps five, times her age. Then again, in the circumstances her experience was many times greater than his.

He moved to the front of the Kinthrong with the other heavy weapons specialists. The orks had pulled back for the moment, and Fyrtor was waiting for the next wave. Lutar's timer measured the uneasy pause with digital precision but made it no easier to patiently await the inevitable next assault. Now and then the aliens fired erratic shots from various places of cover along the hall, but there was no new massing of troops for another push.

'I don't like it,' growled Fyrtor, pacing a little way along the line of his warriors, gleaming hammer in hand. 'Something's wrong. But I guess we shouldn't let the opportunity go to waste. Begin the withdrawal. Rearguard, stay watchful. The orks have something planned.'

Lutar detected the squads moving back along the forge hall to the other gateway. He felt isolated as the distance between the heavy weapons and the others increased, unnerved by the lack of activity from the orks.

'Hari, what's happening below?' Fyrtor asked over the command frequency.

'Quite a mass of foes, I'd say,' the Brôkhyr replied. *'At least four-fifths of their number on the move, in this area anyway.'*

'Get to the hall and we can worry about it on our way back to the ships,' Myrtun replied. Lutar wanted to say something, to let her know he was here, but decided against distracting her. The expedition was going well, but the extraction was a critical phase, and if it went wrong everything that came before was rendered pointless.

'Right you are,' said Fyrtor. He continued his force address. 'Heavy weapons, fall back by pairs, starting on the left.'

Lutar was able to look along the line to see that his fellow Kin were withdrawing, every other warrior retreating ten paces and then standing ready to cover their companion. The ripple of movement reached him, but he was off-numbered in the line, and so the warriors to either side of him withdrew. He felt their departure rather than watched it, focused down the sight of his missile launcher for any sign of enemy attack. Bullets and bright energy blasts sporadically zinged out of the shadows from orks skulking in the pits. There was movement at the far end of the hall, in the darkness that concealed the gates. Lutar switched to a thermal view, just as one of the theyns behind the line issued a warning over the comm.

'Scanner detects new movement, kâhl!'

The horde that burst into the forge hall was made up of the smallest genotype of ork, standing no taller than a Kin's shoulders. Grots. But in the first few moments, Lutar estimated over a hundred of the creatures swarming forwards – some running at full speed, others scurrying from the cover of one corpse pile to the next.

'Hold your fire,' Fyrtor snapped. 'Ready for close combat. A waste of ammunition on these...'

Larger shapes lumbered from the gloom. Some were more

heavily armoured than those that came before, and greater in bulk. Many had heavier weapons – strange-looking energy guns and multi-barrelled cannons, rocket launchers, and wide-bored shell-firers. With them came a knot of heavily armoured orks that towered over the others, wielding more outlandish ranged weapons and crackling, cruel-looking blades, mauls and jagged claws.

'The warlord!' Fyrtor couldn't keep the shock from his voice, and his unease rippled through his Kin.

Lutar felt unease in a more dispassionate sense – algorithms that had been invisibly calculating chances of success and survival suddenly had to revise their conclusions, leading to the return of the momentary uncertainty that had struck him at the commencement of the defence.

With the grots throwing themselves forward, more terrified of their ruler than the guns of the Kin, Lutar found himself caught between two courses of action. If the grots reached the line of Kin, they would bog down the warriors, pinning them in place while their far more dangerous leaders closed in for the kill. If he fired his missiles at them, he would expend vital ammunition needed to deal with the heavier alien warriors.

It was with a grudging respect that Lutar concluded that this had been the warlord's tactic all along. It had counted their numbers and the types of their guns, sacrificing the lives of its warriors to do so, while keeping a greater part of the Kin force occupied in the main hall. Now that it was satisfied the Kin had used much of their stores, it had employed this grots-shielded attack to drive them back.

'Run!' snarled Fyrtor. 'Everyone, get to Myrtun as soon as you can. Re-form in the main hall. Myrtun, clear the stairwell for us, we can't hold them there.'

'Understood, Fyrtor. We'll have a greeting ready for them when they get here.'

The others were following their leader's command. It wasn't a rout. A few warriors here and there fired shots to give the grots pause for thought about charging in, and Lutar did the same, placing a salvo of missiles into the closest mass of small aliens. He barely registered their destruction amid the burst of fire and metal, turning away even as the flames and smoke cleared.

He lumbered into a run while the bellows of the ork warlord echoed down the hall after the retreating Kin, bestial but triumphant.

CHAPTER FIFTEEN

That Which is Lost

'The last of the recovered Kin have been loaded onto the drillers.'

Holgir's report came as welcome news to Myrtun. The High Kâhl replied with an acknowledgement and made a final assessment of the disposition of her Kin around the gateway to the main hall. Sounds of bolters and other weaponry echoed up from the stairwells, and she had positioned a couple of Hearthkyn squads at the top of each to provide much-needed covering fire; her warriors had plenty of ammunition to expend, unlike Fyrtor's throng. From the scant traffic over the comm she assumed that Fyrtor's retreat was proceeding in as best fashion as could be hoped. Brôkhyr Hari continued to warn of an even greater number of orks mobilising from the deeps, with indications that some of them were making their way towards the surface by other routes. It had always seemed unlikely that there was only one way in and out of the abandoned Hold, but Myrtun had not had the time to conduct a proper survey for them, nor the numbers to hold every exit even if she found them.

As when they arrived, speed was the best strategy. Which, for Kin, was not the usual state of affairs. Solid on defence and implacable on attack, they were unfortunately not gifted with notable swiftness of foot. If Fyrtor could not make the hall relatively unentangled, Myrtun would face a grim choice between a counter-attack to get him, risking being cut off from their craft on the surface, or leaving him to replace the Kin that had been recovered from Orthônar's expedition.

'Keep our backs clear,' she told Iyrdin Cabb once again. The Hernkyn had been roving across the hall, looking for ingress points the enemy might use. For the moment all was calm, but Myrtun suspected their adversary was more cunning than she had initially credited. The sneak attacks might well resume when the warlord was at the gate, and probably in numbers not yet seen.

With this in mind, Myrtun's throng was positioned about halfway across the hall, just as Orthônar's had been. The similarities weighed on Myrtun's thoughts. Her predecessor had also counter-attacked against the warlord. It had not ended well. Was she doomed to repeat his failure? Had there been any chance of gaining from this venture since the outset, or would the entire expedition become a huge, bloody monument to her vanity?

The outer ends of the Kin gunline curved around the approach to the gate, furthest away directly opposite the opening, ends forward to create a crossfire if the orks came directly at the centre. If the enemy tried to attack one end of the line, the whole force would move back, to ensure they did not get cut off from the stairs leading to the borers in the hall above.

Ironhelm had settled a little with no foes to attack. He was more lucid than not, but every twitch and glare reminded Myrtun that the veteran was unpredictable, still haunted by the Fane's transmission. He barely responded to his name, and there was no telling what he would do when the orks arrived. Myrtun had already made the decision that if he was insistent on dying here, she wouldn't stop him. She would rather he survived and served her as champion, but she would not risk the lives of more warriors to make that so.

'Fighting's nearly here,' said Jôrdiki. The Grimnyr stood a little to Myrtun's right, the smoking remains of her two CORVs not far away, her wardstaff providing her with physical as well as empyric support. She had the appearance of a true living Ancestor now, her skin pale and mottled, her sweat-laden brow furrowed from her exertions defeating the ork psyker. Myrtun would have sent her back, but there was every chance the warlord had more shamans in its retinue and the Grimnyr would be needed again.

Jôrdiki was right, too. The crash of hammers and axes echoed up the stairs alongside the bark of HunTR bolters and the battle cries of Fyrtor's company.

'Here they are!' shouted one of the Hernkyn theyns from a squad stationed closer to the gates. 'They're coming into the antechamber.'

Myrtun saw them soon after – Kin in void armour of orange and black, just like hers, but bearing badges of the *Canny Wanderer*. The first groups arrived at a run, intercepted by Iyrdin Cabb as they came through the gate, to be assigned places in the waiting formations. They dispersed across the hall, turning to face the foe that pursued them.

The greater part of Fyrtor's throng arrived in a flurry of individuals and pairs, who likewise had no respite but were despatched to bolster the next line of defence. Looking past the protective line of her Einhyr, Myrtun watched in silence as a press of warriors appeared, three dozen or more, firing constantly, the flare from pistols and bolters illuminating first the upper stairway and then the antechamber. A darker red streaked the walls and ceiling as energy bolts spat back, scoring welts across the stones, sometimes striking down a Kin.

A line formed in the adjoining chamber while wounded Kin limped or were carried back through the gate. Grenades went down the stairs, the panicked squawks of diminutive grots and deeper shouts of orks cut off by the boom of detonations and flashes of brightness.

Turning completely, the last group of Kin, Fyrtor at their heart, came racing back towards the hall. Shadows crowded after them, accompanied by the crash of metallic boots, howls of derision and snarls of rage. Trampling over the fallen of both sides, eight monstrous orks arrived up one stairwell while a crowd of smaller aliens piled up the other. Both groups set after Fyrtor with grunts and snapped commands, firing their weapons into the backs of the retreating Kin. A few fell, blasted by energy beams, caught by crackling plasma.

Making it into the great hall, Fyrtor headed for Myrtun, allowing the squads to each side to bring their weapons to bear on the following aliens. But though the bestial orks were no more graceful than the Kin, their bowed legs were longer, and even the armoured creatures covered the ground with surprising speed. Bolts spanged from the armoured plates of the warlord and its retinue, but tore open the flesh of the less well-equipped orks. Heavier weapons spat wrath into the encroaching monsters, but their ruler was protected by a force field that glitched and glimmered with threads of green energy while impacts and beams surrounded it.

Realising he'd be run down if he continued to flee, Fyrtor turned with his remaining warriors, at least a score of them.

While the warlord loomed over them, Myrtun blinked hard, startled by a trick of the light. For a heartbeat it looked as though one of the Kin fighting alongside Fyrtor had no helm within the dome of their visor.

An Ironkin.

A scratch, not long but jagged, just at the crest of the dome. Like Lutar.

She looked away and back, but the illusion remained.

Despite all sanity speaking against it, Myrtun was forced to the conclusion that, though she had no idea how, Lutar was there, among Fyrtor's throng.

Shock swiftly gave way to dread as the warlord and its companions thundered forward. Lutar – she still couldn't quite believe it – lifted an L7 missile launcher and fired at the incoming orks, joining the welter of bolts, shells, and blasts that converged on the immense aliens. Several fell, torn to pieces by erupting rockets and fusillades of exploding rounds, but the warlord continued on, ignoring the sparks and slivers flying from its battered armour.

The creature hit the Kin with a sweep of a red-gleaming axe, a single stroke carving apart the head of one and through the bodies of two more. Its momentum carried the beast past its falling foes, crushing remains under stomping, exoskeleton-clad boots, its backswing slashing through more Kin.

A silent scream rose from Myrtun as she watched that scarlet-wreathed blade connect with Lutar. It seemed to simply pass through his upper arm as if there was nothing there, slicing open armour and brass skeleton without hindrance. The edge cleaved into Lutar's side where a flesh-and-blood Kin's upper ribs would be. Suit and body crumpled like foil, and the impact flung the Wayfinder into the air, to come crashing down some distance behind the ork leader. It paid no heed at all to the carnage, propelled forward by bestial anger, its strides fuelled by the smoke-billowing engine of its armour.

Fyrtor and his Kin were like water at the bow of a ship, parting before the beast's charge, though two more were not swift enough to elude the deadly touch of its broad axe, hewn into sections by a long, sweeping blow.

Myrtun found herself charging forward, firing her gun at the warlord. Her other hand – the one she had lost freeing herself from the clutches of just such a beast – formed into a fist sheathed in silvery skin. Shrieking blasts from her disintegrator careened off the energy shield, forming arcs of green in the air around the monster.

It seemed to recognise her boiling hate and laughed as Myrtun closed. Her body burned with effort, but she ignored every ache and pain that racked her tired limbs, firing again as she raced the last few paces into the melee. The ork's protective field stuttered and the disintegrator beam slashed through leg armour and thigh, turning living cells into an expanding spray of displaced molecules. The laugh became a bellow of anger, and the axe descended with all the inevitability of a sunset.

Myrtun was not without her own defences. The shield-crest that rose from her backpack and over the dome of her helm blazed with unleashed power, sending the axe blade bouncing away trailing red sparks and blue fire. Unbalanced, the warlord stumbled on its wounded leg. Myrtun was not fast, but she had perfected her timing over a long life. Her bionic fist rose to meet the falling chin of the ork leader, bastium alloy smashing into hard bone. She felt the impact like punching the side of a starship, the jolt sending numbing shock up her arm and into her shoulder.

Jaw split open, each side hanging loose from mandibular sinews, half its fangs smashed to pieces, the warlord staggered back, lashing out blindly with the axe, one tine of its double-headed blade missing Myrtun's helm by a finger's width. She stepped inside its reach, thinking to rip out its throat, but she was met by the multi-barrelled gun encasing the warlord's other hand. For an instant, she stared down the smoking tubes. Then white and noise filled her world. A storm of impacts pummelled her shield and armour, driving her bodily back across the hall until she lost her footing on a corpse and fell to the ground.

Blood and drool hung in ropes from the warlord's maimed face as it straightened, vengeful triumph in its eyes.

Jôrdiki threw herself forward, her staff like a spear tipped with fire. One of the warlord's henchbeasts took the blow, perhaps unintentionally as it staggered forward, an arm missing below the elbow, its armour rent in a dozen places from weapons fire and plasma axe blows.

As it fell, another Kin leapt over the crumpling body, carrying a blaze of light.

'For Orthônar!' bellowed Ironhelm as he buried his plasma axe into the head of the ork chief.

Riding the collapsing warlord to the blood-spattered flagstones, Dori hefted his axe and brought it down again, hewing through the creature's helm a second time. He was only dimly aware of the gunfire and shouts around him, oblivious to the other orks and his fellow Kin. Levering free his plasma axe, he stepped back, panting, pulled out his bolt pistol and fired three shots into the remains of the warlord's face, feeling a coolness of satisfaction pouring over the flames of his rage as each round detonated, turning what remained of the head to a glossy dark red and green ruin.

'It's dead!'

The fog of his righteous vengeance lifted and he recognised the voice of Fyrtor, cutting through the thunder of his heart and the wind of raggedly drawn breaths. Dori turned his head slowly, feeling himself crowded by shadows and ghosts. The Fane memories of the long-deceased remained with him, barely seen in the periphery of vision, their voices murmurs and whispers on the edge of hearing. When Fyrtor spoke, their ghostly words echoed after.

'We have Orthônar, and the orks are retreating for now.'

We cannot rest, the dead told him.

We are lost.

Find us.

Dori staggered back from the ork corpses, shaking his head to clear away the voices. He felt fingers on his arm, tight. He looked up the arm and met Fyrtor's gaze, a bloody cut across his cheek, the strain of battle in his eye.

'We need to leave before more of them come.'

'We ain't done yet,' grunted Dori. He pulled himself free, casting his eyes around the hall. The ancient buildings were gone, but a crowd of indistinct shapes flowed towards him, massing around the fallen warlord. Dori thought he saw hands pawing at the body, the wordless moans of the ancient Kin plaintive, harrowing.

'The leader…' he muttered, holstering his pistol to wipe gore from his face and beard. 'Something about the…'

Then his gaze fell upon Myrtun, and he realised Fyrtor had not been speaking just to him.

The High Kâhl knelt over a ruin of void suit and metal, hands resting on the chestplate. Her head was bowed and her shoulders were hunched with suppressed emotion. It was her reaction more than anything else that told Dori who it was she mourned.

'Lutar…?'

One of the Brôkhyr, Thôrdi, came running up, E-COGs struggling to keep up with him.

'Myrtun?' He knelt on one knee beside the High Kâhl and gently pulled her back. 'Myrtun?'

'How is he here?' she muttered. 'What was…? I've known him longer than anyone.'

'Myrtun, it's all right,' Thôrdi said firmly. He stood up, pulling her to her feet with him. The E-COGs gathered around the broken Ironkin and tools flashed – plasma cutters and bolt-screws taking apart the remains of Lutar's armoured dome. 'Myrtun!'

She focused a little more, tearing her eyes away from the ruin on the ground. An E-COG hovered up, claws clutching something roughly oval and glassy, lights flickering within.

'What is that?' Myrtun asked, lucidity returning.

'His neuronic processor,' replied Thôrdi with a gentle smile. He patted the device. 'Everything that is him. It seems undamaged.'

'He can be brought back?'

'Sort of,' said Thôrdi. 'The trauma was real. It will have rewritten some of his circuit landscape. He won't be quite the same. But yes, that's Lutar. We'll take his body too, see what we can do with that.'

Myrtun nodded dumbly and watched with Dori as Lutar's remains were gathered up and carried away along with the rest of the fallen and heavily wounded. All the while, Dori felt the nagging insistence of the Fane-Hold presence as a prickling of flesh and a barely audible tinnitus.

'Good riddance,' snarled Myrtun, looking down at the dead ork leader. Dori turned back to the corpse.

A flash of metal caught his eye. Among the trophies of skulls and bones that hung about the massive alien was a gauntleted hand.

'Orthônar's hand,' he gasped, ripping the severed appendage free from the thong that held it.

The ghosts pushed closer, eager and pleased. The hand reminded him of the moment the High Kâhl had grabbed him and told him to go. Without thought, Dori dragged the ring from his pouch and held it up, seeing his creased face reflected in the many facets of the ruby.

An instant of connection he had not felt at the time. It wasn't just words. Not just the oath, but something else Orthônar had passed to Dori. Finally he understood what was happening. Sort of.

'The ring, it's the key to all of this,' he said dizzily, handing the jewellery piece to Myrtun. 'It has empyric power within it. Placed something inside my thoughts, inside my head. That's why the Fane has been trying to speak to me.'

'Jôrdiki!' called the High Kâhl, beckoning to the Grimnyr. Jôrdiki struggled over the broken ork bodies, weary and hurt. Myrtun held out the ring as she joined them, and the Grimnyr's eyes widened with surprise.

'This was your "key" was it?' she said to Dori before gently taking the ring, eyes fixed on the ruby. 'I can see ward runes in its heart. Ward runes like those in the locks of the Fane here.'

'You think it comes from here?' asked Myrtun. 'What does it do?'

'I think it's an Ancestor Key,' replied Jôrdiki, giving it back to the High Kâhl. 'Like your talisman of office, but far older, more powerful.'

'We cannot stay here,' Myrtun said. Dori looked at the warriors who had gathered around them. There were even more wounded and dead being carried or helped back to the transports. The ghosts had cleared – not disappeared completely, but withdrawn to the perimeter of the hall, watching, waiting.

'We're not done yet,' Dori announced, looking at Jôrdiki. 'We have to take it to the Fane.'

'Happen you're right,' said the Grimnyr. 'But that means getting out of here first.'

Myrtun and Fyrtor marshalled the remaining forces while they withdrew along the hall. One of the borers that Holgir had been going to use to make a diversionary attack was repurposed to pick up some of the force near the Fane. Fyrtor and the majority of the Hernkyn made for the closest drillers, while Myrtun, her companions, and her new Einhyr split off to head for the chamber of the Fane.

'There are orks on the surface,' warned Hari. *'They're heading to the eastern drill site, but they could overrun the landing zone too.'*

'Have everything prepared for lift-off. Send the recovered and wounded back as soon as you can,' Myrtun told him.

'We'll hold the field as long as we can, but don't be taking too long, I reckon leaving won't be as peaceful as arriving.'

Dori could feel the presence of the dead following them along the tunnels and stairs as they climbed up to the Fane.

'I think I have this figured out,' he said. 'The Fane was broadcasting its messages for help when the halls were overrun. Maybe it was processing some recent dead for transmission back to the Votann. Everything has got jumbled up, but somehow that ring acts as a receiver. Orthônar used it in some way to guide us to this place, but when he realised he was going to die here, he used the ring to put a similar geas on me to return.'

'Happen that makes sense,' said Jôrdiki. 'The Ancestor Keys come from the founding of the Leagues, older even than this Hold. Only a score or so of them were made, one for each of the first Votann. This was before we had Grimnyr and the like, back when the Votann was still young too. They could communicate with the captains of the old settler ships with the rings. Like, exceptionally high-powered Votannic channel contact. Seems the rings could also map partly onto the brains of a Kin.'

'I never saw the ring before the expedition,' said Dori, wincing as they mounted another set of steps, wounds old and new sore on every part of his body. 'Where'd Orthônar get it?'

'Most have been lost, of course,' said Jôrdiki. 'A few of the biggest, oldest Kindreds still have theirs, though the Votann don't talk through them no more. Some have been moved about, traded and such.'

Myrtun cursed, drawing everyone's gaze.

'I don't believe it,' she rasped. 'I think I know where it came from. The Enduring Guild of Master Runewrights.'

'The guild that Lekki fellow was representing?' said Dori. His brow creased, and then his eyes widened in realisation. 'That's the debt! They'd given the ring to Orthônar and want it back, or payment for the loss.'

'Why didn't the emissary say anything?' grumbled Jôrdiki.

'Because I didn't listen!' Myrtun's expression was savage with self-criticism. She snarled and shook her head. 'He was peculiar, unsettling, and I thought I had much more important things to consider.'

Dori said nothing, silenced by a flood of guilt as he thought of his own behaviour towards the emissary. If he had but waited a turn, so much more might have been learned and anguish avoided. But if they could have returned the ring, and the source of the contract had been known – if Dori had found out the oath was in fact to return the ring – would they have come at all?

'You wanted to run away, you mean,' said Jôrdiki. Myrtun's mood soured more, but she said nothing.

'So, if we've got this right, Orthônar was told by the Votann to get this Ancestor Key from the Enduring Guild of Master Runewrights, and then to follow its guidance to here. But why? To take back the Hold?'

'Something more than that,' said Jôrdiki. 'Something so important, happen so precious, that Orthônar couldn't share it with anyone.'

'And you didn't find the Fane last time,' said Myrtun, who was wheezing with every couple of steps now. Even so, nobody had thought it better to activate the elevators. Who knew what dangers might be brought up from the depths.

'Aye, that's why I want to take the ring there,' said Dori. 'It's been trying to tell us something all along. Calling out, so to speak.'

Myrtun puffed out her cheeks, which were red with effort.

'And we best do it quick. The orks won't be far behind. Let's not make the lost have fallen for nothing.'

Dori pushed the thought from his mind. It was too much to think that they would get this close and still fail.

CHAPTER SIXTEEN

That Which is Returned

Jôrdiki felt the same sense of awe when crossing the threshold of the Fane a second time. It was as she had left it, thankfully untouched by any alien intrusion. Carved faces – previous Grimnyr or High Kâhls? – gazed down at the party from wrought metal beams above the holographic interface. While Jôrdiki approached, Myrtun and Ironhelm held back a little. The Einhyr spread out along the corridor outside to guard against discovery. Even so, it was only a matter of time before the orks arrived.

'It was the power of the Fane that forced the orks into the lower levels,' she told the others. 'I felt it when I connected with the shaman. Happen the ork psychic field picked up on the same transmissions that Ironhelm's psychomimetic implantation did.'

'My what?'

'The ring placed an empyric engram into your thought patterns, a bit like the code for sealing a file or ratifying a deal, but written in brainwaves. The shaman, happen other orks too because of their generated psychic field, had visions of what they'd done broadcast back at them. They're stupid and superstitious, so they probably thought the Hold really was haunted. Happen the lower they went, the weaker the signal, so they could hide from the dead if they went far enough.'

'So the ghosts really did bring me back to this place to rescue them?' Ironhelm looked in wonder at the Fane's machinery. 'Across the stars and all?'

'I don't think the Votannic signal reached you on the Hold ship, but the engram in your head would've provided its own nudges. But you did the most, being sworn to an oath by Orthônar. Happen he didn't really have a clue what was going on, but when he got the Ancestor Key, he'd have the engram inside too. But he didn't come looking for the Fane, so I don't think he knew truly what he was after...'

Myrtun had approached as they spoke, the ring in her hand. Jôrdiki noticed the Fane's holographic face was now looking intently at the High Kâhl, its stare no longer aimlessly wandering.

'That's unsettling,' admitted Myrtun, meeting the unliving stare of the Fane's projection.

'Put it on,' suggested Jôrdiki.

'You what?'

'You're High Kâhl, wielder of the Ancestor Key now. Put it on. Show the Fane the ring.'

With a bit of ceremony, attention fixed on the semi-transparent apparition of the bearded face, Myrtun took the ring and slid it over a gloved finger. She held it up and a ruddy light sprang from the gem and struck a small, mirrored disc just below the holographic interface.

The Fane's visage seemed to sigh, relief painted across its insubstantial features. A single word croaked from hidden speakers but also manifested inside Jôrdiki's thoughts. Without the interface of her CORVs to channel the empyric power, the Grimnyr felt the latent strength of the Fane. She encountered just a tiny fraction of its full potential, as if she were looking at the slightly rippled surface of a pool that delved far deeper than anyone could ever reach.

+FIND.+

Myrtun stared in amazement as the eyes of the holographic face lit up, becoming nebulae of lights. They expanded, the face disappearing as two star maps grew into the space it occupied, each with a brighter point but riddled with missing patches and static-filled areas.

Jôrdiki jumped forward, pulling an amulet from around her neck to insert it into a matching port close to the holo-interface.

'What is it?' asked Ironhelm as the two maps overlaid each other. Myrtun recognised one, feeling a lump in her throat when she thought of where she had seen it: looking at the charts of the area around the Well of Yrdu with Lutar.

'We're here,' she said, pointing with her disintegrator. Myrtun's bionic arm felt like a weight, barely movable, damaged in the fight with the ork warlord. 'The other point... I don't know.'

Jôrdiki turned around, eyes glistening in the lights of the Fane. She looked awed and terrified at the same time.

'Orks are moving towards the landing zone, we have to leave,' warned Hari. *'We've got grav-coil patrols at the perimeter to keep them back for now, but if they rush us, we can't hold. Once they've worked out what we're doing, they'll come for us with everything.'*

'What is it?' Myrtun asked. She'd attend to Hari in a moment.

'Votann,' whispered Jôrdiki.

'A Votann? Which one?' asked Ironhelm.

'One of the first.' Jôrdiki could barely talk, her whole body trembling. Myrtun realised that the Grimnyr was connected to the Fane and was experiencing something far more profound than looking at a holomap. 'Lost.'

A shiver ran through Myrtun and she realised why Orthônar

had been so secret, why he could not risk news of this spreading, nor hopes being kindled. A Votann, lost to the Leagues for generations, this Hold its last contact with living Kin.

Valuable beyond measure. Perhaps the greatest prize in the galaxy.

Gunfire followed by footsteps at the door behind drew everyone's attention. It was Iyrdin Cabb looking anxious.

'We have to go. Now.'

Myrtun looked back at Jôrdiki. The Grimnyr lifted her interface amulet.

'I have it,' Jôrdiki said, some of the colour returning to her cheeks.

The small tiles on the walls were shattered in places by bullet impacts, las-scorched in others, and cratered by bolt detonations. Lekki hadn't noticed before how the geometric mosaic had formed interlocking knotworks based on the rune of the Enduring Guild of Master Runewrights. Overhead, the lamps – the few that remained among the splintered remnants of the ongoing firefight – were likewise wrought in a design that honoured the Guild by using its symbol. The bulkhead stanchions lining the corridors were decorated with ornate, abstract reliefs depicting the faces of the Guild founders, Ynnok Wise-one and Haykha Anhad. Lekki had always been a function-over-form crafter, as evidenced by the three shuddering E-COGs nestled close to the feet of his Thunderkyn exo-frame. Now, as everything was becoming a broken ruin and the symbols of his allegiance were literally falling to pieces around him, he started to understand the significance of aesthetics. Though never officially recognised as a guildhall, the area of the *Unbreakable Giant* around the field control headquarters – the dorms nearby where the bulk of the members lived, and the common room on the level above – were just as much part of

Guild territory as the *Sparkfly*; the ship was currently two decks down, precariously docked with a tertiary maintenance access bay normally used for E-COGs and single-Kin craft to enter and leave the Hold ship.

This was the Guild, and he was the ranking member here.

Standing just ahead of his exo-frame, the grey bulk of Erkund took up half the corridor, her plasma hammer in one hand, a lascutter held in the other. The gleam of the hammer head and the lascutter's energy cell cast a blueish glow over Lekki's bodyguard and the half-squad of Hearthkyn who huddled behind her, in cover at the junction of two corridors leading to the fields control chamber.

Around the corner were several bodies, of both Kin and the mutant humans that had besieged the Brôkhyr in the control room. The clatter and clang of the boarders' weapons on the armoured door sounded down the corridor, along with the rasp of chainweapons and the shriek of the thick metal. On the other side of the T-junction, Theyn Kylu Keynshot attended two of her injured warriors, their void suits battered with impacts, holed by las-shots. Beside them was a third casualty, his guts blown out by a bolt detonation. An E-COG applied antiseptic salve and coag-sealant to the gaping wound as best it could, but blood pumped to the floor in time to the pulse of the Kin's heart, though with less vigour every beat.

'We can wait them out,' said Keynshot. 'Pick them off when we can. They haven't a chance to break into the control room.'

It seemed like a decent plan for the time being, and Lekki relaxed as much as he could in his Thunderkyn harness. Now and then, one of the Hearthkyn moved forward and looked around the corner. Sometimes they were greeted with the crack of autoguns and zip of lasguns; sometimes they managed to snap off a bolt-shot before being forced to duck back.

Lekki noticed Erkund stiffen, a sign that she was receiving a comm input of some kind. Given that the fields control chamber was just one of several strategic points across the *Unbreakable Giant* being targeted by enemy boarding parties, and now and then they heard the impacts of continued strikes from the Cursed Ones' ships, the Iron-master did not expect the news to be good.

Just then, a heavier tread – a thunderous crash of boots with a long stride – broke the noise of attempted ingress.

'A complication has arrived,' said Erkund, peering around the corner. A sudden flurry of bullets and a las-beam forced her back a moment later. 'A cursed-sworn Space Marine.'

Lekki's heart sank at the news. It had looked hopeless enough trying to get past at least two score of bestial mutants. A renegade Space Marine was a threat of an entirely different order.

'I have more news,' said Erkund, swinging towards Lekki. A stream of digirunic code crackled from her speaker. Lekki caught something glinting gold upon his chest and looked down to see the key amulet had activated.

'What?' His despondency evaporated, his heart racing as he lifted the amulet in a gloved hand. 'How?'

'I have just received a relayed signal from the *Sparkfly*,' announced Erkund. 'Message attached. "Well done, Lekki! We received the confirmation signal from the *Gyrfrost* that the archive has been activated. The search can move on. Myrtun succeeded! In case you have used your Master Key, the unlock cipher is encoded with this message. Hope there wasn't any trouble. Look forward to seeing you back on Svallindrim."'

Lekki didn't know whether to laugh or cheer, and ended up with a choked sob while he grinned stupidly. The feeling of hope lasted just a heartbeat before a metallic voice, deeper than any Kin's and filled with the tone of command, barked something in a language that might once have been human but was no longer recognisable. The mutants answered with grunts and wheezes, one of them jabbering in a far-higher-pitched voice. They seemed agitated about something. The Space Marine replied with a few curt syllables. There was a pause, and then an amplified shout.

Boots thumped and claws scraped on the tiled floor, quickly growing louder along with wheezing, snarls and panting grunts.

'They're coming again,' growled Keynshot, turning away from her wounded squad Kin to prime her HYLas auto rifle. Others readied Autoch-pattern bolters, while Erkund braced herself with hammer pulled back, lascutter ready to activate.

'Defence is no longer sufficient,' said Erkund.

'Agreed.' Lekki powered up his graviton rifle. 'We have to get into the control chamber.'

Ahead, the Hearthkyn were readying to make their attack.

'Wait! Make way!' The Hearthkyn shuffled out of Lekki's path as he stepped forwards in the exo-frame. His E-COGs followed, hissing and clicking. 'COG-2, I need you to go into that corridor and activate your buzzfield. Maintain position in front of me. COG-1, COG-3, follow me.'

The clanking machines bobbed up and down on their anti-grav buffers in acknowledgement.

'What is that pile of bits going to do?' scoffed Keynshot.

'Stand ready,' Lekki replied, ignoring her scorn. He lifted his gleaming hammer in signal to Erkund. 'Ready?'

'Ready,' the Ironkin replied.

'Seriously,' said Theyn Keynshot. 'Leave the fighting to us.'

'It is time to rebuild the Fifth Pillar,' Lekki told her, stepping out into the corridor.

The mutants, twenty or so of them, were almost halfway to the junction and charging headlong. Some slowed in surprise, raising their weapons as the war-rigged Brôkhyr strode into view. In front of Lekki, about two-thirds of the way to the mutants, COG-2 glowed blue. The glow became a glimmering azure barrier that filled the corridor from floor to ceiling, wall to wall. The las-bolts and bullets of the mutants' opening shots hit the field and either fell to the ground or dissipated, their energy absorbed. COG-2 shuddered, shunting that energy through complex converters to increase the depth of the projected barrier. More rounds and blasts slapped against the blue shimmer, and the E-COG started to shiver constantly.

'Make the most of the protection,' said Lekki, opening fire.

The graviton pulse from his rifle passed effortlessly through the uni-directional barrier and hit a particularly hunched, bulky mutant square in the chest. The singularity at the centre of the pulse collapsed, creating a gravitic shell that turned the mutant's own mass into a neutron-dense core, pulling its bones and flesh inwards in a bloody implosion. At his side, Erkund fired her lascutter, the beam slicing the knobbled head from another charging mutant.

'Counter-attack!' yelled Keynshot, rising from the cover of the junction, her HYLas auto rifle spitting sapphire blasts. A mutant with shaggy hair sprouting from between a padded worksuit patched with improvised armour plates went down in the hail of fire, which continued into the lizardine face of the Cursed One following it.

More fell to bolts and bullets, graviton pulses and lascutter beams, but they were nearly at COG-2. Several had wicked axes and swords in hand, ready to smash the machine out of the air.

'COG-3, move and attack, full spread,' ordered Lekki, breaking into a run. The E-COG crackled as it buzzed forward, its field generator flashing a light purple as it passed through COG-2's barrier. When it had reached the other side its swirling power field darkened and grew. With the closest mutant just half a dozen paces away, COG-3's field exploded, smashing down the hallway like a battering ram. Mutants were thrown aside, crashing into the walls and ceiling, crushed to the floor with bones snapping as though run over by a Hekaton Land Fortress.

Most of the mutants were now dead, and Lekki could see to the end of the corridor from his raised position within the Thunderkyn exo-frame. The cursed Space Marine raised its bolter, a grotesque weapon with strange runes carved into its casing, the muzzle shaped like a howling wolf. The warrior's black armour seemed to suck in the light of the fields while the gold chasing gleamed with unnatural hues. As the Cursed One opened fire, the flare of propellant flashed across the leering daemonic face of its helm.

COG-3 was torn to pieces, becoming shrapnel that whirled into more of the mutants. A grief-wrenched bellow escaped Lekki as he powered forward, but his graviton rifle was still recharging. The Cursed legionary fired again, its bolt smashing into the exo-frame around Lekki's right arm, ripping away the mounting for the graviton rifle. He let it go and raised his hammer as the Space Marine drew a power sword with a blade that seemed to be made of smoking amber.

'COG-1, avenge your kin!'

The third of his trio of handmade assistants raced past, a ring of golden energy spooling up around it like a planetary disc. The Space Marine changed position, taking up a guard pose, thinking the E-COG's field was some kind of melee weapon. Lekki growled in satisfaction, and a moment later COG-1 turned off its graviton core and released the whirling field. The golden discus fizzed along the last length of the corridor in an instant, slicing through the Space Marine at chest height. The warrior's powered armour, genetically enhanced physique, and dark pacts availed it nothing against the precisely calculated physics of Lekki's genius.

The mutants still labouring at the control centre door turned at the disturbance. One of them pulled up a long-barrelled autocannon. Lekki felt an eternity stretch out before him as he stared down the darkness of the muzzle, framed neatly against the half-naked, bulbous body of the mutant. He fancied he saw the spark of ignition as the first round was fired.

A spray of dark grey slivers showered over him, accompanied by the staccato crack of autocannon hits against Erkund's armour. Having lunged in front of the Brôkhyr, she now lurched back, hammered by the repeated impacts.

The Ironkin staggered and fell while bolts and las-beams seared past the pair, ripping into the mutants now thrown into defending the door rather than breaching it. Lekki spared them no mind but looked down at the broken parts of Erkund scattered over the chipped tiles of the floor.

'Why?' he asked, stooping over her. Her face was unmoving, her core mechanics exposed by rents in the grey plate of her body.

'It is my… duty…' The words crackled out of her address system without any visible sign that she had spoken. The Ironkin struggled to sit up, managing to force her head closer. 'Use the Master… Key, you idiot.'

Her words snapped him out of the shock that was seeping through his body. With a final effort he pounded forward, broadcasting the door code of the command centre. The portal hissed open in front of him, revealing a cluster of surprised Brôkhyr and attendants, their weapons pointed at the doorway.

Lekki ripped the Master Key from around his neck and lifted it as though it was a beacon torch, parting the Guild members like a lascutter shot through a mutant's belly. He manoeuvred awkwardly in the confines of the chamber and then ejected from the frame, landing heavily outside the kiosk. With a deep breath, he leapt inside and slammed the Master Key onto the activation pad.

Mutants had followed him in and a sprawling fight spilled across the chamber. While the Guild members held them off, some of the Brôkhyr dashed to other stations, turning dials and pulling levers to regulate the surge of energy from the Hearth now flowing through the system.

Keynshot arrived with the remaining Hearthkyn, cutting down the mutants from behind. Stumbling around the chamber, Lekki was bathed in the welcome jade glow of systems coming online all across the *Unbreakable Giant*.

The departure from the Fane was more flight than fight. It was too dangerous to bring in a boring machine and risk it getting overrun, so the Kindred of the Eternal Starforge followed their High Kâhl out of the Hold on foot. Periodically, Myrtun and her companions had to stop to engage the orks dogging their heels all the way back to the surface. Though shaken by the loss of their leader, and wary of the Kin's firepower in the narrow passageways and tight stairwells, the orks held the advantage of numbers and speed when the escape route brought the warriors of the Kindred of the Eternal Starforge into the broader spaces above. Here, the enemy tried to outflank the fleeing Kin, racing through the darkness beyond the lamplight and glare of muzzles and plasma. Yet each time the shadows were not protection enough against the scanners and weaponry of the new Einhyr, and occasionally a determined charge led by Iyrdin Cabb or Ironhelm.

Those that could fight no more were carried by the others, some to their final joining with the Votann, a few to a more hopeful future in the healing halls of the Embyr.

When the group finally exited the Hold through the landing site gates, the sight that greeted them was far from encouraging. Two landing craft were burning, palls of thick smoke obscuring the dawning sun on the flat horizon. Gangs of green-skinned aliens roamed the landing pads and rubble, targeted by speeding Pioneer bikers and a gunship that circled overhead. Two of the Sagitaur transports had been parked up next to the final lander, ready to retreat up the ramp, their guns adding to the storm of plasma and laser that erupted from the craft's defence turrets.

'Coming for you,' Fyrtor announced just as one of the Sagitaurs pulled away from its position, followed by the other, blazing a path straight through the surrounding orks. A Hekaton Land Fortress powered down the ramp behind them, its cannons booming as it hit the cracked remnants of the old star terminal.

Squads of Einhyr spread out to secure the area around the gate, some of them with weapons guarding the rear, and together they waited for the transports to arrive.

'Wouldn't it be quicker to bring the lander here?' Iyrdin Cabb asked.

'Look past the broken tower,' Fyrtor replied.

Myrtun and the others moved to see beyond the remnants of the entrance. Clanking ork walkers were crossing the plain behind heavy guns that had been unlimbered from basic trucks, some of them firing erratically at the landing site, others directed to the skies as anti-air weapons.

'Enemy at the gates,' warned Hari, whose modified Sagitaur was the second of the pair racing towards them. *'Hundreds of them. They must have reactivated the elevators.'*

With a concerted salvo, the two smaller vehicles raced past Myrtun and her group, driving back a mob of armoured foes that had been closing from beyond the other broken terminal buildings.

A bestial shout, almost of one voice, reverberated from the gate tower. Like a froth erupting from the top of a careless Brôkhyr's chemical flask, the orks boiled out of the gateway, shooting and hollering with equal vigour. A salvo of bolts and heavier fire greeted them, but the hardy aliens stormed on, driven battle-crazy by their own numbers, intent on falling upon their enemies no matter what.

'Get in!'

Myrtun looked over her shoulder to see the Hekaton skidding to a stop just a few strides away. The ramp was already descending, Greta at the top with a bolt cannon on a sturdy tripod. She opened fire into the massed orks, heavy rounds tearing chunks off the aliens, turning living creatures to lifeless pulp.

Some of the Einhyr followed Iyrdin Cabb into the Sagitaurs, a few clinging to the outsides when the compartments were full. The others crashed past Myrtun as she waved them aboard the Hekaton, others clambering up the side ramps or clinging to the flanks of the large war engine.

The orks were close behind, shots pinging away from the structure of the vehicle, energy blasts leaving molten tracks on the ramp. Myrtun helped Jôrdiki to the top, and shouted for Ironhelm, who was standing at the bottom of the ramp, axe and pistol in his hands. For a couple of heartbeats he stood there, perhaps contemplating following Orthônar into the hands of the Votann.

'I'm your High Kâhl now,' Myrtun shouted. 'I need you too.'

He turned and ran up the ramp, giving her a nod and a half-smile as he passed. Myrtun followed, giving a thumbs up to Greta.

The Hekaton's balloon tyres scrabbled for grip as the driver gunned the engines. It started to move, but Myrtun saw Greta's eyes widen in shock. Weary beyond movement, turning her head, the High Kâhl saw that half a dozen orks had reached the ramp and leapt onto it. They fired their pistols madly as they charged up the slatted metal, to be met by a hail of fire from the Kin at the top. All but one fell, torn to shreds, but the survivor lunged towards Myrtun, a wicked cleaver aimed at her head.

Greta hit the ork with a full tackle, sending both of them spinning down the ramp and off.

'For my High Kâhl!' Greta shouted, before she and the alien disappeared into the dust cloud left by the Fortress' churning wheels, and then that was obscured by the rising ramp. 'The Ancestors are watching!'

The Hold ship pulsed with returned vigour, from the docks to the control tower, prow cannons to engines. Sheathed in layers of protective energy once again, the immense star fortress slowed, ceasing its retreat. With navigational fields restored, the stronghold started to turn hard. Enemy lances and shells flared from its rejuvenated shields while in the interior, anti-boarding shunts closed off the most vulnerable parts of the ship. Energy that had been used to run away now brought online the massive ion arrays, which had so far remained dormant. Freed from defending Hearth, Forge, Crucible and Fane, the Kindred of the Eternal Starforge turned their minds to purging their home of its invaders.

With the Imperial ships behind them, the enemy had nowhere to run as the *Unbreakable Giant* brought its most powerful guns to bear. Heavy batteries overloaded the void shields of the dragonship first, blanketing it in near-continuous clouds of detonations. As the ion cannons came into arc, the upper decks of the Hold ship were briefly lit by the glitter of artificial starbeams.

Across the expanse of vacuum the daemonship seemed to writhe, more like a living creature than a void craft, blisters erupting into gaping wounds that fountained warp energy from prow to stern. Like a carcass split by a butcher's saw, the dragonship parted along its length, fire and warpstuff combining to burn green and white as it split asunder. Chunks of flaming debris spun away from each into an expanding cloud of ruin.

The *Unbreakable Giant* powered on towards its remaining foes.

EPILOGUE

The clamour of ork voices and the crash of battle that had plagued the otherwise smooth, noiseless space of his dreams started to fade. He felt peace settling across his being. Star charts became stairways towards a brighter light, and he flowed up them.

A sudden surge of energy crackled through him.

Blinking – recalibrating his optical arrays – Lutar found himself looking at the lamps in the ceiling of a Brôkhyr workshop. He turned his head to the right and saw, lying on another bench, the grey-armoured Ironkin that had accompanied the guild emissary. Most of her was still in parts on another bench, but she raised a hand in greeting.

'He's back!'

Lutar felt another spike of energy as he recognised the voice of Myrtun. He sat up, finding himself possessed of a body not too dissimilar to the one that had contained him before. His armour was bulkier, the grey of bastium alloy, and there seemed to be fitting points for more plates.

Myrtun was standing at the foot of the bench-bed, her face a mask of delight. There were others: Brôkhyr Thôrdi, Jôrdiki, Ironhelm, Fyrtor.

The High Kâhl clapped her hands together like a giddy youngster and moved forward to lay them on his shoulders.

'You're back,' she said, more softly. 'My star-guide.'

'My jewel-star... I was foolish. I wanted you to be impressed.'

'I am,' she said. She waved a hand at his new body. 'Something a little bit more combat ready, in case you feel the urge again. We've got quite a journey ahead of us.'

'What happened at the lost Hold?'

'Something amazing!' Lutar had not seen Myrtun so excited for half her lifetime. She was almost glowing with vigour, her grin carving deep canyons in her dark skin. 'A Votann! One that's been lost since the First Truths were being made known.'

'Another adventure?' Lutar could not keep the suspicion from his voice. Myrtun's expression grew sincere.

'Yes, but not one that I'm dashing off to have on my own. I'm High Kâhl by the favour of the Votann, and I have to respect that. No, this time we go all together. The whole Kindred, and whoever else wants to come along.'

'Really?' Lutar took her hands in his. 'We stay together?'

'My oath on it.'

ABOUT THE AUTHOR

Gav Thorpe's long and prolific career with Black Library has seen him write across the depth and breadth of the Warhammer universes. Author of the Horus Heresy novels *The First Wall, Deliverance Lost, Angels of Caliban, Corax,* and novella *The Lion,* he has also recently written the titles *Luther: First of the Fallen* and *Rogal Dorn: The Emperor's Crusader.* His Warhammer 40,000 work includes *Indomitus,* the Dawn of Fire novel *The Wolftime,* and the fan-favourite Last Chancers series, amongst many others. For Age of Sigmar, Gav wrote the novel *The Red Feast,* and in 2017 he won the David Gemmell Legend Award for his novel *Warbeast.* He lives and works in Nottingham.

YOUR NEXT READ

THE FALL OF CADIA
by Robert Rath

Cadia – a bulwark against the forces of Chaos that reside in the Eye of Terror. This proud world stood defiantly for centuries, until it was targeted for destruction by Abaddon the Despoiler in his Thirteenth Black Crusade.

For these stories and more, go to **blacklibrary.com**, **warhammer.com**, Games Workshop and Warhammer stores, all good book stores or visit one of the thousands of independent retailers worldwide, which can be found at **warhammer.com/store-finder**

An extract from
The Fall of Cadia
by Robert Rath

Blood and iron.

Iron and blood.

One lay on the other, and within the other. The slick shine of the iron-rich blood – still warm – on the cold surface of the bell. Two related elements, joined in accidental symbolism.

If records were to be believed, the bell had been forged from blood.

It was said that when Saint Gerstahl – the sacred soldier, favoured patron of the Cadian trooper – fell defending the Gate in the centuries after the Great Heresy, acolytes collected his vitae in a crystal reliquary. There it stayed for centuries, a venerated and lucrative relic on the shrine world christened with his name.

Until, one night, Blessed Gerstahl appeared to the cardinal with a message: he must extract the iron from the tarry, coagulated remnants and forge it into a bell.

A bell that would toll when Cadia was in mortal danger.

The cardinal forged the relic as instructed, then took the bell on a tour of the Cadian Gate, purifying world after world with the vibration of its holy resonance. A fortunate choice, since it escaped destruction when the Despoiler immolated the shrine world – and Gerstahl's incorruptible remains – during the Third Black Crusade.

On Solar Mariatus, two million welcomed the bell. Sobbing

crowds parted to make a path for the fifty Battle Sisters of the Order of Our Martyred Lady who formed its vanguard. In the Derades Subsector, it was said that its chime healed the deaf and straightened crooked limbs. And on Laurentix, in the Belis Corona System, the populace wailed in ecstasy when it tolled a dozen times without being touched by human hands.

That was when the Black Legion descended upon it, in the opening raids of the Twelfth Black Crusade.

The vanguard had sworn to die rather than surrender their relic. And they fulfilled that oath. Their bodies now lay beneath the cold iron of the bell, some resting in its shadow. Chest cavities blown open, limbs severed from the impact of traitor bolt-shells, their own vitae splashed onto the blood-forged iron. It ran in frozen rivulets down the engraved surface, turning the scrollwork and decorative psalms into channels of gore.

They had saved it, in a sense.

Their stoic defence had given Trazyn time to lock the bell and its entourage in stasis, then spirit it to the archival vaults of Solemnace.

Now it hung, unmoving and fastened in time, among the relics of Cadia past. Gazed upon by the unseeing eyes of general officers snatched from the battlefield, zigzag trench-lines full of Shock Troops and a rank of Chimera variants bisected to show internal detail.

Overhead, a squad of Night Lords Raptors arced through the vaults above a lit display of human eyes.

All of them, artefacts of the Cadian Gate. The ephemera of Abaddon the Despoiler's twelve Black Crusades.

Darkened exhibits stretched across twenty-five square miles, a private gallery of humans, exquisitely arranged to please the historical and aesthetic tastes of the alien curator who'd imprisoned them.

Nothing in the gallery apart from maintenance scarabs had moved in over a millennium.

Which is why the soft *pat-pat-pat* of fluid echoed as far as it did.

It fell from the iron surface of the bell like the first drops of icicles melting on the eaves of a hab. Drip. Drip-drip.

Jewelled drops met the upturned forehead of a slain Battle Sister and stained her pale skin with splashes of crimson.

Pat. Pat-pat.

More drops. Coalescing on her brow, trickling into her open eyes.

Blood moved on the bell's skin, collecting in beads like rain on a window and falling in defiance of the stasis field.

And the bell, without propulsion or force, began to swing.

A hand's breadth at first. A sway. Its clapper moving in a soft pendulum arc too weak to do more than scrape the sides.

Then, the arc widened, the violent motion of the bell flinging droplets of blood to either side, spattering the faces of stasis-locked Shock Troopers. Sizzling on the protective fields of lasgun displays. Swaying wider until the bell went fully perpendicular and the clapper inside dropped, its hammer striking the iron of the bell.

Clang.

One.

The blackstone floor vibrated. A rank of medals swayed, its stasis field shorting out. An organic clatter filled the chamber, the sound of ten thousand jaws – held shut by hard-light holograms – shaken so hard that the teeth rattled.

Overhead, the flight of Night Lords Raptors tumbled from the vaults and into a trench display, snapping bones and crushing lasgun barrels. Neither Traitor Space Marines nor Guardsmen reacted.

Clang.

Two.

Trazyn, Overlord of Solemnace, Archaeovist of the Prismatic Galleries and He-Who-Is-Called-Infinite, screamed in rage.

'Sannet! What is happening?'

'Unclear,' answered his chief cryptek, his multijointed fingers dancing across phos-glyph panels. 'Unknown resonance. Macro-seismic. Cracking the vaults, releasing coolant. We've lost the Ooliac sand sculptures.'

'Call the restoration scarabs.'

'Not responding,' Sannet answered, data-chains flashing across his ocular. 'Our nodal program misinterpreted the vibration as a re-interment signal. The legion has entered radical shutdown. I cannot rouse them.'

Trazyn cursed the very wheel of the cosmos. The interval between shocks had been only seconds apart, and while mental speech between he and Sannet was near instant, they were running out of time before the next tectonic shudder would hit.

'It's not tectonic, lord,' said Sannet. 'It's coming from the gallery.'

'Where?'

'The Black Crusades wing.'

'That's only two levels do–'

Clang.

Three.